Sha
Shades of
Shai
Echoes Of Time

TRChowdhury

T.R. Chowdhury &
T.M. Crim

TRIMOON
ECLIPSE

Winter Wolf
PUBLICATIONS

| Cincinnati, Ohio

Copyright © 2017, T.R. Chowdhury & T.M. Crim
First edition: 2011 Loconeal Publishing
First Winter Wolf edition: 2017
Cover Art © 2017, by Lindsay Archer
Interior Image Art © 2017, by Carol Phillips & Miriam Chowdhury
Edited by Jennifer Midkiff
Interior Design by T.R. Chowdhury

Published by TriMoon Eclipse,
An imprint of Winter Wolf Publications, LLC

ISBN: 978-1-945-039-04-1 (paperback)

Shadow over Shandahar:

Dark Storm Rising
Echoes of Time
Whispers of Prophecy
Breaking Destiny
Embers at Dawn
Heroes' Fate

Dark Storm Rising:

Blood of Dragons
Shade of the Fallen
Forging the Bond

The Troubadour's Inn:

(Collections of short stories, poems, and artwork)

Tales from the Hapless Cenloryan

Other work by T.R. Chowdhury
(aka Tracy Renée Ross)

The Chronicles of Rithalion:

Elvish Jewel
Dragon Vessel
Fire Heart

Cat Tales:

The Dream Thief
The Time Swiper

DEDICATION

This book is for my children. They deal with me during all my disgruntled days in front of the keyboard as I handle problem scenes, and the nights I play catch up with all the others. They are there during the times I zone into my world and forget this one, and the times I forget about the laundry, or the dishes, or the following day's packed lunch. My children are my rock, the place I go to when the writing is complete. Every day I feel Blessed to have them in my life, and I could never do this without them.

Miriam, Kamran, Ranlyn and Samir... you are everything to me, and I can't imagine my life without you in it. Wo ai ni *(I love you)*.

~ Tracy

This book is for all the people who have supported me over the years. It's been a wonderful journey, so stick around for my next chapter!

~ Ted

TABLE OF CONTENTS

PART I

PART II

Map of Central Ansalar

● Fortress   ◉ Portal   ● City

Tusbir

Cortubro

Felreve

Durnst

Lake Reneth
Tragesser
Raxel
Kranton
Risset
Wasabe
Ames
Balcazon Hills
Tirnol River
Tirmic Desert
Torrich
Dresdyn
Caldean Forest
Free City of Grondor
Kamden Vandene
Cetuna
Monaf
Strathe Bay

Charron Hills
Nampir
Izran
Corimir
Jerbic
Carmey
Xordrel
Xortec
Hebron Hills
Biske Bay
Drujasu
Das

Skarloc River
Hedrok River
Misemba Hills
Sarringel Mts.
Krathil-Ion
Sheraxi Forest
Raniax Hills
Atandral Forest

Plain of Antipithanee
LAWLESS
Lords River
Sheldomar Forest
Andahye
Ratik Mts.
Ratik
Driscol
Ferent
Sangrilak
Free City of Tambour
Selmist Forest
Donegal River
Bordraas
Aarden

Elvandahar
Karlisle
Bekbor
Calumet

Cortopian
Medea
Entsy
Klevabos
Ticumah
Acrostat
Thirpur
Filopor
Reshik-na
Fazipan
Tarnetta River
Velmist
Bryton Hills
Thenay River
Rotham

Child of prophecy, Warrior of destiny
Into the world a child will come
Born into darkness, she will bring light
Where once there was none
To her cause people will rally
And they will fight the Good Fight
For the birth of a new era
And she will wield great power
That can be harnessed only by the One
Man who has sworn his soul to her
But the undead Master will rise
And into abominable life bring an army
Such as the world has never seen
And that may only be stopped by the magic
Of the Warrior and the sworn Protector

* Excerpt from the Chardelis Prophecies

PART ONE

PROLOGUE

Winds whispered through the towering trees and silver leaves rustled, creating a melody of sound that could soothe and heal the soul. It was a summer wind full of warmth and the scents that could only be experienced at this time of the year. Soon, the heat would dissipate and the air would become cooler. The leaves of most trees would begin to turn color. Shades of crimson, orange, and yellow would suffuse the forests. But not this glen. The leaves from the silver oak never changed color.

Dremathian walked along the forest path. His people called it Krathil-lon, or "silver creation". It was a place of power, a sinkhole for magic. Wondrous things could be done, or undone, in Krathil-lon, and Dremathian presided over it. For the past few years had he been the arch-druid of his order. His predecessor, Father Mesendric, had held his position for over eighty years. Dremathian hoped he would live just as long.

Finally he made it to his destination, a clearing surrounded by mis-shapen rocks of varying sizes, each with a runic symbol engraved on its surface. They were important for the ceremony, but not integral. If the person going through the ritual was gifted enough, they didn't need the runes to help them experience the full power of the tabanakh drink.

However, Dremathian wasn't there to perform a ceremony to make an acolyte into a full member of the druidic order. It was much simpler than that...

The sounds of the forest paused in response to someone's passage. He listened intently, and within the briefest of moments all was normal again. Judging by the time lapse, he knew who it was that approached.

Dremathian gathered some wood from the nearby pile and placed it into the fire pit in the center of the clearing. He looked up as his friend emerged from the surrounding trees and he nodded in greeting. As requested, the young ranger was without the customary presence of Dramati, his corubis companion. He wore the new leather vest and trousers that Dremathian had made for him, and his thick, red hair was tied back at the nape of his neck.

Dremathian pointed to the ornate flask sitting on a flat rock on the other side of the clearing. "Could you get that for me?"

Sirion nodded and sauntered across the clearing. The young man had defied ranger code when he agreed to stay in Krathil-lon longer than necessary to heal from the wounds he'd sustained while helping out with the lycanthrope crisis. Early in Shandaharian history, rangers and druids had worked harmoniously together in their care of the natural world. The druids functioned as guardians of the wilderness, and the rangers as protectors of the druids. Unfortunately over time, fighting erupted between the two peoples. Druids, with all of their many ceremonies, rules and restrictions, wanted to impose that way of life upon their less regimented, and more liberated, ranger counterparts. The rangers resisted, and eventually left the druids to their own devices.

But that was a long time ago and there were very few rangers left. Most of those hailed from the forests, especially the realm of Elvandahar. They often hired themselves out to anyone who needed safe passage through the larger forests. They continued to be protectors, focusing on the flora and fauna of the forest within which they resided. For a long time, no ranger endeavored to protect druids. Not until now.

Sirion brought the requested flask and hunkered down bedside the fire pit. Dremathian caressed the newborn flames with his breath, urging it to grow. Not much longer and a small fire licked at the wood. He looked at the position of the sun and saw that it was almost time. The power of the runes worked best at dusk, when Shandahar's first moon, Steralion, was nearing her zenith.

Dremathian settled himself across from Sirion and removed the cork from the mouth of the flask. He inhaled the scent of the drink, and that simple gesture caused flashes of the visions his gift provided when he drank of the tabanakh. He deliberated taking a sip. It would be a useful tool to see what ailed his friend, but not necessary in terms of the Brotherhood Ceremony. Dremathian looked up and found Sirion staring at him through amber eyes, eyes that reflected the pain in his soul. He made his decision.

Dremathain handed the flask to Sirion. "Take a drink. It may not show you anything, but at least you can share the ceremony with me in every way."

Sirion nodded and placed the flask to his lips. He took a drink and passed it back to Dremathian. The druid watched his friend, knowing what to expect if Sirion received any visions from taking the drink. He doubted Sirion would, for he hadn't drank much, and even with the power of the runes, it usually took more than one drink to receive the visions, even for those who had the gift.

"You defied ranger code and ventured to aid my order with a serious lycanthrope problem. You dispatched the shirwemic with deadly aptitude. In truth, my Brothers and I were astonished by your efficiency, single-mindedness, and strength. After the threat was dissipated, I brought you to my home. I bandaged your wounds and bade you rest. For several days you stayed there, healing from the serious injuries sustained from the shirwemic leader, but when you recovered enough to leave, you chose not to do so. Instead, you took me up on my offer to show you the life of the druids within my order." Dremathian held out his hand, palm up, over the fire. "I was blessed the day I found you Sirion Timberlyn. Over the past several moon cycles you have become like a Brother to me, and today I want to make it real before the eyes of the gods."

Sirion placed his hand within Dremathian's. In a swift motion, the druid drew the ceremonial dagger from the sheath at his hip, flipped Sirion's hand over, and pulled the blade across his palm. He repeated the same for his own palm and gripped Sirion's hand tightly within his. Blood dripped from between their two hands and into the flames. Dremathian then dropped the dagger, picked up the flask, and took a small drink.

His gift exploded to life.

From within the fire the vision took shape in the form of a robust wemic with a thick mane. At first it was strong, wild, and free. It cavorted about in the flames, kicking up sparkling embers as it danced. But within moments it grew tired and weak. It grew sickly and lay on the ashes, its eyes barely able to open. Then it died.

Dremathian released Sirion's hand and sat back on his heels. He regarded his new Brother intently his heart filled with concern. Sirion noticed the shift in his demeanor and frowned. "Something bothers you. What is it?"

Dremathian took a moment to gather his thoughts. Within the time that Sirion had spent in Krathil-lon, Dremathian had noticed something about his friend. Anger. Sirion had a lot of anger that was just biding its time, waiting to be unleashed. It crouched, like an animal, becoming stronger and stronger. Dremathian knew Sirion had experienced difficulties in life and believed the crouching animal within was a culmination of those. He had no doubt this beast would come leaping out of the young ranger one day. He feared Sirion would be unable to control it, and as such, there would be a cost.

If left to run free, the beast would ultimately destroy him.

THE DRUIDS

ortath's easy lope through the tall grasses had lulled her into restfulness, and her thoughts were free to roam as they chose. Laying across the back of her canine friend, Adrianna idly ran her fingers through the thick, ruddy mane that surrounded his neck and chest, loving the silky texture of the fine hairs embedded deep within the mass. Catching her thoughts, Cortath gave a rumble deep in his throat and she smiled to herself, so much enjoying his doting personality. Sheridana had noticed it their first day of travel after leaving the city of Risset. It endeared Cortath to her sister in a way Adrianna never would have imagined, and even better, he liked Sheri too.

For the past two days, the group had been traveling south along the Dresnjik River. On the morrow they would cross it and then proceed along the northern rim of the Vanderess Forest towards the city of Kamden. Adrianna was both relieved, yet disquieted, by the fact they hadn't heard of any activity concerning her father since the day they learned about the deadly conflict outside the city of Torrich. Words spoken by the old gypsy woman, Ami Rayhana, cavorted through her mind... *"The undead lord will not stop until he feels your heart stop beating! For now his vision is clouded, but he will find you again. You cannot run from him forever."*

Adrianna was vexed at her hesitancy to tell Sheridana about Thane. She had intended to do it before leaving Risset, but the timing seemed all wrong. She knew her sister would be upset when she heard what she had to say, and she was loath to place strain on their newfound camaraderie. She'd had plenty of time since then, but tension pervaded the group. Even though Sheridana's daughter, Fitanni, was confined mostly to the wagon, it was difficult traveling in the company of a small child. Likewise, it was almost as hard getting accustomed to the new *adult* traveling companions...

Dinim Coabra and Sabian Makonnen– Sheridana only just tolerated the former and she avoided the latter completely.

However, regardless of any issues Sheri had with the two men, she willingly used her skills to the benefit of the entire group. Dartanyen was impressed by her contributions to the evening stewpot, and Armond and Zorg were appreciative of her willingness to help out with the nightly watches. Since the baby tended to wake her early, Sheri liked to take the last one. It worked out well, because it left Adrianna, Sabian, Dinim and Tianna free to pursue their studies and other necessary activities.

That night the group stopped at a location near the ferry dock along the Dresnjik River. Adrianna saw to the care of the animals while Tianna began preparations for the evening meal. Amethyst gravitated between these two women while Dinim and Sabian laid out the bedrolls. Dartanyen, Armond and Sheridana went hunting, and Carli carried the baby around the encampment in an attempt to stretch herself after a day spent trapped in the back of the wagon.

After tending to the needs of the lloryk and larian, Adrianna noticed Cortath lying at the periphery of the camp. He usually took part in the hunting. Concerned, she went over to him, and right away she realized he was unwell. He gazed at her through lackluster eyes and it was a struggle to get him to move the two handfuls of paces to her bedroll. She stared down at her friend, reminded of the unknown ailment he'd suffered in Risset. She shook her head and chided herself. *We've been traveling with very few stops. Maybe he just needs some extra rest.*

Cortath slept through the evening, but before taking to her bedroll for the night, Adrianna awakened her friend to offer him the last of the stew Tianna had cooked with the ptarmigan the hunters provided. Instead of graciously accepting it as usual, he listlessly turned away, the emotions transmitted to her through their link uncharacteristically vague.

Adrianna quashed down her feelings of unease and lay down beside her companion. She gently stroked the fur around his face as she drifted off into a restless sleep. In the morning she awoke unrefreshed. Turning to Cortath, she noticed he hadn't stirred from his position throughout the night. Frowning, she tried to rouse him from his sleep, but he was either unwilling, or unable, to do so. Through their link, Adrianna sensed that something was seriously wrong.

And she was afraid.

Adrianna didn't hesitate to call Tianna over to her bedroll. The healer knelt beside Cortath and placed her hands on him. After several moments she frowned and shook her head.

"Unlike last time, I sense something wrong. It's something vague, but terribly malignant. I felt it growing during the short time I had my hands on him." She looked up at Adrianna with a sorrowful expression. "He doesn't have an infection, and he hasn't been poisoned. The only thing I can rationalize is that this may be a magic-induced illness."

Fear lodged in her throat and she choked out her words, "Can you help him?"

Tianna sadly shook her head again. "I can't do anything for him. Whoever or whatever is doing this has taken a strong hold. I'm sorry, Adria."

Adrianna knew what Tianna implied by her last statement. If Cortath continued along this course, he might die. Dartanyen approached and stood over them for a moment before giving a deep sigh. "Come on, let's get him into the wagon. We have to leave soon if we are to take the ferry across the river today."

Adrianna nodded and Dartanyen and Tianna left to finish packing their bags. She continued to kneel next to Cortath, her tears falling onto his thick mane. She buried her fingers deep into the fur until finally she reached the soft skin beneath. It was then she felt something. Tracing it with her fingers, it felt like a cord. She hooked a finger under it, and slowly pulled it up through the thick fur. It was black, and made out of leather. She struggled with it for a moment, trying to disentangle the cord from the long hairs. Finally losing patience, she unsheathed the dagger at her side and cut it. She pulled on one end of the cord and it slipped through the fur. When she finally beheld the entire length, she found the reason why it was so difficult to remove. There was a soft leather pouch tied onto it.

The reddish brown bag was about was the size of her fist, pulled together at the top with a drawstring. She felt something inside and hesitated before loosening the top. *What is a leather pouch doing around the neck of an animal? Had Cortath once been a companion to someone else? Had he been a message carrier, and this was his last, undelivered message? He'd never let on about anyone else before me, but then, I never inquired.* Slowly she opened the pouch and dumped the contents into her lap.

The first thing Adrianna picked up was a beautiful signet ring inlaid with tiny shimmering gems. Carved within the gold was a crest depicting a hawk carrying leafy sprigs within its talons. It was definitely worth a small fortune. Next she picked up a long, sharp tooth that she surmised was from a worg or a wemic, and then a whistle made of dark wood. Adrianna put it to her lips and blew into it, but no sound emerged. Finally she picked up a small roll of parchment. She was about to unfurl it when she heard Tianna's voice. "Adrianna, I have your things packed and in the wagon. Let's get Cortath in there now."

Adrianna looked up and saw the healer striding over, Dartanyen and Zorg following behind. Armond was bringing the wagon close to where Cortath lay. "What do you have there?" Tianna asked, crouching beside her.

"It's strange, actually. I found this bag around Cortath's neck. It had these things in it." Adrianna held up the pouch and gestured to the four items spread before her.

"Humpf." Tianna picked up the signet ring and examined it. Suddenly her eyes widened. "Adrianna, did you say that you got this ring from that pouch?"

Adrianna nodded. "Yes, along with these other things."

Tianna put the ring closer to her eyes, narrowing them. "I can't believe this, but it's true."

"What—"

"This ring bears Sirion's house crest," she interrupted. "Only two were made. Anya wears one, and Sirion had the other. I think this one is Sirion's

17

ring!"

Adrianna was taken aback. *How can this possibly be Sirion's ring? Sirion is dead. Why would this animal be carrying it around his neck?* Adrianna silently watched Tianna pick up the pouch and the whistle. "By the gods, can it truly be? Adria, these are all Sirion's belongings!"

Adrianna frowned. "Are you sure?"

"I have no doubt. I've seen Sirion call Dramati with this whistle on more than one occasion."

"But it doesn't work."

"How do you know?"

"I tried sounding it, and nothing happened."

"I'm sure it did," replied Tianna. "Only wemic, worg and corubis can hear the pitch given from this type of whistle. Sirion made it himself. I can tell because he carved Dramati into it. See?"

Adrianna looked to where Tianna pointed. Indeed, there was a carving of an animal on the side. Her friend was so excited, and seemed so sure this was Sirion's pouch, but that didn't explain how it came to be around Cortath's neck. Adrianna looked up to find Dartanyen, Zorg, and Armond approaching. "Come on! Let's load Cortath into the wagon and get going," urged Dartanyen.

"Take a look at this!" Tianna's voice was elated. "Adrianna found this pouch around Cortath's neck, and I think it belongs to Sirion!"

The three men came over and listened to Tianna's explanation. Dinim climbed down from the back of the wagon and joined them, catching the last portion of her description. When he looked down at the pouch and heard Sirion's name, his brows furrowed. "I've seen a pouch similar to that one around Sirion's neck."

"See, I told you! This is Sirion's pouch!" Tianna chortled.

Dinim shook his head. "You know that isn't possible. I told you..."

She narrowed her eyes. "Dinim, I know what you told me, but I'm telling you this pouch belongs to him! This is his ring, his whistle, and Dramati's first tooth. I would know because I've seen these things several times before!"

"But Tianna, what was it doing around Cortath's neck?" asked Adrianna.

Tianna stopped and looked down at Cortath. She looked at his face, into his partially open amber eyes. He slowly lifted his head. Through the link, Adrianna sensed he was aware they were talking about him. Tianna's eyes gradually widened. "Cor... Cortath... he *is* Sirion." She said the words almost breathlessly, like she could hardly believe them herself.

"What? Are you crazy?" said Dartanyen.

"I'm serious. His eyes, now I know why they've always seemed so familiar to me. They are *his* eyes... *Sirion's* eyes!"

Zorg pursed his lips and shook his head. "You *are* crazy!"

"No, maybe not," said Armond in Tianna's defense. "She could be right."

"No way!" said Dinim in exasperation. "I saw him get sucked into that vortex! No one could have survived it!"

"Sirion did," Tianna said plainly.

Adrianna just looked at her wordlessly. Could it really be true? Could Cortath really be Sirion? She stood silently by as the men worked. Cortath barely had the strength to help get himself into the wagon. Once he was inside, she entered and sat by his side. It was covered, so he wouldn't be able to see the familiar sky, and the ride would be bumpy. She would offer what comfort and reassurance she could. Tianna glanced within before they began moving, an expression of indecision on her face. Adrianna was about to ask her to join them, but she left before she could say anything.

It wasn't long before the wagon rumbled to a stop and a series of expletives were emanating from the driver's seat. Alarmed, Adrianna pulled back the flap and saw the angry expression on Dartanyen's face. "What is it?"

"We missed the damned ferry."

Dartanyen proceeded to climb down from the wagon. Adrianna quickly walked through to the rear of the wagon and gazing out, she saw the commuter boat. It had recently pulled away from the shore and was beginning its journey across the river. *Damnation! If I hadn't dawdled so long over Cortath we would have made it in plenty of time. Now we are forced to wait another full day and night, further increasing our chances of being accosted by Thane.*

Everyone felt the strain of their circumstances as they set up camp. Adrianna noticed Sheridana glancing about, probably wondering why everyone was so put out. Dartanyen cast Adrianna some acrid glances before offering to hunt for the stewpot, and she felt worse than ever. No one had been able to say anything about Thane because she still hadn't told Sheridana about him. It placed that much more stress on everyone, and Adrianna regretted putting it off.

A while after midday, Dartanyen and Armond returned with several fat ptarmigan. Adrianna offered one of the birds to Cortath, but he only lifted his head to sniff it before turning away. Through their link she now sensed a raging fever. His body was weakening and his soul was in turmoil. She didn't understand what it all meant, but sensed it would eventually kill him.

Adrianna maintained her vigil. She sobbed piteously, her tears wetting Cortath's fur. Tianna came to sit beside her, and before long her eyes were equally red and puffy. Amethyst, Sheridana, and the men entered the wagon every once in a while, but always left disappointed as Cortath's condition rapidly worsened. Adrianna still nurtured the hope he would miraculously make a turn for the better. She couldn't help it, for she despaired imagining her life without him. No one understood the depth of the bond she shared with Cortath, couldn't even begin to comprehend her loss. She knew Tianna felt that

Cortath and Sirion were one and the same. In truth, Adrianna couldn't allow her thoughts to branch so far. She was losing enough already, and the idea that Sirion was somehow a part of that loss was overwhelming.

The day shifted into early evening. The camp was somber and everyone was keeping mostly to themselves. They had decided to move Cortath out of the wagon, hoping to give him some fresh air. He lay stretched out on the ground, his lackluster, dappled fur laden with an excess of dirt and oils due to insufficient upkeep. His body twitched every once in a while in his sleep, and Adrianna wondered what he was dreaming about.

Suddenly Cortath's body started to convulse, and Adrianna was thrust backward by the force of the muscular contractions. The rest of the group rushed over, Dartanyen and Tianna trying to reach him through the jerking legs. The animal made strange sounds deep in this throat, and his eyes rolled back in their sockets. A deep ache filled Adrianna's chest. She tried to reach Cortath through their link, but his mind was closed to her. Tears filled her eyes and the truth of her reality settled around her, the truth that he was leaving her alone to continue her life without him.

So caught up in her thoughts, at first Adrianna didn't realize the presence of other people in the encampment. Several brown-robed figures rushed over to the scene. One of them, a silver-haired man, gently put his hands on her shoulders and moved her aside. He approached the still convulsing Cortath and knelt beside him. With an expression of intense worry, he placed a hand along each side of the animal's head and leaned in close. He spoke in an unfamiliar tongue, with a cadence that sounded like a priest's prayer or sorcerer's incantation. After a few moments, Cortath's convulsions slowly ceased.

Adrianna immediately knew what these people were– druids.

The man remained poised over him for a while, gently stroking the mane around Cortath's face. He then spoke in Hinterlic, "Sirion, I am here my friend. I will find a way to help you. You are not alone."

Adrianna's breath caught in her throat. The revelation was shocking in spite of Tianna's excited claim earlier that day. Feeling faint, she placed a hand to her forehead. She began to sway and felt a hand at her elbow. Glancing beside her, she saw it was Armond, his green eyes reflecting sympathy. He gave her a faint nod, and after a moment she returned it, silently telling him she would be all right.

The brown-robed men swiftly constructed a litter. She wasn't certain where they obtained the wood and fabric they used, but she didn't care to ponder it overly long. Instead she focused on the conversation the silver-haired man shared with Dartanyen, Dinim, and Tianna.

Tianna's expression was concerned. "Father Dremathian, where will you be taking him?"

"We will go to Krathil-lon, our home in the southern reaches of the Sartingel Mountains. Once there, I hope to find a way to help Sirion."

She shook her head in wonderment. "How did you know where to find him? You came from so far away."

Dremathian nodded. "My dreams brought me here. 'Tis a gift I have, to see things that others cannot." Dremathian paused and then continued in a more hurried voice. "But we must make haste. The longer Sirion goes without help, the more sickly he becomes."

Tianna simply nodded as Dremathian stepped away to confer with two of his Brothers. As they spoke, Dremathian gestured towards Adrianna. She was confused for a moment before she realized he indicated a place behind her. She turned to find that the encampment was not only full of the brown-robed men, but their large riding companions as well.

The beasts were huge, their bodies resembling a combination of a muscular cat and a great bird of prey. Their heads were largely feline, adorned with ruddy-gold feathers. The paws bore the talons of a hawk, and a pair of large, golden wings lay folded against their furred sides. Adrianna stared at them, awed by their majesty and predatory beauty. She had never seen a griffon before, much less a cohort of them. They seemed to be friendly enough, and their manner calm. Atop their backs was strange riding gear and travel packs.

Once the litter was ready, Armond and Zorg loaded Cortath onto it. Adrianna watched as the druids then rigged the litter onto the back of the largest griffon. The ruddy creature turned his feathered head to watch as the men adjusted the litter with varying straps and clips. It would be a heavy load for the beast to carry, but he seemed prepared to take on the job.

The group watched as the druids prepared to leave. Tianna approached Dremathian and spoke to him in a low voice. She then went to the wagon and took her travel pack from inside. Adrianna supposed she couldn't blame her for wanting to leave with the druids. Sirion was her childhood friend, after all. It would be natural for her to want to accompany him. Adrianna felt the pain of loss sweep through her for what seemed like the hundredth time that day. Cortath was leaving her. Upon the backs of the griffons, these druids would take him away, and she would probably never see her dear friend ever again.

Adrianna was about to turn away when she felt a presence beside her. She looked up into the kind face of Father Dremathian. His blue eyes were intent as he regarded her. "Lady, you and your company would do well to consider coming with us to Krathil-lon. I have felt something in the winds, something coming in this direction. I have never felt anything like it before, but I know it is evil, and that it could do you harm."

Adrianna stared at him, startled. Dremathian's expression was one of extreme seriousness. She knew who was coming, and fear rushed through her. Lord Thane had found them, and he was closing in for the kill. Dremathian seemed to know when she made the realization, and he nodded his head minutely. Adrianna returned the nod; it was the only indication Dartanyen needed to start unloading the wagon.

Everyone flew into a flurry of activity, loading the griffons with the group's belongings. Adrianna felt a moment of sadness, hating to leave the lloryk and larian behind, especially the one she called Sethanon. He had been a good mount, and she had come to care for him. She patted the lloryk briefly and wished him well as Dartanyen unstrapped his ropes. When all of the animals had been released, Armond and Zorg slapped them across the hindquarters. They all galloped off together, away from the incoming menace.

Everyone swiftly mounted the griffon to which he or she had been assigned. The creatures were carrying loads that were heavier than usual, but they seemed to have no problems as they began to run. They ran faster and faster, their wings unfurling from their sides. The wind whipped the loose tendrils of hair about Adrianna's face, and she instinctively leaned low over the feathered back. Suddenly she felt a strange feeling in the pit of her stomach, and they were rising into the air. Higher and higher they rose. A feeling of exhilaration gripped her, and Adrianna felt like crying out. Never had she felt something so awesome, so breathtaking. She looked down from the back of the griffon, saw the river winding, serpent-like, across the land. She saw their abandoned wagon, as well as the lloryk and larian they had set free.

But then Adrianna saw something else, something that made a chill rise up her spine. It was Thane. He had almost reached the encampment. With him were his six minions, all of them riding steeds that seemed to be made of the darkness itself. She closed her eyes, thankful to the gods who had afforded them this escape.

For surely she and her companions would not have escaped from her father alive this time.

He slowly awoke.

"Sirion..."

There it was again, the familiar voice that had taken him from deep slumber. He opened his eyes and found himself surrounded by darkness. The darkness was familiar. It was his *aertna*, that place faelin-kind believed existed within every man somewhere between his mind and his soul. It had become his prison when he was sucked into the magical vortex– when his body had transformed from that of a man into a beast. It was the last vestige of him that was a faelin, a part that had slowly been dwindling away as the days passed. And as the place shrank, he had less and less contact with his external senses. His animal nature had become predominant and Sirion was starting to forget who he was. He was sleeping for longer periods of time, escaping from depression and loneliness– letting the inevitability of death have its way with him.

But someone had awakened him.

"Sirion, my old friend... are you there?"

There was the familiar voice again. He tried to place it. It came from his past, this voice. He tried to speak, but nothing came out but a forlorn sound between a howl and a whine. He attempted to project a reply with his mind, but then remembered he was unable to communicate that way with just anyone. For some reason, his connection with Adrianna was different. He had nearly forgotten that fact, his influence over his body declining as his faelin self faded away.

"Sirion, please. I can't help you if you don't choose to help yourself."

The voice stopped. Sirion waited, pensive. Help himself? How many times within the past weeks had he tried to do just that, only to meet complete and utter failure? How could he help himself if he didn't know how to go about doing it? In angry frustration, Sirion began to struggle, pushing at the darkness. He pushed harder, harder than he had since first discovering what he had become.

Sirion opened his eyes. He saw through the distorted vision of an animal. Crouched before him there was a human– no, a half-faelin. The man was familiar to him, wearing a nondescript brown robe. His silvering hair was tied back, and it hung over one shoulder. The man looked deeply into Sirion's eyes and smiled, his expression one of great joy. Sirion also felt happiness, for he hadn't seen Father Dremathian in many years. He started to lift his head, but then lowered it again. It was simply too much of an effort.

It was then he realized it– his body was dying.

"Sirion, it is so good to see you after so many years," said Dremathian. "Here, chew this leaf. It will help you."

He barely had the strength, but he did as his friend requested. The leaf tasted terrible and his guts roiled the moment he swallowed it.

"I am going to help you as much as I can, but in the end, only you can save yourself. Only you can get your life back again, and then, only if you want it badly enough. Your time is limited, my friend. You must hurry! Fight your jailors, climb your barriers, and overcome your inadequacies! Be stronger than you ever have been before!"

Sirion felt a surge of weakness and slowly faded out. He struggled to regain his hold on the outside, but it was to no avail. He plummeted back into the silent, familiar darkness, but Dremathian's awakening had done something to him, and a host of memories came flooding back. It was the years he had spent with his father he recalled first, mayhap because they had been the most defining. It was with Servial that he had met Zandibar, Baltheros, Chans, and the other men who had taught him all he knew about hand-to-hand combat, weapons usage, meditation, and the host of other skills he had learned as a boy. Servial himself had taught Sirion the finer arts of being a ranger, and he slowly earned a name for himself as the years progressed. Finally, memories of his father's brother also arose, and Sirion was filled with hatred. Sydonnia had taken so much away from him the day he murdered Servial. Sometimes he thought to render similar justice one day, just as he'd been trained to do.

Sirion felt himself beginning to slip. The familiar tiredness overwhelmed him, pulled at his consciousness. He was compelled to give in, but Dremathian had said he needed to be strong. Sirion let the memories fade as he struggled against the heavy darkness that pressed closer, closer, closer...

Then he began to feel something. It started out as an ache but it slowly grew. It twined about in his guts like a serpent, growing bigger and bigger. The pain became so much that he could feel his body again, every joint, every muscle, every sinew. The pain wracked through him and he screamed.

SIRION AND CORTATH

T he griffons flew the group across the Dresnjik river into the Kingdom of Durnst. Once there, they continued south along the river until they reached the northern timberline of the Vanderess Forest. The griffons landed and everyone prepared for the remainder of their journey on foot. Adrianna was confused; she could have swore she heard the old druid leader tell Tianna that they hailed from the Sartingel Mountains. So far they had only managed to travel away from their intended destination.

Once a small meal had been taken and their travel packs were in hand, everyone walked briskly through the forest. Every once in a while Adrianna caught glimpses of a ranger or two. They never approached the group, and she imagined they were on friendly terms with the druids. It wasn't very long before they reached a small dilapidated cabin. The druids led them inside, and once everyone was gathered, Father Dremathian uttered a short incantation. The ground beneath them shuddered for a moment before a downward leading staircase appeared.

Once reaching the bottom, everyone hurriedly made their way through the adjoining passageway. Adrianna couldn't help feeling sympathy for Armond, Zorg, and two of the druids carrying the litter holding Cortath. The strain of their burden was evident by the sweat trickling down the sides of their faces and the heavy breaths they took as they struggled to keep up with the others.

Several moments later they entered a large chamber. At the center was a raised platform upon which stood a pedestal with an open book resting on top. A couple of farlo away from the pedestal stood a large oval mirror that measured at least two faelin men tall. The druids stepped up onto the dais, beckoning the group to follow. Father Dremathian walked over to the pedestal and stopped before it. Strangely drawn, Adrianna followed. Dremathian turned to her as she approached. "This book will take us to Krathil-lon. Only there will I be able to help Sirion."

Standing beside the druid leader, Adrianna looked down at the book. There, on the topmost page, she saw an animated wooded glen. The winds moved through the treetops, the silver leaves rustling gently. Below the life-like scene was a phrase written in the words of magic. Adrianna instinctively knew that once the words were read aloud, a portal would form within the mirror before them. It would be an arcane doorway to the place represented on the page in the book. However, she had never experienced such a thing before, and apprehension prickled her senses.

Adrianna looked over her shoulder when Dinim stepped up behind her. He offered a faint smile before they both turned back to Dremathian, the druid beginning his recitation of the words printed below the scene. A gentle wind swept through the chamber as swirls of color began to move through the center of the oval mirror. Within moments, the swirling reached a plateau and stabilized into a shimmering wall of blue.

The druids promptly picked up the litter carrying Cortath and moved towards the portal. Dremathian turned back to Adrianna, his blue eyes taking in her reluctance. "Come. It is not painful–merely disorienting for a moment or two."

Adrianna nodded and began to follow him. Once seeing her move towards the portal, Dartanyen, Armond, and the rest of the group followed suit. Adrianna couldn't help hesitating as she stood in front of the shimmering wall. Somehow, at that moment, she knew her life was about to make another radical change. The others stood behind her, silently waiting. Adrianna took a deep breath and watched as Father Dremathian stepped through the portal.

She closed her eyes and whispered the words from a song she recalled from her childhood, "Put your faith in what you most want to believe in..."

The darkness pressed close. Sirion disliked the proximity, but tolerated it. A floodgate had been opened, and memories coursed all about him like a maelstrom. Where he stood in the center of the convolution, Sirion heard all of the voices and saw the faces of the many people he had known during his forty-eight years. They circled and eddied about him and he waited to get sucked into the recesses of his newly awakened mind.

Without form, Sirion raced through Time. He sped past scenes in his life comprised of people and events that had become important to him over the years: his mother and father arguing as he and Anya looked on... his mother crying softly to herself, her hands over her face, her body shaking with the force of her emotion... his father later speaking with another ranger ..."Servial, don't concern yourself with Lilandria. She is just a woman, and you are the best ranger in these parts. Don't let her spoil that for you."

The scenes shifted. He and Anya playing together among the tall silver trees at home in Elvandahar... his father holding his hands in the proper position on a small bow made just for him... his mother kissing his forehead, her beautiful face radiant with love... Father Dremathian sitting across the ceremonial fire after they had become blood bonded..."Sirion, family is the most important thing a man has. Without family, a man is nothing."

Pensively, Sirion considered the scenes. He felt sadness when he looked upon his mother's loving face. He hadn't seen her for several years. He felt good when he saw Dremathian. He had learned more from him than any other with the exception of his father. Sirion's feelings concerning Servial were mixed. Not once had the man bothered to take him back home during all the years of his training. Sirion had returned to Elvandahar only after his father was killed by Sydonnia.

Sirion's life journey continued... Sirion and his father sitting with the rest of the Bekborian pit fighters, one of the sun-bronzed men leaning towards him, *"Show your opponent no mercy. Be strong, give him all you've got, and utterly defeat him."* The scenes shifted. Sirion sitting across from his father at the evening fire, smiling as Servial told him stories of his youth... facing Zandibar in the ring, the fighter showing him how to evade an opponent's grasp... Baltheros, his large hand on Sirion's shoulder saying, *"When a man is down, and unable to rise, always consider showing him mercy. It portrays strength of character."*...Sirion helplessly watching as his uncle Sydonnia tore out his father's throat... Sirion grasping the werewolf Nora's arm tightly, recognizing Sydonnia's scent on her...*"No matter where you go, I will track you down and kill you."*...

Sirion became angry. The scene of his father's grisly death brought back all of the old fears. No matter what Servial had done to Sydonnia in the past, he couldn't possibly have deserved death, even if it really was Servial's fault that Sydonnia was cursed with lycanthropy. Sirion allowed the rage to consume him. When they finally met, he would show Sydonnia no leniency. The man hadn't just killed Sirion's father, but others he cared about as well. Sydonnia had even threatened Lilandria once, although Sirion knew it to be merely a tactic used to goad him. Somehow, Sirion knew that Sydonnia loved his mother too much to ever kill her.

Sirion moaned in anguish. The much-despised Sydonnia had loved Lilandria much more than Servial ever did. She had always deserved so much more than what Servial had given her. Yet, Sirion had similarly ignored her, staying away between visits much longer than he should. He didn't really know why, only mayhap that he didn't really know what to say...

The darkness pressed heavily on him, the scenes from his life slowing down. Through the rage and guilt, the pressure was crushing, and he gasped. He felt his life slipping away, the voices in accompaniment.

His own voice– *"Do I love myself? That's a silly question. I've never really thought about it. I suppose I do..."*

His father's voice– *"Your life is worthless Sydonnia! You have accomplished nothing, and no one cares about you."*

Anya's voice– *"When I got old enough, and confident enough, I thought about finding you, tracking you down. I knew I would succeed. I wanted so much to see my brother again, despite my anger."*

His mother's voice–*"Life is a wondrous thing, Sirion. It's a miracle, nature's gift to us all."*

Chans' voice– *"Don't judge something upon the words of someone else. Experience it for yourself, and only then pass judgment."*

Sorn's voice– *"Sometimes I wish my life was different, that I could be a normal man with a home and a family. I often tire of the constant traveling, of not knowing where I will end up next, who I will kill on the morrow, or if I will find myself killed instead. What of you, Sirion? Don't you want something different sometimes... something real?"*

Dremathian's voice– *"The world– it is all around, speaking to us. If we open our hearts, we can hear all that it has to say, in all of its many voices."*

Sirion clung to the edge of the precipice, clawing at the substance of his *aertna*, feeling it slip beneath his fingers. And then, with nothing under his feet, he fell, his hands reaching for a ledge that was no longer there. He plummeted through the nothingness, the voices fading away, the scenes from his life shifting into shadow. It was such a shame he never got to meet Adrianna once more as a man.

He could never be the one, the protector who would make all her sorrows undone...

Sensing someone watching him, Sirion turned around. He saw her standing across the street, the woman with moon-colored hair, Lady Gemma Darnesse. She was heavy with child, her belly stretching the fabric of her moss green dress. His interest piqued, Sirion made his way over to her, stopping only when he was a couple of paces away. In spite of her condition, Gemma's beauty was something to behold, her pale blue eyes regarding him intently.

Sirion raised an inquiring eyebrow. "Is there something you wish of me, Lady?"

She hesitated before answering, almost as though considering if she should say anything. The indecision however, was only momentary. Her voice was almost musical in quality, like the burbling of a mountain stream. And much to his surprise, she spoke in the language of Hinterlean faelin.

"You are Sirion Timberlyn, are you not?"

He was surprised she knew who he was. "Indeed I am," he replied as cordially as he knew how.

"I am Gemma Darnesse."

Sirion couldn't keep the small smile from curving one corner of his mouth. "I know who you are, Lady."

Gemma chuckled softly and shook her head. "Of course. It seems everyone knows who I am."

Sirion didn't make a reply. She was right. Everyone did *know who she was. Who wouldn't? Her beauty was legendary in this city.*

She continued, "I have seen you in and about Sangrilak many times within the past few years. We have never met, but since the onset of this pregnancy, I have had dreams about you. Does this not seem somewhat strange?" Gemma's delicate eyebrows furrowed.

Sirion nodded, not really knowing what to say. "Indeed, I see how this must be quite disturbing. But what can I possibly do to help you?"

"I have an ability, a gift if you will, of seeing what Destiny holds in store for us. Perhaps if I speak to you of the dreams, I will cease to have them. Allow me to speak the words of your destiny, and perhaps I can be freed." Her gaze was intent. "Maybe you will be freed as well."

Sirion frowned. He didn't hold much stock in the ranting of seers and soothsayers. Yet, this woman didn't seem to be just another fortune-teller, and she appeared to be genuinely concerned about her dreams. He bowed slightly in acquiescence. "As you wish, Lady."

Gemma gave him a brief grin of appreciation before taking a deep breath. Her gaze turned inward and few moments passed before she spoke again, her voice taking on a mystical quality. "You are meant for more than what you have become. When Destiny calls out to you, it will not be with the voice of the wilderness. You must make a choice, and only in making the right one will you know true happiness. In this you must find your inner strength. I have seen a woman in my dreams. She is meant for you. With her at your side, you are more than just the warrior, the protector, or the hero."

Lady Gemma stopped speaking and slowly came back to herself. She blinked away her vision and smiled, a smile that reminded Sirion of the mother he had left behind so long ago when his father had taken him out on his first ranger run. He felt an upwelling in his chest, the sensation of hope being born. This woman had come to him and given him something he had never known before. He realized he wanted to say something, but Gemma was already moving away down the street. He thought about calling after her, but he didn't know what to say...

.....

Sirion called out to Dramati once more, following the direction in which the faint replies emanated. He wondered why the corubis would not come; Dramati had always responded to his calls before. Through their link, Sirion couldn't sense anything amiss with the animal, so he wasn't worried that Dramati was sick or injured. When Sirion crested the top of the hill he stopped. Dramati lay there in the grass, his body curled around the form of a small child. Sirion's eyes widened with surprise as he approached. It was unlike Dramati to take to another person so well. He was more tolerant of children, and was always gentle, but he was never one to run off with them.

Sirion stood over Dramati and the girl. She was a beautiful child, her hair like white gold. She wore tunic and trousers like a boy, but her small, delicate feet were bare. She had one small fist curled tightly around a tuft of Dramati's neck fur. She was a fair child, but when she opened them, Sirion looked into eyes so dark, he could almost become lost.

The child slowly sat upright and then stood, watching him intently. Her features were familiar, and Sirion recognized her as the late Lady Gemma's daughter. The woman had died in childbed several years ago; this had to be the child she had given her life to bear.

Realizing that he was staring, Sirion stumbled out a greeting. He liked children, and even seemed to have a connection with them, but this one was different. It was as though this one could see into his very soul. The child greeted him in return, and slowly began to approach. Once she was standing before him, she reached out and touched his wrist. He took her small hand within his larger one, and he couldn't help but smile. The girl smiled in response. She was a beautiful creature, so much like her mother.

.....

Sirion smelled the young woman before he saw her. He was so attuned to her scent, he would know it anywhere. Then he saw her– a graceful step here, a shy glance there, a glimpse of her soft throat, her pale hair plaited in a long rope that hung down her back. A long dark cloak streamed behind her as she moved down the main thoroughfare. Like always, Sirion considered stepping up to her, speaking to her, letting her take notice of him. But then he remembered his physical state: his tousled hair, dirty hands, and grimy clothes. He reeked of the wilderness, his own body odor, and mayhap even the blood of some of the trolags he'd slaughtered the day before.

So Sirion just watched like he did every time he saw her. Her beauty, so much like her mother's, took his breath away, and her fragrance was like croxian to him. He remained an aspect of the shadows across the street from her, and she never knew it was he who observed. She just looked around from time to time, knowing only that someone watched.

.....

Sirion walked across the street to Volstagg's inn. The night seemed to be a busy one, the patrons staying a bit longer than usual. They knew the Wildrunners were back in town, and the rumors preceding them were interesting ones. Upon entering the establishment, he smelled a fragrance he hadn't encountered for a long time. His brows drew together. It couldn't be... she had gone to the city of Andahye almost a decade ago. But there she was, sitting at the bar, speaking with Volstagg. His heart hammering in his chest, Sirion began to make his way over. Volstagg saw him and grinned. Sirion approached and took the seat beside the woman he knew as Adrianna. Her scent was overwhelming; he hadn't the opportunity to get this close to her in such a long time.

Tiredly, Sirion placed the large sack he'd been carrying on the counter. It contained much of what he and the rest of the Wildrunners had earned within the past few moon cycles. It would go towards the expansion of the inn.

Volstagg picked it up appreciatively and placed it beneath the bar. Then they began to speak in earnest, using his native tongue. He felt her watching him, her dark gaze speculative. At a break in the conversation he turned toward her. He caught her gaze, her dark eyes widening in surprise. He heard her quick intake of breath, raised an eyebrow, and turned away. Gods! She was more beautiful than he remembered!

Sirion struggled. He was drowning, but he wanted so much to make it to the surface. He felt a sudden rush, and fueled by determination, he began his ascent. He felt the muscles working in his arms and legs, and he felt his heart pumping fiercely in his chest. He wanted to live! He wanted to see the world again... to run bare-foot through the forests of home... to hear the song of the wind in the trees, to feel the cool waters of Lake Tashinade wash over him after a refreshing rain. He wanted to have something real, something for which to come back after a long run. He wanted to live his own life, not just simply accomplish those tasks set out for him by others. He wanted to be more than just the best there was at what he did. He wanted to be more than what he had been primed by his father to be. He wanted to be more than just a warrior, and more than just a hero. One day he wanted to be a husband, and a father.

Sirion pushed aside the darkness and the oppression. He kicked harder and he continued to move ever upwards. He felt the blood rushing through his veins and an exhilaration he had felt only as a boy, learning the ways of a ranger in the forests of Elvandahar. He thought of all the things he wanted to see again, and all the things he had never seen but wanted to see. He thought of his mother and his sister, of Volstagg, Sorn, and Dremathian. He thought of all of the people who had loved him in his life and who had given him the will to endure, to face his daemons, to accept what he had become, and to realize what he could be. He thought of Adrianna, and hope for the future surged through him.

Sirion wanted to live, and at the end of that life he wanted to look back on it and be complete.

The group walked towards the sprawling building. The druids called it an apoptos, and it was the center of the of the druids' lives in Krathil-lon. The structure was very open, having as few walls as possible while still maintaining some security from the elements. Tall columns supported the ceilings, many of them sporting ivy with arrow-shaped leaves and orange flowers. Adrianna followed her comrades up the stairs and into the building. Magnificently carved animal statues silently looked on as they walked towards the main hall where they would break their fast. Once there, she listened as everyone talked among themselves at the table.

The group had spent the past several days in the silver glen. It was a beautiful place, and Adrianna had filled her time with walks along the forest paths, studies in the library, mealtimes with her comrades, and opportunities acquainting herself with her neiya and reestablishing her bond with Sheridana. She spent her nights sleeping alone. During the weeks leading up to his sickness, she had grown accustomed to the warmth of Cortath's body curled around her, the rise and fall of his breaths, the tickling sensation of the soft furs of his mane brushing her cheek, and the long tail laid protectively over her. She tried to smother her feelings of loneliness, but it was difficult. Dremathian was doing his best to help Sirion break free from his bestial prison so he could walk Shandahar as a man once more. It would be good to see Sirion, and she looked forward to it, but she would never see Cortath again.

And her dreams had returned.

Time had crept slowly by and there was no sign of either Sirion or Dremathian. The group had asked several members of the druid order about both, but the answer was always the same– Sirion was very ill, and Dremathain was trying his best to save his life. Tianna was in a state of constant agitation, and was difficult to be around. Zorg and Armond worked to develop their weapons techniques in sparring practices, and Amethyst snooped around the place like a shadow. Dartanyen helped Sheridana hone her skills with the bow, and Dinim and Sabian could often be found in the library.

Tianna was the first to notice Father Dremathian's presence. When everyone else finally turned to look in the direction where her attention was drawn, all talk ceased. Everyone focused on the arch-druid as he approached the table, his countenance stoic. "About three nights ago, Master Sirion finally returned to us. Only today has he been strong enough to accept visitors. He is presently in the meditation chamber if you would like to see him."

Everyone rose from the table. Tianna was the first to reach Dremathian. "Thank you so much! You have worked a miracle!"

"No," replied the old man with a tired smile. "Only gods perform miracles. I am merely a man. Sirion did most of the healing himself. I just guided him along the way."

The group followed the druid through the halls. Adrianna could feel Tianna's excitement as she walked beside her. At the end of the corridor Dremathian opened a set of doors and the group walked into a large room. It was virtually unfurnished with the exception of a sprawling, ornate rug in the middle of the floor. Lying upon it was Sirion's corubis companion, Dramati. He regarded the group intently as they entered, but didn't move from his spot. At the far end of the room there was a large window, and leaning beside it, looking out, was a man.

His skin was the color of pale bronze. He wore no tunic, only a pair of tawny trousers. His back and shoulders were muscular, and his shoulder-length hair a fiery chestnut. He moved his body away from the wall and slowly turned around.

For a moment no one said anything. Sirion slowly appraised them, his amber gaze traveling from one face to the next. Standing back behind the rest of the group, Adrianna watched him. Her heart thumped in her chest as she looked upon familiar eyes. She thought she'd never see Cortath again, but he was right here standing before her in the form of a man.

"Sirion..." Tianna launched herself towards him, her arms out-stretched. He steeled himself for the impact before she nearly knocked him from his feet. She wrapped her arms around his neck. "By the gods, I have missed you."

Sirion's voice was deep, deeper than Adrianna remembered. She could hear the hint of amusement in his tone. "Hello, Tianna." He chuckled and embraced her heartily, the muscles of his arms flexing as he lifted her feet from the floor.

Sirion just held her for a moment. Tianna's body shook within his embrace, and he knew she was weeping. He swept a comforting hand over her back and hair, and his tone was soothing. It took him another moment to finally pull himself away. He placed a forefinger on her trembling lips. "Shhhh, everything is well now."

Tianna swallowed heavily and shook her head. "I thought I had lost you..."

Sirion put his hands on the sides of Tianna's face, wiping her tears away with his thumbs. "I know, I know. We will get another chance to talk later." He patted Tianna's shoulder reassuringly and stepped towards the group. He grinned. "It's good to see everyone."

Dartanyen was there to meet him halfway. "And even better for us to see that you are well again, my friend."

The two men clasped one another's arms in greeting. Sirion was a bit surprised when Dartanyen then took it further by stepping closer to wrap his other arm around his shoulders in a brief embrace before stepping back again. Sirion was heartened by the simple gesture; he felt that he had truly been missed by these people even though they had met only twice before being separated by duty.

Behind Dartanyen were Armond and Zorg. Each of the men greeted Sirion the same way, patting him on the back and expressing their delight to see him hale and whole once more. Dartanyen then introduced him to Amethyst, Sabian, and Sheridana. They had never met him prior to his miraculous transformation and gave a simple nod in acknowledgment. Sirion returned the gesture.

It was then he realized someone was missing. His eyes scanned the group. *Where is she? Why isn't she here?* He had asked Dremathian about her, so he knew Adrianna had come with the rest of the group through the portal system. As he lay in recovery, he'd thought of this day, the day he would be reintroduced to the people who had accompanied him during an especially pivotal time in his life. And the one he'd looked forward to seeing most wasn't there.

Mayhap she doesn't care as much as I imagined she might.

As disappointment set in, he focused beyond the group of friends surrounding him. He let out the breath of air he hadn't realized he was holding, and he smiled.

Adrianna slowly approached from the rear of the chamber. She was radiant, just as she had been that evening in Sangrilak when he first saw her again after so many years. He remembered treating her coldly that night, aloof and a little standoffish. He had regretted it later, berating himself for being such a lloryk's ass.

The memory faded into the back of his mind and he stepped around the others to meet her. At that moment, it felt like just the two of them were there. He didn't hesitate as he might have once done and he reached out and took both her hands into his own. The behavior was unfamiliar, for he hadn't experienced many women in his life. There had only been Joselyn, and she'd been the one doing most of the approaching.

Sirion inclined his head to her. "My lady Adrianna."

She responded in kind, her gaze intent. "My lord Sirion."

He looked into her eyes. They were piercing, and seemed to see into the very depths of his soul. "I am glad to see you are well."

Adrianna nodded and replied almost hesitantly. "It seems you are not much worse for the wear."

He shrugged. "Appearances can often be deceiving."

Sirion immediately sensed a shift in her demeanor. She quickly took her hands from his and stepped back. "I suppose you are right."

Sirion was taken aback. At first he didn't recognize the reason for her abrupt withdrawal. But then his thoughts caught up to the situation at hand. *Damnation! I'm such a fool! Adrianna is still thinking about the beast she had called Cortath.* As he understood it, she had befriended him in his animal state and they were almost inseparable. His offhand remark had made her remember how illusory that had been.

Compelled to right his mistake, Sirion gently took her shoulders and leaned in close, placing his face alongside hers. He then spoke softly in her ear, "You know I have been wanting to thank you for–"

At that moment, the doors to the chamber suddenly opened. Sirion looked up as Dinim strode towards them. He had a huge grin on his face.

"By the gods, Sirion, it's so good to see you!"

The enchantment of the moment abruptly gone, Adrianna took a step back from Sirion. She watched a strained expression briefly pass over his face, but then he was smiling back at Dinim and moving forward to greet him.

"Hellfire, I thought you had been lost. It has been so difficult–"

With a slight shake of Sirion's head, Dinim broke off the sentence and placed his hands on Sirion's shoulders. He then continued speaking, deftly choosing another topic. "Damn, we really need to feed you something. You are thin as a silver oak sapling."

Sirion chuckled and then began to laugh. It was infectious, and soon the rest of them were joining in. It wasn't long before everyone was talking all at once. Adrianna felt more than a bit overwhelmed, but she was glad everyone was coming together. She heard expressions of gratitude from Sirion, followed by questions concerning his well-being from the group. She finally heard Dartanyen suggest they all go to a place where they could sit down. On their way out of the meditation chamber, Sirion grabbed his tunic. He seemed a bit shaky, but kept up with the others as they proceeded to the dining hall.

Everyone sat for a while over food and ale, Dinim sharing with Sirion about what had happened to the rest of the Wildrunners after their final battle with Gaknar and Tharizdune. Tianna stayed at Sirion's side, her eyes never leaving him. Dartanyen and Armond began to share details of their journey. It wasn't long before Adrianna excused herself from the table, patting Dartanyen on the shoulder to remind him not to say anything to Sirion about Thane. He only nodded as she left.

In the semi-darkness of early evening, Adrianna walked back to one of the cabins the group had been sharing since their arrival to the glen. Once entering, she went to her room and closed the door. With a deep sigh, she seated herself on the bed. It was good to see Sirion strong and robust after his ordeal, but she missed Cortath. She couldn't bear to stay and listen to the tales the group would probably tell about how they met him in the Vanderess Forest. She leaned back on the pillows, letting her body melt into them as she pondered the reunion. She envisioned Sirion once more, the color of his eyes, the ripple of muscle across his chest, the shape of his mouth. She closed her eyes...

A knock on the door startled her from sleep. She struggled to collect herself as she rose from bed, her heart beating a staccato rhythm. She wondered who was there, but knew the answer before the words left her lips. "Wh– who is it?"

"It's me." There was a pause, "Sirion."

Adrianna swallowed convulsively, and the muscles in her stomach tightened.

She went to the door and opened it with a shaking hand.

Sirion stood at the threshold, looking handsome as ever. "I hope I haven't disturbed you." His brows came together in the beginning of a concerned frown as his gaze swept over her pale face.

She stood aside. "No, not at all. Please come in." She caught the floral/musky scent of his bath soap as he stepped past her, and she wondered why he had come. Once closing the door, Adrianna just stood there, not knowing what to say.

"How have you been?" The words came simultaneously from two throats. It seemed to lessen the tension and they both grinned.

"I am well, thank you. Here, sit." Adrianna removed her travel pack from the nearest cushioned chair and motioned him over to it.

"Thank you." He seated himself in the chair and she sat across from him on the edge of the bed. "So how have you found it here in Krathil-lon?"

Adrianna gave a wistful smile. "This is a wonderful place. I have never been anywhere quite like it. I feel restful here, at peace, able to think more clearly. Despite the circumstances of our arrival, I don't think I've ever felt more relaxed." Adrianna stopped and looked down at the floor. She hadn't meant to put it like that. She didn't intend to imply that it had been burdensome for her to come.

"Yes, this glen is quite wondrous. I first came here several years ago when I was a much younger man. I met Dremathian, and we became good friends." Sirion smiled. "Krathil-lon has become a sanctuary for those who know of its existence. The order takes care of this place so that it may continue to serve those who need it most. It is a place of power, and magic abides here, unharnessed."

Once realizing he hadn't taken offense to her statement, Adrianna relaxed and listened to Sirion's voice. It was deep and soothing, one she could get accustomed to rather quickly. "The journey here wasn't a difficult one, I hope. Unfortunately, I don't remember most of it."

She grinned and her voice became animated. "No, it wasn't bad at all! It was exhilarating to ride on the back of a griffon. It was one of the most tremendous things I've ever experienced. The one I rode even seemed to like me. It was humbling, actually, in a way that is difficult to describe. I..."

Adrianna let her words die away. She suddenly remembered who she was talking to and she felt a moment of discomfort. This was Sirion, a member of the Wildrunners, someone who had become a hero in the eyes of all who knew of him. He had traveled all over Ansalar and had probably ridden his fair share of griffons. The many things he had seen, the things he'd experienced– she would probably never come close to matching. He studied her intently, his lips pulled up in a half smile. He was so self-assured and confident while her guts were busy working themselves into knots.

The silence stretched out for several moments and she wiped her damp palms on the bed sheets. Adrianna didn't really know what to say; Sirion was a stranger to her after all. But then she remembered the short camaraderie they had shared on the veranda of Volstagg's inn and the messages they had sent to one another. Then there was the fact that Cortath had known her in ways no one else ever would. That thought alone was a bit daunting, for he had known her innermost mind. He'd known her heart.

Sirion's expression was solemn when he finally broke the silence, like he had some idea what she was thinking. "You know, there are some things I remember, and many more I do not. However, one thing I know for certain is that you were there for me, a companion when I needed one the most. I will never forget that."

Sirion looked away and stirred in his chair, exhibiting signs of uncertainty for the first time. He suddenly seemed so normal, like any other man. "The animal you called Cortath is something that exists inside of me. He emerged when I was at my weakest, and his dominant animal nature began to take over. I slowly began to lose the part of me that made me a man, but because you were there, the transformation could never be entirely completed. You kept me from the brink, and I am indebted to you."

Sirion looked at her once more. His eyes were shadowed, and Adrianna could see how hard it was for him to speak to her about how dire his circumstances had been. She reached out and placed her hand on his where it rested on his knee. "No. You owe me nothing. What we shared was good for me too. Cortath healed me in ways I can't begin to explain. I'm glad I was able to help you just as much as you helped me."

Sirion nodded. "Thank you. That means a lot to me."

Adrianna looked at him and then down at her hand. When she realized it continued to clasp Sirion's hand, she pulled away. He slowly rose from the chair. "Well, I suppose I had better go. I feel like I haven't slept for about a year."

Adrianna followed him to the door. "I'm glad you came. It was good to talk."

Sirion opened the door. "Indeed it was. I shall see you tomorrow."

Adrianna nodded. She watched as he made his way down the hall towards the front of the cabin and realized she had one last thing to say. "Sirion..." She paused until he turned around. "...welcome home."

He gave her a wide smile, his eyes sparkling warmly in the torchlight. "I *am* home, aren't I? It feels good to be here."

Visions In Fire

In companionable silence the sisters walked through the silver woods, enjoying the ambiance and taking advantage of the fair weather. The air was cool, much more so than it had been when the group was traveling through the more southerly Kingdom of Durnst. There they had been experiencing the heat of midsummer with very little wind and hardly any rain. But since arriving in Krathil-lon, they had noticed a sharp decrease in temperature as well as days where rain was the chief climatic event. Unaccustomed to so much cold so early in the season, Adrianna didn't want to contemplate what the area would be like during the winter months.

In less than three days, the group would be leaving the sanctuary of the secluded glen. Sirion was rapidly recovering from his ordeal, and Dremathian had given them his blessing to travel when they were ready. Adrianna found she was quite loath to leave. Once they were away, the ugly reality of her life would rear up to slap her in the face and the peaceful serenity of Krathil-lon would very quickly become a distant memory.

Adrianna's thoughts were suddenly interrupted by the sound of someone speaking somewhere in the trees ahead. She shared a brief glance with Sheridana as they moved quietly forward. Once getting closer, the women realized it was a voice raised in anger. Another, much younger, voice replied and an argument ensued. The two women glanced at one another again and nodded, both agreeing to eavesdrop.

"You are a disgrace, Lucien. Your actions have proven to me that you aren't ready for the Tabanakh Ceremony. You are not ready to become a part of the Brotherhood."

Adrianna and Sheridana peered through a break in the foliage. They lay in a depression made by the roots of a large silver oak tree, watching a man and his tyro. The two stood in the center of a clearing surrounded by large rocks, each with a runic engraving. The boy was on the verge of manhood, about the age of fifteen or sixteen summers, and the man was about the age of Father Dremathian, maybe a bit younger.

"I think you are being too harsh on me, Brother Donavan. I wasn't the only one. The other boys were there too."

"That is the key word, is it not? Boys. You, Lucien, are no longer a boy, but one who is supposed to become a man this very evening. All of the others are younger than you by at least a year or more. You fell in with them, following them like an unschooled pup." The man pursed his lips. "You are not ready for the ceremony."

The young man looked away from his mentor, crimson coloring his cheeks. He was angry and ashamed. Adrianna's heart went out to the boy. He had made a mistake, and now he would pay the harsh consequences.

Brother Donavan held out an ornate ceramic jug. "This drink is very powerful, meant only for those who are ready. Those who drink it will experience visions of the past, present, and future. Only those who are strong enough will be able to understand the visions and use them in order to meet his destiny one day. I will tell the others we won't be having a ceremony tonight. You will simply have to wait until you have grown a bit more."

Brother Donavan turned away, placing the jug near the firepit beside him.

"But Brother, I'm ready. I just know it!"

The older man held up a hand, palm facing the boy. Lucien was immediately quiet. "I have made my decision. There will be no ceremony. You are dismissed."

Once more, anger flashed across Lucien's face, but the emotion was short lived. Shame quickly settled over him once more, and he dejectedly turned and left. In silence the sisters patiently waited, making not a move lest they be discovered. Finally Brother Donavan stood. His shoulders were slumped, and his face bore an expression of sadness. Adrianna realized it had been a difficult decision for him to make. The man left the clearing, probably to tell his brothers about his decision.

Adrianna and Sheridana lay there for a few moments more, just to be certain he wouldn't return. Then they rose and entered the clearing. Beside the firepit, the ceramic jug still sat. Sheridana turned to her. Right away, Adrianna could tell what was in her sister's mind. Pensively she regarded the jug. They didn't know what type of drink it was, only that it caused one to experience strange visions. It could also have other side effects, and maybe even make them ill. For some reason, Adrianna found she really didn't care. It was a druids drink, and she doubted it would affect her. She shrugged and then nodded to Sheridana. A smile lit up her sister's face and she couldn't help but smile in return.

Maintaining their silence, the women approached the fire pit. Lying on the ground nearby was a pile of dry wood. Sheridana broke some of the larger pieces in half, and then placed them onto the weak flames within the pit. Soon the fire was gaining strength. Adrianna picked up the strangely shaped jug and passed her nose over the lip. The drink had an unfamiliar scent. Looking at Sheridana, she slowly placed her mouth to the opening and took a swallow. The drink flowed down her throat, making a warm path to her belly. It tasted like nothing she had ever imbibed before. She handed the jug to Sheridana, who also took a swallow. The two women then smiled conspiratorially.

The sisters sat opposite one another in silence, the fire between them. The red, orange, and gold flames were nearly hypnotizing and Adrianna realized the drink was already influencing her. The flames could easily put her into a trance if she would only allow it. After a while longer, she knew it would happen whether she wanted it or not.

The women began to feel warm. Tunics were the first to come off, followed by trousers. All that remained were smallclothes and ornamentation: the serpent coiled about Adrianna's upper arm, a golden torc about Sheri's throat, a delicate platinum bangle circled Adrianna's ankle, and wide golden bands enveloped Sheri's arms just above the elbow. Long pale and dark tresses were gathered and bound with combs and leather strips, while sweat ran in rivulets down slender bodies.

The women swallowed more of the forbidden drink while they continued to feed a fire that blazed hotter and hotter. Impurities flowed from the pores of their skin, bathing them in a shimmering sheen of sweat. Without them realizing it, late afternoon had darkened into evening, and the pale form of Steralion hung over them. Still maintaining their silence, the women regarded one another from across the fire. Adrianna noticed pale scars crossing Sheridana's left side and thigh. They looked to have been made by a large predator. Belatedly, Adrianna realized Sheridana would notice similar markings upon her. She hesitantly brought her gaze back to that of her twin. Indeed, Sheridana's eyes had settled to the healed wound that started between her breasts and continued down to her navel.

Yet, the sisters continued to say nothing. The fire burned on, and the sweat trickled. How long they sat there they didn't know. The flames danced before their eyes, the tendrils twisting together lovingly, caressing one another with a soft touch here, another touch there, until Adrianna could see forms within the depths. It was two people dancing. The couple swirled about in the fire, the woman's long gown flowing behind her. Or was it her cloak?

Adrianna leaned forward, hoping to see the figures in more detail. It was then the scene changed. She saw what appeared to be a dragon in flight. She frowned, for dragons were creatures that many believed to be the stuff of myth. Sitting astride the dragon's back was a person, an arm raised in victory. Adrianna scoffed inwardly. Nowhere in history had she heard of a man flying on the back of a dragon. Although she had to admit musingly, it would be a wonderful experience.

Aware of the heat, Adrianna jumped out of her reverie. She had been very close to the fire, too close in fact. She glanced at Sheridana, saw that her sister was in her own trance. However, she was still aware and began to speak.

"I remember my life before I left Sangrilak. I spent much of my time in training. Father taught me the sword, while our uncle, Ian, taught me the bow. Father would often instruct others who wished to learn the art of swordplay. Frequently my skill was pitted against them. More often than not, I wasn't good enough, and Father would be angry with me, wanting me to practice even more.

He wanted me to work harder despite the fact I trained in things other than the blade. By the end of each day, I was so tired, I sometimes didn't care to eat my evening meal. I became distraught with my lot in life, and it was Ian who often came to offer comfort. He would tell me tales from his young adventuring days and that Father hadn't always been such a harsh man. He told me Father had once loved a woman so much, a part of him went with her when she died.

I also remember a time soon after our departure from Sangrilak. We began to travel with a group called the Dawn Treaders. With them was a man who taught me hand-to-hand combat. By that time, I had become rather skilled with the sword and the longbow. My skill was appreciated even by Father. The three of us spent two years with them. Very often, Ian and I would be the ones hunting for the evening stewpot. As a result, we spent much of our time together.

It was in the Free City of Grondor that we met up with a group called Thritean's Pride. It was with them we spent the next four years. The last year, Father abruptly left the group to pursue other interests. It was only then that Ian and I refused to deny ourselves what we had known for over two years. We were lovers up until the fateful night that took him away from me forever."

Adrianna's gaze locked onto the dancing flames of their fire and a vision begin to take shape. Her heart thundered against her ribs. She wanted to look away, but Sheridana had somehow enfolded them within a terrible nightmare, weaving it tightly about them. She shared it the only way she knew how, with the one person whom she once shared a mother's womb. Adrianna was able to see what Sheridana saw, and much more.

"Ian and I were hunting. We were on the trail of a leschera that would feed the group for at least three days. I got the feeling we were being watched, but before I could mention it, someone leaped from the nearby brush and hurdled into me. I instantly knew it was a man. With my face in the dirt and a knee between my shoulders, I smelled more than felt his nasty breath on the back of my neck. Something sharp raked across my left side before he released me. He unsheathed my blade as he stood, and I just managed to flip over onto my back as he stabbed downward just below my shoulder, pinning me to the ground and rendering me helpless.

The man's leathers were black, as was the chain mail vest over top. His most distinguishing feature was the horned helm that covered most of his face. When he turned away, I saw two of Ian's arrows sticking out of the man's back. With unnatural speed, the warrior reached Ian and swept the bow out of his hands. He backhanded Ian across the face, making him spin almost full circle before falling. But Ian swiftly got back to his feet. I still remember the song of bespelled metal sounding through the air and the soft glow the weapon exuded in the approaching darkness. The man laughed, and I couldn't help thinking it sounded eerily familiar.

Ian swung the sword. With a clawed gauntlet, the dark warrior took the weapon. I screamed when I saw the blood flowing from the deep gashes in Ian's forearm and hand. I plead for him to stop when the warrior took Ian by his tunic and raised him from the ground. With incredible force, the warrior threw him into a nearby tree. Even now I can hear the sickening crack of bone followed by the sound of him falling.

The warrior turned to me and I sensed him smiling from behind his helm. "Now you will watch him die and his tormented voice will haunt you forever."

I struggled. I tried to pull the sword free of my shoulder, and nearly fainted with the pain. I screamed again as I watched the dark warrior walk over to Ian. I knew he was going to do something terrible. He knelt beside Ian and cut into his belly. The warrior slowly proceeded to disembowel him.

Ian's agonized cries raked through me. I desperately tried to remove the sword, screaming and sobbing with frustration. It slowly began to move, and I hoped that Ian would still be alive when I finally managed to reach his side. The warrior turned to watch me as he continued pulling at the entrails, and I knew he still smiled.

Finally the warrior stood. He said something to me in an unfamiliar tongue and then walked away into the surrounding darkness. It wasn't much longer before I managed to pull the wretched sword from my shoulder. Overwhelmed with weakness, I somehow crawled to Ian's side. I instantly knew he was dead. I kissed him one last time, his lips still warm with the pale echo of life. I then put my head on his chest and it felt like I cried forever."

Adrianna only vaguely realized Sheri had stopped speaking as she continued to stare into the dancing flames. The acts she saw were horrific, and the one she saw executing them even more so. Somehow, Adrianna was able to see what Sheri saw, and more, she knew the identity of the dark warrior.

It was Thane.

Adrianna's body shook as Sheridana continued.

"Thritean's Pride found me there at Ian's side. Joshua was somehow able to keep me from Death. For many days he worked over me, praying to his goddess for the power that would make me well. Finally the physical wounds healed, and I was able to run with the Pride once more.

But I became reckless and withdrawn. Whatever wounds I suffered in my mind were still there, festering deep within me. I became more a liability than an asset. When I realized this, I decided to leave the group. They tried to stop me, but my mind was set.

It wasn't long before I began to notice the changes in my body. I worked as a hired mercenary while I denied a truth I already knew. I ceased my idiocy when I could no longer fasten my trousers.

I was pregnant."

Adrianna regarded her twin through wide eyes. The knowledge of Fitanni's parentage was overwhelming coming so soon after discovering Thane's horrific act. Inwardly Adrianna struggled, for she had yet to say anything about their father to her sister at all, even after all these weeks. Adrianna had put off speaking about Thane's descent into madness because she knew it would be devastating. Sheridana had shared something with their father that Adrianna never had, a relationship that would only ever be a void in Adria herself. She knew the time had finally come; Sheridana needed to know that both she and her daughter had become a part of Thane's destructive plan.

Adrianna looked back into the fire. The flames were still strong, licking the wood that fed it. She couldn't help watching it, for it seemed to draw her in. Once again she began to see images, visions of people she didn't know, places she had never been. As she continued to watch she struggled within herself.

Sheridana wasn't the only one with secrets.

Sheridana watched her sister and waited. The fire reflected in Adrianna's pale hair, making the color appear a ruddy gold. Her dark eyes stared into the flames, and there were times she could swear her sister saw something within. Adrianna had said nothing about what she'd told her, but she half expected the lack of response. With the drink running through their veins and the fire between them, the air had an aura of ceremony to it. This wasn't a time for discussion; it was a time for speaking about what lay in the soul.

Sheridana knew that Adrianna had much to speak. The weight of it hung about her like a dark cloak, damping her spirit. Sheri could see it in her eyes by the constant twinge of sadness she saw there. She could see the same sadness in Adrianna's smile, in the way she moved, in the very essence of her. Sheridana reached out to place another piece of wood on the fire and the flames enveloped it hungrily. She was afraid Adrianna's secrets would soon envelop her the same way.

Sheridana looked back up to find her sister staring at her intently. Adrianna's voice was as forlorn as the expression reflecting in her eyes.

"I have seen the new face of our father. It has become just as hideous as his soul. Even now he hunts me down for a crime he feels I committed against him on the day of our birth. He burned the house we lived in as children, and Mairi and Hafgan were still inside. Volstagg was beaten, and his inn wrecked in his search for me. Others have also fallen at his hand and I fear more are to follow. Knowing I had nowhere to turn, Dartanyen, Armond, and the others have pledged themselves to my safety, hoping to keep me alive long enough for Dinim and I to find a way to thwart him.

"I now believe it is not only I for whom Thane searches. I have somehow divined the images of the event about which you spoke. The laugh of your dark warrior was familiar because you have heard it many times before. It was our father who killed Ian and left you to bleed to death in the forest. By now it is very possible he has learned of your survival and that a child has been produced by your union with our uncle. Mayhap it has made him hate us all the more."

Sheridana stared at her sister in shock. *No, she is wrong. Adria is terribly mistaken. Our father would never do the things she claimed. It is simply that Adria doesn't know him... Yes, that must surely be it. Sure, Father seemed a bit sullen and withdrawn during his final days with the group, mayhap even a bit unpredictable. But to kill people, to kill his own brother, just wasn't possible.*

Where was her father now? What had become of him? Sheri had wondered about Thane since the night he never returned to the encampment. She could never really understand why he had left without giving her some kind of farewell. Now that she thought about it, she recalled Thane being more irritable at the end, more argumentative, especially with Ian. And then there were the malicious glares she would see every once in a while, as though Thane *hated* his brother.

Sheridana lowered her head in her hands. The laugh, that wicked laugh that was so familiar to her, was just like Thane's. She suddenly remembered the deep voice of the dark warrior, remembered the way he moved as though he might have a mild limp. Sheridana had been there at the battle during which Thane had injured his leg so badly that it was never the same again.

Sheri felt as though her heart was breaking. *Oh gods... why is he doing this? How can he hate us so much?*

The truth was like a scythe sweeping through her. She recalled how Thane was never able to let go of her mother's memory, recalled the terrible things he would sometimes say about Adrianna. Sheri would always bite her tongue, never wanting to say something retaliatory that would bring Father's wrath down on her.

And if she were to be honest, she had always been a little afraid of him.

Sheridana fought to collect herself and looked back up at Adrianna. By the pained expression on her face, Sheridana could see what it had taken for Adrianna to finally tell her about their father. Adrianna had hidden the knowledge for so long; Sheridana understood why she did it. She might have done the very same if their positions were reversed, but it didn't mean that she wasn't angry.

Sheridana solemnly regarded the woman kneeling on the other side of the fire. She had seen the scars, saw Adrianna's moment of clarity when she realized Sheridana had noticed them. She knew her sister still kept something from her, something dark. She watched Adrianna from across the fire, waiting for her sister to shuck her cloak of pain and loneliness, to divulge her secrets the way she had hers. Sheridana had shared everything, had nothing left to hide. She deserved the same confession.

"I'm waiting, Adrianna. I know there is something more you have yet to tell me."

Adrianna felt a moment of surprise. When did her twin become so perceptive? She suddenly felt her head began to spin and she had to remain still for a few moments before the dizziness passed. "I don't know what you're talking about."

Sheridana regarded her with a doubtful expression, but Adrianna's thoughts were no longer on her personal trials. It was time to return to the cabin. She was beginning to feel ill, either from the drink, the heat of the fire, or both.

Sheridana rose from her position on the other side of the fire and moved to stand over her. She gave a deep sigh and frowned. "Adrianna, I know you are keeping something from me. I can see it in your eyes. I have laid my very soul open to you, yet you still continue to shut me out."

Adrianna turned away from her sister. This was not something she was ready to share. Her gaze inadvertently went back to the flames. Immediately she began to see something begin to take form there, something she knew she didn't want to see, much like what she experienced when Sheri began her recitation of Ian's death.

Unable to pull her eyes away from the mesmerizing flames, Adrianna felt her heart begin pounding in her chest. *Oh gods, no. I can't bear to see those men, to visualize what they did to me. Feeling it had been more than enough–*

Sheridana's voice broke the reverie. "Eventually it will begin to haunt you, this thing you hide inside of yourself. It will whittle away at your soul until nothing is left but pain and emptiness."

Adrianna heard the petulance in Sheri's voice, the underlying hurt. She struggled to breathe, to control her rapidly beating heart. *What in the Nine Hells is going on? What manner of fire is this that it shows me such terrible things? What was wrong with me that I see such terrible things within it?* But then she remembered what Father Donovan had said to the boy. *Oh yes, it is just the drink showing me these things.*

Adrianna shakily rose to her feet to stand beside her sister. Sheri just watched her through impassive eyes. It was still dark, but by the position of the moons, she knew that dawn would soon be approaching. Adrianna shook her head. "I really don't know what you are talking about..."

Sheri's frown deepened. She stepped closer to Adrianna, grasped her upper arms, and shook her. "This secret you keep will eat at you until nothing is left," she shouted. "But you won't listen to me. Hells, what do I know? Just remember, you are the one who has placed this barrier between us, and it will keep us apart until you tear it down!"

Shocked by her outburst, Sheridana released her sister. Too late, she saw the paleness of Adrianna's face, realized the clammy coolness of the flesh of her arms where Sheri had gripped her so tightly. Adrianna weaved on her feet before crumpling to the ground.

"Oh gods, Adria?" Sheridana knelt beside her and felt her neck for the telltale pulse that indicated the heart was still beating. "Adrianna, please be all right!" Her hand shook, so it took a moment for her to find it, but it was there. She thought back through the night, in particular, about how much of the drink they had imbibed. In truth, she couldn't really recall. Time's passage had been swift; she could hardly believe that morning had come already. Along with her lack of memory, she blamed the drink for that.

Sheridana tried to rouse Adrianna and was finally able to get her awake enough to carry part of her weight. As they began to make their way back towards the cabin, Adrianna stopped to vomit. Sheri berated herself for her stupidity before gently urging Adrianna onwards. She should have noted the tell-tale signs that Adrianna had reached her limit. They had been easy to see, only she had been too blinded by her anger to recognize them.

With Adrianna's weight leaning heavily against her side, Sheridana stumbled along the path. She was soon exhausted, but struggled to hold her sister upright as Adrianna lost consciousness again. *Oh gods, what was in that drink?* Just as Sheri was about to let her sister fall, someone was there to grab Adrianna's other side.

Sheridana turned in surprise. "Sirion," she breathed, "What are you doing here?"

He raised a brow. "I can ask you the same thing." He looked down at Adrianna and frowned. "What in Hellfire is wrong with her? Where are her clothes? Where are *your* clothes?"

Sheridana just stood there, not knowing where to begin.

Sirion shook his head. "Never mind, you can figure it out on our way back to your cabin." He placed his other arm beneath Adrianna's knees and lifted her up. He cradled her against his chest and strode swiftly along the path.

Sheridana was silent as they walked, her mind riddled with guilt. *It's my fault she's sick. Even when we were children, Adria rarely found trouble unless I was there.* It wasn't long before they reached the cabin and she opened the door for Sirion. He carried Adrianna to her room and laid her gently on the bed. The motion was too much. Sirion barely managed to step aside as she turned to her side and retched on the floor. She moaned pathetically as she heaved over and over again, nothing coming out because there was nothing left.

When Adrianna was finished she lay back on the pillow. Her face was deathly pale, and her body shook just as much from the force of her heaving as the chill her body felt without anything to cover it. Sirion brought the blankets up to her chin and turned back to Sheridana, his eyes bright with incense.

"You care to tell me what happened now?"

"We were in a clearing surrounded by large stones. There was a jug that contained some kind of drink. We didn't think anything about it when we drank from it."

His eyes widened. "You're telling me that you go around drinking strange brews without knowing what is in them? You ever think it may be poisoned? Are you that daft?"

Tears sprang to her eyes. "We heard one of the druids talking about the drink. He said only that it would give one visions, nothing else. Please, is Adria going to be all right?"

"How much did you drink?"

The tears slid down her cheeks. "I... I don't know. I can't remember."

He pressed his lips into a thin line. "Go get Father Dremathian. He will know how to help her."

3 Brinaren CY593

Adrianna awoke but made no effort to rise from the bed. She could tell that it was still early, the golden rays of dawn just beginning to adorn the morning sky. She wasn't eager to rise. Her body ached, and her throat was parched. She recalled the terrible sickness she'd endured the day before and how she felt every time she moved. She didn't want to take any chances.

"Ahhh, you are finally awake. I was wondering when you would."

She turned to find Father Dremathian sitting beside her bed, his lips curved into a smile.

"Good morning Father."

She regarded him speculatively. He was able to divine her thoughts and his smile broadened. "No, nothing is wrong. You will be just fine, my dear."

"Then why are you here?"

"Your sister was tired, and Sirion had preparations to make for his departure with you and your comrades tomorrow morning. I offered to sit here for a while since they would not leave you alone."

She nodded. She wondered why he mentioned Sirion, but she was stuck on the fact that there was another reason why he was there. She simply had to practice patience, but in the meantime she could ask questions. "Why was I so sick?"

"The tabanakh drink is a very powerful tool. It is meant to be taken in sips. You ingested far too much of it."

"So Sheri was ill as well?"

"No."

"She drank just as much as me. Why did I become sick and she did not?"

"Because the drink only has such severe effects upon those who have a propensity for certain... ah... encumbrances."

"You must be referring to my Talent. That is interesting, for I have never heard of a drink that can determine a person's Talent before. You should take it to Andahye. The Elders would love you forever."

Dremathian shook his head. "No, I'm not referring to your Talent."

She frowned. "Then what are you talking about? Please be plainer with me."

"The reason you were affected so strongly by the drink is because you have another gift besides your Talent. People who are drawn to the druidical orders tend to possess some measure of this gift, but most others haven't even an inkling of it. In truth, it is quite surprising to find one who is so strongly gifted outside the druidical sphere."

Adrianna was silent.

"You have the gift of Sight. Contrary to popular belief, this gift isn't just the ability to see what will be, but also to see what is and what was."

Taken aback, she continued to regard him for a moment. "You must be mistaken. I'm not a Seer."

He narrowed his eyes. "You can honestly lay there and tell me you saw nothing in the fire the night before last?"

She swallowed convulsively. *So that wasn't a dream after all...*

"Listen, I know this is all very new to you, but I can help you with your gift. I implore you to stay here with me here in Krathil-lon. I haven't had one in many years, but I will take you as my tyro. I want you to join my order."

Adrianna was stunned. "You can't be serious?"

"Does it look like I'm joshing you?"

She looked into his eyes, saw the sincerity reflected there. She considered his proposal for a moment but then discarded it. "I'm sorry. There's a part of me that wants to accept your offer, but it's for the wrong reasons. I want a place to hide from Thane, but you hope to discover a tyro worthy of your teachings. Indeed, it would be great to stay in this wonderful place, but with my unresolved problems, I can't possibly do that."

Dremathian put a hand on her shoulder. "My order will help you against Thane. You know, violence isn't always the means one should use to defeat their enemies."

She nodded. "I understand, but you don't know my father the way I do."

He rose from his seat. "Just think about it before making your final decision. And remember, there are many paths one can take to fulfill one's destiny."

Sirion watched from hooded eyes as Adrianna walked into the dining hall. She was dressed for travel, wearing dark brown trousers and a beige tunic with a burgundy sash. Her long hair was braided and coiled on the back of her head, a change from the way she usually kept it in a thick plait that lay down her back. She walked over to the largest table and chose a honey bun from the large platter of sweet breads, fruits, and nuts. She then sat down at another table with her sister.

As Adrianna slept away the effects of the tabanakh drink, Sirion had decided to making his way back south to his home realm of Elvandahar. Sirion needed to let his family know he had survived the battle against Gaknar and

Tharizdune. His sister had gone home to tell their family about his death, and he felt the intense need to go there to rectify the tale. However, once being apprised of their situation with Thane, Sirion invited the group to accompany him there, telling Sheridana that it would be a good place for her to keep her baby, at least for a while. He explained that Elvandahar was very well protected, and that the baby would be safer there than anywhere else.

Sirion's gaze flicked to Dinim as the man moved to seat himself beside Adrianna. The Cimmerean began to speak with her in an easy-going tone, teasing about her slightly disheveled appearance, her decision to fall in with her sister to drink the tabanakh brew, and her condition the morning after. He got her to smile and Sirion couldn't help staring at her for a moment. Her beauty stilled his heart in his chest, and an ache lodged there. She had a good rapport with Dinim, and Sirion could easily see the Cimmerean was attracted to her. This fact bothered him more than it probably should.

Sirion was aware of Adrianna's rejection of Dremathian's offer to stay in Krathil-lon. The arch-druid had much to teach her, and most likely, Adrianna could learn to be a powerful member of the order. But for now, her life's calling lay beyond the silver glen. She had other things to do before harnessing herself to the natural world. Having heard accounts given by her comrades, Destiny called her to a much darker place.

Sirion shifted his gaze when he felt someone sitting down beside him. He turned to see that it was only Tianna. The young woman smiled as she put a plate down on the table in front of him. "Here, eat this. Dinim is right, you are thin."

Sirion regarded her dolefully. He felt discomfited by the almost maternal attitude Tianna had begun to adopt towards him. He already had a mother, and thus didn't need another. Yet, she had been acting strangely in other ways as well. On several occasions he'd found her staring at him with a forlorn expression, and seemed a bit preoccupied with the clothes she wore and the arrangement of her hair. She was no longer the child he remembered, but to him she would always be the little girl who had chosen to follow him around during the time she was but an orphan with the Order of Reshik-na in Elvandahar.

Sirion regarded the plate set before him. He wasn't hungry, but would humor Tianna and eat at least a small portion. Picking up a fig, he tossed it into his mouth as the rest of the group finally filtered into the hall. Behind Carli and baby Fitanni, Amethyst was the last to enter. Her tousled appearance gave one the impression she had just awoken and donned her clothing on the way over. The petulant expression on her face also spoke that she hated the fact that she had been awakened so early in the day. Dartanyen and Armond seemed well prepared. They joined Sirion at his table and began to discuss with him the length of their journey.

By the time Dremathian entered the hall, everyone had broken their fast. The platter of honey buns had been emptied of its sweet contents, and the pitcher of tobey's milk had similarly disappeared. Water flasks had been filled, and food packs divided among all. Everyone turned their attention to the arch-druid as he approached their tables. "I see that you are ready to embark on your journey to Elvandahar. I wish you the best of fortune and freely give whatever blessing I may."

"We will need all of the luck we can get," said Dartanyen. "It is going to be a very long trip, especially without lloryk and larian. I'm thinking we will reach the northern tip of Elvandahar in about three weeks. After that, the going will be slower as we move through the forest."

Dremathian nodded. "I have another way. If you choose, you are free to use the portal system we used to bring you here. It will be no imposition for me to take you there."

Dartanyen was thoughtful for a moment before shaking his head. "No, that will only take us further away from our destination. It will be best if we just leave on foot from here and go south across the plains of Cortubro. It is a relatively safe journey, and will only cost us some time."

Dremathian smiled. "You don't understand. The portal has more than one destination. It actually has several that are scattered about Ansalar. One of those destinations is here, and another is obviously the Vanderess Forest. A third destination exists in the junction of the Selmist Forest and the Bryton Hills located in the Kingdom of Karlisle."

Pensively, Dartanyen regarded Dremathian. "That would save us almost two weeks."

Dremathian nodded again. "Come, let me take you to the portal."

The group walked through the halls of the apoptos. Adrianna followed behind Sirion, his pack hanging crazily from only one shoulder. He wore a sleeveless brown tunic, black trousers, and a black studded leather vest. His fiery chestnut hair was tied at the nape of his neck, and he wore the signet ring Adrianna had found in the pouch about Cortath's neck.

It was more than embarrassing to know Sirion had been witness to her semi-clothed state the morning after her rendezvous with the tabanakh drink. She'd cringed when Sheri shared the account with her and she could only hope that his opinion of her hadn't been too terribly tarnished. The vertical scar that ran down the length of her torso was difficult to miss; surely he wondered who had put it there, and why. A flood of shame suffused her at the memory of how it got there, and she felt sick inside. But she pushed the feeling away and just focused on walking

Several corridors and a downward staircase later, they reached the portal room. Dremathian walked over to the pedestal holding the open book.

Adrianna followed him, still intrigued by the arcane properties contained within. She watched as he turned to the next page. On it she saw the image of a large citadel. Its highest towers seemed to reach the sky. Adrianna leaned in to look closer. It was familiar to her somehow, yet she knew that she had never seen a place like it before. Dremathian turned the next page again. She saw the image of a cave situated in a deep wood. This would be their destination. She looked up to find the rest of the group standing near the platform in front of the portal brackets.

Dremathian began to read the words at the bottom of the page. A slight breeze wafted through the room, pushing the errant tendrils of hair from her face, a whisper of magic and power from the creator of the portal. The current between the brackets began to move, and just like before, Adrianna watched until it turned into a wall of shimmering blue. Zorg and Armond were the first to walk through, followed by the others. With the large corubis, Dramati, at their side, only Sirion and Sheridana turned back. It was then she realized she hadn't moved from her place beside Dremathian. She looked up at the man to find him watching her.

"You know my offer still stands," he said, a gleam of hope in his blue eyes. "You are welcome to stay here. There is much I can teach you. I believe you could even be my successor one day."

Adrianna shook her head. "You know that I cannot."

Dremathian smiled. "Go in peace, then. And may the sun shine upon you."

Adrianna inclined her head in a gesture of respect before walking away from the pedestal. She stepped up onto the platform as Sirion and Sheridana turned and walked through the portal. Doting as ever, Dramati waited patiently as she paused to situate her pack over her shoulders. She put her hand on his withers and together followed their comrades.

Adrianna felt a slight wrenching as she was sucked within, very unlike the first time she had traveled in this fashion. She momentarily wondered if she had done something wrong, but then she was stumbling into a cool place. Before she could fall, she felt a hand at her elbow. There was a flare of light from a torch being lit, and she saw that it was Sirion there beside her. A brief flutter swept through her chest when he didn't release her arm right away.

Their eyes met and locked. They stood there for a moment, each regarding the other. It was Sirion who finally broke contact, but not before he gave her a barely perceptible nod. Adrianna felt a calm pass over her. Mayhap she hadn't really lost Cortath after all.

NYXLARIAN

*T*hane bellowed into the crisp morning air. *"Up! Up, Sheridana! You are drooping again."*

His young daughter raised her blade to where it should be, just in time to parry a blow from her older brother.

"Gareth, stop being so easy on her! She won't learn a damn thing if you are going to pussyfoot around her whenever she's training."

Gareth grimaced but obeyed, and his next hit was harder, making the sword spin out of the girl's hand to land on the ground half a farlo away.

Sheridana screwed her face up into a scowl, holding her wrist in her other hand. *"Dungheaps Gareth! He didn't mean you had to be a buffelshmut and disarm me!"*

As she stalked over to the blade and picked it up out of the dirt, Thane couldn't help the grin that turned up one corner of his mouth. She was a little spitfire, that one. One day she would be a force to be reckoned with, that was for sure. Already she had the makings of a brilliant swordsman. Her stance was good, and her grip too. She was eager to learn, and she had stamina. She just needed a bit more strength, but that would come over the years as she continued her training.

Thane walked over to Sheridana and looked down at her. Deep blue eyes stared up from a face kissed golden by the sun, her cheeks red from exertion and irritation. Her long, dark hair was braided and lay down her back. *"Do you know why I push you so hard? Why I tell Gareth and Ian not to coddle you?"*

She shook her head.

"It's because I see great potential in you. But potential is only that until it is tapped and shaped. You will never be the warrior I see you can be until you struggle, until you sweat, cry, and bleed. Only when you have done these things can you ever be the warrior I see in you."

She nodded.

Thane grunted. *"Hit me."*

The girl frowned.

Out of the corner of his eye, he could see that something had caught Ian's attention and his brother was walking towards the trees to the left of the clearing. Thane nodded. *"Come on, hit me. Hit me as hard as you can with the flat of that blade."*

Sheridana hesitated only briefly before obeying. She sunk into combat stance and swung as hard as her small arms could. Thane smacked the blade away with one hand. *"Again!"*

Sheridana swung once more and he did the same. "Again!"

After several rounds of this, the girl was breathing hard, and sweat trickled down her temples. She was about to swing again when Thane found his attention on Ian, who stood at the treeline. "Oi!"

Sheridana stopped and Thane narrowed his eyes. He began to walk towards him. "Ian, what do you have there? Is it one of those pesky kids again?"

Ian slowly turned around. The expression on his face looked pained before he schooled it into one of nonchalance. His hand gripped the upper arm of a child, one the same height as Sheridana. Golden curls tumbled around her shoulders, some of which were caught up in a haphazard braid that fell down her back. She wore tunic and trousers like a boy, and they were streaked with dirt from hiding in the shrubbery.

Rage suffused him, rage tinged with a pain that would never subside, a pain that reminded him of the greatest thing he had ever had... and lost. "What the Hells is she doing here?"

"Thane, it's alright. She was just watching."

Thane reached them and pulled the girl out of Ian's grip. It was wrong that she looked so much like his beloved Gemma: her hair so pale it was like a ray of moonlight, her lips finely sculpted, her face already so beautiful even though she was only twelve summers old. She looked up at him from wide, dark brown eyes, the only feature that made her different than her mother.

He shook her so hard she stumbled. "I've told you to stay away from me," he growled.

"I... I'm sorry. I didn't mean to..."

He vaguely felt Ian put a hand on his arm and tell him to stop. Gareth had rushed over as well, and Sheridana. He heard their voices, like flies buzzing.

His grip tightened and his jerked her forward. "I've told you, I never want to see you. Ever." Tears pooled at the corners of her eyes and trailed down her cheeks. "I've hated you for as long as you've been alive. You want to know why?"

A strangled sob escaped her throat.

He leaned close, his nose barely an inch from hers. "Because you killed her."

Thane came free of his reverie, the last vestiges of his vision falling away. The vision wasn't really that, but a memory of the long-ago past. As an Azmathous, he never slept, but his mind would wander as he rested, often coming to settle upon his brother and his children. His brother was dead, killed by his own hand a couple years ago. It had felt good to feel Ian's life trickle between his fingers through the blood of the entrails he'd torn from his belly. Gareth he hadn't seen in years, for the young man had disappeared even before Thane had left Sangrilak for good. It was Sheridana and Adrianna that he dreamed of the most, the twin daughters he had gained when...

...when he lost his wife.

Sheridana, the oldest twin, he'd managed to embrace, taught her the ways of a warrior. The younger one, Adrianna, had been the difficult one, the one that he felt ultimately killed Gemma. He'd rejected her, right from the start, had never been able to forgive her.

And now... now his hunger for her death had grown to unfathomable heights.

Thane's hands clenched into fists, his leather gloves creaking. He imagined the smell of her fear, the sound of her distressed cries, the feel of her throat collapsing within his hand. He imagined the scent of her blood, her pleading for her life, the sight of her struggling to take her last, pained breaths. These thoughts invigorated him, kept him going zacrol after zacrol. He'd lost her at the Dresnjik River, but it was only a matter of time before he picked up her trail again. And if nothing else, Thane had time.

The day had been a warm one, much warmer than what the group had become accustomed to in Krathil-lon. And being that much further south than their original location north of the Vanderess, it was definitely a climate shock. Immediately after leaving the small cave that held the portal chamber, they shucked their cloaks. The men had the added advantage of removing their tunics. They traveled for the rest of the day after leaving the cave, moving north towards the Denegal River. Once crossing it they would be within the realm of Elvandahar.

From her bedroll, Adrianna watched as the rest of the group lay down for the night. Along with Dartanyen, Sheri was taking the first watch. It would be followed by the one overseen by Sirion, and the last would be taken by Armond and Zorg. Through bleary eyes, she watched as Tianna settled onto the bedroll she had situated near Sirion's. Adria felt a twinge of regret sweep through her. It was easy for her to see that Tianna was in love with him. She had gone out of her way with the preparations for the evening meal, and she had sought out his company on the few occasions he walked with the group during their travel that day. Sirion was a good man, and she would do well to have him by her side. Naturally, Adrianna couldn't help but feel slightly envious.

Her eyelids become heavy. *Yes, Tianna would certainly do well to have Sirion as her husband. Hellfire, the man is renowned throughout Ansalar as a member of the now-legendary Wildrunners. That's without mentioning he's a paragon in his professional field.* Sirion had spent most of his day scouting ahead of the group to be certain the path was a safe one. Every once in a while he would double back astride the back of his corubis companion. With every return, Dramati approached Adrianna to offer her a greeting and get an ear rub. She appreciated this affection, yet Sirion had noticed and he regarded her with an air of speculation.

Adrianna breathed deeply as she finally fell into sleep.

She slipped silently within the low-lying brush. She remained alert, ever vigilant for any sight or sound that may herald potential danger. She could already smell them; their scent was all around her. But this time she would escape; she could already savor the taste of freedom. Carefully she continued to slip away from the camp. Each moment that passed took her farther away and made her success more palpable. Suddenly, in the trees to her right she heard the snap of a branch. She stopped, rotated her ears toward the sound, and sought to detect any more movement. After a few moments she moved forward once more. It must have been another animal. She took one step, then two. With the third step, she heard the harsh snap of metal and sharp teeth sank into her right hind leg. She was suddenly swung up from the ground. She felt the muscles in her hindquarters tear and the bone shift from its socket. She screamed in agony, pain shooting up her leg and into the dislocated hip.

Wildly, the golden fox vixen writhed within the cruel hang-trap as she struggled to free herself. She heard their laughter she saw them step from out of the surrounding trees and bushes. She became still and the blood flowed thick and warm up her leg into the soft fur of her belly. One of the men grabbed the other hind leg and swung her. The movement brought renewed agony and she mewed piteously.

She had failed. She would never have her escape, and they would have their way with her, as always.

From his place before the banked fire, Sirion was on the alert. He waited for a moment and then heard the noise again. Glancing in her direction, he heard Adrianna moan low in her throat. Silently, he continued to sit there. He heard her moan again, the tone indicating someone who was in pain. He then heard a shuffling noise and knew that she sought to escape something. Sirion stood from his place and saw Adrianna thrashing about. Her moans intensified and began to take on an edge of fear.

Sirion quickly rose and padded over to the young woman. He knelt beside her. "Adrianna... Adrianna wake up. 'Tis is naught but a dream."

Much to his dismay, she continued to thrash about, her movements becoming more desperate. "No... no... please..." She breathed fearfully and then groaned once more.

Sirion leaned in close, placing a gentle hand on her face. He instantly felt wetness. Rubbing a thumb beneath her eye, he realized she was crying.

Suddenly determined to end the dream, he cupped her jaw in his hand. "*Shendori*, wake up." Sirion paused for a moment in mild surprise. The term of endearment had come naturally in spite of never having spoken it before. In Hinterlic it meant *pretty girl*, a word he'd heard his father use for his mother a few times when the fighting was at a low. "Adrianna, 'tis only a dream."

She called out in desperation using a language he didn't recognize. Briefly he wondered how many languages the woman knew how to speak. Her thrashing intensified and Sirion swung a leg over to her other side. Straddling her, he sat back on her legs and put a restraining hand on her shoulder. He continued to hold her face in the other hand. In his most soothing voice he spoke again, "Adrianna, wake up. I am here to help you."

She finally pulled herself free of the webs of the dream and with a deep breath she opened her eyes. She lurched upright and found Sirion there leaning over her. Her face almost smacked into his, but she stopped just in time. He was close, so close, that his lips almost touched hers. Her heart beat double time, not just from the nightmare, but the surprise of finding a man hovering over her in the middle of the night. And it wasn't just any man...

Regaining her senses, Adrianna began to feel more than just his breath against her lips. She felt the pressure of his legs against her hips and the warmth of his hand on her side. For a moment, neither of them spoke. Then Sirion broke the silence. "You were dreaming," he said in a low tone. "I tried to awaken you, but you sleep deeply."

Feeling a bit flustered, she replied hurriedly. "Yes, my old master used to tell me that. He said that it was one of my only shortcomings."

Sirion slowly pulled back. "Are you going to be all right? Can I get you anything?"

Adrianna gave a tremulous smile and lied. "No, I think I'll be all right now. Thank you."

With a sense of hesitancy, Sirion returned to his watch at the barely flickering fire. Adrianna readjusted herself on the bedroll, still recovering from his proximity. Even now she could feel him kneeling over her...

It wasn't long before reality gripped her tightly within its cruel embrace. The dream had been so intense, the pain so real. Her leg ached as though it recovered from a past injury, and the rest of her... Adrianna swallowed heavily. No longer was she enveloped by the security of Krathil-lon, no longer was Cortath there to act as a dream chaser. She could hope that it was a solitary event, that it wasn't a herald to anything more.

But she knew better...

The day was hot, even for the moon cycle of Brinaren, making the day seem longer than usual. Amethyst, Tianna, Sheridana, and Carli immediately took advantage of the nearby lake, leaving the men to tend to the evening meal and other chores. Adrianna had only enough strength to spread her bedroll and sprawl on top of it. She was certain her exhaustion had much to do with recent sleepless nights, but she didn't wish to complain and make anyone worry. She still had hope the dreams would pass, and mayhap she wouldn't be forced to ask Tianna for any of her foul-tasting sleeping draughts.

She drifted off and on for longer than she thought. When she finally awakened, everyone was already in their bedrolls with the exception of Zorg, who was keeping the first watch. Beside her lay a bowl of the stew that had been made for the evening meal and she smiled at the thoughtfulness. She was hungrier than she thought and the stew was soon gone. She laid back on the bedroll, but it wasn't long before she thought of how dirty she felt. She should have bathed earlier, but sheer tiredness had won out. Now that she had it on her mind, she knew she would get no rest until she had bathed.

Her decision made, Adrianna rose from her place. She passed Zorg, nodding deliberately in the direction of the lake so he knew where she would be going. He raised a hand in acknowledgment and she left sight of the encampment as she continued towards the water. As she walked among the moonlit trees, she unlaced the ties of her vest. Despite the mark of her shame, it would have been nice to bathe with the others. But now, now it would be even better under the pale glow of the eldest lunar sisters, Steralion and Meriliam. She stopped at the edge of the lake. The waters shimmered silver, and a fine mist hovered about the surface. She slipped out of her trousers and pulled her tunic over her head. First one bare foot, and then the other stepped into the cool waters. Smiling at the soothing feel, she removed her smallclothes and tossed them in a heap on top of everything else.

Adrianna walked deeper into the lake, luxuriating in the sensation of the water enveloping her body. She immediately began to feel better, the sweat and dust from her travels washing away. The soft, silty ground beneath her feet dropped precipitously, and it wasn't long before she was up to her shoulders. Closing her eyes, Adrianna tipped her head back and allowed herself to submerge.

From his place across the fire, Sirion watched as Adrianna left her bedroll. He followed her with his eyes, saw her nod to Zorg as she walked into the copse of trees within which the lake was secluded. He lay there for a moment, wondering if he should go after her. *Despite making Zorg aware of her whereabouts, Adrianna should know better than to leave the safety of the encampment alone at night. I need to be on guard, make certain no harm came to her just as I would for anyone else in the company.* Then, motioning for

Dramati to stay, Sirion picked up his cloak and rose from his own bedroll. He sauntered by Zorg and gave him a nod much like Adrianna's had been. He caught the surprised expression on the big man's face as he passed in the same direction Adrianna had gone only moments before. But the warrior said nothing, simply returned his attention to polishing his sword.

Sirion shook his head. He continued, moving swiftly and soundlessly. *Would I do this for any of the men? Yes, if I noticed they carried no weapon, I would follow a man out to the lake. The fact that she is a woman and without a weapon, well, that is even more a reason to follow.*

The trees stopped right at the edge of the lake. One behemoth had fallen, the trunk hovering over the water. Sirion remained concealed among the trees as Adrianna finished removing her outer clothing, depositing them at the base of the fallen trunk. He suddenly had no wish to disturb her. Sirion knew what would come next, told himself he should look away to afford her at least some measure of privacy, but he kept his eyes riveted as she removed her smallclothes.

She was like a goddess, her hair shining in the light of the moons, her pale flesh radiant, the shape of her backside perfect. She stepped into the pool and he continued to watch, transfixed, as she became submerged into the water. Lathering it with the small handful of soap she had thought to bring with her, Adrianna washed the dirt and grime from her hair, followed by her body. Afterward, she relaxed for a few moments and simply floated.

Before long, she began to make her way to the shore. Twisting her hair to wring out the excess water, Adrianna slowly waded out of the lake. Sirion's eyes drank in the vision of the woman before him. She was quite possibly the most beautiful creature he had ever seen. Her small, slender form was magnificent in every perfect detail, and the droplets of water glistened as she slowly stepped towards him. He had seen Adrianna almost completely naked once before in Krathil-lon, but it had been nothing like what he saw now.

It wasn't until she was completely out of the water when she realized she wasn't alone. Sirion had stepped out of the trees, and when she looked up, she saw him standing a short distance away. Surprise flitted across her face and she brought her arms up to conceal her breasts. Struggling to control his body's reaction, Sirion stepped towards her, his cloak extended. She remained still until he reached her and then she silently turned so he could wrap the cloak around her shoulders. He felt her tremble beneath his touch and his control almost slipped. He so much wanted to touch her, to run his fingertips over the fullness of her lips, the contours of her neck and shoulders, the softness of her breasts.

Sirion slowly turned her around to face him. "You should have brought a cloak. You would have made your clothes damp wearing them so soon after bathing." She drew the cloak more tightly around her. He stepped back a pace

and put his hands at his hips. "And you should have told me you meant to leave the safety of the camp. It's my duty to protect you, and I can't do that if I'm not aware you're gone."

She lowered her eyes from his face with a chagrined expression. He instantly felt the lloryk's ass, for he hadn't intended to make it sound so harsh. He'd only meant to express his care for her well being. *Ah Hells...*

Adrianna didn't know what to say. Sirion had been awake, watched her leave, and felt compelled to come after her. He had a valid point; she was a lone woman out in the middle of the night beyond sight of the camp. Although, in her defense, she'd indicated to Zorg where she would be. Certainly he would have come looking for her if too much time had passed without her return.

Even more, why had Sirion waited to announce his presence there at the lake?

Adrianna gave an inward sigh. *We've been traveling together for only a few short days and I'm already doing the wrong thing. That's without mentioning the dream from which he'd awakened me a couple nights ago. Then there was the morning in Krathil-lon he'd found me and Sheridana stumbling back to the cabin...*

Oh gods, he must think me a complete imbecile.

Adrianna struggled to contain the urge to cry as she brought her eyes back up to meet his. "I... I'm sorry. I didn't mean to–"

She was interrupted by his forefinger against her trembling lips.

"Shhhh, don't be," Sirion spoke in a whispered voice. He took her hand in his. "Come, let's just get you back to camp."

Sirion bent to sweep up her clothes before leading her back into the encampment. Zorg raised an inquiring eyebrow as they passed him by on their way to their bedrolls. Adrianna felt embarrassed. She knew what it must look like, she wrapped in Sirion's damp cloak and he holding her clothes under one arm.

Sirion laid the clothes down beside her bedroll and turned back to her, his amber eyes regarding her solemnly. He reached out and swept a stray curl away from her face and behind her ear. "May your dreams be well." He then moved away to his own sleeping place.

Adrianna settled herself down to comb and plait her hair. When she was finished, she took a moment to don her smallclothes, followed by her nightgown, beneath the barrier of Sirion's cloak. After finally lying down on her bedroll, she cast a glance in his direction. He was still awake, staring silently into the glowing embers of the banked fire.

Before them, a half day's ride to the north, the forest of Elvandahar awaited. Walking, it would take them longer depending on their pace. The journey across the river had been an uneventful one, as ferry trips tended to be, and Adrianna's sleep had been restless the night before. The morning found her even more tired than usual, and she kept to herself for most of the day as they walked. She couldn't help thinking about her dreams. They were disturbing and her mind continually sifted through them. At her worst, Adrianna was no longer sure what was real and what had been fabricated by her overwrought mind. Her dreams about the original event had become so diverse, and so abundant, it was difficult to keep them separated.

Adrianna closed her eyes. What had caused them to return so intensely? After so much time? She'd had a few when she first left Andahye, but they had been nothing like the night terrors she'd experienced the first several moon cycles after the event, or the ones she faced these past couple of nights. It was like a flood gate had been opened, and she was being inundated by a deluge that had been waiting for the opportunity to burst forth. Certainly it couldn't be the tabanakh drink, for she'd begun to have them before she drank it. But could the drink have made them worse? Opened her mind to the horrors she faced on a nightly basis? Or was it that she'd lost Cortath, the one being she thought could really protect her? That was silly; Dartanyen, Armond, and Zorg were accomplished fighters, and Dinim a powerful sorcerer. She was more than protected. And Sirion was there...

Someone fell in beside her and she turned to find one of the men she'd just been thinking about. Dinim gave her a smile, but she had a hard time returning it. "Anything I can do to help, beautiful?"

She shook her head and grimaced. "I don't feel beautiful."

He put an arm around her shoulders. "Well, you are. You also look tired. Let me take your travel pack."

"No, you have your own to carry."

"Who cares? I can carry two today. You're tired; let me help."

She frowned. "I'll feel bad if I let you do that, so no."

"Then I'll take the choice away from you." Dinim pulled her to a stop and lifted the strap off of her nearest shoulder, sliding the pack off her back. Dinim then slung it over his shoulder, took her hand, and continued to walk. "Care to tell me what's bothering you?"

She hesitated, not really wanting to say anything. She had never told anyone about the dreams or the event that caused them. "Eh, it's just some bad dreams."

He nodded. "Yes, I have those every once in a while. Growing up in the Underdark was rough. I get to relive it a little every few nights."

She looked up at him, her interest piqued. "How do you deal with that? Don't they keep you awake?"

He shook his head. "Not anymore. I learned to control them, how to recognize when I was in a dream and shake myself out of it."

"How do you do it?"

He was thoughtful. "First I learned to recognize that I was actually in a dream by figuring out the qualities that make them different than reality. If you pay close enough attention, you can pick them out."

"What kinds of qualities?"

"I don't know. I can't describe them. But they are there."

"Thank you. I'll try it."

Dinim walked with her for the remainder of the day, and once the group was ready to stop and set up camp, he laid out her bedroll and set her travel pack beside it. He winked at her as he left to help set up camp. No one said anything as she just lay there, quietly watching their activity. Late afternoon passed into night and everyone sat quietly around the evening fire before heading to their bedrolls for the night. Adrianna had remained in hers, keeping busy by reading one of her books. Once it was dark, it was harder to fight sleep and the words blurred together despite the light she cast.

She looked towards the fire. This time Armond sat there, gazing into the flames, his swords within easy reach. She focused on him, so much wanting to remain awake, afraid of what her dreams held for her this night. Her eyelids grew ever more heavy, and they closed for longer and longer periods. She promised herself she would only close them for a moment...

The fronds parted as she slithered through the tall grass. Slowly she moved, the muscles of her body contracting together to push her through the waving foliage. She felt the cool ground beneath her belly, and she found herself yearning for warmth. Mayhap she would find a nice, flat rock. Then she could curl herself atop it and allow the gentle rays of the sun to touch her scaled hide.

However, there was something she wanted even more than the sun. Freedom. She wished to escape from those who sought her... those that would brutalize and kill her.

Suddenly, she felt a vibration of the ground. Someone was close, and moving nearer. She increased her pace, no longer worried about stealth. But then they were upon her. She dodged one blow, and then another. The clubs only narrowly missed her as she slithered first in one direction and then another. Fear coursed through her and she increased her pace even more. But it wasn't enough. The third blow didn't miss. She felt the hammer fall heavily, crushing her body beneath its hideous weight. When the weapon lifted, she tried desperately to flee, but her body was slowed by the massive wound that had crushed her bones. She felt the thick flow of blood coating the grass as she struggled to maneuver herself into a tight coil.

The hammer fell again, and she felt the terrible agony of her body being crushed. As always, there would be no escape. She would suffer the cruel torment they would inflict on her. Then she would die. It was easy to believe that death would be preferable than to live and remember the atrocities that had been done.

Adrianna suddenly sat up, her body shaking uncontrollably. Her heart beat wildly and sweat dampened her under-tunic. Her gaze raked through the camp, praying her tormentors wouldn't be there. Once she realized where she was, and whom she was with, she began to calm. The dream had been so vivid, and the pain so agonizing. Hoping she hadn't made too much noise, she looked about the camp once again. Across the fire, she saw Sirion watching. His gaze was intent, and she could see the questions lurking in his eyes. *Oh gods, what is he thinking?*

"Adrianna, are you all right?"

Adrianna turned towards the sleepy voice. "I'm fine, Sheri. It was just a bad dream. Go back to sleep."

Sheridana turned over, wrapping an arm around Fitanni. On the baby's other side slept Carli. The girl was still sleeping soundly, and Adrianna was glad not everyone had been awakened. She lay back down on her bedroll and curled onto her side. There was no indication that anyone else had been roused. She was tired, but no longer so tired that her fears wouldn't keep her awake. So she just lay there with her eyes open, staring into the night.

The group walked among the silver trees. Elvandahar was a beautiful place, but unlike the glen from which they had come, it was uncomfortable, the thick canopy overhead trapping heat and moisture. Adrianna hoped there wouldn't be many more days like this one, where the humidity was so thick, it was suffocating.

But more than the insufferable heat, lack of sleep made her sick and weary. Her dreams were no longer just a thing of the night. They had become a part of her days, and no matter where she turned they would not leave her. She thought she saw shadows at the periphery of her vision, lurking in the trees, and sometimes she thought she heard something.

She feared her sanity would soon become forfeit.

Adrianna looked up when she noticed someone walking beside her. Her sister smiled and Adrianna had to struggle to return the gesture. "Adria, are you all right? I've noticed the past couple days you haven't seemed to be feeling well. You're falling behind, and we've begun to slow down."

Adrianna turned away to look back at the ground. "I'm sorry. It's just that I am a bit tired. I'll try harder to keep up."

Sheridana frowned and put the back of her hand to her forehead. "You are flushed and feel a bit warm. Maybe I should let Dartanyen and Sirion know. Perhaps we can stop early today."

"No. I will be fine. I don't want to hold everyone up."

"Well, if you say so. But just remember, no one will mind if we have to stop because you are ill."

Adrianna finally found it in her to offer a sincere smile. "I know."

With a pat on her shoulder, Sheridana walked ahead to return to the front of the line with Dartanyen and an oblivious Tianna. Quite truthfully, Adrianna was rather pleased to have the healer so preoccupied with her infatuation for Sirion. She didn't want the extra attention Tianna's concern would bring. Adrianna struggled to keep pace, and by the end of the day she was exhausted. However, when she wearily lay on her bedroll for the night, she was loath to fall asleep. The dreams were so real, and while she was trapped within them she suffered the way she did that horrible night almost nine years ago.

Tears flowed, unchecked, down her cheeks, and she angrily wiped them away. *Damnation! Why am I so weak?* She wanted to be strong like Sheridana, yet, looking deep within herself, she felt that she was lacking. Her fears ruled every aspect of her life, and she had no idea how to take control of them.

For half the night she lay there, until Shandahar's last moon, Hestim, made her appearance. Finally her body gave in to the fatigue, and Adrianna slept.

Through hazy vision, she saw the men in the near distance. They were human, with unkempt hair and unshaven faces. Their trousers were worn, and their studded leather vests had seen better days. She immediately turned and ran through the trees. Her heart thumped wildly against her ribs while branches tore at her clothes, face, and arms. As desperation enveloped her, she moved faster and faster. Suddenly she found herself beginning to change and, within moments, she was a golden hawk. Her arm muscles unfurled expansive wings and the wind lifted her from the ground. High above the trees she flew, screeching her defiance at the men below. She felt the sun's rays upon her glorious feathers and her heart soared with the victory of her escape.

Abruptly she felt a pain blossom in her chest and she instantly faltered. She then felt a second arrow rip through her right wing. She began to plummet from the sky and, by the time she hit the ground, she was a woman again. The men were there, waiting. They beat her until she could hardly breathe, punching her in the belly, slapping her face, and tightening their hands around her neck until she thought she might expire from lack of air. They released her so she could fall to the ground, then brutally kicked her. She felt a crack followed by a sharp pain in her side and she knew her ribs were broken.

It was her punishment for trying to escape again, and it was a warning that they would kill her the next time.

A strange haze enveloped Adrianna, trapping her within the fabric of the nightmare. Yet, from someplace far away, she heard someone calling her name. She recognized the voice and struggled to awaken. From without, Adrianna vaguely felt her body being shaken. The thick mist suddenly tore and she was released. As though submerged in a deep pool of water, she pulled herself to the surface and finally broke free.

Adrianna's consciousness was abruptly thrust back into her body. It trembled from her efforts, her breathing was labored, and she was covered in sweat. "I was a hawk... I was flying away and I still couldn't escape. I tried so hard... to get away... Her body convulsed with the force of her weeping and she struggled to breathe.

Sheridana held her tightly. "It's all right. We are here for you." She spoke a few more nonsense phrases that Adrianna discarded... nonsense she discarded because she knew better.

The nightmare meant to have her one way or another, and she had to sleep sometime.

Sirion knelt on the other side of her bedroll. His brow was pulled into a concerned frown, and his eyes reflected the worry he felt. Behind him stood Tianna.

She finally stopped crying and attempted to collect herself. Sheridana pulled back. "Are you better now?" Adrianna looked into her sister's eyes and nodded. "You had me frightened," she continued. "It sounded like someone was torturing you."

Adrianna shook her head. "I'm fine now. Please, I apologize for waking everyone. It was just a really bad dream."

Sheridana scoffed. "It sounded like more than that. Why don't you tell us about it? Maybe it will help."

"No." Adrianna almost shouted the word. "Just... just go back to bed. I'll be fine. I just need some good rest, that's all."

Adrianna watched Sheridana purse her lips in frustration, and then heard her give a deep sigh as she rose from beside the bedroll, saying nothing as she moved away back to her own bedding. Sirion also rose. He regarded her pensively for a brief moment before returning to his own place.

Once she was alone, Adrianna allowed the tears to come. *Oh gods, what is happening to me? The dream seemed so real this time, and I was barely able to escape!* She pulled the blanket tightly around her, felt chilled even though it was the middle of the warm season. The thought that she might really be sick didn't enter her mind as she continued to lay there, staring into the star-littered sky.

Break Free

Sheridana watched as her sister walked behind the rest of the group. A summer cloak was wrapped about her slender body, the hood pulled over her flaxen hair. The face that peered from within was almost frightening. Adrianna's eyes were large and dark in their sunken sockets, her complexion a pallid gray, her lips without color. Dramati walked beside her and she caught herself against his side as she stumbled for the third time. Already she was having difficulty keeping up with the group, and they had been walking for hardly more than an hour. Sheridana knew she was sick, but Adrianna refused to allow them to stop. From where he walked nearby, Sheridana saw fear written over Dinim's usually confident features. Sheridana was afraid too, afraid the thing haunting Adria would eventually succeed in killing her.

The day passed slowly, Sirion leading them through the silvery forest of his childhood home. The group was unusually quiet as they continued through the trees. Thankfully, the weather had cooled, but the sky was shadowed gray where they could catch glimpses of it through holes in the canopy. Sheridana turned when someone approached to walk beside her. It was Dartanyen. He usually stayed in the front, so to have him at the rear of the procession meant he was concerned.

"Is she all right?" he asked.

She shrugged, struggling to hide her frustration. "I don't know. She won't tell me anything except that she's having some bad dreams."

Dartanyen seemed to deflate and Sheridana was reminded of how much her sister had come to mean to the other people in the group. His expression became pensive. "Do you think she's been ensorcelled?"

Dinim approached to walk on her other side. "No, I don't think so. I already cast a *Detect* spell and didn't see anything."

Dartanyen shook his head. "Then what could it be? It seems so much more than just a few nightmares."

The three of them just looked at each other for a moment. No one knew what to say. Dartanyen was right; it was much more than just nightmares that beleaguered Adrianna.

Much more.

Later that night, the group sat around the evening fire, drying themselves from an earlier downpour. Looking towards Adrianna, Sheridana saw her sister had placed her bedroll in a spot removed from the rest of them. She sat on the blanket, knees drawn up beneath her chin. Her head rested wearily on the hands she had folded there. She looked so weak, and so tired. Food had been offered, but Adrianna refused it. When Sheridana tried to argue the issue, Adrianna had become angry and told her to go away. With a sense of futility, she now sat with the rest of the group when all she really wanted to do was make her sister well again.

"Something is seriously amiss. Has she shared anything yet? Anything at all?"

Sheridana looked over at Armond. He regarded her with a concerned expression. All she could do was shake her head. Adrianna would tell her nothing. Every one of her inquiries had ended in rejection.

"You don't know anything at all?" he asked in consternation.

Sheridana scowled darkly. "At this point, you know her better than I do. Go ahead. You figure her out. She won't talk to me."

"Sheridana, we are just trying to find out what could be wrong. This is so unlike her," said Tianna.

Sheridana shook her head. "I know. I'm sorry. It's just that I don't like to see her this way."

"None of us do," said Dartanyen.

"And she won't tell me anything. I feel like she's hiding something from me. If I only knew what it was, I think I could help her."

Dartanyen gave a sympathetic nod. "I suppose all we can do is wait. We will decide whether she's fit enough for travel in the morning. If she isn't, either we can stay here, or we can build a makeshift litter."

Sheridana's lower lip began to tremble. "It's just... I love her so much. We used to be so close."

Oblivious to the talk, Adrianna sat on the edge of her bedroll, Dramati curled behind her. She watched the activity of her comrades: Tianna and Amethyst preparing the evening tea, Dartanyen and Sirion going out to see if they could catch something for the stewpot, Carli and Sheridana playing with Fitanni. As the evening wore on, dinner was prepared. Zorg, Armond, Sheridana, and Sirion looked over their weapons and armor. Food was given to her but she wasn't hungry. She offered her portion to Dramati, and he only ate it when she insisted.

Laying back against his furry side, she watched the group settle in for the night. His warmth staved off much of the chill she felt. Sirion looked in their direction every once in a while, but didn't seem to mind that his companion had abandoned him. Darkness fell and she remained upright, unwilling to lie down for fear of what her dreams would bring. But exhaustion gripped her in its relentless embrace and, just like the night before, her eyelids grew heavy. Perhaps this time she would finally die. After so long, her attackers might win after all.

She stared at the fire, the flames licking at the fresh piece of wood Dartanyen added to the blaze. It began to blur and her body swayed until she allowed herself to rest all her weight against Dramati. "Please, dear gods let this be over. Please..." Before her head settled back against the pillow of fur, her mind was focused inward on a battle that would only end with the rise of a new dawn.

Darkness enveloped her and Adrianna floated in the void, waiting. Just as before, the mist rolled over her, submerging her within its layers. The scene that dominated her dreams for so long was set before her. However, the trees seemed to become smaller as her form shifted into that of a kyrrean, larger than life in all her feline majesty. With a mighty voice she roared her defiance. This time, she wouldn't attempt an escape. She would not flee. With courage she would face her enemies. She had come to realize she was stripped of everything she held dear: her happiness, her pride, and her sanity. She had nothing to lose anymore, and everything to gain.

The kyrrean eyed the men that emerged from out of the trees. They drew their swords and began to slash at her. She felt the massive muscles of her hindquarters coil as she leaped at the men, felt the tension as she extended her claws. Valiantly she fought, using teeth, claws, and brute strength against her enemies. But the men were skilled, and she finally fell to the sword blows. She lay in a pool of her own blood, panting her life away. She became a woman once again, and the men beat her mercilessly.

They meant to kill her.

They would not leave her for dead this time.

Adrianna screamed. Her body convulsed and her legs kicked out in an attempt to escape some unseen pursuer. Sirion rushed over, Sheridana just a footstep ahead. She took Adrianna's shoulders and shook her, hoping she would awaken. Adrianna screamed again, recoiling from the touch. Sirion could hear the raw fear in her voice, the terror. Dramati just lay there and made whimpering sounds in the back of his throat.

Finally the young woman opened her eyes. Adrianna was awake, but not, existing somewhere in between. He could tell by the distant look of her eyes. But suddenly they found focus. Adrianna swiftly reached out and gripped her sister's arm, pulling Sheridana down towards her. Her teeth and lips were colored red with blood from biting the inside of her mouth.

Her voice was a whisper. "They killed him, Sheri. They killed Nahum. Now I have no one to keep them from me."

Hunkered with her side pressed against his, Sirion felt Sheridana's body spasm with shock. Adrianna's eyes filled with tears and regained their lost look. She gave a deep ragged breath and released Sheridana's arm, her body slumping against Dramati's side. Sirion swallowed past the strange lump in his throat as he watched Sheridana take her in her arms. Her voice was broken. "Adria... Adrianna. Please wake up. I am here for you this time."

Sirion gave her a moment before putting a hand on Sheridana's shoulder. Her tear-filled eyes were agonized when they swung up to meet his gaze. Once seeing his expression, she let Adrianna fall gently back. She moved back to allow Sirion the space he needed to kneel beside Adrianna. He had already noticed that her face seemed unusually flushed and he put the back of his hand to her cheek. He could hardly believe the heat he felt. *Dear gods, no wonder she's delusional, speaking in half-sentences that can't be properly understood! She's raging with fever!*

Sirion instantly scooped Adrianna into his arms and carried her across the encampment to his own bedding. Tianna's bedroll lay close by, and it would be easier for Adrianna to be brought to her than for Tianna to move all of her things across the fire. He lay her atop his blankets, and Tianna was at his side the next moment. She knelt beside Adrianna and placed a wrist at her brow.

Adrianna moaned and her body shuddered. "Why Sirion, it feels like she has a fire raging inside her!" Tianna exclaimed.

Adrianna knew she was trapped and that this time she wouldn't awaken. It was a hell she'd created for herself, trying for so long to flee from those who she thought pursued her. The dreams had come, each one slightly different from the next, and the theme was always the same. One time she was a wily fox, hoping to use her wits to free herself. They set a trap from which there was no escape and crippled her. Another time she was a slithery snake in the grass, hoping to silently slide past those who watched. But they saw the parting fronds and smashed her with their clubs. Yet another time she was a hawk, hoping to fly away so high they would never reach her. But they shot her out of the sky with their arrows. The last time she was a fierce kyrrean. They battled her with their swords. They wounded her, and when she finally fell, they tied her up and stripped away her pride. Then they tried to break her spirit so that she would never try to escape again.

Now, it was too late. She was tired... so tired. All she could do was turn around and fight the final battle. In a way she was happy, for she had already won. Her death would finally release her.

For the third time she turned to look behind her, and once again saw no one there. Dusk was falling, and it was time to find a place to camp for the night. The road to Andahye seemed empty save for herself and Nahum, but Adrianna was anxious nevertheless. After a while they broke off from the main road, entering the protective covering of the trees. Nahum's eyes widened just as a large human man barreled into her from behind.

Adrianna fell forward. She bit her lip as her jaw hit the ground, and the grit in her mouth told her she had broken a tooth somewhere. For a brief moment she was stunned, but then began to struggle for the dagger she had tucked into her knee-high boot. She was successful at evading thick-fingered hands and pulled out the dagger, but she wasn't quick enough. He moved his forearm just in time to intercept her backward stab.

The dagger cut deeply into her attacker's arm and he hissed a string of epithets. He swung her around, and she saw the fiery anger in the man's eyes as he backhanded her across the side of her head. Through bleary eyes Adrianna saw Nahum and the other two men. It was the end for her old mentor and he regarded her from soulful eyes as he crumpled lifelessly to the ground. One of the humans kicked the body, and then put his sword through Nahum's chest.

"No!" Adrianna cried out.

There was another curse, followed by a thump to her head.

Darkness reigned.

.....

She awoke to find herself hanging upside down. There was pressure at her belly, and she realized she was slung over someone's shoulder. Her hands were bound behind her back, and her braid hung beside her face, hitting her jaw with each step deeper into the darkening forest.

The men were large, their clothes dirty, their faces hairy, and they stank of their own filth. Her head ached with every step her captor took and she felt a cool wetness at the side of her face. She had never felt fear so strongly in her entire life, even when Hafgan had raised his hand to her in anger. Yet she dared not scream, for she had the dreadful feeling no one who cared would hear.

Eventually they reached an encampment. The man holding her over his shoulder threw her onto the ground. The force of the impact bruised her backside and made her head throb, but she immediately tried to scramble away.

One of the men kicked her in the ribs and all three laughed. "You aren't going anywhere sweetie, not before we're finished with you."

They made a few more lewd comments, bound her ankles, kicked her a few more times, and then sat around the pit that would become their evening fire. As they sat there and talked for a while, she had a horrible thought of what the men had in mind for her that night. Adrianna tried desperately to get her wrists free of the bindings. Her efforts served only to make the cord bite through the flesh of her wrists until she felt the stickiness of blood on her palms.

The hours passed. By the time the men stood from their fire, Adrianna's desperation had reached new heights. The rope at her wrists was so wet, and her flesh so swollen, she could no longer move her hands. Shocks of pain swept up her arms when she defied enough to move and her skull ached with awesome ferocity. She felt like she was going to die.

Adrianna would soon come to wish she had.

The largest of the men approached. His long hair was dark and stringy, and his hairy skin colored a light brown. He bent down, cut the bindings at her feet, grabbed her arm, and hauled her up. The sickening pain made her stomach churn, and when he noticed the bloodied bindings he gave a mocking laugh. He dragged her nearer the fire and the other two men. Once there, he cut the bindings at her wrists.

Pain surged through Adrianna's hands. She held them out in front of her as she realized she was free. Her heart leaped, and in fear and panic she darted from the fire and began to run. But the men were prepared for that. The hairy brown one was behind her faster than lightning. He caught a fistful of hair and her head snapped backward with the force. He roughly hauled her around to face him and put his long, wicked dagger at her throat.

"Dumb bitch. I said you can't go anywhere. Besides, I haven't had my fun yet." He pressed the cold metal tip to her flesh and she felt a painful sting followed by a trickle down her neck. He removed the tie from her thick braid and loosened the hair from its prison. He gathered a handful of the pale curls and leaned close to bury his face in them, his hands roving over her body to settle on her breasts and backside.

She trembled, uncontrollable shudders that consumed her body. He said something, but the pounding in her skull was so loud, it drowned out most of his words. Finally, he mumbled something about "preserving her pretty hide" and pulled her against him. Instinctively she struggled, and for her efforts she was awarded a backhand to the side of her head. As Adrianna fought to regain her senses, he savagely cut through her tunic. She felt the long-knife slice the flesh between her breasts before she was shoved to the ground onto her back. The man went down with her, tearing at her smallclothes.

Adrianna continued her struggle and one big hand wrapped itself around her throat. She tried to disengage the fingers, but the more she fought, the tighter his grip became. With his other hand he began to work at her leggings. She was afraid to move when it became too difficult to breathe, and tears streamed down her temples into her hairline. When he had the pants away, and she was about to expire, the man pinned her thighs to the ground with his knees and released her throat.

Adrianna gasped for air and the man placed the tip of his long-knife to the deep cut on her chest between her breasts. She hissed involuntarily as fresh blood welled from the wound and ran beneath the curve of her breasts to drip down her sides.

"Think yer better than us, do ye, faelin bitch? Even though yer blood be the same color as mine? I been waitin' a long time fer this."

She trembled as the knife continued its way down her torso, blood welling up to trickle down her sides. He didn't apply much pressure until he was below her navel. She began to struggle again as the man put his large hand on her chest and held her there as he cut downward into the delicate skin. Again he laughed, mocking her, enjoying himself at her expense. His eyes were filled with what she had come to recognize as lust, and he dropped the knife to roughly probe between her legs. Her renewed efforts to escape seemed to increase his excitement. He grinned maliciously and growled as he put his stinking mouth over hers. He thrust his tongue between her lips and she gagged at the taste of him.

Finally the man grew bored of his game. With a heavy fist, he struck Adrianna upside the head. While her senses reeled from the blow, he untied the fastenings of his trousers, parted her legs, and lifted her hips. The breath left her chest when he forced himself inside and she screamed as the searing pain tore through. He laughed as he worked over her, and she wished he'd succeeded in knocking her senseless. Every thrust was torture, and her agony only seemed to enhance his pleasure.

It seemed like hours passed before the man was finished. Adrianna could no longer understand his words, and her vision was blurred. She cried piteously when the one with yellow hair came to take the first man's place, and the pain began anew. Only when the third man moved over her did her mind finally whirl away into sweet oblivion where she felt nothingness.

Adrianna later awoke sometime in the middle of the night. Her movements caught their attention, because the men came to her almost immediately. She felt as though the inside of her body was being torn apart as each of them took another turn. After they were finished, they beat her until she could barely endure the pain just to breathe. And when the first rays of the sun crested the horizon, they left her there to die.

And their vile faces were burned into her memory forever.

How long she lay there, shifting in and out of consciousness, she didn't know. Her body was broken and she was dying. She barely managed to whisper to herself, "The only thing that can save me now is something magical..."

Slowly opening her eyes, Her sister sat there beside her, chin resting against her chest. Adrianna couldn't stop the moan that escaped her lips when she tried to move. Her body ached so much, it felt as though she had been raped and beaten all over again. Sheridana jerked her head up and regarded her through red-rimmed eyes. She placed a hand at her brow and Adrianna shivered with the coolness of it.

"Adria, please speak to me," Sheri implored, her eyes wet with unshed tears.

Her voice was the barest whisper, "Everything is so clear to me now. I know what I need to do— what I've always needed to do. If I fail, I will die trying. I'll die a warrior's death, even though I don't wield a sword."

Sheridana grasped her hand and pressed it to her cheek. "No, please don't say that."

Adrianna blinked, her vision starting to become gray. Sirion had come and he knelt behind her sister. It was so good to see him. His amber eyes were so full of concern. She suddenly wished she'd known him when she was younger. Somehow, she knew that he would have allowed no harm come to her.

Then they were gone. Adrianna's mind spiraled away. Images passed before her, images of her father, of Hafgan, and of the men who had used her so brutally. She hated them, yet hated herself even more for her fear of them, a fear that had dominated her life for so many years. But she refused to be weak anymore. She would finally take the self-worth Master Tallek had tried so hard to give her. She would take the Talent she'd been given at birth and use it the way she'd been taught. She would step up to take the place meant to be hers. She knew she had a long way to go, but at least this was a start.

Adrianna would give herself a chance at life by defeating the ones who haunted her dreams.

The forest path was the same one she always dreamed about. Within the trees surrounded her, the men were there, watching, waiting for the right time to launch their ambush. She was alone. Nahum wasn't with her for he had died many years ago. Adrianna walked along that same ordained path. Unlike the times before, she made no attempt to protect herself from what was to come. She didn't shift into an animal. Nor did she draw her dagger or attempt to use a sword. She had tried all of those tactics, and more, over the passing years.

This time, she would use a new weapon.

She closed her eyes in concentration as she continued to walk. She grasped the metal ore in her hand and spoke the incantation to an Armor *spell. Right after, she began the casting of* Shocking Grasp. *Just as she completed the final words of the incantation, the first man jumped out of the nearby brush and knocked her to the ground. Much to her delight, she didn't suffer as she always had before. Her body felt less vulnerable, as though a thick layer of something covered her. She felt the man on top of her convulse with the shock that passed through his body. He fell away from her, gripping his sides and moaning in agony.*

Adrianna stood up. The other two men stepped out of the trees and regarded her for a moment, wondering what was happening to their comrade. Then they advanced toward her. Adrianna reached into the pouch at her hip and found the coil of rope lying within. Meanwhile, she retreated from her adversaries. They smirked maliciously, their companion easily forgotten. The blond man drew his dagger, and the other took a garrote from his satchel. Adrianna began the words to her Bind *spell, hoping she would remain out of their grasp until the spell was complete.*

However, the men were in no hurry. They advanced slowly, grinning widely as they got closer. The blond man made a lunge for her, but by then the spell was complete. He roughly grabbed her arm as she threw the glowing rope, commanding it to bind him within its coils. It obeyed her, swiftly unfurling to twist around him. The man stared at the rope, fascinated, as it bound his arms against his body. When he realized what was happening, he looked at her in surprise. With a bitter smile, Adrianna plucked the dagger from his immobile hand just as the other man stepped up behind her. Before she could react, he reached around her and placed the garrote at her neck.

The cord bit into her flesh and she reared back, the back of her head hitting his chest. She began to choke, and in desperation, she maneuvered the dagger until the blade pointed backward. Then she plunged it into the man behind her. He yelled into her ear and the garrote loosened from about her neck. She pushed him away and he briefly fell back, but then he snarled and leaped at her. Adrianna just barely managed to dodge out of his way and he careened past. Without a backward glance, she turned and ran. She passed by the bound man and then the one she'd shocked at the beginning of the skirmish. He'd recovered from her spell, but made no move except to follow her with his eyes.

Adrianna ran into the relative safety of the trees. After several moments she hid under a fallen oak and waited. It wasn't long before the men came looking for her. A strip of cloth had been tied around the leg of the one cut by the dagger and the other had been released from the confines of her magical rope. They were angry...

Adrianna whispered the final words of her incantation. Fatigue washed over her and she hoped it would work. She had never summoned anything before, but it was worth a try...

Then she heard it. A sound she'd heard only a few times in her life. Her excitement was tangible; she could feel it rising in her chest like a coiled snake about to strike. The sound was a humming that got louder and louder as it approached. The men finally heard it as well and they stopped to look into the trees behind them.

The swarm of whirigs emerged from among the leaves. The men began to swing their arms, and then to yell. The shouts heightened in pitch as the large insects started to sting them. Adrianna crawled from beneath the fallen tree and left, unnoticed. She was lucky her Summoning spell brought the whirigs. Each casting brought something different and she couldn't have asked for a better ally.

Adrianna ran for as long as she could and then slowed to a walk. Her heart was light as she continued her journey to Andahye. The darkness hovering over her soul fell away and was left on the road behind her. Her only regret was that Nahum wasn't there with her as he should have been.

But he would remain alive in her memories and in the victories she would experience because of his faith in a young half-breed girl from the outskirts of Sangrilak.

With a deep breath, Adrianna opened her eyes. A few midmorning rays managed to shine through the silver leaves of the thick canopy, and one had settled onto her face, making her blink. She shifted out of its direct light and glanced about the camp. Sabian sat a few farlo away, his back to a large tree. He was reading a book, as always. Tianna was before the fire, stirring something in the pot hanging over it. On one elbow, Adrianna levered herself upright, her mind giving her images from the night before. Surprisingly, she felt better than she had in several days.

However, her alertness came with a sense of anxiety. Adrianna once more looked around the camp. *What exactly happened while I slept? Did I speak out loud? I was definitely out of my mind if I did. Does everyone think I'm a lunatic? Where is Sheridana?* Adrianna glanced down at the bedding beneath her. She studied the blankets for a moment and realized they weren't hers. With a frown she looked back up to see that Tianna had risen from her place by the fire and was making her way over.

"Adrianna, how do you feel?"

The sorrowful expression on Tianna's face brought the reason for her anxiety to life. *Oh gods, she knows. That means I was talking in my sleep. That means the rest of the group knows too.*

Tianna knelt beside her and placed a cool palm to her brow. "Your fever has broken. This is a good sign. You were gone for over two days."

"Gone?" Adrianna shook her head. "What are you talking about? What's happened to me? Whose bedding is this?" She lifted the corner of one of the blankets.

Tianna regarded her intensely for a moment before replying. "It's Sirion's. He brought you over to his bedroll the night you went into your delirium. You've been resting here ever since."

Adrianna's breath caught in her throat. *Sirion. Oh gods, he knows about me too.* She suddenly felt sick to her stomach, wished she could sink into the ground. She put an arm across her belly, tears springing to her eyes. She felt like such a whore, even more so now that she knew her comrades were aware of how she'd been used.

Tianna watched Adrianna fold into herself and witnessed the self-recrimination pass over her face. She instantly felt a surge of sympathy. She wanted so much to reach out to her, to help her, but Tianna felt so much of her own hurt. She had silently watched while Sirion, the man she loved more than anyone, brought Adrianna to his bedroll and tended to her. He'd even slept beside her, as though his presence would somehow help. Mayhap it did;

Tianna was certain it would have helped her had she been as sick as Adrianna had been.

Tianna reached out and put a hand on her friend's shoulder. "Adrianna, you've been ill. Here, let me get you some tea–"

Adrianna shook her head. "No, I don't want anything. Please, just leave me."

Tianna shrank back from the despair she heard in Adrianna's voice. Her frail shoulders slumped forward and tears slid down her pale cheeks. Dinim arrived back into the encampment after some time at the nearby creek, and realizing Adrianna was awake, an expression of relief washed over his handsome face. But once noticing Tianna's stoic expression, his expression changed. His eyes were full of questions as he knelt beside her at Adrianna's side. She only shook her head and he turned his full attention to Adrianna.

Dinim touched her shoulder. "Adrianna, I understand everything you are feeling. I swear I do, and I can tell you all about it. But today I'm here for you." He slowly pulled her towards him and into his embrace. Tianna watched as Adrianna's body began to quake, her sobs intensifying. She hit her fists against Dinim's chest. "I'm so lost. I beg you, please help me."

"Ssssh. You are not alone."

Adrianna put her arms around his neck and fiercely clutched him tight. He responded in kind, crushing her against him. Tianna stepped back from them, not really understanding what transpired between them. What was most important was that Dinim could help her friend in a way that she could not. Tianna didn't entirely understand Adrianna's plight, and she was glad of that. She didn't want to contemplate how she would have been able to deal with the trials Adrianna had been forced to endure.

Tianna noticed some movement at the periphery of the camp. The hunting party had returned. Sheridana and Dartanyen carried a leschera between them and Sirion carried a brace of burbana. Not until the hunters laid down their kills did they realize Adrianna had awoken. Sirion was the first to notice. With his longbow in one hand and a quiver of arrows over one shoulder, he stood there for a moment to take in the scene across the encampment. Tianna watched the multitude of unreadable expressions pass over his face before he slowly made his way over to Adrianna and Dinim. However, having seen the shift in Sirion's focus, Sheri joyfully rushed past him and was the first at her sister's side.

"Adrianna, I am so glad to see you have finally awakened!"

Adrianna pulled away from Dinim and turned to embrace Sheridana. The two sisters held one another for a long moment before Sheridana finally pulled back. She brushed the back of her hand against Adrianna's cheek as she spoke in a tremulous voice. "Come and sit at the fire we're building. You've been sick and the fresh meat we brought will be good for you."

Tianna stood back as Sheridana and Dinim helped Adrianna from Sirion's bedroll. Weakened from the terrible fever, she struggled just to stand. With a sinking sensation in her chest, Tianna noticed Sirion still watching Adrianna, his expression solemn. She could sense something about his demeanor, but couldn't quite place exactly what it was.

Swallowing past the strange lump in her throat, Tianna turned her attention back to Adrianna. Her friend's eyes regarded Sirion as she allowed Sheridana to lead her towards the larger fire that Zorg and Armond worked to build. They would use it to roast the leschera meat being prepared by Dartanyen. Tianna felt her heart lurch in her chest and was overcome by the same feelings she'd begun to have since the group left Krathil-lon, feelings she tried to shake away the moment she sensed them.

Unfortunately, it was becoming so much harder to do that.

The group moved deeper into the forest. After getting adequate rest, the last vestiges of her fever had abated, and Adrianna was feeling well enough for light travel. While she suffered in her delirium, the group had constructed a litter upon which they had carried her. Zorg and Armond joked about how terribly heavy she'd been, and made a big rumpus about how happy they were to leave the litter behind. Adrianna couldn't help but smile at their antics, and she felt better knowing they would be treating her no differently than they did before her bout with insanity.

Walking beside Tianna, Adrianna took in the magnificent silver oaks towering overhead. The bark was a dark gray, but it was the color of the leaves that gave the forest its nickname, the Silverwood. Sometimes, when one looked up, it was almost blinding, each leaf reflecting the light of the sun off its surface. Adrianna found she rather liked the forest. She much preferred the surrounding trees as opposed to the walls behind which she had lived her life thus far.

From where he walked ahead of them beside Dramati, Sirion suddenly held up a hand. Adrianna and Tianna instantly obeyed his cue to stop, and the rest of the group followed suit behind them. From out of the shadows of the trees ahead, emerged a retinue of faelin. Each carried a cocked crossbow, and a quiver of bolts at his or her shoulder.

"Greetings, wanderers. Please state your house and your business." The speaker was a typical young Hinterlean man. He had light brown, curly hair. His eyes were a dark brown and his skin tone bronzed. Adrianna could see that he was somewhat nervous about them, although he seemed to regard Sirion with more than a little interest. Within moments, Adrianna realized that nearly the entire troupe was composed of young individuals, each barely out of adolescence.

"Greetings to you as well. I hail from the house of Timberlyn." Sirion stepped forward as he spoke, displaying his signet ring. "My business is my own. However, I wish to know the whereabouts of my mother, whom I have not seen for a few years."

The young man's eyes widened. He swallowed anxiously and turned to look at a comrade who had stepped up beside him. The second young man shook his head and shrugged his shoulders. He also seemed to be agitated. The first man looked back to Sirion. "Did you say the House of Timberlyn?"

Sirion's brows furrowed. "Yes, I did. What is it to you?" He paused to give them a chance for a reply. "Listen, we really don't have the time for this. Just by looking at me, you should be able to see that I probably hail from this realm, and that's without my ring." Sirion gestured behind him to the rest of the group. "These people are with me. We have urgent business, but I need to know the whereabouts of Lady Lilandria Sariansee Timberlyn."

Once more the young man glanced at his companion and then replied. "My Lord, Lady Lilandria resides at the center of Elvandahar in the Sherkari Fortress."

Sirion frowned at the title with which the young man addressed him but said nothing about it. "Thank you. I know the way there. It's about six days journey from here, is it not?"

"Yes, my Lord," replied the man. "You know that we are in dangerous times. I apologize for interrupting your journey. Travel in peace." With that said, the young Hinterlean and his retinue began to melt back amongst the trees.

His frown deepening, Sirion put up a hand and stopped them. "Wait. What is this danger you speak about?"

"We've been having trouble with some lycanthropes. Their leader is powerful, and they have finally begun to infiltrate the communities surrounding Alcrostat."

Sirion narrowed his eyes. "Who is this leader? What do they call him?"

"They call him Sydonnia, my Lord. The monster is evil and cruel. He has no mercy."

Sirion tensed minutely, then nodded. "Take care and keep safe."

The young man nodded and left. Without hesitation, Sirion gave a forward wave of his hand and the group proceeded onward. Adrianna recognized the name. It was the one from a message written in blood she'd received from a strange man before leaving Sangrilak three moon cycles ago. He'd been looking for Sirion, and she never knew the reason why. She believed she was soon to get her answer.

The trees became larger and older as they moved deeper into the Silverwood. When it rained later that day, the shimmering kaleidoscope of silver overhead sheltered them. They encountered no one. If anyone lived in the areas through which they passed, they didn't make themselves known.

That evening, the group chanced upon a small clearing. Everyone set up camp, glad to have a place to sleep where they wouldn't have tree roots digging into their backs, or spiders falling from the bushes onto their faces as they slept. Soon they had a fire going, and Tianna prepared the evening meal from the remaining leschera they'd brought down two days ago. The men busied themselves by tending to their weapons. Zorg and Armond were soon joined by Sheridana and Dartanyen. Sirion took his own weapon and went to the far side of the clearing where he began to do some exercises. He caught the attention of the others, and it wasn't long before everyone was joining Sirion, starting a friendly sparring competition.

With avid interest, Adrianna watched as Dartanyen and Sirion squared off with their staves, and Sheri and Armond with their swords. Adrianna was especially interested in the quarterstaff spar, for she'd received some formal training with that weapon while she was an apprentice to Master Tallek. Sirion's proficiency was excellent, and he far outranked Dartanyen with his ability. Dartanyen took his defeat in good stride, and soon Tianna was taking his place to face Sirion.

Curiously, Adrianna looked towards the fire to see that the meal had been completed, and that it awaited their attention. More time had passed than she realized. However, she had no inclination to take herself over to the pot, much too interested in the sparring match. She noticed Tianna's sloe-eyed expression, and she wore a low-cut blouse that displayed her ample cleavage. But Sirion seemed oblivious to these seductive efforts. He made quick work of his beautiful opponent, offering her some pointers as he soundly defeated her. Amethyst, Sabian, and Dinim came to sit next to Adrianna, bowls of steaming stew in their hands. Dinim offered one to her, and she gratefully took it.

It was then she saw Sirion jogging over, holding up one hand, panting for breath after his sound defeat of Tianna. "Wait! Adrianna, I noticed your interest in watching our games with the quarterstaff. Would you like me to show you a few things?"

Surprised and pleased by the invitation, Adrianna nodded and placed her bowl back into Dinim's hands. "Thank you. It will be good for me to get back into practice again."

Sirion seemed taken aback. "You've had some training then?"

She nodded. "Yes, when I was an apprentice in Andahye. It is customary for the students to have some training with a weapon, usually a quarterstaff or dagger. I chose the quarterstaff because my master preferred it."

She rose from her place when Sirion gestured her forward. She couldn't help feeling some excitement; it wasn't every day one had the opportunity to train with one of the most renowned rangers in all of Ansalar. She followed

Sirion into the circle that had been drawn for the matches and she caught sight of Tianna. Her friend had a dejected expression on her face. Did she want Sirion to participate with her in another match? Or had she hoped to keep his attention for just a little while longer? Regardless, Adrianna was a little worried about her friend. Tianna so much wanted Sirion to see her as his equal. Adrianna saw Dinim hand Tianna the bowl of stew he'd previously offered to her. She began to feel a little better when Tianna sat down beside him and began to eat.

Adrianna turned back when Sirion handed her one of the makeshift staves he and Dartanyen had found in the forest. Adrianna took it and assessed its weight and feel. It was heavier than she would have preferred, and it wasn't balanced. Yet, it was acceptable for a match such as this and she would adjust to the weight quickly enough. Sirion took a place opposite her and she made herself ready for his attack.

The spar ensued. After only a few moments, Adrianna knew she was severely outmatched. Sirion was a master with the weapon, his skill outranking even the master with whom she'd learned the basics of the art. But Sirion didn't compete with her the way he had with Dartanyen and Tianna. Instead he acted as a teacher, giving her suggestions on how she should hold her weapon, how she should place her feet, and how she should position her hips and spine. After a while she began to tire. He pressed her for only a short time longer before he called a halt to her training.

Sirion smiled when he came to take the staff from her. "You did well. Perhaps we can make a habit of practicing before the evening meal."

Adrianna returned the smile. "I would like that. Thank you, Sirion."

Adrianna was thoughtful as she slightly inclined her head before turning away. Sirion seemed so different from the man she had met in Sangrilak a few moon cycles ago, so different than the man he had been portrayed by others to be. There was something about him, a sincerity when he regarded her. It reminded her of the way Cortath used to look at her and she felt a twinge of sadness.

But there was something else.

Adrianna glanced back. Sirion was still standing there, watching. His amber eyes seemed to reach into her very soul. She couldn't help feeling that a little bit of Cortath had returned to her. Mayhap she would have some measure of his companionship again after all.

FOREST REALM

T he group continued their journey through Elvandahar. It was warm, but cooler than it had been previous days, a foretelling that autumn would arrive soon. Halfway through the morning, Sirion stopped the group with a raised hand, making the motion that indicated silence. He then closed his eyes and raised his face. His nostrils flared as he sniffed the air, and his body stiffened. There was danger afoot.

Sirion's eyes snapped open. He looked into the trees before him, the path they had chosen to take into the Hinterlean city of Alcrostat. From out of the shadows emerged a man. He stood in the path and waited. Sirion bade Dramati move forward, and the rest of the group silently followed. As they approached, seven more men stepped out of the forest. Sirion kept his eyes fixed on the first man, his father's brother, Sydonnia. Sirion knew that the others were his lycan followers, men that made up his pack. Most likely, another score of them lay in wait somewhere nearby, watching to see if an attack would be made.

It had been many years since Sirion saw Sydonnia last. And within those years, Sirion wasn't surprised that his uncle had finally chosen to secure a solid foothold in Elvandahar. It was a damned good way to lure Sirion to him, but little did Sydonnia know that his nefreyo had been unable to respond to the plight of the Silverwood. Until now.

Sirion approached his uncle with a staying hand at Dramati's withers. Sydonnia's smile was one of self-fulfillment and victory. Sirion stopped a few farlo away, raking his gaze over the unkempt man before him. He was large for a Hinterlean, and hairier. It was the curse that made him that way. His boots were over-worn, as were his vest and trousers. His dark hair was long, gathered by a strip of leather at the nape of his neck. Disgusted, Sirion looked into eyes that had hardly any soul left to them.

"Sirion, I knew that you would come eventually." Sydonnia gave a malicious smile, his feral eyes full of contempt.

"Yes, uncle. I am fully aware of the goings-on here, the panic you have probably created. The people are afraid. In this you have found power. I suppose it's the only way you can attained it."

Sydonnia's smile was immediately wiped away, followed by a hideous frown. "Just like your father, you are. So arrogant. Haven't you learned anything Sirion? Haven't you learned what it's like to be more than just a tool, a thing to be used to kill?"

Sirion clenched his fists, but said nothing.

Sydonnia got a faraway look in his eyes. "You are wrong, dear nefreyo.

Had I wanted or needed power, I could have easily attained it. Your mother, she hailed from a very influential family. Had she chosen to stay with me, I would have married into that family. With Lilandria, I wouldn't have needed anything ever again..."

Sydonnia snapped his eyes back to Sirion and narrowed them. "You know I hate you. You are a symbol of my ultimate failure, a memory of what I should have been. I loved Lily more than life itself, but Servial took her from me, charmed her into loving him. He only wanted Lilandria because I loved her." His voice shifted into a growl. "You shouldn't even exist."

Sirion flinched inwardly. He now knew what he had always suspected. Damn his father. Sydonnia was right. Had things gone the way they should have, Sirion would never have lived. Sirion felt a momentary pang of pity for the man standing before him, the man that was no longer a man. Once he may have been something good, something beyond the ordinary. But now Sydonnia was nothing but a monster, killing wantonly for his own selfish pleasure.

Sydonnia cocked his head to the side and smiled once more. Sirion was instantly on guard, wondering what his uncle had in mind for him. Sydonnia had surely known of his presence the moment they entered Elvandahar. He had chosen this time for them to meet, had set his plan into motion days ago.

"Ah, but enough of my past," said Sydonnia. "It is much more interesting to focus on yours, Sirion. There are so many things you left behind for others to find," Sydonnia's smile widened, "and those things have betrayed you."

Sirion tensed and his nostrils flared. A sliver of fear knifed through him and he was instantly on edge. *What can he possibly be talking about?* Sydonnia's attention suddenly shifted focus on something behind him. Sirion could only imagine what it might be, and his thoughts instantly went to Adrianna. *Gods no, please don't let him recognize her...*

His feral gaze was piercing, but finally he looked back to Sirion. He raised a hand and made a beckoning gesture. A brief moment later, a beautiful half-faelin woman emerged from out of the trees and Sirion's breath caught in his throat. Her hair was light brown, but shone golden in the rays of filtered sunlight. Her complexion was pale, and her ears were rounded. Her body was slender, and her mesmerizing blue eyes were set in a slightly angular face. She walked with the grace of a leschera, softly and quietly over the vines littering the forest floor. He swallowed heavily and clenched his lower jaw. It was Joselyn.

He hadn't seen her for many years. She wore pale yellow robes and a silver circlet at her brow. The talisman she wore at her throat designated her as a druid, one who had made a promise to protect and preserve the wilderness. She was as beautiful and alluring as he remembered, gracefully stepping up to Sydonnia's side. Sirion knew he must look the fool. Even knowing that he should expect anything from his uncle, he'd been caught off-guard.

Joselyn spoke in her musical voice, a voice he had always admired. "Hello Sirion."

He struggled to compose himself. It was so difficult to believe she had succumbed to Sydonnia, for druids generally had no taste for the unnatural. "Hello Joselyn," Sirion replied with a nod. He strove to keep his face expressionless. "Time has treated you well, I see."

With a tinkling laugh, she gave a smile that didn't quite reach her eyes. "Oh Sirion, charming as always."

Sirion cocked his head. What game was she playing, flaunting herself before him as his uncle's consort? Hells, she was a disgrace to the druidical order, and a dishonor to herself. "But not half as charming as my uncle," replied Sirion.

Joselyn flushed and averted her gaze. Sydonnia shook his head with a smirk. "My dear nefreyo, don't be so hard on her. She didn't know if you would return for her. She wanted– *needed* a man in her life." Sydonnia grinned, gripping Joselyn about the waist and pulling her against his side.

"I didn't," said Sirion, regarding Joselyn intently. "I didn't return for her. I came to see the end of the dung-eaten lloryk's ass who has created mayhem in my homeland. Joselyn and I said our farewells a long time ago." Sirion raised an eyebrow at her pointedly as he said the last. Once more the woman averted her gaze.

"Well, then you won't mind knowing that she has been my lover for over three years." Sydonnia put a handful of light brown hair to his nose. "She is a feisty little thing. She says that I am the best she's ever had." Sydonnia kissed Joselyn's neck and glared at Sirion triumphantly.

Sirion returned his gaze to Sydonnia. "It is just like you to want another man's scraps."

Sydonnia glared menacingly. "I'll kill you," he growled. "It is only but a matter of time."

"You can try. At the end we will see who is left standing."

Sydonnia grunted. "I will come for you. Then I will finally be rid of you after all this time. I wish I'd finished the job all those years ago." Sydonnia said the last in introspect, almost as though to himself.

"Well that's your problem now, isn't it?" Sirion stepped away from his nemesis and back towards the group.

The reply was pitched so that only he would hear, sounding like nothing more than a whisper. "No, it's my promise."

Sirion glanced back to find that his uncle was gone. So was Joselyn, as well as Sydonnia's pack. Sirion gave a deep inward sigh. He would need to prepare for what was to come.

Later that night, the group sat around the evening fire. Since their encounter with Sydonnia, Sirion had been more solemn than usual. Adrianna had caught him looking in her direction a time or two, his expression unreadable, and he'd been on constant guard. He picked at the fire with a twisted sapling, shifting the kindling around when Tianna added more. Dartanyen sat down across from him, silently watching until Sirion looked up. He nodded at the unspoken question.

"I know you are all wondering about the man we met today. I appreciate you all waiting until now to ask about him, especially since he's difficult for me to talk about. We have a long history together, Sydonnia and I, but I'm sure you all have figured that out already."

Silence reigned for a few moments as he collected his thoughts. Adrianna imagined he was sifting through the things he should leave off telling them.

"Many years ago, before my birth, Sydonnia became afflicted with the curse of lycanthropy. You may have heard of shirwemic before, people with the ability to shift their shape into the form of a wemic, only much larger, and much more aggressive. Sydonnia was one of the first of his kind, and over time he has become very powerful."

Thinking back on it, Adrianna recalled hearing about such creatures while she studied in Andahye. They made for interesting conversation, for no one knew how, or when, they originated, only that the condition had something to do with a misuse of magic.

"About twenty years ago, Sydonnia finally accomplished one of his life's goals– to kill his brother, my father. He almost killed me as well, but for some reason, chose to leave me alive. Dremathian found me and brought me back into good health. That was how our friendship started. Since then, I have become a lycan hunter of some renown. Cities all across Ansalar have hired me to help take care of one lycan problem or another. Sydonnia heard about this and has made it very clear he wants to meet me again. My assumption is that he wishes to finish off what he began two decades ago."

The flames crackled in the ensuing silence. "Is that why he's here in Elvandahar? Hoping to get to you?" asked Armond.

Sirion nodded. "Maybe in part. The rest is because he has learned to hate this place for reasons I can only speculate about."

Dinim ran a hand through his thick black hair. "So what are you planning to do?"

"I'm not sure. But the first thing I need to do is see my mother. As far as I know, she still thinks I'm dead."

Dinim raised an eyebrow. "You know, you could have sent a message ahead."

Sirion shrugged. "I felt this one was best given in person."

"You want to double up on watches until we reach the fortress?" asked Dartanyen.

"Definitely. Sydonnia has a plan for me and I don't want to make it easy for him to execute it."

The morning of their tenth day in the Silverwood, the group walked beneath the city of Alcrostat. The journey to the fortress had been a long one, and Sirion looked forward to its ending. Since their meeting with Sydonnia, the nights had been difficult, the howls of the wemic making everyone restless. The days were almost as hard because the lycan scent of Sydonnia and his pack were everywhere. For Sirion, it was nothing less than an olfactory overload, and he was constantly on edge.

By midday they finally approached the Sherkari Fortress. It was magnificent to behold, a palace in the trees. Even though he wasn't a spell-caster, he could feel the magic surrounding the place, and knew that powerful protective wards were a primary defense in case of attack. He couldn't see them, but he was certain that Elvandahar's best archers watched from above, making certain to keep the fortress safe. Other magicks had been used to bend and shape the trees so as to make a bastion of architectural beauty. High within the forest canopy, structures could be seen, each one connected to the others by elaborate bridges constructed of living wood and vines. A series of platforms and pulleys existed for the purpose of lifting people from one level to the next. Two isterian, or palace guards, stood before the platform that would take them up into the fortress.

The isterian both bowed before Sirion. "My Lord, your arrival has been foretold. Your lady mother awaits you," said the one on the left.

"Yes, welcome home my Lord," said the one on the right.

Sirion frowned and cast Dinim a sour glance. The message he'd wished to deliver in person had been demolished. "I appreciate the show of respect, but my name is Sirion."

The isterian said nothing as they stepped apart to allow the group onto the platform. The men then took the ropes on either side and began to hoist them up. Looking at the faces of his companions, Sirion saw they enjoyed the scenery as they moved higher and higher into the silvery trees. As they got closer, they marveled at the expansive interconnecting bridges. Many of the other structures were people's homes. Some of them were small, and others so large they spanned two or three treetops.

When they reached their destination level, the group was met by more fortress guards. The first spoke to Sirion with a gesture towards a bridge leading to the right. "Lady Lilandria's solar is this way, my Lord."

Sirion gave a sigh of exasperation and heard the second isterian address the rest of the group. "Come, follow me this way. I will show you to your alcoves." Sirion nodded for the group to follow the guard as he followed the first one across the bridge. His gaze trailed Adrianna where she followed behind the rest of the group. He was relieved that she had recovered from her illness, and she had even begun to regain some of the weight she had lost. Unexpectedly, the young woman turned back and met his gaze. He thought he saw the slightest hint of a smile before she rounded a curve and disappeared from his sight.

With another sigh he turned back to the guard walking ahead. He wondered why they were being so formal with him, for the grandson of a hamza didn't ordinarily require so much ceremony. It was irritating to say the least, and he hated having to correct people. He also wondered why his mother was there at the fortress. The last he remembered, she had taken herself back to the domain of Kleyshes after his father's death. Even though Servial had left her long before, Lilandria remained in the daladin they had once shared together until the bitter end. Sirion respected her for it, but wouldn't have thought less of her if she had moved on long before. Servial had been a terrible husband, and a despicable father. The least Hinterlean society expected was for Lilandria to return to the domain of her birth.

For quite a while they walked through the interconnecting bridges of the fortress. He had never been there before, but he didn't bother to look about as the others had. He was far too nervous, his thoughts focused only on seeing his mother again after so many years. Finally the isterian led him up to a large alcove. The wealth inherent in the décor told him that someone of importance resided there. Once approaching the door it was pulled open by the guards that stood on the other side. Keeping an impassive expression, Sirion entered. He was led through into the next room and it was there the isterian stopped.

"Lady Lilandria, your son is here to see you." The guard then gave a slight bow and exited the solar.

Sirion turned to regard the profile of the small, slender woman out on the terrace. She wore an exquisitely embroidered gown in varying shades of yellow and green. Her contrasting copper-gold hair was plaited in a thick rope that hung to her hip. Emeralds glistened from within the plait and hung from delicate arched ears. Sirion suddenly realized why his father had favored her. Not only had Lilandria been chosen by another man, but she was very beautiful. When she turned to face him, his breath caught in his throat. His mother looked so much like she had when he saw her last. She regarded him solemnly at first, but then he saw a tiny tear escape from the corner of her right eye. Guilt washed over him. *By the gods, why did I stay away so long?*

With long strides he rushed over to Lilandria and put his arms around her. His voice was low. "Mother, I have come to show you I am well. I know Anya has been here to tell you otherwise, but she doesn't yet know I survived our battle."

She trembled in his arms and her voice quavered. "Two days ago, when the scouts came bearing the tale that you lived, I refused to let myself believe them, afraid my hopes would be raised for nothing. But here you are, standing before me, holding me in your arms like I dreamed you would."

Sirion clutched her more tightly against him, his heart lurching in his chest. He swallowed past the painful lump in his throat and blinked his eyes free of the tears that threatened. He inhaled the scent of her and memories from when he was still but a child overwhelmed his senses– memories before Servial had taken him away from her.

"I will never leave you again," he whispered.

Lilandria wrapped her arms around his neck and kissed his cheek. "I believe you."

Finally they stepped apart. Sirion continued to hold her hands, knowing that she didn't want him to let her go. "I am also here to serve the realm, Mother. I am here to aid in the removal of the lycanthrope threat."

Lilandria looked deep into his eyes. "My son, you *are* the realm."

Sheridana stood beside her sister before the looking glass. Truth be told, Adrianna was quite possibly one of the most beautiful woman she had ever seen. Every plane, every angle of her face was perfect in every detail. Her features were small, delicate, and slightly canted brown eyes were framed by lashes so long, they touched her cheeks. Her chest was small, but pushed up by the support of the gown she wore, it was decorously concealed by the cream-colored velvet swaths. She was slender, and usually had enough curves in all of the right places. With time those would return as long as she continued to eat well.

The gowns they had been given to wear for dinner with the King and Queen were gorgeous. Sheridana honestly didn't believe she'd ever worn anything so exquisite. The fabric was the color of rich cream. At the sash and neckline, the dresses were adorned with swaths of medium brown velvet and the bodices and hems artfully decorated with darker brown embroidery. The excess material at the waists were gathered at their backs and fell in thick waves. Around their throats were ribbons of dark brown lace, and from them hung golden drops each containing a stunning ruby. Similar drops hung from Adrianna's earlobes. Golden clasps pinned similarly colored brown stoles to their shoulders. One of the palace servants, or hralen, bound Adrianna's pale hair onto the crown of her head with golden combs beset with rubies. A few tendrils of her hair escaped and hung in loose curls at the sides of her face. Looking at their images, Sheridana could hardly believe how different they looked and she wondered if the rest of the group was being transformed the same way.

She wondered what Sirion would think...

Sirion. After their encounter with Sydonnia, he had become slightly withdrawn. She supposed she couldn't blame him. Regardless, just as he said he would, Sirion had taken the time every evening during their travel time to teach Adrianna the quarterstaff. It was only when they practiced that Sirion seemed to open up, and he endeavored to teach her all he knew. As the days passed, Sheridana noticed that Adrianna anticipated the sparring sessions just as much as Sirion did. She didn't quite know what to make of this increased interest, but felt it must have something to do with the companionship her sister missed so much with Cortath.

But Sheridana was perceptive. She knew that the handsome ranger watched Adrianna through more than just the eyes of a mentor. In fact, he watched her more than he did any other member of the group. His insistence that he watched over the group merely to protect them was moot with Adrianna. Not only did he look after her wellbeing, but in Sheri's estimation, he looked at her the way a man looks at an attractive woman, one that he would like to know better. Sheri grinned. *Much better.*

Sheridana bent to kiss her sister at the lips. They were becoming close again, much like they were before she had left with their father. It was a harsh lesson she had learned, and she would never leave her family again. Never.

Sheridana felt Adrianna take her hands. "You are beautiful," she said.

Sheri smiled and kissed the tops of the hands that held hers. "So are you."

Adrianna shook her head and grimaced. "Sheri, I don't feel right. I feel so out of place."

Sheridana was about to respond when a knock sounded at the door. The hralen opened it and one of the isterian stood there. The man paused for a moment, staring into the room, then finally found his voice. "The Lady Queen wishes your company for the evening repast." Sheridana and Adrianna stepped away from the mirror and to the door. "If you would please come with me."

The two women followed as the guard led them across the interconnecting bridges. Along the way, they stopped to collect the other members of the group. First was Armond, and then Dartanyen and Amethyst. Looking at the girl, Sheri had never seen someone so transformed– or so out of place. She was stunning, her red gown accenting her bronzed complexion and dark hair. She looked like a woman instead of a girl, and even the stoic Armond glanced twice. Amethyst was extremely uncomfortable, however, and she kept bringing her hands to the shortly cropped hair that feathered away from her pretty face.

They collected Zorgandar next. His hralen answered the door, and finally he stepped through, obviously put out. "Ya wouldn' believe how long it took for 'em to find somethin' ta fit me. They finally had ta go to the former isterian captain. It seems he's human, and big, like me." Zorg's gaze took in the rest of the group, contemplative. "I hope they didna have this problem with you."

Sheri smiled widely. "I am glad to say they did not."

Zorg relaxed. "O' course not. You'd be an easy fit."

The group then went to Sabian's alcove, followed by Dinim's and then Tianna's. The healer wore a pale purple gown, trimmed with a darker shade of the same color. As usual, Tianna was the epitome of beauty, and she would portray herself as such throughout the evening, especially to one Sirion Timberlyn. Sheridana had been watching the other woman and knew she had romantic feelings for him. More than once, she'd noticed Tianna playing on Sirion's masculine side. Much to his credit, the man didn't respond to her sexuality, and appeared to view her only as a younger sister.

The group finally made it to a large structure that appeared to be a common area. Once entering, they saw that it was a dining hall. They paused to look at the magnificence of the large alcove, for not only was it lavishly decorated, but it had the capacity to seat hundreds at once. Slowly, everyone made their way to the table. At the center was a sizable array of breads. Everyone seated themselves, each of four isterian holding a chair for Amethyst, Tianna, Sheridana, and Adrianna. They waited only a few moments before the Lady Lilandria entered. On her right arm was Sirion. Behind them strode the King of Elvandahar.

Everyone stood and bowed upon the entrance of the Lady Lilandria, Sirion, and the King. When the three of them were seated, the rest of the group again retreated to their own chairs. Sheridana watched Sirion discreetly. His thick red hair had been tamed, and the parts that escaped curled at his neck. His clothes were befitting those of a member of the royal family; his trousers and vest were made of black leather and his hunter green tunic was made of silk. A crimson sash hugged his narrow hips and from it hung an ornate long-knife.

King Thalios sat at Sirion's right. His hair was curly and dark, pulled back at the nape of his neck with a silken cord. At his brow rested a splendid crown. Embedded within the platinum were five jewels: a ruby, a sapphire, a diamond, an emerald, and a golden topaz. She had once heard that each jewel represented one of the five domains of Elvandahar and wondered if it was true. At his side was Lilandria. He held her hand where it rested on the table and his eyes shone with devotion. She was a beautiful woman, and it was obvious where Sirion got his good looks.

Sirion looked around the table and when his eyes came to rest on Adrianna, they widened. By the gods, she was the most beautiful thing he had ever seen. It was more than the dress she wore, or the jewels. It was the way she smiled, the way her eyes seemed to brighten when she saw him, the way she moved with careful grace. Apart from his bond with Dramati and his choice of profession, he had never felt so good about anything his entire life.

"Welcome to Elvandahar."

Sirion tore his gaze from Adrianna to look towards the head of the table-at the man who had become his father though marriage. As the group nodded solemnly to the King, Sirion shivered involuntarily. He didn't want to be the heir to a realm, didn't care for such responsibility. He wasn't made for it, the call of the wilderness much too strong in him. Sirion didn't crave power; he had no use for it. He felt that someone else could rule the Hinterlean people better than himself, someone with patience, truth, and compassion.

But who would that man be? Who would reign after Thalios? Not just anyone. If Sirion rejected the throne, it would be offered to Anya. He doubted she would accept it based on the same premise that he rejected it. Knowing Thalios had no heir, other influential families would attempt to claim the throne once he was unable to rule. There would be political strife until the most powerful candidate dominated. After much deliberation, Sirion had devised the solution to his predicament.

Sirion thought back to the day before, after his reunion with his mother. After spending many hours deep in conversation, Lilandria had taken Sirion to meet the man who had chosen her as his wife. The King had greeted him and welcomed him into his house. Thalios was friendly, yet wary, most likely wondering why Sirion had returned after so many years away. Sirion knew he would wonder the same things were he in the King's position, so he'd gotten straight to the point.

"My Lord Thalios, decisions surrounding my family have not always been the best. However, as a result of recent experiences, I've come to realize the error of my ways. I decided to come home, and once here, I came across someone who has been causing a great amount of trouble for you. After some contemplation, I've decided that I might be of aid in helping you to eradicate it. I implore you to accept my services."

Sirion had waited. Impassively, the Hinterlean king regarded him for several moments before turning to pace the chamber. Meanwhile, Sirion continued to stand his ground. Finally Thalios spoke. "I thank you for your desire to help our cause. To be truthful, we have had very little impact on the threat. And with each passing day it grows out of control, like a plague." He stopped and looked Sirion in the eye. "I don't know how you could possibly help. The lycan are extremely strong, more than any normal man, and they heal at an astounding rate. They change their shape at will, into kyrrean, wemic, or alothere. It's like a disease, taking some fully within its hold while sparing others. Social status is no boundary, for members of my own household have succumbed to it. Villages have been marauded, women raped, men and children killed. They take whatever they want whenever they want it. Throughout the past five decades we have been dealing with this threat from time to time. But now it is worse than ever."

Finally Thalios had come to stand before Sirion, his brows pulled into a frown. "So, how do you imagine you can help me?" Thalios asked the question not out of speculation, but as an end to his tirade. There was an air of disbelief about him, tinged with desperation. The King of Elvandahar was at a loss, felt that he had failed his people.

But that was all about to change.

Sirion had regarded the other man intently for a moment before feeling the corners of his mouth turn up into a malevolent smile. "My Lord, I have spent many years of my life in pursuit of lycanthropes. I have discovered the weapons that will harm them, and learned their strengths and their weaknesses. I have hunted them down and killed them without mercy, taken from them what they so wantonly took from others.

Thalios nodded. "So I have heard. Please excuse me for being the pessimist."

"You ask me how I can possibly help you. I tell you that today is one of the best days of your life."

Sirion now regarded the man standing at the head of the table. Thalios spoke with a warm voice full of assurance. It was a good voice, one that would easily calm people. "Sirion has told me that you wish to help rid Elvandahar of the threat that terrorizes us. For this I thank you." The King raised his wine glass and the rest of the table followed suit. "You will be richly rewarded for your efforts. I offer a blessing for a quick end to the lycanthrope menace."

Everyone raised their cups and drank in acceptance of their new responsibility. Barely a moment later, the meal was served. The food was delicious, roasted fowl accented by mildly seasoned vegetables and legumes, fresh grains, and pale wine. Adrianna relished the new aromas and flavors. As they ate, lively conversation ensued. Adrianna didn't join in, content to simply listen to the talk. The king seemed to be a good man and cared strongly for his people. Sirion's mother also seemed to be very genuine. She was different from her son, a social being in contrast to his more solitary nature.

Adrianna suddenly had the feeling she was being watched. Glancing about, she finally saw Sirion regarding her from across the table. She met his gaze. His amber eyes didn't waver from hers, but continued to watch her. She felt her cheeks begin to flush and she noticed a slight smile playing at one corner of his expressive mouth. She finally turned away, feeling self-conscious. At the same time, she wondered what he thought about the gown she wore.

Adrianna chastised herself. She felt like a silly girl who had become entranced with an older man. Why would Sirion care about the dress, especially when Tianna was seated directly across the table from him? Her friend was the epitome of loveliness, and this thought had been substantiated when she saw the appraising glances from all of the men they passed on their way to the hall.

Finally the meal was over. The food remnants were cleared away and replaced with several casks of wine. The men drank and told tales of their adventures. It wasn't long before Thalios and Lilandria retired for the night, swiftly followed by Sirion. Adrianna also rose to leave. Nodding to her comrades, she excused herself from the table and was escorted back to her alcove by one of the isterian. Later, she lay in bed and thought about Sirion. What was it about him that drew her? She also thought about the woman Joselyn. *What had she shared with Sirion? Did he love her?* It was quite apparent that the woman still cared for him in spite of the years that separated them...

Adrianna walked the path leading to the thermal spring. It was a place she came to visit at the beginning of every day she spent at the fortress. She knew she wouldn't always have such a luxury, so she took full advantage of it. Most mornings she saw other women on the path to and from the pools to bathe, but this day it was unusually quiet. She had almost reached the spring when she heard movement from the path behind her. She turned and saw that it was only Tianna, who was walking quickly to catch up.

Adrianna smiled as her friend approached. Since the night of her delirium, she and Tianna hadn't found much opportunity to spend time together. She had come to miss Tianna's company, her carefree nature and spirited personality. But Adrianna knew it lay deeper than their arrival at the fortress, Sheri's addition to the group, or Adrianna's sickness. It was Sirion. Tianna had begun to place all of her energies into her pursuit of him, and had allowed their friendship to fall into a lull. Adria supposed she couldn't blame her. Sirion was a good man and would make a wonderful husband and father.

The two women walked to the edge of the pool and removed their clothing. They then stepped into the warm waters, sighing as they sank up to their necks. They waded there, in the center of the pool for several moments, neither one saying anything.

Finally Tianna spoke. It was almost abrupt, as though she had been working herself up for the moment. "Adrianna, what is Sirion to you?"

Adrianna turned towards her friend in surprise. "What do you mean?"

Tianna regarded her intently. "I mean, what does Sirion mean to you?"

Adrianna stared at Tianna, noting the tension around her mouth and the seriousness of her gaze. Contemplatively she considered Tianna's question. Even though she had thought quite a bit about Sirion, she hadn't really thought about what he might mean to her. She supposed that she was attracted to

Sirion, but who wouldn't be? He was a very handsome man. He was also intelligent, worldly, and a paragon within his field of expertise. He was nothing short of a legend, and that fact only served to make him all that much more appealing. However, despite those things, she supposed that all that she truly wanted from Sirion was his friendship, especially knowing Tianna was in love with him. Aside from a few twinges of envy, Adrianna supposed she was fine with the concept of Tianna and Sirion as a couple. Although, she knew that once that concept became a reality, her attraction to him would become a liability.

"Tianna, you know that I hardly know the man. What could he have possibly come to mean to me within the past three weeks I've known him? Really, what is going on?"

Tianna gave a heavy sigh. "Oh Adrianna, I know that you're right, but I had to ask, just to be sure. I know that he sees me as just a child, but I so much want him to recognize the woman I've become. I love him so much, and I know that I can please him, if only he would give me the chance."

Adrianna smiled. "He will, Tianna. You'll see. He just needs some time. He has been through so much, and needs all of the support you can give."

Tianna nodded and grinned. "I feel so much better. I should have spoken to you sooner. You always know what to say." Tianna wiped a stray tear from her cheek.

Adrianna returned the smile then began to wade out of the water toward the towel she left at the side of the pool. "Come on. Let's get some breakfast. I'm famished."

As she dried herself, Adrianna continued to think about Tianna's question. What did Sirion mean to her? She didn't really know, but she knew that she needed to find out.

The talisman glowed red in the darkness of the alcove. Although the communication link had been severed, the object continued to bear the residual effect and would not diminish for another few moments. He placed the talisman deep within his travel pack, far from any prying eyes. He would be a fool to keep it near the top, where someone might catch a glimpse of it. It wasn't something he wanted others to see, for fear they may recognize it and discover the true reason why he traveled with the group.

The fold continued to be in a state of dissension. Since Gaknar's destruction in his fight against the Wildrunners, the priesthood had begun to disintegrate. Gaknar had been powerful and had borne the ability to guide the fold into a new era. Since his loss, a nebulous void had replaced the goals for a future of prosperity and power. When Gaknar failed in his attempt to bring Tharizdune into Shandahar, all of the hard work that had gone into that endeavor was swept away. And without a leader, the priests began to bicker, and no one knew what the fold was destined to become.

Without the light cast by the talisman, the alcove was plunged into darkness. Since arriving at the fortress, it had been easier for him to communicate to his allies in the priesthood. He didn't need to be constantly on guard, afraid of someone happening upon him while he was working with the talisman. Despite Gaknar's loss, he still had his orders. He would stay with the group, monitor them, and report their activities.

It had been Gaknar himself that had brought him into the conclave. Most of Gaknar's followers had been priests, but there were a few necromancers who had allied themselves with him as well. As one of the only spell-casters within the priesthood, he was a valuable asset. He was well rewarded for his efforts, and he felt the cause to be a good one. Currently, his efforts seemed to coincide with those of the group and he was in little danger. He hoped it would last, but knew it would be unrealistic to believe it would. It was only a matter of time before their interests began to conflict with his. There would be problems, and he would have to deal with those issues when they arose.

Until then he had an easy road. He wasn't concerned about Lord Thane, or even the mess they'd walked into by coming to Elvandahar. Trouble seemed to follow these people around like a lovesick corubis cub, but he was learning how to steer clear of their encounters. The girl Adrianna was more interesting than he'd originally thought and he'd shared this with his allies. When the time came he imagined he just might be bringing her back to the fold with him.

SYDONNIA

A drianna stood on the alcove terrace. Creeping vines twined all around the structure, enveloping it in leaves and little yellow flowers. The gentle wind caressed her face and lifted the hair from her neck. Breathing deeply, she inhaled the smell of the forest, heard the rustling of the leaves, felt the sway of the trees all around. The treetop fortress was nothing like she had ever experienced before, awesome in its immensity and its proportions, exceptional in its beauty and majesty. Her lodgings were magnificent. The bed was blanketed with luxurious furs: blue foxes, silver hares, and black mink. The pillows were made of the finest material and stuffed with knapseed-pod silk. The canopied bed arched high overhead, silver tassels hanging from the four posts at the corners. Beautifully woven rugs adorned the wood flooring, and colorful tapestries hung on the walls. Only a thin curtain separated the interior of the alcove from the exterior balcony. She felt the light fabric sweep about behind her as the winds blew it about.

For several days the group had been residing in the fortress. Every afternoon, with the exception of the first two, Sirion had continued her quarterstaff training. Just today they had fought an exceptionally good match. The training was intense, much more so than it had ever been before. Adrianna remembered feeling energized. Perhaps she was getting better! Sirion had seemed to be working up a sweat, and his expression was of one who had become focused on his task.

Sirion swung his staff. His strength was overpowering as he bore into her, and with a savage twist, her staff was torn from her hands. It spun in the air a couple times before landing in some nearby foliage. Adrianna stumbled back and Sirion followed her onto the ground. With her weight, and a bit of his, applied to her backside, she cried out.

Sirion quickly disengaged and knelt over her, his brow creased his worry. "Are you alright? Did I hurt you?"

She blew away some of the hair that had come loose from their ties to hang in front of her face. "No, I'm fine. I was just a bit startled."

He put a hand at her back and helped her upright, then gently wiped the hair away from her face. There was a pregnant pause before his hand brushed against her cheek, and she felt a momentary rush that made her heart skip a beat. His face moved closer to hers, ever so close...

"Sirion! Adrianna! Good morning to you both. I thought I'd find you here."
Dartanyen had hailed them as he stepped from out of the trees. Sirion's gaze had been intense as he rose and offered her a hand. After helping her up,

he'd reluctantly stepped away to speak with Dartanyen. Breathless, Adrianna had vacated the area, leaving the two men to their discussion. She'd gone in search of a bath, hoping to cleanse away the sweat, but continued to think about her response to Sirion. She'd *wanted* him to kiss her.

Adrianna felt warm wetness at the corners of her eyes and placed her hands on the balustrade to steady herself. Her guards came crashing down and she realized Tianna's fears were founded. Sirion had become something special to her– more than just a hero, more than just a legend. He had become a man.

By the gods, I'm falling in love with him. She couldn't deny it anymore, even though she wanted to. She'd been attracted to Sirion for quite some time, and had come to enjoy his company. She was loath to admit she cared so much for him, especially when she knew he loved another woman.

The tears escaped from behind her closed lids. Adrianna bowed her head, felt the wetness become cold on her cheeks as the wind touched it. Joselyn. Sirion might hate what the druidess had become, but continued to love the woman she had once been. And then there was Tianna. Even if Sirion no longer bore an inclination for Joselyn, Tianna was there. She was beautiful, engaging, and witty. Sirion would be a fool not to realize that.

Dear gods, what is happening to me? Just a week ago I was entangled with insanity, and now this...

Sirion stood in the shadows, breathing the sweet scent of her as the winds carried it to him. Her moon-colored hair played about her shoulders and back, her nightgown a dark contrast to the pale gauzy fabric of the curtain. Lilandria had asked him about her, knowing with a mother's intuition there was something about Adrianna that captivated him. He'd told her nothing except that she was someone he'd met when he was last in Sangrilak. His mother wasn't satisfied with this response, yet she wisely said nothing.

With a bowed head, Adrianna leaned against the railing of the terrace. Even though he was tired from hours of deliberation and strategic planning, he wanted to come and see how she fared. After speaking with Dartanyen following their disrupted spar earlier in the day, he'd intended to look for her, but was accosted by other responsibilities that required his attention.

So he hadn't been able to come. Until now.

Yet, Sirion was no fool. He knew it went much deeper than a simple inquiry after her wellbeing. He had felt something between them while he knelt over her after their fall, something more than just mere attraction.

Sirion shook his head, feeling torn. Even though he harbored romantic feelings for Adrianna, thoughts of the half-faelin druidess Joselyn kept him awake at night and haunted him during the day. He remembered how much he'd once cared for her, and the times they had shared together. It had pained him immensely to see her standing at Sydonnia's side as his consort. It was difficult to believe she'd *chosen* the path of evil, for druids were much immune to the disease of lycanthropy.

Many events had taken place over the time that separated them, but most importantly, Sirion had been swept up in that magical vortex. He'd faced his true self and found it lacking. He had discovered that every man needs other men, and that those of faelin and human kind weren't meant to walk alone. He'd broken the mold set forth for him by his father and become the man he'd always dreamed he would be. He had set new standards for himself and lived by the rule that his life would be what he made of it.

And through it all, he had finally found that thing for which he had been searching a long time.

Sirion stepped out of the shadows and onto the balcony. Adrianna didn't move. He thought surely she must have heard him, but then remembered exactly how silently he could step. He ached to reach for her, but hesitated. What if he was wrong? What if the connection he sensed earlier was only something his mind fabricated? What if she really didn't care very much for him at all? Sirion breathed deeply. He'd come this far. He was damned if he allowed his few opportunities to act on his instincts pass him by. He'd missed out on too many other things in the past. Sometimes a man just needed to take the chance...

He gently spoke her name. "Adrianna?"

Sirion wanted her to turn toward him, so much wanting to see her expression, hoping to read something there. He put a hand on her shoulder, but she still didn't turn. He sensed a sadness emanating from her, and she trembled beneath his palm. Guilt suffused him. *I hurt her. I should have come sooner. I'll need to get her to the nivorlan...*

"Adrianna, we have healers. I can take you to one right now." He stepped closer, brought a hand to her hair and gently ran his fingers through it. He felt the softness of her skin as he brushed it away from her neck. He took a deep breath and silently exhaled. As always, he was intoxicated by her presence. He leaned closer, closer– *I need to stop. I'm tired and I drank too much wine with dinner. I need to take a step back and harness myself.*

Adrianna sensed his presence just before she felt his hand on her shoulder, followed by the same type of rush she'd felt after their spar. A lump came to her throat and the tears burned there, waiting to be unleashed. His hand was gentle as he moved it through her hair and then down the bare flesh of her arm. She felt the warmth of him close behind her. She knew she should turn around, or at least make some kind of response, but she didn't want to let him see her crying like a babe. The warmth intensified as he stepped even closer, followed by the feel of his breath on the curve of her neck. Her heart stuttered when he unexpectedly placed his lips there. *Oh gods, what is he doing?*

Adrianna inhaled sharply when he took her shoulders and began to turn her around. She resisted for a moment, but then surrendered. Just as she knew they would, tears fell the moment she faced him. She could see the questions in his eyes, yet he said nothing as he pulled her close. She melted against the solid wall of his chest and rested her head against his broad shoulder. Sirion wrapped his arms around her and she felt safe. Within his embrace, she felt nothing could ever harm her.

But then she remembered the way he had looked at the woman Joselyn and her grief was renewed. *What will I do when he chooses to go back to the beautiful druidess? What will I do if he chooses to go to Tianna?*

Sirion pressed Adrianna close, her proximity making him reckless. Again he pressed his lips to the curve of her neck, inhaling her distinct scent overlaid by the floral perfume of her bath oils. Since the night he'd eavesdropped on her at the lake, he'd awaited this moment. It felt like he was in a dream; the air around them seemed surreal and his body tingled where it touched hers. He moved his hands along her sides to rest at her waist. Her gown was modest, leaving much to his imagination, and when she placed her palms on his chest, his flesh rippled at the light touch. He tightened his grip and pulled her hips against him. His breath quavered when she slid her hands up over his neck and into his hair, fueling the fire burning within him. Through the fog of desire Sirion vaguely remembered she'd been crying, that she was obviously upset about something. Even now he could feel her tears dampening the thin fabric of his under-tunic. He hated to think she might be unhappy, and disliked it even more that she felt the need to hide it from him. He made a growling sound deep in his throat and tilted her face up just enough so that his lips captured hers.

Adrianna gripped the front of his tunic in her fists, returning his kiss with matching intensity. He lived in the moment, a moment he never would have imagined a mere year ago. Holding her securely in his arms, Sirion slowly led them off the terrace and into the privacy of the alcove. He slid his hands from her waist to the curve of her backside. She was soft and pliable against him, responding with a passion he never would have imagined. He felt the warmth of her breath against his lips, the gentleness of her fingertips as she caressed his face. Sirion backed her into the room until they reached the canopied bed, then gently pulled her down with him.

Sirion wrapped his arms tightly around her as he continued to kiss her mouth, her nose, and her eyelids. Adrianna gave a soft moan as he moved over her, and she ardently returned his embrace. She moved her lips from his mouth to the sensitive skin at his throat, her hands kneading the fabric of his tunic, her hips and legs moving against his. Her movements were beginning to drive him wild, and he knew that he should stop.

He *needed* to stop, but he didn't want to. Sirion wanted Adrianna so much it hurt.

Adrianna's heart thundered against her ribs. Instinctively, she knew that Sirion wanted her; she could feel it in the way that he touched her, the way he kissed her. She wanted him too– wanted him in a way that was unfamiliar, for she'd never felt the need to have a man before. It was both frightening and invigorating at the same time. A part of her wanted to tell him to stop, but the other, bigger, part never wanted it to end.

Suddenly there was a knock at the entryway.

Sirion grudgingly dragged his mouth away from hers and hovered for a moment. His chest rose and fell against hers with each ragged breath and his amber eyes smoldered. Sirion lowered his face to hers, about to resume their activity, when the knock sounded again. Once more they paused, but the moment was gone. Her ardor began to slip away, and she saw reason return to his eyes. She shifted uncomfortably beneath him and he immediately moved away. They both stood from the bed, smoothing their hands over clothes and hair.

"Adrianna, are you awake in there? It's me, Sheri."

Irritated, Adrianna turned towards the voice. "I'm awake now," she grouched. "What do you want?"

Sheridana seemed not to notice. "Dartanyen wants to see us all in his alcove, something about–"

"Right now?" Adrianna interrupted with a frown. "Yeah. I'll meet you there." She cursed beneath her breath. "Just give me a few moments."

She turned back to find Sirion watching her, his demeanor distant and withdrawn, his gaze unreadable. "I am glad to see you weren't harmed from our spar earlier this afternoon."

The feeling of sadness infused her once more and she abruptly remembered– if not Joselyn, it would surely be Tianna. By his manner, she imagined he regretted what had just taken place, and she wondered what exactly that was. "Um, yes. I'm fine. Thank you for the concern."

Sirion nodded. "I will see you tomorrow."

Adrianna nodded as he walked out of the bedchamber towards the entryway. He looked back for a moment, his expression indecisive, but then he was gone. She just stood there for a moment, not really knowing what to think. She considered regretting what had happened, but quickly realized she couldn't do that.

She loved Sirion, and she could regret nothing they had shared together this night.

29 BRINAREN CY593

Sirion scouted ahead, walking silently among the trees. Just that morning, the group had left the sanctuary of the fortress, amply equipped with all Sirion had told Thalios they would need for their mission. Zorg, Sheridana, and Armond had been given Savanlean-made plate, the best that could be made upon all of western Ansalar. It was lighter than other armor, leaving the warrior feeling less encumbered. Sirion and Dartanyen were both given new studded leather vests and Hinterlean-made arrows. Everyone's packs had been stocked with new supplies, as well as fresh bread, cheese, and the eukana mix that the Hinterlean rangers ate when they were on extended missions outside of the forest.

Sirion continued to walk. He was accustomed to riding astride Dramati, but this day he left the corubis behind with the others. He was aware he was being followed and had been for quite some while. It was the scent that gave her away. He knew her smell just as well as he knew Adrianna's. After several moments of trying to ignore her, he finally stopped. With a sigh of frustration, Sirion put his hands at his hips and slowly turned.

From behind one of the gigantic trees, Joselyn emerged. Sirion felt any ire he'd been feeling melt away and he stood motionless as she gracefully approached. Her supple body was easily seen beneath the sheer silk of her gown and long, light brown hair spiraled down to her hips. It was threaded with tiny white chamdaroc flowers, their scent thought to have intoxicating qualities. Joselyn only stopped when she was close beside him, much closer than common protocol, and he quickly discovered her scent was indeed intoxicating, much as he remembered it.

She placed a hand on his chest. "Sirion?"

He remembered that voice. It was the low, seductive one she used when she was unsure of his mood, or when she sought to placate him. He looked down at her, took in the slight pout of her lips, the rise and fall of her breasts beneath her gown. He could see the blush of her nipples through the thin white fabric. He knew she wore it purposefully to thaw his resolve against her.

"What do you want, Joselyn?" He stepped back and she let her hand drop to her side.

She continued to pout. "Why didn't you return for me, Sirion?"

The question should have surprised him, but nothing surprised him anymore.

He gave a heavy sigh. "You know why. We had an agreement. Neither of us was willing to give up his or her profession for the other. Either that, or we were unwilling to compromise. Each of us wanted to be the best at our chosen vocations. We had no future together."

Joselyn regarded him intently. "You really believe that?"

Sirion frowned. "Yes, it was spoken between us." Sirion sighed again and lowered his head. He continued in a lower voice. "You left the order, then."

For a moment there was silence. Her voice cracked, "Yes."

"Why, Joselyn? Why did you do it?"

She looked up at him beseechingly. "I did it because I yearned for you to return to me. The order was a constant reminder that I had chosen it above you. And then Sydonnia came. I knew you would eventually seek him out. Only, I never realized it would take so long. I thought maybe you would come if you knew he'd taken me."

Joselyn stopped speaking, and lowered her head. "But you never did."

Sirion looked at her, pale chestnut tresses framing her lovely face. "Joselyn, I never knew you were with Sydonnia until I arrived here several days ago. Hells, how would I have learned of it sooner? Regardless, there is nothing more between us. You had to know I would never accept you under these circumstances."

She looked up at him, tears at the corners of her blue eyes. "I hoped you would. I prayed you would have me back at your side." She paused and her eyes widened. "There is another woman?"

Sirion hesitated. Thoughts of Adrianna raced through his mind, of what they had shared the other night, of a passion he'd never felt so strongly before. Sirion shook his head, and then nodded. "Perhaps, but what is it to you?"

"I thought so. I saw her that day, watching you." The tears spilled down her face. "And Sirion, it means everything to me! Please have me back. I can prove to be so much more than I ever was before. You know I can be what you need. That other woman, she won't understand the calling of your profession the way I do. Please–"

Sirion shook his head and pursed his lips. "No, you have chosen the path of corruption. Despite your claim to have been in wait for me, you shared my uncle's bed and became his consort. You sullied yourself with the stink of his filth. I can smell him on you even now."

Joselyn made a mewling sound and wiped at the tears. "Do you love her?"

Once more, Sirion paused. He knew the answer, felt he had always known it. But he didn't wish for Joselyn to know, afraid she might use that knowledge against him– she who had chosen the easy path.

"Perhaps. But it isn't really any of your concern."

All of a sudden she was standing close to him again, too close. "She can't possibly mean to you what I once did. We have a past together, and I want you so much. Please don't make me beg." Joselyn gave another little mew and seductively pressed her body against him. She wrapped her arms around his neck and ran her fingers through his hair. Then she took his lips with hers.

At first Sirion responded to her kiss, much as he always had before. But this time it was different. It was *wrong*. Sirion pulled away, replacing the distance between them. "Go back to my uncle, Joselyn. You can no longer manipulate me the way you did before. Once, I may have loved you. But now you have defiled my memory of you and I feel shame."

Her eyes widened and her voice was imploring. "Sirion, please—"

He cut her off. "No. You have chosen your path." He then turned abruptly and walked away.

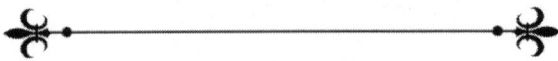

Tianna silently looked up at the sky. Evening was approaching. Already she could discern the pale shape of Steralion through the canopy above. Seated before the small cauldron, she poked at the growing flame beneath it. Given a bit more time, the fire would heat the pot enough so that she could begin the evening meal.

Tianna gave a disheartened sigh. For two days the group had been attempting to track down Sydonnia. That first morning, Tianna was quick to perceive a change in the relationship between Sirion and Adrianna. There was a tension between them that hadn't been there before, and she caught them glancing at one another when they thought no one else was watching. They didn't speak to one another very much, their conversations limited to the business at hand. Tianna knew something had happened, but couldn't decide what it might be. She only hoped it wasn't one of the more disturbing thoughts going through her mind.

However, the strange relationship between Sirion and Adrianna wasn't the only thing weighing on her. It was her family. After passing through Alcrostat, the group moved into the domain of Filopar. They began to see the effects of the lycanthrope menace on the people who lived there. They lived in fear, keeping to themselves and staying inside their tree-top homes, hoping that any lycan that came by would leave them alone. Many places had been severely ravaged. The group learned that the domains of Filopar and Mirpur had been the most affected, especially the area where the druids of Reshik-na resided.

Reshik-na was a place located within the southernmost region of Filopar. The order of druids that lived there was one of the most beneficent upon all of Ansalar. Several years ago, during a mission to the farthest reaches of the domain of Mirpur, the druids had found the child Tianna at the site of a village decimated by some unknown threat. The druids had taken Tianna back to Reshik-na, and she came to live in the house of Father Domick. Withdrawn, and constantly wary of others, Tianna didn't thrive. She became more sickly and frail until the day a young ranger by the name of Sirion Timberlyn arrived. He became the medicine that ultimately made Tianna well. She blossomed under Sirion's protective wing, and she started to show an inclination for the art of healing.

However, when Tianna began to approach adolescence, she realized she wasn't motivated enough to live the strict life of a druid. She left the order and journeyed to the city of Sangrilak. There, she entered into the priesthood of Beory and began to study herbal medicine in earnest. Within only a few years, she advanced in the ranks of the priesthood and became a qualified healer. Within that period of time, Sirion had come to visit her in Sangrilak, but she never forgot the times they had shared together in Reshik-na. As she developed into maturity, she finally recognized her true feelings for him. Since then, she had slowly endeavored to win Sirion's heart.

Tianna continued to poke at the growing fire, her thoughts turned inwards. She was worried about Father Domick and the rest of the druids in Reshik-na. She loved them like they were her family, for she remembered no other, and she couldn't help but think that they needed her.

"Is something bothering you, Tianna?"

She looked up from the fire to find Sirion standing over her. Her heart quickened for a moment before it settled again. "I feel so torn. I want to help you find your uncle, but I also feel that I should go to my family. I need to be certain they are all right."

Sirion crouched beside her. "Then go, Tianna. Nothing is holding you back."

"But you need me. Who will be there if you, or anyone else, gets hurt?" Tianna stopped, glancing in Adrianna's direction.

Sirion took Tianna by the shoulders. "We will be fine. Go, your people need you more than I do."

Tianna turned back to Sirion, questions in her eyes, but she asked none of them, afraid of the answers. "But what I really want is to be with *you*," she whispered.

But Sirion didn't hear as he rose to make his way back to the unsheathed shortswords lying on his bedroll. "When you go, just be sure that you take someone with you. You shouldn't be traveling alone," he said over his shoulder.

Tianna remained silent. Her loyalty to the people who had taken her in as an orphan was strong. But her desire to be with the man she loved was stronger. She felt an overpowering urge to stay, hoping that her presence would keep the inevitable at bay. But something was happening whether she wanted it to or not, her presence or no. She could see the connection between Sirion and Adrianna, and knew they hardly perceived it themselves. She felt the tension between them, and recognized it as the attraction they attempted to ignore.

She had to go. If her only reason for staying was to try to keep Sirion and Adrianna apart, then she would be doing herself, her people, and possibly Sirion and Adrianna a disservice. Of course, it wasn't her only reason for staying; she knew her help would be greatly welcomed in the fight to come. But she also knew, with every fiber of her being, that her people needed her more.

"I will be leaving in the morning then," she said.

Sirion looked back at her. "Who will be going with you?"

"I don't know. Perhaps the King can spare some men."

Sirion put his hand beneath his chin, stroked it for a moment, and then replied, "Perhaps, but I don't trust them. At least one of us should go with you." Sirion looked around at the rest of the group. They were all preparing for the night, laying out bedrolls and blankets. Sheridana had picked up Tianna's slack and was busy preparing the evening meal, and Zorg conducted a perimeter check.

After a few moments Armond spoke up. "I will go with you."

"Excellent," replied Sirion. "I will send Dramati back to the palace with the message that we need three of the king's best men to accompany you. They should be here by morning." Sirion removed a parchment from his pack and wrote a quick note. He called Dramati to him, and the corubis allowed the message to be tied around his neck. Sirion held the animal's face in his hands, gazing into Dramati's eyes. Then the corubis was gone, bounding back into the forest through which they had trekked that day.

Sirion looked up to find Tianna still watching him and he smiled. "You had better get some rest. You have a big day ahead of you tomorrow."

"Will you come for me when your task here is through?"

Sirion chuckled. "Of course. We can't remain too long without our healer now, can we?"

Sirion's good humor was infectious, and Tianna felt herself smiling in return. It was one of the reasons why she cared for him so much. Despite his often stoic demeanor, he was able to make her smile when nothing else could.

She went over to Armond and they quickly discussed their plans for the next morning. Then she took Sirion's advice and went to bed. Whatever was meant to happen would happen. No matter how much Sirion had come to mean to her, she couldn't make him see her as anything more than the little girl he had met over twelve years ago.

But, at least for now, she could still hope.

Sirion dropped his pack beside Zorg's and looked out into the forest. Just that morning, Tianna and Armond had departed for the southern reaches of Filopar in the company of three of Thalios' men. Just as he predicted, Dramati and the warriors had arrived in the early hours of the morning, and even before everyone was awake, Tianna and her escort were gone. Tianna had embraced him before leaving, kissing him on the mouth before quickly turning away. Sirion was a bit surprised, for she'd never been quite so demonstrative before. He decided she was distraught about her journey to Reshik-na. In light of their situation, he couldn't blame her.

Sirion frowned as he felt the tension in his body beginning to build. They were close. He'd noticed signs of a lycan pack, and could some-times smell Sydonnia's distinctive odor. Sirion glanced cursorily about the encampment, told Dramati to stay there, and walked into the forest. He would just take a quick look. Perhaps that was all that Sydonnia wanted– to catch him alone. It wasn't the best scenario, but he'd taught the rest of the group his distinct calls on their way to the fortress. Dartanyen knew them quite well and was able to respond with his own reply calls.

Sirion's footfalls were silent as he moved. He allowed his senses to extend outwards, to encompass the world around him. Then, not only did he hear the wind in the trees, he heard the movement of the animal life in the leaf-litter, saw the scat of a leschera, followed the tracks of an alothere, and smelled the scent of rain on the wind. Suddenly he realized he was being followed.

"Sirion?"

He turned around to face Adrianna. She stopped, and stood about half a farlo away. He heard the fear in her voice when she spoke his name, the unspoken questions. Now he saw the same reflected in her eyes.

"Sirion, where are you going? Is something out here?"

He pulled his hand through his hair. He probably shouldn't have left like this, without telling anyone. His thoughts were so full of Sydonnia, he couldn't be bothered to remember anything or anyone else. "No, I don't think so. I just wanted to be sure before we camped for the night."

Adrianna nodded. "Do you want me to leave you alone then?"

Sirion regarded her solemnly for a moment before his lips pulled up into a small smile. "No," he replied. "I always enjoy your company."

A flash of surprise swept over her face when he took her hand. A weight lifted off his shoulders as they walked together in silence, making a wide circle around the periphery of the encampment. He felt badly about being so aloof, but he didn't know how to deal with the pressures of facing Sydonnia coupled with the intense emotions he felt in her presence. He hoped this would end soon and he'd be able to give her the attention she deserved. They walked for several moments before she spoke again. "Sirion, what's going to happen?"

He turned to look at her. "I don't know."

He wanted to give more of an answer, but the alarm it might cause was unnecessary. He had some idea of how events could play out. His uncle was very cunning and his strength equaled that of several men. It was very possible he wouldn't return to the group in one piece, much less alive. He'd lied to Tianna when he told her to go; the group would be very hard-pressed without her healing abilities. But he just couldn't stand to keep her there when the needs of her family were too real to ignore.

Suddenly Sirion was afraid. If he lost against his uncle, Sydonnia and his minions would come for the rest of the group in retaliation. Adrianna would be a valuable commodity for Sydonnia, not only because she was beautiful, but because she had meant something to Sirion. And then there were the others. The lycan would certainly crush them.

Sirion fiercely ran his fingers through his hair and then clenched his hands into fists. Adrianna startled with the force of his expletive. "Ugh! Why me? Of all the people on Shandahar, why me? My life has been nothing but hardship. You never asked, but I know you've thought about it. You wondered what Sydonnia meant when he said that I was a killer."

Adrianna regarded him impassively. She said nothing, just waited for him to continue.

Sirion shook his head. "For years my father trained me to be a fighter, a damn good one. He took me to some of the best warriors he knew. I trained every day, stopping only when we were on the road to my next mentor. But even then it wasn't a real break because he was the one who taught me all my skills as a ranger. It was all done for one purpose– to kill his brother. He knew I was the only one who could do it because he was too weak to do it himself." Sirion chuckled dryly. "Servial was always the selfish one."

Sirion stopped on the path. He saw the compassion in Adrianna's eyes and was glad she had decided to follow. He needed someone to listen, and she proved she was good at it. Before he realized it, she was closing the distance between them, wrapping her arms around him in a gentle embrace. With a small smile he reciprocated, and she put her head on his shoulder. Holding her made him feel so much better about what he had done a few nights ago when he took advantage of her.

Finally they stepped apart. "We should go back," she said. "The others will be wondering about us."

"You go on ahead. I will follow in a moment." Sirion gestured for her to go on without him. "I just need to be sure the area is secure." Adrianna nodded in reply and turned away towards the encampment.

Sirion stood there for quite some time. Memories of his days as a boy went through his mind. He couldn't recall a time he hadn't known the terrible story of how Sydonnia was made into the monster Sirion had come to know as his uncle. *What exactly had happened all of those years ago? Did Servial really betray his own brother? I suppose I'll never know. Servial is dead, and soon Sydonnia will be as well, gods willing.*

Sirion knew when he was being watched. All his senses on the alert, he slowly began moving in the direction Adrianna had taken back to camp. Moments later, from out of the darkening shadows before him, two forms stepped out from among the trees. The brawny faelin eyed him speculatively. "Your day of reckoning has come," said one.

Sirion's mind reeled. *Adrianna! By the gods I'm such a fool! I knew Sydonnia was near, but I allowed her out of my sight to return to the encampment alone. What was I thinking?* He was about to call out to her when he sensed a third man stepping up behind him. He felt the point of a sword at the center of his back. It was possible he could take the man down, but there were probably others waiting in the trees.

"I wouldn't do that if I were you," the man growled. "Besides, it's too late. Sydonnia already has her."

"Where is Sirion?" Dartanyen looked around the camp with a frown. "And Adrianna?"

Sheridana looked up from her plate, also glancing around the camp. Both Sirion's and Adrianna's packs lay at opposite sides of the fire. Neither one had unfurled their bedrolls, telling her they'd been gone a while. Dramati lay beside Sirion's pack, his head on his paws. Sirion must have told him to stay there.

A bad feeling suffused her. She saw Dinim looking around the camp then back at her. Almost as one, they stood. "I don't know."

"I'm thinkin' I remember seein' Sirion head off innat direction when we first got 'ere," mentioned Zorg, pointing into the trees to the right of the camp.

"But that was over an hour ago," said Dartanyen.

"What about Adrianna? Did anyone see her leave?" asked Dinim.

"I can only assume that she must have followed Sirion," said Sheridana. Dinim frowned. "Why would she do that?" His voice sounded oddly strained.

Sheridana glanced at Dinim. She wasn't going to spell it out for him. Besides, he knew just as well as she what had begun to transpire between Sirion and her sister, whether he liked it or not.

Dartanyen put his hands up. "It doesn't matter," he said. "Let's just find them before our light is gone."

Sheridana shivered involuntarily as she watched Dartanyen get his weapons and vest. He was right; the sun was beginning to set. They would have the light of Steralion, but it wouldn't be enough. This night, the air was cooler than usual. Unaccustomed to the mild chill, she slipped on her cloak and couldn't help but wonder if Adrianna had hers.

"Well, we might as well all go," said Zorg. "If they're in some kinda trouble, they're gonna need as many o' us as possible."

"This is ridiculous," grouched Amethyst. "Sirion is a big boy. I am sure he can take care of himself."

"And what about Adrianna? She doesn't know how to protect herself against a lycan!" Dinim snarled.

"I am sure that the ever-so-brave Sirion would come to her rescue," Amethyst spat nastily.

"Amethyst," shouted Dartanyen, "Shut your face. We don't need your censure right now. Just get your belt and let's go."

Amethyst stomped over to her bedroll, mumbling under her breath and shaking her head. Sheridana rolled her eyes. Sometimes Amethyst could be a great person to have around, but when she was sick or just simply tired, the girl was best left alone. She wondered which one it was, and then thought it might be neither. Human women tended to be rather hateful during their menses. Perhaps it was Amethyst's moon-time.

The group filed out of the camp, Dramati in the lead. Sheridana found herself wishing Tianna and Armond were with them. She and Armond tended to be at odds much of the time, but she respected him as a fellow warrior. In spite of her increasing exasperation with the man, she was glad they were on the same side. She often wondered if he felt the same.

Sheri's agitation increased as they walked, the shadows lengthening with the setting sun. She heard a whine in front of her and Dramati looked back, his head and tail held high. He sensed something. The snap of a branch to her right warned her of something approaching. She drew her swords from their sheaths at her back just as an arrow came slicing through the air, embedding itself deeply in Dramati's left side. He cried out as he fell, immediately trying to tear the arrow free of his flesh.

Sheridana ran over to Dramati as she heard shouts from the others behind her. Just as she was about to reach him, she found her way blocked. She jumped to the side as the large form lunged for her. It barreled past and she did a quick turnaround, smacking the broadside of her right sword onto the person's back.

Quick as lightning, the man turned to face her, and she was met with a terrible visage. The man was no longer simply faelin. His skin was grayish, and short wiry hairs sprouted from the exposed flesh on his arms. The eye-teeth in the lower jaw were elongated, coming up over the upper lip. His muscles were hyper-developed, and Sheridana was certain he could easily overpower her. But the most frightening thing about him was his eyes. They were black as pitch, seemingly without emotion. The man looked like he shifting into an alothere, a large wild boar that liked to make its home in the forests of Central Ansalar. It was about to move towards her when a shrill scream pierced the air.

It was Adrianna.

Sheridana's heart skipped a beat and her flesh turned cold. But it was the distraction she needed. She ran past the alothere-man, back towards the group. She saw Dinim running towards her, and in the distance behind him were five other monsters that had Zorg, Dartanyen, Amethyst, and Sabian surrounded.

As Dinim flew by her, he grabbed her hand and they sprinted in the direction from whence they had heard Adrianna scream.

Adrianna screamed again. She didn't mean to; it just happened. She liked to think mayhap it would turn out to be a good thing, for the group may have heard her, or even Sirion. However, when she saw the expression on Sydonnia's hideous face, she instantly changed her mind. He grabbed her roughly by the arm and hauled her to him. His breath stank and she couldn't keep from averting her face, squeezing her eyes tightly shut. He was terrible to behold, not quite man, not quite wemic. And he was strong, so strong she was certain he would break her if he squeezed even the littlest bit more.

Sydonnia chuckled maliciously in her left ear, sending chills down her spine. "Little whore," he spat, his spittle drizzling her face. "My nefreyo, the philanderer. It seems he always has a woman hanging around."

Adrianna stiffened. Noting her reaction, Sydonnia laughed again. "But don't worry, my dear. I will have you. I am beginning to sicken of Joselyn. She is a weak woman, not worthy of the powerful icon I will soon become."

She trembled, the situation terribly reminiscent of the one she'd endured several years before. With a surge of desperation, she began to struggle. Sydonnia tightened his grip, and she cried out. He laughed as he watched her puny attempts to escape, but then suddenly stopped, roughly taking her face in his large hand and holding it still. He studied her intently, his feral eyes narrowing into slits.

"We have met before, have we not?" Adrianna nodded her head, eyes wide. "When? Where?" Sydonnia demanded.

"At the Inn of the Hapless Cenloryan, several moon cycles ago."

Sydonnia frowned. "No, no. It was some other time, some other place."

Adrianna shook her head. If she'd met him before, she would have remembered.

"I know I've met you before, but it doesn't matter now. My nefreyo will be here any moment. I will kill him and finally be rid of my treacherous brother's male offspring."

The last Sydonnia said disdainfully, a smirk on his ugly face. His teeth were yellow, the canines elongated and sharp. His eyebrows had thickened, as had the hair everywhere else on his body. His stature had increased, and his muscle mass had nearly doubled.

Adrianna remembered what Sirion had taught them about lycan sitting around the campfire one night. Sydonnia was in his transitional form, the one he assumed before reaching animal state. He was very powerful in this hybrid form, having the best of both faelin and animal worlds. Adrianna made no reply, barely able to tolerate his proximity. He was an abomination, a freak of nature, a monster created by parents to scare their children into obedience. He was an anathema to her, and she would escape him at her earliest opportunity. If needed, she would then help Sirion kill him, just to be certain the world was rid of such an abhorrence.

All of a sudden, there was a commotion in the near distance. Sydonnia barked an order to one of his men to have it checked out. He gripped her tightly and dragged her down the trail. *By the gods, I have to get away. He will surely kill me.* Adrianna began to struggle again. He snarled and raised his hand. Then, from out of the trees before them, Adrianna heard Sirion's voice. "Don't you dare touch her. I swear I will cut your hand off and shove it down your throat."

An evil smile washed across his hideous face. "Sirion, it is so good of you to join us."

The commotion behind them got closer, and within moments, Sheridana and Dinim emerged on the scene, three shirwemic following close behind, while Sirion and his own captors came out of the trees to the right of her and Sydonnia. His hands were bound behind his back. Two shirkyrrean followed, each holding one of his arms. In the other hand, each held a sword to Sirion's back.

Dinim watched Sheridana recklessly sprint towards Adrianna and her captor. Sydonnia barely had time to position himself for the attack before she was upon him. She slashed out with her longsword, slicing across his forearm and driving him back. Meanwhile, Sydonnia released his grip on the struggling Adrianna. He snarled in anger, and with his wickedly clawed hand, reached out and gouged Sheridana's shoulder and upper arm, sending her spinning to the ground.

"Sheridana!" Dinim ran to her side and began the incantation to his spell, weaving the strands of magic between his hands. Suddenly a large weight slammed into his back and he pitched forward. *Damn it all...*

With his face pressed into the dirt, Dinim helplessly watched as the other shirwemic stooped to pick Sheridana up. His hybrid form had progressed, and his face was more wemic-like, as were his legs and hands. With some hidden reserve, she lunged for her sword, screaming in fury when he grabbed her before she could reach it. She fought until the monster wrapped his large, clawed hand around her throat and began to squeeze.

Dinim struggled against the weight on top of his back as the shirwemic leered. Somehow, the clasps of her plate had broken, and the armor had slumped down over her hips. The monster snarled, opened his maw wide, and sank his teeth into the vulnerable flesh above her left breast.

Sheridana shrieked and almost dropped the dagger she'd extracted from its sheath about her upper thigh. She raised it above her head and slammed it down into the foul creature's neck. She was sprayed with dark red blood as the shirwemic screamed, the sound of his voice a long drawn-out howl. Her throat released, she started to fall. Awkwardly she caught herself and scrambled against the shirwemic, struggling to keep the blood-slicked dagger in his neck.

Dinim suddenly felt the weight of the other shirwemic leave his back. He jumped up in hot pursuit, drawing his shortsword as he ran. The shirwemic reached his injured companion, reaching out towards Sheridana. Dinim called out a warning just as a crackling black bolt of energy passed before him, striking the monster about to attack Sheridana. Dinim jumped back and looked into the trees to his left. Adrianna was standing there. She wore an expression he had never seen on her face before.

Sheridana continued to hold on to her weapon, resisting the lycan's attempts to be rid of her. She was at risk, not only because she had already suffered his bite, but because she knew he would eventually use his clawed hands to escape from her. But she refused to let go. Her weight pulled the weapon down, tearing the flesh of his neck, severing the blood vessels. Each moment that passed made him weaker, more vulnerable to other attacks.

And then it happened. She felt the shirwemic give one last valiant attempt to disengage. His claws raked across her unprotected side just above the fallen plate. She hissed with the pain and her grip on the dagger begin to slip. All of a sudden she felt something topple into them, and they went down in a tangle of arms and legs.

Sheridana struggled against the heavy weight. The smell of the shirwemic was rank and panic threatened. She felt a hand grasp her upper arm and she looked up to see Dinim trying to help her out from beneath while Adrianna pushed against the weight of the lycan. When she was finally free, she picked up her closest sword. She looked down at the monster where he knelt, a hand held against the jagged wound to his neck. Without a second thought, Sheridana swung her sword in a shallow arc. His head rolled onto the ground, the body slumping to rest beside it.

Breathing heavily, the three of them stood there for a moment. As they looked on, the bodies of the dead shirwemic slowly reverted to their faelin state. Sheridana saw the other one had been gutted, and by the look of Dinim's blade she knew who had been the one to do it. She stepped up to the body and severed the head from the neck. With creatures this powerful, she simply didn't want to take any chances.

Sheridana gave her companions a wan smile as they turned away from the bodies to go in search of the rest of the group. The bite wound above her breast throbbed mercilessly and the claw wounds along her side burned as though on fire. She could only pray nothing would come of them.

Darkness had fallen. The area was lit by tall standing torches set into the ground. Sydonnia circled his brother's son. In so many ways, Sirion Tidus Timberlyn reminded him of Servial. It was the way he was built, slender and lithe, although with an undertone of physical power that had never existed in Servial. It was the way he held himself, self-assured and confident. And it was his eyes, the same dark gold that Servial's had been.

Had been. Sydonnia had killed his own brother. He had killed Servial when the rage took over, at a time when he could no longer bear the burden of his curse, to live the rest of his days as a monstrosity, to never know the true joys of life, to never hold Lilandria in his arms as he had so long ago. She had been his good friend until Servial came along. He had wanted her like he'd never wanted a woman before. But Servial had to take her away...

Sydonnia narrowed his eyes speculatively. *Oh yes, Sirion looks like Lilandria as well. He has her hair color, her charisma, and her heart. Even more, he has honor and nobility of spirit that Servial never possessed. Lilandria has both of those qualities and somehow passed them to her son before Servial took him from her– took him to make him into an assassin.*

"My brother's whelp. So long have I dreamed of this moment, dreamed it in every detail, down to the feel of you expiring in my hands. I hear your pleas for mercy in my ears, even now." Sydonnia grinned.

Sirion remained impassive. "Your dreams are nothing more than that– dreams. I would never plead to you, not even for my life."

"Oh, I know you wouldn't plead for *your* life. Once, it would have been for Joselyn's. Now it would be for the life of the young woman you call Adrianna." Sirion stiffened as Sydonnia continued. "It's such a shame she got away. I so much would have loved to hear her scream, and to see you grovel before me to spare her life."

Sirion frowned. "You are lucky she escaped, Uncle. I would have tormented you for all of the days of forever had you harmed her."

Sydonnia maintained his grin. "Ah, so Joselyn was right. You *do* love the Savanlean woman."

Sirion didn't dignify Sydonnia with a reply. It figured Joselyn would open her big mouth. In every way now, she had betrayed him to one of the only men who could possibly kill him. But he wouldn't think of her now. To do so would be folly, and she would end up being the death of him.

"Joselyn, that bitch. I'm glad that I left her when I did. Does she service you as well as she did me? I do remember you saying that she was 'feisty'."

The smile left Sydonnia's eyes. "She serves me well enough."

Sydonnia resumed his circular path, but Sirion refused to be taken in by his uncle's ploy to make him nervous and lose focus. He'd used the same strategy himself, back during his days as a lycan hunter. "Really Uncle, why are you here? After so many years, why do you feel the need to have control in

Elvandahar?"

Sydonnia regarded him intently for a moment before giving a shrug. "I got bored of roaming about western Ansalar without purpose." He gave another toothy grin. "My pack has slowly grown over the years. It will be fun to see the realm slowly buckle as I continue my attacks. You know how powerful we lycan can be. There is little hope of the king eradicating us."

Sirion frowned. "So, this is the life you really want?" he said gruffly. "I'm certain you've acquired quite a bit of gold over the years. Have you never considered trying to find a cure? Paid handsomely enough, there may be someone out there who can save you."

Sydonnia suddenly stopped and Sirion could feel the anger pulsing in the air between them. "Save me? Find a cure? Why would I want someone to find a cure? What do you think would happen then? What life would I have? I would be an outlaw! Do you know how much blood is on my hands?" Sydonnia shook his head. "Most of the people I have ever cared for are gone, and the ones that remain have become my enemies. Even your mother hates me. Do you think I would give this up now? All that I have worked for? I will someday rule this place, sitting on a throne of pain on top of a mountain of bones!" Sydonnia suddenly reached out to grasp the front of Sirion's tunic, bringing his face close. "I don't want saving, not now. All I want at this moment is the battle I have craved for so many years."

Sydonnia pushed Sirion back and let out an ear-splitting howl. The hairs on his scalp prickled, his body responding to imminent danger. Sydonnia walked around him again, one hand on Sirion's left shoulder. Sydonnia paused behind him.

"That battle begins now, Nefreyo."

There was a tug at the bonds around his wrists, and Sirion felt them fall away. His breath paused in his throat as Sydonnia stepped in, bringing his face close. He spoke in a low, anticipatory voice. "Run, Sirion! Run!"

He needed no urging. He bolted from the clearing, away from the light and into the darkness of the forest. He knew Sydonnia would be close behind, that his uncle wouldn't give him much of a head start– only enough to make it good sport. Sirion ran as fast as he could, his thoughts focused only on survival.

Adrianna, Dinim, and Sheridana made their way quickly through the trees towards the location they thought the group to be. Darkness had fallen, but the moon above them, Steralion, offered at least some light, and it would be even lighter when the second moon, Hestim, rose to join her sister. Dinim thanked the gods they had found Adrianna when they did. He didn't want to consider what may have befallen her in the captivity of the lycan leader. *Hells, the*

strength of any one of the monsters was enough to overpower at least three normal men.

Dinim shook his head, his thoughts moving down a different route. He was impressed with the higher level spell Adrianna had cast. She couldn't have known what effect *Enervation* would have on the monsters, but she had used it anyway. It was a wonderful strike of good luck– or mayhap skill, and Adrianna was becoming more of the mage Dinim imagined she could be, the mage Master Tallachienan *knew* she could be.

Walking alongside him, Sheridana stumbled and he reached out to steady her. The heat of her flesh burned beneath his hand. He stopped in mid-stride. She stopped with him, placing a fever-warm hand on his shoulder to steady herself.

"What is it?" asked Adrianna, stepping up to them.

Dinim put the back of his hand to Sheri's brow and felt the fire growing within her. Then he remembered. His gaze dropped to her chest and he groaned. "Damn, the fever has already begun to set in. Sirion always said it was quick, but I didn't know it was this quick."

Adrianna put a hand on her sister's arm. "What do you mean?" She looked up at Dinim, her eyes wide.

"Sheri was bitten by the lycan. She has begun the ordeal of fighting the disease. Either that, or succumb to it."

Dinim watched the fear play across Adrianna's face before she turned to her sister. "Sheri, come on. We have to hurry and get you back to the group. You need to rest."

"Rest," mumbled Sheridana. Dinim caught her as she began to collapse. He picked her up in his arms and he and Adrianna again moved in the direction of the group. Within only a few minutes they heard the sounds of battle from up ahead. They walked a short distance closer before Dinim laid Sheridana down, and looked to Adrianna.

"You go," she said. "I will stay with Sheri."

He nodded and sprinted in the direction of the fighting. On his way, Dinim passed the bodies of two lycan. One was covered with a plethora of boils, lesions, and seeping abscesses. He knew it to be the work of Sabian. Both were headless and had reverted to their faelin state after death, just like the ones they had killed earlier. About a farlo away from the two bodies, he stopped at the still form of Amethyst. He knelt beside her and felt at her neck for a pulse. It was there, but she bled from a claw wound to her back and side. He pursed his lips, knowing he couldn't afford the time it would take for a field dressing. Dinim tried to staunch the flow, but felt hurried knowing that the others needed him. In the end, he wrapped the girl in his cloak and left her.

Dinim rushed forward and entered the scene just in time to see Dartanyen go down. Meanwhile, Sabian finished casting a spell. The electricity slammed into the shirkyrrean standing over Dartanyen, knocking him a farlo through the air. The lycan landed heavily and was still. Dinim quickly made his way over to the creature and cut off the head just as the shirkyrrean began to stir. Zorg continued his battle with the last of the monsters, sweat pouring down his face. Dinim began the incantation to his *Enervation* spell with a grin, already knowing the effect it would have.

When the black bolt of energy struck the lycan, the creature instantly began to diminish. It seemed like it was a painful process, for he clutched himself about the midriff as the spell took effect. Zorg used the opportunity to run the creature through with his broadsword and the lycan fell to his knees. Zorg withdrew the sword from the shirkyrrean's belly and lopped his head off, disposing of the threat just like all the others.

Dinim, Sabian, and Zorg gathered together at the center of the moon-lit battlefield. Zorg looked around. "Where are Sheri and Adria?"

"Back there," replied Dinim, pointing behind him. "Sheridana was bitten, and the fever has taken hold. If the wound gets too infected, she may die. But she will need to fight the disease no matter if the wound goes septic or not. I passed Amethyst on the way over here. She has also been injured, but I think it's just a claw wound."

Zorg nodded and headed in the direction in which Dinim pointed, while Sabian went to get Dartanyen. Finally everyone was gathered at one location, the injured either carried or dragged there.

Adrianna cleansed Sheri's wound. She poured some water onto one of the soft cloths Tianna had given to her before she left, then took a pouch from her pack and rubbed a green powder onto it. She applied it to Sheri's wound and kept it there.

Dinim hunkered down beside her. "What is that?"

"I'm not really sure. All I know is that Tianna told me to apply it in this fashion to any wounds anyone sustained."

Dinim nodded. "Then you will also want to see to Amethyst and Dartanyen. Both have lost a lot of blood."

Adrianna nodded in reply. "I will see to it then."

She made to move away when Dinim took her arm. Surprised, she glanced back at him. "Adrianna, I'm glad you are well."

She smiled and placed the unbloodied back of her hand to the side of his face. "I was happy to see you had come for me."

Dinim swept a tendril of curling hair away from her face as he returned the smile. He then rose to make his way over to Zorg, who was having trouble wrapping his arm. Adrianna watched him for a moment before moving to Amethyst's side to tend her injuries, followed by Dartanyen. They would both be very sore when they awoke. She wished she could do more, but all she had was a drink they could take, one Tianna had shown her how to prepare.

Later, while the rest of the group slept, Adrianna put the pot over the fire, filled it with water, and added the herbs Tianna had provided. She sat there and stared tiredly at the dancing flames while allowing the concoction to boil. She gave the drink to Sheri, Amethyst and Dartanyen before going over to awaken Dinim for his turn at the watch. She then went to her bedroll. She lay there, wide-eyed, while Dinim shuffled around the camp. Finally he settled against the trunk of a tree, his sword across his knees and a book open beside him. She watched him for a while, and was about to turn around to find a better sleeping position, when she saw movement out of the corner of her eye. She focused on the darkness of the trees and finally made out the form of a large animal.

Her heart leaped in her chest, but then subsided. It was Dramati! Where had he been? Adrianna crept away from her blankets and slipped over to him, meanwhile keeping an eye on Dinim. The man didn't move, didn't even look in her direction. Adrianna ran her hands over Dramati's body, felt the matted fur, and caked blood. He snuffled her hair as she inspected him the best she could in the pale light of the moons. The night would be over in a few hours. Then she would be able to tend his injuries. *But why was he here? Why wasn't he with Sirion?*

Adrianna spoke Sirion's name to the animal and Dramati quickly stood up, his curved tail waving rapidly. It was apparent he wished to go to his companion. Adrianna crept back over to her bedroll, picked up her pack, and slung it over her shoulder. Dinim remained motionless. She passed Sheri on her way back to Dramati, stopping to place a hand on her sister's face and kiss her fevered brow. Adrianna hated leaving her, but her desire to be with Sirion was overwhelming.

Adrianna finally approached Dramati. He crouched to the ground and she took his fur in her hands and pulled herself onto his back. Memories of riding astride Cortath tumbled through her mind, but she shook her head. *Sirion. It was upon Sirion's back I had ridden.*

"Dramati, take me to Sirion," she whispered.

Dramati heard and he was up and running swiftly through the forest.

THE BUNKER

The sky lightened with the arrival of daybreak as Sirion continued through the trees. Between runs he'd rested for short spurts of time, just enough to get his wind back and to give his body a chance to reclaim some stamina. It seemed Sydonnia had done a thorough study of him, knew he was endurance trained. He sought to strip that endurance by beginning their battle with a chase. Sirion had considered turning around and facing his uncle when it first started, but then thought better of it. He knew of an abandoned outpost not much further away and thought he might be able to use it to his advantage.

Sirion gave his uncle the chase he wanted. He continued to run, the shirwemic not far behind. The sun began to rise, and it wasn't much later before he reached the expansive outpost. Once there, he circled around to the rear and entered the main bunker through a concealed door. Inside, he took stock of his situation.

The building was an absolute wreck– if one would even call it a building anymore. The walls were crumbling and stones littered the floor. Much of the ceiling had collapsed, allowing the outside world to encroach upon the inside of the structure. The main room consisted of broken tables and chairs, some old candelabras, shards of broken pottery and glass, and some musty piles of fabric. Outside, Sirion heard a series of howls, followed by one long drawn-out one. They were close. He unfastened his quarterstaff, Stalker, from his back harness. Now it was only a matter of time.

Sirion waited in the center of the dilapidated room while the staff thrummed in his grip. The lycan were right outside; the ensorcelled weapon could feel their nearness. He placed both of his hands, side by side, in the middle. He visualized his will and Stalker began to glow. A moment later, the staff slid apart and there were two blades. He positioned them, crosswise, before him just as the front door splintered open. In strode Sydonnia.

"My, my what a place we have found here. It's interesting you would choose this bunker to be the place of your downfall. It was once a vast military stronghold, one of the last to be retaken in the Krish-Alneez. It is also where I used to meet your mother. It's funny how things come full-circle, is it not?" Sydonnia's lips turned up into a bittersweet smile, his eyes taking on a far-away cast. "It's always so unfair when life brings you down to nothing." For a brief moment his expression was saddened and his shoulders slumped, but he was quick to snap out of his contemplation and smiled when he took in Sirion's battle-ready stance. "I have been waiting a long time for this."

"So have I," Sirion replied. "But killing you will bring me no pleasure."

Sydonnia drew his massive blade. He was big enough, and strong enough, to wield it single-handedly. "Let us begin, shall we? I'm just *dying* to know how powerful a fighter my brother created to be my nemesis."

Sirion cocked his head. "Well, pay close attention. You will see it only once."

Sydonnia suddenly sprang, swinging his greatsword over his head in an arc. Sirion stepped back only to hit a nearby table. Forced to flip over it, he swiftly rolled backward. When he landed on the other side, he found that his balance was skewed, and Sydonnia quicker than anticipated. He grunted with the impact of the pommel of his uncle's sword in his gut, and fell back between two more tables. He landed and rolled underneath one, disappearing into the shadows. He was fortunate for the ability to hide, for the building was largely unlit despite the morning light outside streaming through the cracks in the ceiling.

Sydonnia began searching around, toppling tables and other dilapidated furniture as he went. Sirion caught his breath, and when his uncle's back was turned, he leaped from the shadows. Sydonnia managed to block his first attack, but Sirion's second blade cut deeply into his left thigh. In spite of the wound, Sydonnia swiftly made a retaliatory slice across Sirion's belly. The studs embedded in the thick leather vest took away much of the impact, but the sword was still able to penetrate the places in between.

Sirion fought to control his expression as they circled one another. The wound burned horrifically, but he schooled his features into an expression of nonchalance, unwilling to give anything away to his opponent. He focused on predicting what Sydonnia would do next. He feigned a thrust that resulted in a similar attack. Sirion spun into Sydonnia, parrying that attack with one blade while slicing into Sydonnia's arm with the other. He used his momentum to continue his spin and placed the blades together lengthwise. Stalker glowed briefly and once more became a quarterstaff. Sirion then dropped to the ground and swept at Sydonnia's feet. The lycan stumbled, but turned it into a roll in an attempt to alleviate ground impact. By then, Sirion had risen and was taking advantage of Sydonnia's vulnerable position. He swung in an upward arc, and with a loud *smack* Stalker connected with the side of Sydonnia's head.

Sydonnia fell to his knees. He growled menacingly as Sirion backed away, breathing heavily from the assault. The lycan slowly rose to his feet, ignoring the blood trickling down the side of his face.

"You are better than I imagined you would be," Sydonnia sneered. "Servial must have paid someone handsomely to teach you so well. It's a shame he can't be here to see the fruit of his labors." Sydonnia spoke a word under his breath and a pair of hooks sprang from the crossbar of his greatsword. Without warning, he lowered into a half-crouch before leaping upward with a mighty thrust of his legs.

Sirion's eyes widened and he just barely positioned himself to block the powerful downstroke. As their weapons met, Sydonnia ran his blade alongside Stalker, capturing the staff within one of the wicked hooks. Before Sirion realized it, the staff had left his hands and was spinning across the floor with Sydonnia's sword, soon disappearing from sight.

Sirion cursed under his breath. Sydonnia definitely had the upper hand now. He tried to dodge out of reach, but his uncle grabbed his shoulder and delivered a harsh uppercut. Sirion felt the air leave his chest as he flew backward, his rear hitting the floor a moment later. Sydonnia swiftly followed. Just as he reached Sirion's side, Sirion picked up a heavy candelabrum laying nearby and swung it at Sydonnia's face.

Startled, Sydonnia tried to block the blow. It still managed to hit him in the temple, and with a grunt Sydonnia dropped to one knee. Still struggling with the pain in his belly, Sirion scrambled to his feet and rushed to the nearest stone pillar. He untied the rope of the chandelier still attached to it and let it go. He watched it descend upon his uncle with a massive crash, shards of pottery scattering in all directions. Once some of the dust had settled, Sirion slowly walked towards the downed chandelier, one arm around his middle. Blood from the earlier wound had begun to soak through his vest. He coughed and squeezed his eyes shut against the tearing sensation from deep inside. He tasted blood and knew he was broken. If he survived this day, he would surely need a priest.

A massive rumble suddenly filled his ears, and the floor beneath his feet began to give way. He barely had time to comprehend what was happening before he fell into darkness...

Dramati slowed his pace to a walk. Stealthily he moved through the trees, his eyes and ears alert for any signs of danger. The pale rays of dawn scattered through the mist and settled over the 'scape, creating an eerie quality that made her shiver. She had a feeling they were close and signed for Dramati to stop. He crouched to the ground and she slid off his back. He regarded her steadily from golden eyes as she took his face in her hands. "Dramati, stay here. Wait for Sirion and I to return for you." Adrianna knew that a corubis could be a great companion to have at one's side in dangerous circumstances, but he'd been wounded in his fight with the shirwemic. She doubted he had the strength to endure a similar encounter. She could tell he wasn't happy about it, but he lay his head on his forelegs, the gesture telling her he would wait.

Adrianna continued alone through the trees. After walking about a farlo, she reached a clearing. Before her was a series of dilapidated buildings. Once, it may have been some type of fort or outpost, but now it was just an old ruin.

Adrianna continued to move with caution. She could see the place was occupied, several men moving about the area in and about the ruins. Some of them were in faelin form, while others were hybrids. There were probably even more of the lycan moving around in the surrounding forest.

Adrianna stopped for a moment, pondering what move she should make next. *Sirion is inside, probably in the largest building. There's an expansive clearing between me and the building, but perhaps if I keep to the trees until I reach the rear, I can to get inside undetected.*

Adrianna moved as quietly as she could through the trees. The world continued to get lighter with the rising of the sun. It was a longer walk than she thought it would be and she hastened her pace. She had to stop a few times to avoid being seen, hoping each time the breeze carried her scent away from the enemy. Finally she was there, at the rear of the largest building. No one appeared to be in the vicinity and she gave a small sigh of relief.

Sirion slowly picked his bruised and battered body up from the floor. He coughed, and when he wiped the back of his hand across his chin, it was red with blood. Glancing about, he was momentarily pleased to see the glint of Stalker lying in a pile of debris less than half a farlo away. Hearing movement to his left, he was disturbed that Sydonnia had already succeeded in standing and was making his way over.

Sirion wasn't fast enough. Sydonnia picked him up by the throat and slammed him into the nearest wall. He gasped for breath while the lycan then reached down to grab one of his legs. Choking, Sirion felt his lower half swinging up to the side. Sydonnia held him that way for a moment, throat in one hand and leg in the other, before finally hurling him away. He crashed through an old wooden door to land in a heap beside a stone staircase, gasping for breath.

Sydonnia followed. He stepped through the splinters of the door, and came at Sirion, his mouth open wide. His hybrid form was progressing, beginning to appear more and more beast-like. Barely having time to react, Sirion picked up a splinter from the floor near him and shoved it into Sydonnia's maw.

The lycan reared back and a mighty roar rent the air. Sirion galvanized his aching body into action and darted between Sydonnia's legs towards Stalker lying in the distance. He reached the weapon and opened it, the blades separating from one another in a fluid hiss, and turned just in time to watch Sydonnia cast away the splinter, blood streaming down the corner of his mouth. With a snarl his uncle charged and Sirion met him halfway. A meaty fist swung towards his face but Sirion ducked. With a forceful jab, he brought Stalker upward and there was a crunching of bone as it struck Sydonnia's wounded jaw.

The lycan lurched back, his ear-piercing wail reverberating throughout the basement. Hate shown in his blood-red eyes, and his muscles clenched in anticipation. Once more the two circled one another, each sporting a multitude of battle wounds that could still be seen in the dimness. As Sirion watched, he noticed his uncle was healing, injuries from the beginning of their battle rapidly fading. He'd seen it in other lycanthropes, but hadn't expected to see it so soon. His uncle was definitely in a class by himself, far exceeding the abilities of other lycan.

Suddenly, right before his eyes, Sydonnia disappeared into the shadows. Sirion cursed and panicked. He glanced about for a moment, hoping to see any sign of his whereabouts. He then did what any amateur would have done– stepped into a shaft of light.

Sirion saw him too late. Sydonnia rushed from out of the shadows, grabbed Sirion by the tunic, and threw him into a nearby pillar. It was a supporting structure, and it cracked under the force. Sirion fell heavily to the floor, holding his ribs. More were broken– he could feel the press of them against his air sacs with every breath he took.

Sirion continued to lie there while Sydonnia came at him again. Time slowed as his uncle bent over him. Somehow, Sirion had retained his grip on one of his blades. With the last bit of strength he possessed, he struck.

The weapon went deep. It passed between Sydonnia's ribs and into his chest to pierce his heart. The lycan slumped over the blade while the old pillars holding up the ceiling began to crumble. Sirion fell back, the pillar behind him falling over-top him, protecting him from the rest of the ceiling as it came tumbling down.

Adrianna approached the building and walked slowly along its length. She hadn't noticed an entry on her way over, but she hoped there might be a concealed door somewhere. Using her faelin-sight, she carefully searched the stone walls until she met with success. Grinning in satisfaction, she stepped behind the foliage growing in front of the hidden doorway and slipped into the dark, narrow space between two stone walls. She quickly made her way through the short corridor. Debris crunched beneath her feet, and she frowned to herself. *What is a structure built of stone doing in the middle of the forests of Elvandahar, a realm consisting mostly of people who live in the trees?* She reached a bend in the corridor and was about to step around it, when a thunderous crash reverberated throughout the structure, making the floor beneath her feet shudder ominously.

Adrianna hurried forward into what appeared to be a main chamber. Awestruck, she stopped to look at the chaos that lay before her. All over the ground were shards of pottery, glass, and wood. Rusted sconces dangled precariously from their old anchors, and tables, chairs, and other furnishings lay overturned. In the center of the chamber there was a massive hole in the floor with clouds of dust rising from it.

Adrianna immediately began casting a spell. She walked carefully towards the collapsed flooring as she spoke her incantation, and at the finish, she ate a dried spider from her pouch. She instantly felt the change in her body. She would be safer now that she had the ability to climb the walls, floors and ceilings with the agility of one of the creatures she had consumed.

Adrianna removed her boots, tied the laces together, and slung them over her shoulder. She carefully stepped up to the rift and crouched, steadying herself with her hands. She continued to the edge and then looked down into the opening. Through the dust and darkness, she could see a wide pillar holding up part of the remaining floor. The sound of crunching debris alerted her and she snapped to alertness and looked into the darkness. Within moments a woman emerged from the shadows. It was Joselyn.

Adrianna tensed. *What the Hells is she doing here? I don't need to deal with this right now when Sirion is down in this hole, probably needing my help. But I dare not take my eyes from this woman long enough to begin making my way down.*

Joselyn finally stopped a few arm lengths from Adrianna and regarded her intently, then she looked down into the hole. Adrianna took the opportunity to get her bearings and to carefully make her way over the edge.

"Please wait!" Joselyn rushed closer. "Take me with you. I can help."

Adrianna paused. She didn't have time for this. How Joselyn could possibly help was beyond her, unless she had some healing skills. Adrianna wished she were a mind reader so she could be certain of the other woman's sincerity. "I don't know how far the drop is."

"Can you carry me?"

Adrianna raised an eyebrow. "As far as I can see it, you are bigger than me.

You might take me right off of the pillar." "Couldn't you just try? Please?"

Adrianna sighed heavily. "Fine. Come on." She was so gullible. Joselyn looked so desperate and pitiful, she couldn't help but agree. But nervousness pervaded. She could very easily fall with the added weight of the druidess.

Joselyn gingerly climbed onto Adrianna's back and they slowly began their descent. Adrianna stifled a moan as she progressed, wishing she'd never agreed to this insanity. Sweat beaded her brow, and a couple of times she almost slipped. Joselyn at least had mind enough to put her own hand onto the pillar to steady them. About three quarters of the way down however, Adrianna could hold them no longer.

As they fell, Adrianna wished she'd cast her *Featherweight* spell.

Adrianna caught the brunt of the impact as they hit the floor. Joselyn rolled away when they landed, helping at least to remove the possibility of crushing her under her weight. Adrianna slowly stood and kicked at the rocks, cursing to herself. Her head throbbed, and when she felt at the sore spot, it revealed a hand covered in blood.

Joselyn rushed passed her and Adrianna followed. The two women made their way over to a pile of rubble a short distance away. They searched among the debris, but much of it was much too large for women of their stature to lift. After a few more moments of poking around, Adrianna heard a low moan. She turned toward the sound and caught a glimpse of shining metal between two large stone fragments.

"Sirion!" Adrianna knelt at the rocks, scrabbling to move them. She only succeeded in shifting a couple of the small ones before she lashed out at a larger one, cracking her knuckles and making them bleed. In frustration she put her face in her hands. She breathed heavily and felt the wetness of her tears in her palms. *Sirion will die beneath these rocks; they were much too heavy for him to remain beneath them for long.* She tried to calm herself-to think rationally. *If only the stones were lighter...* Abruptly she stopped. *Yes, I have the means to do that!*

Adrianna found her calm and began to concentrate. She beckoned to the magic as she spoke the incantation to the *Featherweight* spell, weaving it as she wrote a small rune in the air. She then placed her hands above the rocks and debris lying over Sirion. Briefly they glowed a pale amber. Barely a moment later she was lifting away the rocks and glanced up when Joselyn moved to her side to help.

It took longer than she would have liked, but finally she removed the rock that rested atop the remains of a pillar. Beneath it lay Sirion. She leaned over the large fragments, putting her hand in the hollow beneath it to touch his hand. "Sirion?"

He stirred. His eyelids fluttered open and he moaned as though in great pain. His voice was broken and he struggled just to speak. "Adria... Adrianna. You... must go... dangerous here."

"Sirion," her voice cracked. "I'm here to help you."

"Adria... please..." Sirion stopped, his eyes focusing on something behind her.

Adrianna turned to find Joselyn standing there.

The druidess shouldered past her and knelt at the fallen pillar. "Sirion, let me help you. You know I can. Here, let me just move this last stone..."

Adrianna took a deep calming breath. Now wasn't the time to be concerned about Joselyn's motives or Sirion's reaction to her presence, but it was difficult not to feel like such a tool. With her heart in her throat, Adrianna squelched down her feelings of inadequacy and helped Joselyn get Sirion out of the hollow. A moment later she felt a chill creep up her spine. Someone was watching...

Adrianna looked down at the rocky debris all around her. Barely an arm's length away from the disturbed area around Sirion, she caught sight of some shiny dark metal. Following it with her eyes, she noticed it connected to a hilt, and realized it was a sword. Not far away she saw an identical hilt protruding from a dusty leather vest. Her eyes traveled up the vest and into a hideous, leering face.

Quick as lightning, before she could even think about moving out of reach, a large hairy hand grabbed her wrist. Adrianna screamed as Sydonnia pulled her down, the overwhelming stench of blood making her stomach turn. She struggled, striking out with her free hand. He slowly brought himself upright and twisted her arm, easily ending her assault. He pulled her against his chest, put his face to the curve of her neck, and inhaled. Adrianna squeezed her eyes shut, blocking out the images her mind concocted to torment her.

Sirion heard Adrianna shout and saw her disappear within the surrounding rubble. *Oh gods, no!* In desperation, he begged his broken body to move. He struggled to breathe and his sides screamed in protest as he pulled free of the rock. Joselyn was there, helping him out of the hollow the pillar had created for him when it fell.

He crouched there for a moment, watching. Sydonnia held Adrianna captive against his bloody chest. She was limp in his arms and Sirion felt a rush of fear course through him. *What has Sydonnia done?* But then she moved and he let out a gusty exhale despite the pain. Sydonnia said something to her Sirion couldn't quite hear through the muffled sensation in his ears, and the lycan laughed raucously when she started to struggle in his grip.

Sirion's fear shifted into anger. He noticed the hilt of one of his blades protruding from Sydonnia's upper abdomen. How the man was able to move and function so well after such a wound was a mystery. Such a hit would have been fatal to any other man, maybe even any other lycanthrope. But Sydonnia was different, his will to live fiercely strong. Or was it the curse that sought to keep his body alive? Sirion didn't know, neither did he wish to contemplate the possibility, as his gaze searched for the other half of Stalker in the debris. Finally locating the weapon, he struggled into a standing position, Joselyn supporting him. His eyes riveted upon the blade, he roughly pushed away from her and lunged towards it.

Joselyn grunted as she lost her footing and fell. Cursing under his breath, Sirion quickly turned towards Sydonnia. His uncle's gaze was focused on him. "Ah, Sirion. You have proven to be more tenacious than I thought. But now I have something you may want." Sydonnia took a fistful of Adrianna's pale hair and jerked her head back. She made no sound, but he saw her dig her fingernails into the leather of Sydonnia's vest. Her eyes were tightly closed. Behind him, Sirion heard Joselyn regaining her feet. *Damn her, damn them both! What possessed them to follow me down here, and how did Adrianna get to the bunker in the first place?* Sirion thought quickly– Adrianna's life would depend on it. He began to speak, sought to keep Sydonnia occupied while he slowly made his way over to the partially hidden blade.

"Uncle, why don't you let her go? She has nothing to do with this."

"She has everything to do with this!" Sydonnia spat. "I will make you suffer the way Servial has made me suffer all of these years."

Sirion kept his body moving, swaying back and forth, making it seem he was weak and that it was difficult to keep himself in one place. Much to his disgruntlement, it wasn't too far from the truth.

Sirion raised his arms from his sides. "But I'm not Servial. Servial is dead. You killed him. If you wanted to torment someone, why didn't you torture my father when you had the chance?"

Sydonnia growled, "I was too angry to toy with Servial then. All I wanted was his blood. And now, you are the closest thing to Servial I have left. His blood runs through your veins. My wish is to take that away from him, even in death. He will have left nothing of himself behind in the world to show that he ever existed."

"But what about Anya? I do have a sister, you know."

Sydonnia shrugged. "I will hunt her down and kill her. She will be easy to dispatch."

Sirion shook his head. He was close to the blade now, so close. "It seems you have everything figured out."

"I've had many years to think about it."

"But you've forgotten one thing."

Sydonnia grinned maliciously and tightened his grip on Adrianna's hair. "I much doubt that, Nefreyo. I rarely forget."

"My son. I have a son. Servial will live on through him."

Sydonnia's eyes narrowed and his smile dissipated. He pulled back on Adrianna's hair. "You lie! You have no offspring!"

Sirion gave a heavy swallow, hoping Adrianna wasn't hurting very much. "You are wrong. There is a period of time in which you were unaware of my whereabouts. Is that not true?"

Sydonnia grimaced disdainfully. "That may be true, but I happen to know you have no son."

Sirion cocked his head to the side. "There was a woman. I didn't know her long, but I took her to my bed. Very recently I have discovered she has borne me a son." Sirion shrugged. "It's too bad you don't know where she is, Sydonnia. Your plans are moot. I have a successor to my bloodline and Servial will live forever."

Sydonnia's face suffused with anger. "Liar! Liar! I will kill you once and for all! I'll kill *her*." Sydonnia lifted Adrianna from the ground, much as he had picked up Sirion earlier, by one arm and one leg. Sirion swiftly crouched to retrieve his weapon. The hilt vibrated in his hand, the weapon wanting to taste Sydonnia's blood as much as Sirion wanted to spill it. Sydonnia easily lifted Adrianna above his head. With sickening clarity, Sirion knew he meant to crush her against the rocks strewn all around them. Unhesitatingly, Sirion sprinted towards his uncle, and barely a moment later was barreling into him. His right shoulder bore most of the impact, and his already bruised and battered body screamed at the abuse. His blade entered Sydonnia's lower gut and Sirion twisted it as they fell.

Sydonnia screamed in agony. Adrianna was flung backwards and she managed to hit the rocky ground without breaking her back. She struggled to right herself and hissed when she put her weight onto her left hand. She looked towards Sirion and Sydonnia. They lay in a bloody, crumpled heap on the rocks, barely moving.

Adrianna began to stumble towards them when she heard shouts from above. She looked up at the breach in the ceiling, noticed a familiar rumbling sound that reminded her of another time, another place. She glanced all around her, felt the trembling of the ground beneath her feet, the particulate debris falling from all around. The ceiling was going to collapse, the entire ceiling. The structural integrity of the place had been violated when the supporting pillars were destroyed. Adrianna cupped her hands around her mouth. "Get out! Get out of the building! The ceiling is going to cave in!"

Once more Adrianna turned towards Sirion. Sydonnia had risen and was standing over the body of his nefreyo. Joselyn was at his side, desperately pleading with him to spare Sirion's life. Sydonnia swung at her angrily and she fell. She stayed where she landed, moaning and sobbing piteously. Sydonnia crouched over the still form of Sirion, who appeared to be dead. Adrianna felt the scream rise in her throat as Sydonnia opened his mouth and lunged...

Sirion waited. He felt the rocks beneath him shift as Sydonnia crouched over him. He tightened his grip on Stalker, biding his time, waiting for just the right moment.

Then it came. As Sydonnia lowered his head, Sirion swung Stalker up in an arc. The blade swiped across the underside of Sydonnia's neck. Mouth open wide, Sydonnia continued to come at his throat. Sirion had just enough energy to move his head to the side as his uncle landed on top of him. As the head rolled away, the blood from the severed neck poured over Sirion-onto his face, neck, and chest. He strained to breathe with the weight of the heavy body, weakly trying to push it off.

Sirion's consciousness wavered. In the near distance he heard Adrianna's voice— something about the building collapsing. And then she was there, tugging at Sydonnia's headless corpse. In vain she attempted to move the body, but it was to no avail. Tears streamed down her cheeks and she grimaced in pain.

Suddenly, others were there– Dinim and Sabian taking away the body of Sydonnia. Sabian knelt to help Sirion up, while Dinim led Adrianna away.

Joselyn threw herself over Sydonnia's corpse, wailing uncontrollably. Sirion tried to clear his head, attempted to focus. He thought he saw dust and grit falling from above. He shook his head, hoping to clear his vision, but it was still there. Sirion saw several rangers. One of them retrieved his blades and another tried to take hold of Joselyn. She lashed out and he retreated, shaking his head. He left her at the body of Sydonnia, rushing ahead with the others. Sabian urged Sirion to follow, his voice urgently insistent. The two made their way through the main chamber and into a passageway. After a few moments, Sirion began to hear a low rumble in the distance behind them, and Sabian began to move even faster, urging Sirion onward.

Sirion and Sabian finally entered another chamber. There was an exit passageway in the wall of the basement and Sirion saw the others enter. Sirion struggled to move, his body being dragged, in part, by Sabian. A ranger up ahead saw them struggling and ran back. He took Sirion's other side and the two men lifted him from the ground and carried him towards the passage.

All of a sudden, in the distance behind them, there was a shout. Sirion's heart skipped a beat. "Wait... wait!" he rasped. "That's Joselyn!"

Sirion struggled to be set down and Sabian and the other man fought against him. "Sirion, no! The building is coming down; we can't stop now!" The rumble intensified and the rocks rained hard. The dust began to clog their nostrils and they coughed. Sirion doubled over in pain, and in spite of his protestations, the men carried him away into the waiting passage. Just as they entered it, the ceiling behind them came crashing down, the impact knocking them over. The torches went out and the corridor was thrown into darkness.

Sirion lay in there in the passage, his breath labored. Joselyn was gone forever– buried beneath the ruins of the old outpost. She had called out for him to help her, and he hadn't come. His chest constricted with emotion. She was dead. She had failed him in every way imaginable to him, but he'd failed her as well. Sirion's mind spiraled away and faded to dark.

The small group of travelers walked through the city streets. They knew that the 'others' were there, for Anya had tracked them all the way from the Terrestra River. Until now, the group had been unable to catch up with them, and all they needed to do now was find a way of taking them unawares. The group knew the city wasn't the best place to have a fight, but they didn't want to wait until these 'others' their 'doubles' to wreck another inn, kill another man, or lay waste to another field.

Triath glanced around at his companions. They all looked bedraggled and weary. For the hundredth time, he caught himself searching for the faces of the others and mentally berated himself. Arn, Laura, Breesa and Sirion were all dead at the hands of Gaknar and his fell priests. The group really could have used Dinim Coabra's help, but he'd been unable to locate the sorcerer.

Hells, he'd been loath to contact everyone else too, the last remaining Wildrunners: Anya, Naemmious and Sorn. They all wanted– no, *needed*–to get on with their lives. However, they had unfinished business Triath couldn't manage alone. The actions of their doubles had become more and more deadly, and they were causing extensive damage to the cities and villages in and around the realm of Torimir.

All had responded to Triath's summons. Anya had been the farthest away, having gone back to Elvandahar. Sorn and Triath had returned to Sangrilak, their city of origin, and Naemmious had gone to Ferent, the city closest to the hills south and east of the Tangir River. All agreed they needed to do something about the 'evil' Wildrunners, and so, for one last time, they found themselves in one another's company. Now here they were, making their way through Entsy, wondering how they were going to defeat their enemy, an enemy that knew them as well as they knew themselves. The group had done poorly in previous encounters, and that was when they still had Sirion, Arn, and Laura with them. This reality weighed heavily, but they strove to stay lighthearted. The Wildrunners had always persevered before, and this time would be no different.

"Hey, how about this one?" said Sorn, stopping in front of an establishment with a sign that read, "Silver Serpent Inn and Tavern".

Anya hiked her travel pack back up over her shoulder. "It looks good to me."

The foursome entered the building and procured two rooms for the night. They then settled down to discussing how they would find their doubles without being noticed, and how they would go about defeating them. As the conversation wore on, Triath became more and more despondent. Perhaps they would have to wait for the enemy to leave the city, and then try to catch them unawares in the middle of the night. But that sounded like a stupid idea, and he knew it.

If only they had been able to find Dinim.
If only they had Sirion.

DOUBLE THREAT

Hearing another sniff from beside her, Adrianna glanced at her sister from the corner of her eye. Sheridana pined for the daughter she had left behind in Alcrostat over three days ago. While recovering from her terrible sickness, she'd spent as much time with Carli and Fitanni as possible, knowing the two of them would be left behind in the safety of the fortress while she attended her duties. Adrianna had often joined them, happy for the opportunity to spend time with family. She'd come to view Carli as a younger sister and was glad baby Fitanni had someone to look after her while Sheridana was gone, someone who truly loved her.

Adrianna was certain she looked almost as pathetic as her sister. Sirion was constantly in her thoughts, and she wished that her mind would stop pondering him so intently. She tried not to let his disinterest bother her, yet she was unable to shake her disappointment. He rarely spoke to her, hardly looked at her, and barely managed to even acknowledge her presence. Granted, these days Sirion didn't speak much to *anyone*, and spent much of his time scouting ahead of the group and keeping contact to a minimum. Regardless, his avoidance of her had been noted, for she'd caught the strange glance or two from many of the others. They had chosen not to comment, but it was still a strain.

That evening everyone sat around the fire, silently eating their meal. The evenings were getting a bit cooler, and Adrianna was glad the heat of summer was beginning to abate. The group had traveled southeast across the northern border of Filopar. By mid-morning tomorrow they hoped to reach Reshik-na, where they would meet up with Tianna and Armond. Letters sent back and forth via messenger hawk had revealed that Tianna's aid was greatly appreciated. Working diligently alongside her family, she helped those in desperate need of her skills. Adrianna wondered if the order would require her services longer and if Tianna might feel obligated to stay behind with them in Elvandahar.

A bit later, Adrianna lay down on her bedroll and stared across the fire. On the other side was Sirion, his back turned away from her. Tears found their way down her cheek to wet the blankets beneath. Since the battle with Sydonnia, Sirion could hardly stand to be near her, even when she'd gone to see him while he was recovering from the terrible wounds he'd sustained in the fight. He'd lay abed for over a week, but she stopped seeing him when he showed no interest in having her there at his bedside. At first she attributed it to Joselyn's loss, but finally realized it was much more than that when he accepted visits from the other members of the group with grace and affability.

However, her feelings for him remained unchanged and she fought to keep him out of her mind. Despite their attraction to one another, and the camaraderie they had once shared, any relationship between them seemed to be misbegotten. It seemed that Sirion felt nothing but dislike, his attitude towards her aloof and cold. It reminded her of the Sirion she had first met in Sangrilak all of those moon cycles ago after coming home from her apprenticeship in Andahye. Regardless, she would try not to let her emotions interfere with what needed to be done. When the time came, if they survived their inevitable encounter with Thane, the group would disassemble...

...and hopefully she would never see Sirion Timberlyn again.

Tianna knew the moment the group made their arrival. The children squealed with delight, something they did only when visitors came. She was impressed with her friends' punctuality, or more likely, Sirion's accuracy; it was midday, just as the letter she had received a few days ago had stated it would be when they arrived.

Hearing the commotion, Armond stepped outside of the cabin and together they waited until they saw Sirion and Dramati emerging from out of the trees, trailed by a group of excited children. Right away she could tell something was wrong. It was the set of his shoulders, the furrow of his brow, and the dark cast to his amber eyes. Just the way he walked was indicative of something terribly amiss, and his face was pale through his typical sun-bronzed complexion.

Tianna stepped down the steps and rushed to his side. She wrapped her arms around him and held him for a moment. "Sirion! I'm so glad to see you. I've been worried."

He rubbed her back and gingerly pulled away. "I'm still healing, but I'm doing well." He gave her a smile that didn't quite reach his eyes. "See, your fears were unfounded."

She gave him an incredulous stare, his comment taking her aback. *Of course I have cause to worry. If he is still recovering from battle wounds...*

The rest of the group turned the bend and Armond stepped past her to greet them. Within moments, everyone was together again and snippets of the past two weeks were exchanged. As the talking continued, Tianna felt Sirion's tension increase. Finally he raised a hand and whistled to get everyone's attention. "If we start now we can cover enough distance to stop early and talk around the fire tonight."

Everyone nodded agreement and gathered their travel packs. Tianna raised an eyebrow when her father approached. "Please, I would like to invite everyone to my cabin for supper. My wife has been cooking all morning and it would be an honor. "

Surprised, Tianna looked over the rest of the group. They just stood there for a moment, not knowing what to say. Finally Dartanyen stepped forward. "I apologize for our rudeness, but your invitation was unanticipated and we have a long road ahead of us. However, we gladly accept. It will be our last big meal for a while."

It wasn't long before everyone was eating heartily of freshly baked bread, succulent fowl, spicy legumes, and an impressive array of fruits and sweetmeats. Afterwards, they remained to talk for a short time over some mead while the remainder of the meal was packed away for them to eat the following day while they traveled. Father Domick monopolized the conversation.

"The most recent lycan attack took place the day before Tianna and Armond got here, however, the surrounding area had been suffering several days before that. In our endeavor to help the people who were victimized, many of us had also been injured. None succumbed to the curse, but a few had died. When Tianna arrived, she offered god-blessed skills many of us don't have at our disposal. There were some she was unable to save from permanent impairment, but none died beneath her tender ministrations." Domick turned to her and smiled. "When we received word you would be coming, I implored her stay behind with us. Someone with her skill would be especially appreciated in my order."

Everyone turned to look at her and she blushed under the scrutiny. A pregnant silence ensued until she felt a hand on her shoulder. She turned to look at the man seated beside her, his expression the epitome of seriousness. "This is an important decision, Tianna. We will not begrudge your choice to stay."

She breathed deeply. Sirion was close, so close she could see the minute lines in his face, the texture of his lips, the balance of color in his eyes to make them so beautiful. She placed a hand on his face and exhaled. "I've already made my decision. I want to remain with you and the rest of the group. I gave you my word when I chose to accept this responsibility, and I will see it through to the end."

For a moment Sirion's gaze was conflicted, but then he gave a nod. He looked at Father Domick and the older man gave a disappointed smile. "I was afraid she would say that. My daughter has always been one to see to her responsibilities."

Sirion returned the nod. "It makes her a gem in a world full of ordinary rock."

Tianna preened with the praise as everyone thanked Father Domick for his hospitality. They gathered their travel gear and she said her farewells to her family and friends. With whatever daylight was remaining, they needed to travel as far as they could. She would find out more about their destination when they stopped for the night.

The group traveled as late into the day as they dared. It was already dark when a suitable camp was found and a fire started. Leftovers from the midday meal were taken out, and as everyone sat around the growing flames, Tianna heard the story about Adrianna and Sirion's capture by Sydonnia, the battle with the lycan, and Adrianna's subsequent escape with the help of Dinim and Sheridana. Dinim recounted the story almost as well as any bard, leaving out none of the details. He told of Adrianna leaving the safety of the encampment in the middle of the night upon the back of Dramati, and Sirion's rescue by her and Joselyn. He left nothing out, ending the story with the battle with Sydonnia's pack outside the bunker, the final collapse, and Sirion and Sabian just barely making it into the escape tunnel before the ceiling caved in on them.

Avidly Tianna listened to the tale. Adrianna's actions didn't go unnoticed by her, and she even saw Dinim casting her friend a glance or two as he recounted the story. His expression was one borne of mixed emotions, and Tianna was unable to understand the meaning behind the glances. However, Adrianna's expression seemed indifferent, and she barely even looked up while the story was being told. Sirion also had an impartial expression, his attention apparently absorbed by the weapon he was busy cleaning in his lap. Tianna felt the strangeness of it, for the account was focused primarily about them. She wondered what else was going on, what hadn't been spoken in the tale, unknown by the storyteller.

For two more days the group traveled through Elvandahar. The tree density gradually thinned as they moved farther east. The timberline ended at the shores of the Terrestra, and once there, they would travel northward along the river for about another day. Once they crossed the river, the group would continue to journey north to the city of Entsy. There they would be able to stock up on food and supplies, and maybe even purchase some larian with the gold that Thalios and Lilandria had given them for their help against the lycanthrope menace. Without Sydonnia there to lead them, Thalios hoped they would become fractioned and that the raids would die down. Either they would leave the vicinity, or the rangers would slowly eradicate them.

As the days passed, the group developed a need for long-sleeved tunics and thicker vests and cloaks with the unusually swift approach of the cold season. The nights were more difficult for they didn't have enough of the thicker blankets they needed to keep warm. They built larger evening fires, hoping to provide more heat, and they situated their bedrolls that much closer to it and to each other.

Blankets and clothes would be only a couple of the things the group would need to purchase once they reached the city. They passed villages along the way, but the people tended to be wary of travelers in general, especially those in mixed company. The sight of humans and faelin traveling together was rare, one that many people never got the opportunity to see. So the group simply passed the villages by, not even bothering to ask if there was an inn.

Tianna watched Sirion and Adrianna as they traveled. There seemed to be no indication of the relationship she imagined forming between them before she left to go to Reshik-na. This discovery heartened her. Perhaps she could make one last play for Sirion after all. She would set aside her innuendos and feminine enticements and bluntly tell him how she felt.

Once the group reached Entsy, they immediately sought out an inn and paid for their rooms. Dartanyen made certain they chose a decent one, knowing they would be spending at least two or three nights there. Having arrived at midday, they leisurely got situated their respective rooms. They bathed at the communal bathhouse, ate a small meal, and then went in search of supplies. Tianna followed obligingly behind the rest of the group, for she didn't have a particular destination in mind, and went where everyone else led. As they made their way through the streets, she continued to think about what she would say to Sirion. She would wait and bide her time until the setting was just right.

A prickling sensation on the back of her neck interrupted her musings. It was the feeling she always got when she was being watched. She glanced about the busy city street, searching for the source of her unease, but saw nothing out of the ordinary. With a shrug she returned her attention to the group, and seeing they had moved further ahead, she hastened her pace to catch up.

Later that evening, Tianna regarded Sirion across the table He leaned back in his seat, his meal barely touched. As usual, his expression was indecipherable, but she got the impression he was bored. For the past two days she'd been contemplating the moment she would approach him. However, Sirion had made it difficult, continuing to remain distant and aloof. She knew she shouldn't approach him in his present state, and wondered how she would break through his stoic indifference. Something was amiss with him, seriously so, and she was determined to find out what it was. She just had to find the right time.

Tianna allowed her gaze to travel from Sirion's face down to his chest. He had removed his studded leather before dinner, providing her a good view of his lean muscular shape beneath the light fabric of his sleeveless tunic. She couldn't suppress the sigh that escaped her lips, imagining the feel of his arms around her, the contours of his chest beneath her palms, and the sensation of his mouth over hers. Tianna's gaze continued downwards until her view was blocked by the table. But she knew what was beneath it— finely shaped legs encased within tight fitting leather trousers. Suddenly, the image before her eyes shifted. Tianna swung her gaze back up to Sirion's face to find him watching her. He raised a questioning eyebrow and her cheeks burned with embarrassment. *Damn! I hope my expression didn't give away my thoughts! I have to be more careful.*

Armond suddenly sat bolt upright in his seat. He placed his hands on the table and sat there for a moment, saying nothing, an intent expression on his face. Then he turned around in his chair, facing the table behind him and the three human men sitting there. "Excuse me, but what was that you just said?"

The man sitting immediately behind Armond turned around. He looked at him questioningly before answering. "Just a rumor. I heard a tale about a horned warrior who has been wreaking havoc throughout the realm of Monaf."

All other conversation at their table stopped. Beside her, Tianna noticed Adrianna leaning forward in her seat, her complexion pale. Sirion had also abandoned his relaxed position, and sat straight in his chair. Everyone's attention was riveted on Armond and the man with whom he spoke.

"Did you learn any other details about this warrior?" asked Armond.

The man inhaled deeply. "They say he is an abomination— no longer human— and that he travels with a group of other men who are the same as he. The dark warrior and his band have destroyed villages and ransacked towns. They have no mercy, killing indiscriminately."

"Does this warrior have a name?"

The man paused and shook his head. "I'm not certain—"

One of the other men from the other table suddenly spoke up. "Lord Thane." The man paused and then continued. "Rumor has it that he is searching for a young woman, and that he won't stop until he has found her."

Tianna heard Adrianna's breath catch in her throat. Her father continued his search for her, killing anyone who happened to be in his path, cutting a swath of destruction as he made his way across the continent. Sheridana stared at her from across the table, eyes wide, a multitude of emotions reflecting there, most of which were sadness, loathing, and fear.

"Where did you hear these rumors?" asked Armond.

The first man spoke again. "I started hearing the tales in the city of Driscol before I came here. The two towns I passed through had also heard the rumors. They said that the dark warrior and his band have been making their way westward through Monaf."

Armond nodded. "Thank you for the information. We were thinking of going that way. Now we know to be careful."

The other man nodded and turned back to his comrades. Armond did the same, his expression solemn. His gaze sought out Adrianna and he regarded her intently for a moment. "It seems we shouldn't stay here overly long." He spoke quietly, his voice barely perceptible over the background noise of the inn.

"He has gone on a rampage," said Dartanyen. "Remember, he lost our trail south of Torrich. He probably wasn't very happy about that."

Sheridana clenched her hands clench into fists. "We need to put an end to this!"

"Don't worry, we will," Dinim replied. "But we can't rush into this. We don't have enough information. Let's just focus on getting our supplies, and then on finding out as much as we can about Thane: his strengths, his weaknesses, where he gets his power, and how he formed his band. All of these answers will be integral in his defeat. If we don't know anything about Thane, he will surely destroy us."

Sirion nodded. "Dinim is right. We need to gather as much information on Thane as possible. But in the meantime, let's get some rest. In the morning we will restock our supplies and decide where to go from here."

Almost in unison the group rose from their table. Everyone, with the exception of Armond and Dartanyen, left the common area and went up the stairs to their rooms. Adrianna and Sheridana went to one, while Amethyst entered the one she would be sharing with Tianna. Further down the corridor, Tianna watched Zorg go into one room, Dinim and Sabian into another, and Sirion into a third. She waited for a few moments longer, just to be sure he was settling into his room, then slowly walked down the hall. This was the only time she would have to speak with him. Starting tomorrow, everyone would have all of their energies focused on Thane.

Tianna knocked on the door, and immediately received a response. "Who is it?"

Her heart pounded against her ribs. "Tianna."

Within a brief moment the door was opened."What is it? Is something wrong?" Sirion's face bore an expression of concern, his eyes searching the hallway behind her.

"No, nothing is wrong."

Sirion furrowed his eyebrows. "What is it then?"

"I just wanted to talk to you for a short while."

He sighed. "Can't this wait until tomorrow?"

She pouted. "Please?"

He sighed again and opened the door wider. Tianna stepped into the room and he closed it behind her. Sirion removed his travel pack from a red cushioned chair and gestured for her to sit. Tianna did so, and watched Sirion as he seated himself across from her on the bed.

For a moment there was silence. Tianna fought to collect her thoughts, suddenly forgetting how she had decided to angle the conversation. Patiently Sirion waited. When he finally realized she wasn't going to say anything, he sighed for a third time. "Tianna, what is this about? What do you need to talk about that can't wait until tomorrow?"

"It can't wait until tomorrow because you will be busy tomorrow."

"Tianna, I am always busy."

"You aren't right now," she pointed out.

"That's because I was about to go to bed."

Tianna picked at a nail. "Sirion, I need you to talk to me."

He slapped his hands down on his thighs. "I *am* talking–"

"No, I mean *really* talk. You're holding something back, and I want to know what it is. Since Reshik-na, I've noticed a change in you. You've become so distant, so withdrawn from everyone. I know something happened during your battle with Sydonnia, and I want you to share it with me."

Sirion regarded Tianna intently, noticed the obstinate expression on her face, the rigid set of her shoulders. She intended to get him to talk to her, even if it meant a fight. If he still hadn't been so upset about the events that took place during and after his fight with Sydonnia, he might have even cracked a small smile. She was a tough one, his Tianna, and he was glad to have her on his side.

"You already know it was a bad fight." He saw her relax and he continued. "We met in an abandoned fort and fought there until the floor collapsed beneath us. I became trapped beneath the rubble. Joselyn and Adrianna dug me out." Sirion paused in his recitation. Tianna waited patiently. She had heard this part of the story already from Dinim's recitation several nights before. "Somehow, Sydonnia gathered enough strength to grab hold of Adrianna. I focused whatever energy I had left on getting her away, then finally succeeded in killing him. The ceiling started coming down. Dinim and Sabian arrived, and we all ran to escape from the collapse. Somehow Joselyn got left behind."

Sirion paused, the ache in his chest rising up to engulf his heart. *I should have had her back. This may have never happened if I'd just swallowed my pride and had her back.* "She called for me. I wanted to go back for her, but I didn't have the strength. We barely made it into the tunnel before the bunker collapsed."

Tianna regarded him for a moment before moving from the chair to the space beside him on the bed. Dinim hadn't told the part about Joselyn. Either he didn't know what had happened, or he wanted to spare him the heartache– probably the latter. She put her arms around his shoulders and lay her face in the curve of his neck. When she finally pulled away, she took his hand and held it. He gently squeezed her fingers, expressing his gratitude.

"I can understand why you have been so upset. But Sirion, it wasn't your fault."

He shook his head. "I failed her. She called for me, and I didn't come."

"You were *unable* to come. You were severely wounded, Sirion. I heard about the extent of your injuries. You can't blame yourself."

"But I do, and I always will." Sirion looked up and into her eyes. "Somehow, I feel responsible for her death. Because of me, she lies beneath a pile of rock and debris."

Tianna shook her head. "No. That's not true."

"She came to me a few days before my confrontation with Sydonnia. She bade me to have her back by my side. I refused her. If only I had taken her back, this would have never happened."

"You don't know that. Perhaps Fate would have taken her from you anyway."

Sirion shook his head. "I don't know. Maybe..."

"Besides, she made choices in her life, choices that didn't involve you. Why would you drop everything in your life for her, when you know that she wouldn't have done the same?"

Sirion stared at her for a moment. "It seems you've become wise in your advanced years."

Tianna pressed her lips into a thin line. "Don't make fun of me, Sirion. I'm serious."

"So am I," he replied solemnly.

Tianna sat back for a moment, a myriad expressions passing over her face. "Sirion, there is something I must tell you."

He cocked his head slightly. "I'm listening."

Tianna opened her mouth to speak, but then seemed to change her mind. A heartbeat later, she abruptly leaned forward and placed her lips to his.

Surprised, Sirion fell back. She followed him down onto the bed and intensified the kiss. His mind reeled with shock and he struggled to find coherent thought and get his body to move the way he wanted it to. He tried talking, but only a small sound made it out, something akin to a pathetic groan. He shifted beneath her, hoping to get into a position that would give him the leverage and strength needed to hoist them up, when he noticed someone else was in the room.

His heart leaped in his chest. *Oh gods...*

Sirion suddenly found the strength he needed and sat upright. Tianna fell back, and seeing the direction of his gaze, turned to where he was staring. Adrianna and Dartanyen stood at the entrance to the room. Adrianna's face was pale, too pale, and her voice a strangled whisper, "I... I'm sorry. I didn't mean to intrude." She turned and swept past Dartanyen out of the room.

For a split moment silence reigned. "Sorry, Sirion. I didn't mean to interrupt. I didn't know that you two... well... you know." Dartanyen just shook his head, turned, and left, closing the door behind him.

Sirion jumped off of the bed and glared at the woman sitting on it. "Tianna, what has come over you? What possessed you to do that?"

She shook her head, eyes wide. "I... I just wanted to tell you, to show you how I feel about you."

For a moment, all Sirion could do was stare. It suddenly all began to make sense– the way she watched him when she thought he wasn't looking, the conversations about the future, the change in the way she dressed, and even the way she moved. Sirion swept his hands through his hair. "By the gods, Tianna..." Then he stopped and shook his head. "Just go."

Tianna stood slowly from the bed, tears in her eyes. Once more Sirion ran his fingers through his hair. *Damn! Now he'd gone and made her cry.* She slowly walked to the door, opened it, and left. He just stood there in the center of the room. He couldn't get the image of Adrianna's face out of his mind, the hurt he'd seen mirrored in her eyes. He had to find her, explain there was nothing between he and Tianna.

Sirion opened the door and swept out into the hallway. He was brought up short by the presence of Dartanyen. "Where did she go?"

Dartanyen pointed down the hall. "Tianna went to her room."

"No, I mean Adrianna. Where did Adrianna go?"

Dartanyen frowned. "I think she may have gone outside. I hope she comes back soon; within the hour it will begin to get dark."

Sirion nodded and then turned back into his room. If she'd left the inn, he needed to get his leather and Stalker, just in case. By the time Sirion made it out of the room again, Dartanyen was no longer standing outside. He rushed down the hall and then down the stairs. At the bottom he met Dartanyen again. This time Armond was there too.

"Do you want us to go with you?" asked Dartanyen.

"No, just leave it to me. I'll bring her back. Get some rest. We have a long day tomorrow."

Dartanyen was concerned, but he only nodded as Sirion made his way to the front of the inn and out the door. He stopped once he was out on the veranda and looked up and down the street. *Which way would she have gone?* Frustration burbled from within and he gave a heavy sigh before choosing to turn right. He skipped down the steps and out into the street. *I need to hurry. The shadows will soon lengthen with the approach of dark, and I don't know Entsy the way I do some other cities. Anyone could be out there.*

Hearing the door open, Amethyst turned from the window. She had just opened it so that she could get some fresh air, knowing it would make her feel better. Not to mention, she would have the perfect opportunity to spy on the two men talking out in the street below. Tianna abruptly swept into the room and fell onto one of the beds, sobbing hysterically. All Amethyst could do was stand there for a moment, wondering what in the Nine Hells had happened to make her so upset.

Amethyst walked across the room to the door, opened it, and looked up and down the hall. A few doors down she saw Dartanyen and Sirion talking. She pulled back into the room but continued to keep the door open, hoping to hear what they were saying. To her dismay, she heard a door close and thought the men had probably gone back into their room. Then she heard footsteps coming in her direction. Amethyst quickly closed the door, being careful not to make any noise. She stood a few moments with her ear to the door, waiting for the person to pass by. Amethyst glanced over her shoulder at Tianna, who was still lying on the bed. The woman continued to cry with her face in a pillow, not noticing Amethyst standing at the door. After another couple of moments had passed, she very slowly opened it again.

Amethyst poked her head out into the hall, looking in the direction where she'd seen Sirion and Dartanyen talking. She saw no one. She sighed almost imperceptibly, wishing she knew what was going on. Suddenly, she heard a door open and quickly pulled herself back into the room and closed the door until just a crack remained. She put her face to the crack and peered out. She saw Sirion rush by. Right after he passed, Amethyst opened the door slightly wider, just enough to see that he was going down the stairs. She darted out of the room and to the stairway. She pressed herself against the wall at the top of the stairs and listened. She heard Dartanyen's voice, and then Sirion's in reply, stating that he would bring someone back to the inn.

Amethyst heard the front door of the inn opening and she rushed back to her room. She swept across the chamber and over to the open window. Looking outside, she saw Sirion standing on the veranda, looking pensively up and down the road. She watched him make his decision and head east down the street. Glancing behind her at the woman on the bed, Amethyst saw Tianna turned away, her body and head covered by a blanket. Amethyst slipped out of the window and onto the roof. Quickly getting her bearings, she crouched and swung off the edge. For a moment she hung from the gutter and then dropped.

Amethyst cushioned her fall, immediately going into a crouch when her feet touched the ground. Then she was up and running in the direction Sirion had taken, sprinting to catch up. It didn't take long to see him walking briskly down the street in front of her. Concerned he might notice he was being followed, she began to follow him more discreetly, widening the distance between them and keeping herself close to the buildings.

For quite some time Amethyst followed Sirion. It became less and less difficult for her to stick to the shadows as night approached. This was her element, and she felt at home in these darkening places, not the reticence most others would begin to sense at about this time in the evening. And Sirion was the same as most other people. She noticed a hastening to his pace and an increased focus on his objective. She continued to wonder what that objective may be, and also where her curiosity was taking her.

Only time would tell.

Adrianna walked briskly down the street. She just needed to get away– to escape from Sirion, who had been such a lloryk's ass, Tianna, who acted like the world revolved around him, Dartanyen, who had seen her in a moment of weakness, and everyone else just for being associated with her. She felt sick to her stomach, and her throat and chest were so tight with suppressed emotion, they ached.

By the gods, what has Sirion done to me? He turned my world upside down that night at the fortress. What had he been thinking? The way he'd kissed me made it seem as though he'd truly cared. Why did he do it? Why did Sirion start something he had no intention of continuing later?

Even more important, why do I care so much?

In the distance behind her, Adrianna began to hear someone calling. She quickened her pace, not wanting anyone to catch up. She needed to be alone with her thoughts, just for a little while longer.

"Adrianna... Adrianna, please stop. We have to talk."

Damn, it's Sirion. He's the last person I want to see. There is nothing that he can say that will ease the hurt. Besides, she don't want him to see me cry. Adrianna quickened her pace even more, almost into a slow run. She glanced behind her and saw he was rapidly closing the distance between them. She thought about trying to lose him in the alleyways, but then thought better of it. Hells, the man was a tracker; he would probably still find her even though the city streets weren't his native terrain. It would only prolong the inevitable. He would stop her and make her listen to him whether she wanted to or not.

Adrianna stopped and turned around. It took Sirion only a few moments longer to catch up. She kept her face impassive, hoping to give nothing of her inner turmoil away. "Adrianna, what you saw back at the inn– it isn't what you think."

Adrianna regarded him intently for a moment, fighting to keep her blank expression. He must surely consider her a fool if he thought she would believe that. She shouldn't have bothered to stop. Adrianna turned away and continued down the street.

"Adrianna, you have to listen to me." Sirion matched his stride with hers. "Tianna came to me, claiming she just wanted to talk. Before I knew it, she was on top of me. I swear... I had no idea she had that type of feeling for me."

Adrianna continued to walk, taking in Sirion's words. *Was it true? Maybe, but he'd seemed so... so involved in his activity with Tianna. It was hard to believe he hadn't been participating with equal intensity.* Suddenly she felt his hand on her arm, urging her to stop.

"Adrianna, you have to know I don't feel that way about her. I only have feelings for you."

Adrianna stopped and turned back to Sirion. She searched his face, finding only sincerity there. Tears began to pool in her eyes and he closed the distance between them. He wrapped his arms around her and she lay her head on his shoulder, allowing him to hold her. In that moment, she never wanted him to let her go.

For several moments Sirion and Adrianna remained in their embrace. She took in the feel of him, the scent of him. He was so quiet, but she longed to hear his voice in her ear, murmuring to her the way he had that night back in Elvandahar. She vaguely noticed his smell was different than usual, not the spicy/ musk she liked so much. His arms around her were warm and strong, but had a firmness she didn't remember them having before.

All of a sudden, Adrianna felt a prick on her upper arm. "Ahhh." She abruptly pulled away. "Something pinched me." She put her hand to her arm and rubbed the area.

Sirion looked at her with a strangely concerned expression that didn't quite make it to his eyes. "Are you all right?"

An odd sensation swept through her and she began to sway, putting her arms out to steady herself. Sirion gripped her shoulders and she put a palm to her forehead. "I... I feel something wrong." Sirion's face blurred and her voice sounded thick. "Wha... what's happening to me?" She pitched back, and then there was only blackness.

Sirion caught the woman as she fell into his arms. Grinning, he looked down into her face, her beauty almost taking his breath away. Then he looked back up at Sorn, who continued to hold the small dagger in his hand. He saw his friend smiling too, the import of what they were doing making them giddy. Swinging her into his arms, Sirion carried Adrianna into the nearest alleyway. Although the streets were nearly deserted, he didn't want to take the chance of anyone seeing them. He was glad the woman had chosen this path, it being in the older section of the city and made up mostly of buildings dedicated to business and storage. As most of the tradesmen had gone to their homes for the evening, the place was empty.

Sirion could still hardly believe what the day had brought him. He and Sorn had been rather shocked to see Sirion's double walking through the streets of Entsy. Rumor had led them to believe he was dead. When they recovered from the initial surprise, they had followed him and the people with whom he associated. Sirion experienced his second shock when he saw the woman Adrianna. Remembering his double had an inexplicable attraction to her, Sirion knew he had to have her.

While Sirion returned to the 'Wildrunners' to tell them his double was still alive and in the city, Sorn followed the other Sirion until he and his comrades walked up to the place at which they were staying, The Golden Griffon. Via telepathic communication with Triath, Sorn had let Sirion know where he was, and after bathing and cropping his hair shorter to match that of his double, Sirion had rejoined his companion. Sorn had discovered the rooms in which the other people were staying, and he easily spied on them by going from window to window along the rooftop.

After that it was a waiting game. The initial plan had been to wait until the women fell asleep for the night and then take Adrianna from her bed. However, Sirion had received his third shock when Sorn later rushed back to him, telling him Adrianna had caught his double in a com-promising situation with the young woman, Tianna. Sirion couldn't believe his good luck. Beckoning him to hurry, Sorn had then explained that Adrianna had fled the establishment. The two men followed her from a distance, waiting for the right time to approach. When she entered the older section, the men closed in.

Once in the alleyway, Sorn sheathed the dagger and took Adrianna's other side. Together, the two of them carried her through the side streets to The Snorting Gorgon Inn located not far away. As they walked, Sirion couldn't keep from smiling to himself. If he knew his double, the man would come searching for this woman as soon as he realized she was missing. He didn't know what the man was doing with Tianna, nor did he care, but his double was a fool to let this one get away. With just one glance, Sirion was smitten and knew he was going to keep her.

It wasn't long before the two men were approaching the inn and Sorn called for Naemmious. It was easy to get Adrianna to Sirion's room, there being only a single storey to the establishment. Sirion and Sorn passed her to Naemmious through the open window located at the back of the building. The half-oroc then lay her down on Sirion's bed before leaving the room to inform the rest of the group.

Sirion silently stood over her, his loins tightening with desire. Gods, he wanted her more than any woman he'd ever laid his eyes on. He'd noticed the effect she had on the other men in his company, and possessive irritation surged through him. Hearing the door open, Sirion turned to see Triath, Anya, and Laura enter the room. Triath wore an expression of malicious glee on his face-even his single, black, soul-less eye appeared to have emotion. Laura grinned at him conspiratorially, and Anya just looked bored.

"I had to come and see her for myself," said Triath. "It will only be a matter of time before your double realizes we are here. When he comes for her, we will be ready. Without his companions to back him up, he will be easy to dispatch."

"But what of the sorcerer, Dinim? I saw him in the company of this new group with which my double has aligned himself. The Dimensionalist is powerful."

Triath's grin widened. "Don't worry about the magic user," he interrupted. "I will take care of him. Now, I will leave you to your... business. I'm sure you have much to orchestrate."

Anya rolled her eyes in Sirion's direction and then glared at Triath. Laura stepped up to Sirion, pulling something out from within her robes. She handed him a bundle of sheer fabric, a brazen expression in her eyes, her lips curved up in a seductive smile. He immediately knew what it was, and he felt his own mouth curve upwards.

"Tsk tsk. He will probably molest her before he gets it on her," said Anya scathingly.

Sirion heard Triath begin to snicker as he swung a contemptuous glance at his sister. "Fine, bitch. Why don't you put it on her?" he said, throwing the cloth at her.

Anya caught it and then tossed it to Laura. "Sorry, that's more like a chore for Laura. I might just kill her before I get it on her." Anya then turned and left the room, followed by a chortling Triath and a solemn Sorn. Once the door was closed behind them, Sirion turned to Laura. Comprehending the demand in his eyes, she proceeded towards the bed.

Sirion walked down the darkening streets, his mind a maelstrom of concern and confusion. *Blast! Where is that woman?*

It was so hard to believe things had worked out this way. She'd gone and run off to only gods knew where. Sirion shook his head. *This is my fault. If I'd paid more attention to Tianna, I would have realized her feelings for me and put a stop to things before they went too far. Now, here I am, tracking down Adrianna in the middle of the night. Well, not quite the middle of the night...*

Sirion shook his head again just as he noticed a small group of people coming towards him from down the street. Suddenly on alert, he considered turning down one of the alleyways, just in case they wanted trouble, but then thought better of it. The chances of that were slim, and besides, he wouldn't want to miss an opportunity to ask if they had seen a woman fitting Adrianna's description this evening.

Sirion slowed as the group came closer. There was something familiar about them– the unusually large size of one of the men, and a patch over one of the eyes on another. Recognition suddenly washed over him, and he felt his heart stutter in his chest. *Hells, these people are what remain of the Wildrunners.*

Sirion stopped in the street, watching as they approached. Then he saw Sorn take notice of him, and he put a hand on Triath's arm. The Wildrunners slowed to a halt. Sorn said something, and Anya shook her head. Naemmious said something as well, and once more Anya shook her head. She then started toward him. Sirion couldn't help but smile to himself. *She knows it's me. Even though she believes I'm dead, there's a part of her that knows it's me standing here in the middle of the damned street.*

Once she was about a farlo away, Anya stopped. Her eyes were wide. "Sirion, is that you?"

Sirion felt his mouth pull into a huge grin. He swiftly closed the distance between them, and when he reached her, took her in his arms in a tight embrace. "It's me, Anya. It's really me. I survived the vortex."

"By the gods!" Sirion heard the shaking in her voice. "I can't believe this is true! There have been so many times I wished–" Anya suddenly stopped speaking and pulled back from him, tears running down her face. "Sirion, where the Hells have you been?"

"It is a long story, and I would like to tell you about it, but I'm looking for a friend of mine."

"Sirion, can it really be you?" Hearing Sorn's voice, he turned towards the rest of his friends. The men embraced one another, each one expressing his joy upon seeing his comrade hale and whole. Everyone wanted to know how he'd survived and where he'd been all this time.

Sirion only shook his head. "Listen, I can talk all you want when I've found my friend. She is out here somewhere, and I need to find her before it gets dark."

Triath raised an eyebrow. "Who is this woman and why is she roaming the streets alone at night?"

Sirion sighed. "Her name is Adrianna. She's a member of the group I've been traveling with. She's of half-faelin descent, and has long, curly blond hair. She was wearing a green long-tunic and trousers when she left. Have you seen her?"

Everyone shook their heads.

"Damn! Where could she be? I have been searching for at least two hours. I have a bad feeling..." Sirion stopped speaking when he noticed Sorn casting a pointed glance at Triath. "What? What's going on?" Sirion put his hands on his hips.

Triath sighed. "Brace yourself, my friend. You aren't going to like it. For several weeks now we've been on our last mission together. We've been tracking our doubles and we followed them into this city."

Sirion's eyes widened. "Are you telling me that our doubles are here?

Now?"

"That is exactly what I'm telling you."

Sirion swept a nervous hand through his hair. "My friend might not be able to tell us apart. Do you know where they are staying?"

Sorn grinned maliciously. "Hmph, do we know where... of course we know where they're staying! Courtesy of my skills, of course!" Sorn sniffed emphatically. "They are holed up at the Snorting Gorgon Inn. It will take us a little while to get there, but it isn't too terribly far."

"Then what are we waiting for?" asked Sirion. "Lead the way."

"What about the group you've been traveling with. Couldn't they help us?" inquired Anya. "You know how much trouble our doubles have been in the past–"

"We don't have time," Sirion interrupted. "If my double has found Adrianna and taken her to the Snorting Gorgon, she is in great danger."

Sorn frowned. "How do you know?"

Sirion regarded his friend intently. Since his near brush with death, things had become so much clearer. He had wanted Adrianna for a very long time, and most likely, his double would find her just as enchanting. Sirion had her best interests at heart. Most definitely, his double did not. "Trust me. Her well-being is imperiled every moment she stays with that damn bastard."

AMENDS

Adrianna struggled to awaken. Her mind felt sluggish, as if it didn't want to bother coming to awareness. After another moment or two, she began to experience sensations, erotic ones that were both wonderful and bothersome at the same time: wonderful because they felt good, and bothersome because she didn't know what was creating them. Waves of desire swept through her, and she felt a mouth on hers, a pair of arms encircling her, and hands that seemed to be everywhere at once. Adrianna heard moans, and as she started to embrace alertness, discovered they were coming from her.

"Sirion..." Adrianna moaned his name, struggling to move her apathetic limbs. She heard an answering reply deep within Sirion's throat, felt his hands kneading the flesh of her thighs and backside, his fingers precariously close to her femininity. This realization made her nervous, yet the sensations those fingers invoked made her arch towards him for more.

"Sirion?" Confused, she said his name again, hoping he would stop before she was swept away by the power of her lust. Sirion moved over her and a pressure parted her thighs. Suddenly, her awareness sparked. Adrianna felt as though she rose up from within a deep well. Her senses heightened, and her body protested beneath him.

"Sirion. Please... stop." She found that it was difficult to speak, and even harder to move. She was finally able to turn her head. Just half a farlo away, on the wall nearest the bed, she saw herself in a mirror. She was wearing a sheer gown of shimmering gold. On top of her was a shirtless Sirion, his head between her bared breasts. Her eyes widened. She didn't remember receiving a gown like this, much less putting it on.

"Sirion..." Adrianna began to struggle, her mind finally having some control over her limbs. She felt the passion drain away, fear rolling in to take its place. "Sirion, please stop!" Adrianna pushed at him and he finally looked up at her. The expression on his face nearly unnerved her. It didn't look like the man she'd come to know. His eyes seemed wild somehow, almost fanatical.

"Mmmm. I want you." He lowered his head to kiss her, but she jerked away.

"Sirion, no. I feel sick. I don't remember..."

Sirion's brows furrowed. "I'm not stopping now," he growled. "You brought me this far, and I mean to have you."

Shocked, all Adrianna could do was stare into his eyes, eyes that were flat, unyielding, and without emotion. With a firm grip, Sirion pinned her onto the bed, his weight bearing down on her. The silvery scar running the length of her torso burned, as though in remainder... Fear gripped her insides and she resumed her struggle. She kicked her legs, twisted her hips, and arched her back, desperately hoping to dislodge him. Then, all of a sudden, he reared up, pulled back his hand, and slapped her across the face. Hard.

For a moment she was still. Adrianna saw the cruel curve of his lips and the maniacal gleam in his eyes. She heard the staccato beat of her heart and the raggedness of her breath. She felt the warmth of the tears falling into her hairline and the trickle of blood that crept from her nose. But what she really wanted was to see, hear, or feel nothing. Detatching herself, Adrianna turned away from Sirion and her body went slack. She felt his lips at her neck and the pressure of his knee between her legs, but it was as though from a distance, like it was happening to someone else.

Abruptly, something changed. She felt Sirion's weight lift away and she looked up to find him standing in the middle of the room. She heard a flurry of activity from outside in the hall as he quickly refastened the ties of his trousers. He then donned his tunic and leather vest. Then she heard it again, this time louder. There was a definite commotion outside. He snatched Stalker from its position near the desk, and then looked towards the bed. Narrowing his eyes, he grabbed a rope lying nearby. Adrianna quickly tried to scramble away, but he viciously seized first one wrist and then the other, binding them together and then to the headboard of the bed frame.

"We will continue this when I come back. And believe me, I *will* be back." Sirion took a fistful of her hair and pulled her into a brutal kiss, his teeth cutting into her lower lip. When he released her, he pushed her roughly back onto the bed. She saw blood on his mouth as he turned away and her lips stung from the abuse. When he was gone, her tears began anew. Of course she couldn't be absolutely certain, but she knew he wasn't *really* Sirion. Maybe something had taken control of his mind, or mayhap he was doing this to her because...

She swallowed heavily. The fact that he'd almost raped her weighed heavily, and she couldn't rid herself of the images her mind concocted.

With a cry, Adrianna pulled savagely at the rope tying her to the frame. The binds bit into the flesh of her wrists, but she didn't care. Like an animal, she writhed upon the bed that had become her prison. She pulled so hard at the rope she felt her wrists pop. She struggled until she had no strength left, and finally she just lay there, her body bathed in sweat, her breaths labored. She put her tongue to her lips and felt where Sirion had cut her with his cruel kiss.

Now all she could do was wait– wait for him to come back and take her.

Amethyst watched the lady archer, Anya, climb the scaffolding to the top of the roof of the Snorting Gorgon Inn. The establishment was nothing like she was used to getting since she'd been traveling with the group. It was small, and while it wasn't a dilapidated mess, it was in need of some repair. The scaffolding was one example, and in many places it had broken away from the side of the building.

Amethyst saw the man before Anya did and resisted the urge to cry out an alarm. She frowned when she saw how much he looked like one of the men from the small group of people with whom Sirion had allied himself and wondered what the Hells was going on. Sirion muttered a string of epithets as the two on the rooftop began to scuffle, and within moments, patrons were pouring out of the establishment to see what was going on.

Amethyst watched Sirion and his companions enter the building before swiftly following. Just as she reached the entrance, she heard fighting break out from the inside. Keeping to the walls, especially those places in which she could also hide behind tables, she slowly circled a melee that looked like something from out of a misbegotten nightmare. The man on the rooftop wasn't the only one who looked like a member from Sirion's new group of friends. The rest had been inside the inn, and they were now fighting like their lives depended on it.

A man who looked like Sirion emerged from a hallway at the rear of the main room and Amethyst made her way over to it. She imagined Adrianna had to be back there somewhere in one of the rooms. There was a part of her that wanted to stay and help in the fighting, but deep in her guts she knew Adrianna needed her more. She walked slowly down the hall, trying each of the doors as she came to them. Many of them were locked. Those that were not, she opened and had a quick look about to be sure no one was there. Finally her efforts paid off. At the end of the hall she came to a room with an unlocked door. She opened it and poked her head inside.

Despite her clothing, or lack thereof, Amethyst knew right away that the woman lying on the bed was Adrianna. Her face was turned away, but it was the pale hair that gave her away, for Amethyst knew no other with tresses so distinctive. She entered the room and went into a crouch, noiselessly shutting the door behind her. Adrianna's eyes were closed and her breathing heavy. As Amethyst approached the bed, she saw Adrianna's belt of pouches lying on a nearby table and grabbed it. As she drew closer, she saw a sheen of perspiration over Adrianna's body and congealed blood circled her bound wrists and stained the sheets beneath. Remembering how terribly Adrianna had suffered at the hands of men in the past, a surge of sympathy suffused her.

Once reaching the bed, Amethyst stopped and rose to her knees beside it. A sheer gown was twisted about Adrianna's hips, exposing her nudity. Her chest rose and fell with deep inhalations, and a thin, white scar ran between her breasts down to the part of her belly hidden by the fabric. Tears flowed from beneath closed eyelids. It was impossible for her to lie comfortably, the rope that bound her much too short, causing her head and shoulders to remain suspended above the pillows.

Amethyst's heart stuck in her throat and she suddenly found it difficult to speak. "Adrianna?"

The other woman's eyes sprang open and she lurched back on the bed.

"Ssssh, please don't be frightened. It's only me, Amethyst. I have come to free you."

"Free me?" Adrianna's brows came together in confusion. Her words were slurred, almost as though she was drunk.

Amethyst nodded. "Yes. I even retrieved your belt," she said, setting down the only bit of clothing in the room that belonged to the woman, the pouches releasing strange fragments of the components inside. She slowly placed her hand on the bed. "I'm going to climb up here and I'm going to cut that rope, all right?"

Adrianna just stared at Amethyst for a moment, as though her mind needed the extra time to understand what had been said. Then she gave a slow nod. Amethyst climbed onto the bed and crawled to the headboard. When she took the rope in her hands, Adrianna gave a drawn out hiss.

Amethyst let go of the rope. "Oh, gods. I'm sorry Adrianna. I'll try to be more careful."

When the rope was finally cut, Adrianna lay back on the bed for a moment, cradling her wrists to her chest. Amethyst glanced about the room, hoping to see some of her clothes.

Adrianna's voice was low and shaky. "Thank you."

Amethyst blinked in surprise, not expecting gratitude. It gave her a good feeling that spread throughout her chest. *Finally I've done something right.* "You're welcome."

Adrianna unsteadily rose from the bed and slowly fastened the belt about her small waist. Amethyst shook her head. "Damn Adria, I wish I had something for you to wear." She glanced down at her own clothing, a smoky gray blouse and a pair of snug, coal black trousers. Adrianna didn't even have small clothes beneath the filmy gown she wore. The material left absolutely nothing to the imagination.

Adrianna sighed, still shaking her head as if to clear it. "That's all right. No one will even notice. They are much too busy trying to kill one another."

Amethyst looked back up to find Adrianna grinning slightly. She returned the grin but remained skeptical. "I dunno, men can be such–" She jumped when a loud crash suddenly sounded from outside the door. Within moments the sounds of battle could be heard approaching from down the hallway. Adrianna become tense beside her and Amethyst instinctively reached out and took her hand. She was surprised by her response but didn't ponder it too long as she glanced around the room. "We can leave through the window. There's a scaffolding that we can use to get to the ground."

Adrianna's eyes were wide. "What's going on out there?"

"Sirion is here, the *real* Sirion. He and some others are fighting the people who must have brought you here."

Amethyst watched her think about this as the shouting and clanging of steel got louder. *Damn, what the Hells did they do to her?*

Adrianna looked longingly at the window, but then turned away. "They came for me."

Even though it was more a statement than a question, Amethyst gave an answering nod.

Once more, Sirion swung at his double, grimacing with the pain in his forearm. The bastard had clipped him at the beginning of the fight, and the damned cut dripped blood all over the floor. He bore into his opponent, his sword straining against its counterpart, his face only inches away from that of his double. The man still had blood on his lips, blood that had been there when the fight began. Out of the corner of his eye, Sirion glanced down the hall from where he'd seen his double come when the fight broke out. Somewhere, in one of those rooms, was Adrianna.

Sirion pushed his double and, with a massive shove, knocked the man to the floor. However, instead of following up with another blow, Sirion took the opportunity, however small, to glance around at the scene. The friend closest to him was Sorn, who was having the unfortunate experience of skirmishing with anti-Anya. Across the room, he saw Naemmious at combat with anti-Arn, and Triath and anti-Triath seemed to be locked into a battle of minds, their mental struggle apparent by their expressions of deep concentration. As his double lurched back up, Sorn managed to get a good kick in at anti-Anya. The woman flew backwards and hit the wall behind her.

Sirion seized his opportunity. "Sorn, go find Adrianna! She's somewhere down this corridor!" He deflected anti-Sirion's next blow and then ducked and rolled. He came up behind his double, blocking any chance the man had to give chase. Sorn rushed into the corridor and quickly began checking the doors.

Anti-Sirion gave a shout, "Naemmious, to my chamber!" He then turned back to Sirion, a grimace spreading across his face. He licked his lips, tasting the blood that was there. He spoke in a drawl, "She tastes sweet, and feels even sweeter. You were a fool to let her get away from you!"

Sirion gave a low growl. "Effin bastard! What have you done to her?"

There was a crash and Sirion glanced down the hallway to find anti-Naemmious standing over the fallen form of Sorn. *Damnation...* Sirion blocked a blow from his nemesis just in time, staggering under the strength behind it. Anti-Sirion continued to drive him back, further and further into the hallway, and then he stumbled.

Sirion fell back against the wall and anti-Sirion pushed past him, his maniacal laugh receding down the hall. Sirion regained his footing and sprinted after. As anti-Naemmious stopped at a door at the end of the corridor, Sirion caught up to his double. He reached out an arm, and with all the force he could muster, he knocked anti-Sirion into the closest chamber.

Amethyst cringed when she heard someone fumbling at the door. *Oh gods, Adria's abductor has returned. What will he think about two captives instead of just one? Really, that window would have been the perfect escape route.* She thought she heard Adrianna whispering something to herself as the door abruptly swung open. Amethyst blinked through wide eyes as a huge man burst into the room. He was hairier than any human, and his lower jaw jutted out to expose elongated canines that rested over his upper lip. Barely another moment passed before she felt a surge of... something....

A glowing bolt left Adrianna's hands, the electrical power rushing towards the big, ugly man. The energy struck him in the chest and he was cast back through the doorway. The impact of solid flesh and the crunching of bone against unforgiving stone was heard. The stench of charred flesh filled the air, and when the smoke cleared, the man could be seen slumped against the corridor wall, a blackened hole in his chest. His skull had hit the wall upon impact, and blood ran down his temple and face. His eyes were open, but were no longer bright with the presence of life.

With a massive exhale, Amethyst turned back to Adrianna, her eyes wide with wonder. The sorceress was closing one of the pouches on her belt, the materials therin expended. Without speaking, Adrianna proceeded to walk out of the room. She didn't even pause at the body as she strode past it. Amethyst just followed behind and whispered to herself, "Damn, that was so awesome..."

The two men grappled on the floor, each one beating the other with his fists and issuing malicious epithets. Within moments of being in the room they heard a crash followed by a large thud. The two men looked towards the sounds, and intuitively knew they came from the room to which anti-Naemmious had sought access. Suddenly anti-Sirion acquired the upper hand, straddling Sirion with a dagger to his throat.

Anti-Sirion grinned. "It's a shame you never had her. She is good, very good."

Abruptly freeing his arm from beneath the weight of his opponent, Sirion knocked the dagger from out of anti-Sirion's hand, sending it across the room. "I'm going to kill you," he growled.

Sirion wrapped his hands around the throat of his double, and anti-Sirion followed suit. Once more they tumbled about on the floor, each one seeking to end the other. They hit a table, sending it falling on top of them. A lamp crashed to the floor, and the flickering candle rolled over to the window.

Sirion took one of his hands from around his double's neck and picked up the splintered leg of the table. He hit anti-Sirion hard across the face. The other man screamed and reared back, holding his jaw in his hand. Sirion scrambled up off the floor, only to be brought down again by his opponent. He squirmed and kicked against the other man, hoping to get away, when suddenly Sirion inhaled the scent of smoke. Anti-Sirion noticed it too and they both glanced at the flames climbing up the thick fabric that outlined the window.

By the gods, the place is on fire!

In spite of the seriousness of the situation, Sirion snatched the chance to kick anti-Sirion in the face. His double grunted with the impact as Sirion rose from the floor, looking wildly about for the dagger he knew to be in his general vicinity. Too late, the realization that it had already been found struck him just as anti-Sirion lurched up from the floor with a malicious grin distorting his battered face. The dagger gleamed within the light cast by the growing flames as it arced towards him. Sirion dodged the lunge, and anti-Sirion stumbled. Sirion snaked out his hand, hoping to capture the dagger, but anti-Sirion gripped it too tightly.

Once more, the two men fell to the floor. For a moment no one moved. Finally Sirion lifted himself off of his double. He quickly turned the man over and found the dagger deeply embedded in his chest. Anti-Sirion struggled to take his last breaths, and his eyes were already becoming vague. Suddenly noticing the increasing warmth, Sirion looked at the inferno that had begun to encompass the chamber. The cheap tapestries hanging on the walls had all caught flame. Disoriented for a moment, Sirion glanced wildly about the room and then through the open doorway. Lying on the floor on the other side was Adrianna.

Heart racing, Sirion ran out of the burning room. Once out in the hallway, he knelt before her. He was relieved to see that she was breathing and that her eyes were open. "Adrianna, are you all right?" Without waiting for answer he continued. "Come on. We have to move away from here, let someone know that the building is on fire." Sirion took her arm, urging her to her feet. He tugged at her, but while she did not pull away, she was moving slowly and uncoordinated. .

"Adrianna... Sirion. Are you two all right?" Amethyst rushed down the hall, calling out to them.

"Get back, Amethyst!" he shouted. "The room is on fire!" Sirion swept Adrianna up into his arms and rushed away from the room just as the flames began to emerge behind them. Beyond Amethyst, the rest of the Wildrunners had gathered. Sirion saw Triath take Amethyst's arm, urging her back down the hall. Resisting, she continued to wait until Adrianna and Sirion had nearly reached them before she allowed Triath to take her through the tavern and out of the building.

By that time, others had arrived, men carrying large buckets of water to put out the fire. Sirion carried Adrianna down the steps of the establishment and into the chilly evening air. He set her down; immediately feeling the cold, Adrianna shivered and wrapped her arms around herself. It was only then he realized what she was wearing.

The sheer fabric of the dress she wore demanded his stare. Through the diaphanous material it was easy to see the contours of her breasts, the shape of her waist and her thighs. He watched as she sat down on the steps of the inn, wrapping her arms around herself. He saw the red marks where her wrists had been savagely bound. *Hellfire, what did that man do to her?*

Sirion stepped back over and knelt down before her. "Adrianna, are you all right? Is there anything I can do to–" He reached out a hand to touch her and suddenly Adrianna reared back. Awkwardly she stood up and backed away from him, fear reflected in her eyes.

Sirion held out a hand, palm up. "Adrianna, I just want to help. Here, let me give you my vest." Sirion began unfastening the buckles of his leather as he stepped towards her. He reached out again, hoping to put an arm around her shoulders to keep away some of the chill, but Adrianna pushed away from him.

Her voice was anguished. "Don't touch me!" Tears rolled down her cheeks and she continued to step farther away. "Just... just stay away from me. Haven't you done enough?"

Dumbfounded, Sirion just stared. Her body shook with emotion, and she was folded inward, her arms wrapped around herself. Sirion glanced at the remaining Wildrunners and Amethyst. They were silent as they watched the scenario playing out before them. When Adrianna turned and rushed down the street, Amethyst broke away from the rest and went after her.

Sirion stared after them, his mind enveloped in disbelief. After a few moments, Triath stepped up to him and put a hand on his shoulder. "Let's go back to your inn. Sorn will follow the women to be sure they make it back there."

Sirion only nodded before following Triath and the others.

Through the remainder of the night and well into the next day, Adrianna slept. When she finally found the desire to get out of bed, it was almost midday. For several moments she felt disoriented. She struggled to recall all that had happened the night before, and cringed in shame once it all came rushing back. Once discovering she still wore the gossamer gown, she stripped it off and threw it into a shimmering heap on the floor. Then, her body shaking, she stood in the middle of the room.

Adrianna didn't know how long she remained there, but eventually she had enough presence of mind to find decent clothes to wear. She got dressed and then sat on the chair next to the window. Time slipped by without notice. She didn't think about much of anything as she sat there; it was easy to simply exist without thinking much of anything.

Finally Sheridana came. Her sister said nothing as she brought another chair over to the window and sat down. She reached out and took her hand, making certain not to touch the dried scabs encircling her wrists. They remained that way for quite some while. Adrianna appreciated Sheridana's silent presence there beside her, and even more, the warm hand enveloping hers. As the time passed, she found the muzziness in her mind finally melting away.

She didn't stir until she feel the urge to eat. Sheridana had left a short time ago, and Adrianna thought her sister must have felt the same. Adrianna poured some water into the washbasin and splashed it onto her face and neck. It felt good to wash away evidence from the evening before. She wrapped her wrists in cloths, not wanting any visible reminders, and combed out her hair and let it be, unwilling to take the time to plait it again.

It was late afternoon by the time Adrianna made her way out of the chamber. The smell of roasting meat wafted up the stairs, making her belly rumble. She wondered if Sheridana would still be there. Her question was answered when she was brought up short by the conversation going on as she neared the bottom of the stairs where it entered the common room.

"It's called esfexanar. The poison can be used in many ways, but the quickest way to get a response is to apply it to the tip of a blade or an arrow and make it penetrate the skin. If too much of the poison is used, it can cause death, but in very small amounts it can cause the behaviors you see in your sister."

Adrianna stood motionlessly on the stairs. She didn't recognize the man's voice, and she wondered who would be talking about her.

"But how long will the effects last? It's been over twelve hours," said Sheridana.

"Depending on the amount they used, she could remain this way for the rest of the day."

So there *had* been something wrong with her. Adrianna felt a little bit better knowing there was a reason for her unnatural listlessness.

"I just hate to see her this way. And we still don't know what happened except what Amethyst told us. She just found her lying on that bed..."

"Now Sheridana," Dartanyen interrupted. "Don't get upset yet. It's possible he didn't get that far with her." His voice took on a macabre edge, "And, as a bonus, he is dead."

Adrianna frowned. She'd heard enough, not to mention, she felt like such a creep standing in a stairwell listening in to a conversation that didn't include her except in the third person. She stepped backwards a couple of steps before continuing back down, making certain to make enough noise for them to know she was coming.

She found her companions seated at a large table. Others had joined them, and she recognized the people as Sirion's sister and their friends. She was surprised to see them there but realized why she'd heard an unfamiliar voice. Food and drink had recently been brought to the table, and everyone was serving themselves from the large platters. There were greetings all around as Sheridana made room for her at the table between herself and Amethyst, quickly snagging a nearby chair and sliding it into place.

Adrianna sat down and noticed too late that Sirion sat directly across the table from her. Next to him was seated one of his Wildrunner companions, the one with the eyepatch. Glancing around, Adrianna noticed that Tianna avoided looking in her direction, but Dartanyen, Armond, and Zorg all expressed interest in knowing how she was feeling. She smiled with the genuine nature of their inquiries, and hated to tell them her arms ached from trying to escape her bonds and that she had a headache from whatever poison they'd used. So she told them all was fine, and that she felt much better after her rest.

The food disappeared quickly, and the drink even more so. Even Sirion participated in the imbibing of significant quantities of mead and ale. The companionship was good, the two groups getting along with one another rather well. At first, there wasn't much talk of the evening before and Adrianna felt grateful for that. Instead, the Wildrunners told stories of their earlier days. The ones about Sirion tended to be the most humorous. She couldn't keep the grin from her face, but she continued to avoid any possible eye contact with him and barely looked in his direction. It was difficult with him sitting right across the table, but she managed.

Unfortunately, the conversation took a natural shift to the individuals the Wildrunners referred to as their 'doubles'. The man with the eyepatch, Triath, explained the history behind their existence, as well as the trouble they had caused the Wildrunners ever since.

"Our efforts to see an end to these people culminated in the battle at the Snorting Gorgon Inn last night," Triath continued. "With Adrianna's abduction by Sirion's double, we no longer had the time to think of a suitable strategy, but everything worked out better than we thought it might." Triath grimaced. "Well, except for the fire. That was expensive."

There were chuckles all around the table. Adrianna shifted un-comfortably in her seat. *If only I hadn't run off like that, Sirion's double may never have gotten the chance to take me.* Some of his words flashed through her mind and she recanted. *I don't know, maybe he would have still found a way to get me.* She inadvertently cast a look in Sirion's direction and found him regarding her intently, his arms crossed at his chest. Recollection of her response to him the evening before came to the forefront of her thoughts and her mind recoiled. She took a deep breath and slid her eyes past him when Triath began to speak again, refusing to be drawn into his gaze.

"But this was our last mission together," he said. "We agreed to disband once our doubles were destroyed. It's about time we returned to our homes. Through the years we have sacrificed so much to our causes, not to mention the lives of our friends." Triath lowered his head and Sorn clapped him on the back and nodded his agreement.

There were a few moments of silence and then Dartanyen spoke. "We should probably be leaving the city soon. The faster we find out all we can about Thane the better. Dinim took a look around the library here today and found nothing of use. I suggest we head in the direction of Driscol. It's larger than Entsy, and more likely to have a bigger library."

Sabian spoke up. "You know, if we are looking for libraries, what about the one in Andahye? It is quite extensive, and more likely to have the resources we might need since it is a city dedicated to arcane knowledge."

Dartanyen became thoughtful. "You have a good point."

Dinim shook his head. "I don't believe we will find what we're looking for there. I think it's best if we go ahead and move towards Driscol. The city has a really good library that might even rival the one in Andahye. If that gives us nothing, I might know of someone who lives nearby there that might be able to help us."

Dartanyen nodded. "All right. What does everyone else think?"

Armond and Zorg nodded their agreement, as well as Sheridana. "It sounds like a good plan to me," she said.

"Well, let's get some rest tonight and tomorrow focus on getting our supplies. Then we can stay one more night and leave early the day after," said Dartanyen.

"Maybe we can buy some larian, at least one or two to help carry our packs. The journey would be much easier," suggested Sheridana.

Armond nodded. "That sounds good."

"Oh Adrianna, before I forget, I wanted to tell you that I have a book you might be interested in," said Dinim. "It even has a spell in it that you haven't seen yet."

Adrianna looked over at Dinim and smiled. "That would be great. Whenever you're ready just let me know."

"Are you sure that's a good idea? Maybe you should focus on getting some rest," said Sirion. "You've been through a lot the past day or so."

Surprised, Adrianna turned towards him. His expression was unreadable, but she sensed his statement had very little to do with her ordeal the evening before. "No, I'm fine. It will be good for me to get my mind off of things."

"Adria, are you sure? Maybe Sirion is right. You do look rather tired," said Sheridana thoughtfully.

Adrianna swung her gaze to her sister and frowned. The conversation struck a frayed chord, and irritation swept through her. "Actually, I don't recall asking Sirion for his opinion, and as much as I value yours Sheri, you're just going to have to trust me when I tell you I'm fine." Adrianna raised an eyebrow, and looked at Sirion pointedly.

The rest of the table became quiet as the ranger's eyes darkened. "You didn't ask me for help with your father either, but here I am."

For what felt like the hundredth time, Adrianna felt the hurt swell inside of her. He made it sound like it was such a chore to be there. *Hells, why does he bother if he is so miserable? Is it some odd sense of obligation? Mayhap because Cortath would have stayed by my side?* "Perhaps you shouldn't be here then."

Sirion's gaze was stony. "Perhaps I will just return to Elvandahar with Anya. I can see now that my help isn't appreciated," he said in a low voice.

Adrianna replied without thinking, anger fueling words driven by threadbare emotions. "Fine, go back to Elvandahar. Actually, that would be great. I won't be forced to watch my friends groping one another for the next few weeks."

There was a moment of stark silence before Sirion responded in a raised voice. "Why are you acting like such a child?"

Adrianna's eyes widened with mock astonishment. "Me? I'm acting like a child? What about you, Sirion? You've been ignoring me ever since the fight with your uncle, constantly scouting ahead of the group, not talking with anyone, and growling when you do?"

Sirion scoffed. "That's right. What would you know? You have no idea what I am going through, because you didn't have to kill *your* uncle."

Adrianna stared at him through wide eyes. "Well, mine is already dead, so I guess I can't include him in our little quarrel." She didn't pause when she heard Sheridana take a swift intake of breath. "I suppose we will be equals when I'm forced to kill my father, because I'm certain that's what it will take to keep him from murdering me, my sister, and my neiya."

Adrianna rose shakily from her seat and looked around the table. "Excuse me everyone. Perhaps I'm tired after all." Her voice sounded puny, even to her own ears. She turned and walked swiftly out of the common room. Her chest felt heavy and sobs caught in her throat. *Damn Sirion! Because of him, I'm crying yet again. Within the short time I've known the man, I've cried more than I have in the past twenty years.*

Adrianna swept up the stairs and into her chamber, slamming the door behind. Her breath came in ragged gasps, and she felt sick to her stomach. Wrapping her arms around her belly, she leaned back against the door. It was wrong of her to say some of those things to Sirion, for she'd made his ordeal seem so much less than what it really was. But he'd been equally wrong in his reply. They had managed to treat one another very poorly within the space of only a few short moments.

Now, when she and the others needed Sirion the most, he was going to leave.

And it was all her fault.

Dinim and the rest watched as Sirion stood from the table and followed Adrianna out of the room. For a moment there was silence, and then a voice spoke up. "I'm going to bet that Sirion wins this one. Damn, was he *angry*." Sorn's lavender eyes glinted, and his mouth pulled up into a small grin.

Triath smiled. "Yeah, he was pretty mad, but the lady was too."

Sorn reached into his belt pouch and pulled out a gold piece. "I'm betting Sirion wins the argument."

"No way," said Sheridana with mock indignation. "Adrianna will surely win this one." Smiling, she pulled two gold out of her own pouch and set it on the table.

"I agree with Sorn. Sirion will take this fight. He isn't one to lose, not even to a lady," said Naemmious, putting his pouch onto the table.

"What the Hells are you all doing?" said Armond. "You're going to take bets?"

Amethyst gave a girlish giggle and grinned widely. "Why not? This is as good a reason as any."

Armond frowned. "This isn't right. Two of our good friends are up there right now, both very hurt and confused. I can't believe you people are going to exploit that."

Zorg clapped Armond on the back. "C'mon, Armond. Loosen up a bit. It's jus' a bit of friendly gamblin'. I vote that Adrianna wins the fight. She 'as more spunk in 'er than most people realize."

Naemmious shook his head. "Well, you obviously don't know Sirion very well."

"Don' have to. I know Adrianna," replied Zorg.

"Well, I know my brother. He won't back down. I say Sirion will win this one," said Anya, bringing her own pouch to the table.

Sabian cackled with glee. "I'm with Anya. Sirion will win the argument. I don't think Adrianna is up for the fight."

"Come on, Triath, what do you think?" asked Sorn.

Triath narrowed his eyes for a moment. "I don't know. Maybe no one will win."

Naemmious guffawed. "You know better than that Triath. You and Sirion have had your fair share of scuffles. Possibly even more than your fair share."

"I suppose I should lay my own wager," Dartanyen interrupted with a sigh. He made it seem like he was a bit put out, but the sparkle of amusement in his eyes gave him away. "I say Adrianna will win the argument. Zorg is right, she has fire in her. What say you, Dinim? Who do you think will persevere?"

Dinim frowned, feeling vaguely out of sorts. He cared about Adrianna very much, maybe even loved her. At one time, she might have felt the same for him, but since Sirion became a part of the group, things had changed. The attraction that manifested between the ranger and the sorceress was one not easily explained, and at first Dinim refused to see it.

Now he had no choice.

However, the recent turn of events couldn't be ignored, and because of this *thing* going on between the two of them, Adrianna's life had been endangered not just once with Sydonnia, but again with Sirion's double. He hated that. Dinim glanced away, not wanting his feelings to be seen. Over the past several days he'd tried to convince himself that Adrianna wasn't all his mind made her out to be, and had even tried to come up with some things that weren't so good about her. Even under such scrutiny, Dinim found it difficult to find much negative about her, except for one thing...

She was weak.

It was something Dinim had realized right away. It was the way she carried herself, the way she let others make decisions for her, and the way she went about life in general. Her confidence in her skills and abilities was meager, and her self-esteem laughable. She contributed very little to the decision-making process, although she may have spoken up once or twice. For someone of her Talent, Dinim had expected something... well... *more*. Instead of making her stronger, her experiences in life seemed to have made her weaker, and her inability to truly apply herself was depriving her of the power that lay just below the surface.

Yet, despite this key flaw in Adrianna's personality, he had begun to fall in love with her. Deep inside, he knew this flaw could be overcome, and he fancied himself the one who would break down those walls. Recently he'd been forced to accept he might not be that person. It would be someone else, and the fact that it might be Sirion Timberlyn rankled him to no end.

Anger crept through him like a hungry kyrrean hunting for its unwitting prey. He was angry with Sirion for being such a pile of umberhulk dung and at Adrianna for allowing him to be that way with her. And now her ability to win a battle of wills was up for debate, making his opinion of her public.

"Sirion will win the argument," he growled. "I agree with Sabian that Adria isn't up for the fight."

The moment the words were out of his mouth, Dinim regretted saying them. He saw Sheridana's eyes widen with surprise, and Zorg raised an arched brow. Dinim sighed to himself and tapped his fingertips on the table. *Damn, I can never win.*

"And what about you, Tianna? What do you think?" asked Sorn.

Everyone swung their eyes in her direction. Tianna sat there for a few moments, a myriad expressions passing over her face. "Perhaps Triath is right. Maybe they will both win."

Sorn put his hands on his hips. "Now why would you think that? We all know Triath is a freak and that he would believe something like that, but not an intelligent creature like yourself. Now come on, be honest."

"Hey friend, don't push it," growled Armond. "This is a stupid bet anyway. Let the lady be. She's been through too much lately to be bullied around by the likes of you."

Sorn narrowed his eyes. "And what do you mean by that?"

"Hey, hey, hey," interjected Dartanyen. "Cut it out. We aren't here to fight. I thought this was just for fun."

Sorn held up his hands. "Yes, you're right. This is all just for a bit of friendly gambling. So, we have Dinim, Sabian, Naemmious, Anya, and myself in favor of Sirion. And we have Sheridana, Amethyst, Zorg, and Dartanyen in favor of the lady. Let's put our money where our mouths are." Sorn then flung his bag in the center of the table. The others followed suit.

"Wait a minute," said Armond. "Put me in favor of Adrianna."

Sheridana smiled. "I knew you would come around."

Armond frowned and grumbled incoherently as he threw his own money pouch onto the table.

Sirion slowly opened the door to Adrianna's room. Within the wan light cast by the lamp, he saw her pull the covers up around herself. He paused at the doorway, not knowing what to say, not knowing how to breach the distance that had grown between them. They had been walking along a path of camaraderie, one he'd hoped would ultimately take him along one even deeper. He knew the distance was his own doing, for he had rebuffed her efforts to comfort him the day after that fateful battle.

Even now he could feel the fear, coiled like a serpent in his chest, waiting to strike. It was the fear of knowing he wouldn't be able to live the rest of his life with the knowledge that her life had been forfeited for his. It irked him that she had so flagrantly dismissed his wishes to stay behind with the rest of the group while he fought Sydonnia. However, another part of him was touched that she had wished to remain by his side, even in the face of such adversity.

But he had chosen the path of anger made easier by Joselyn's loss. He pushed Adrianna away in spite of her attempts to soothe him, and he'd remained cool towards her, almost as though to punish her for her disobeying him. Then last night happened. Once again he'd been faced with his worst fears. He hated himself for this vulnerability, not realizing that such emotion was the byproduct of loving someone more than oneself. And then, when the fighting was finally over, and he saw her dressed in that flimsy gown, his senses had gone wild.

My double was right. I am a fool for letting her go.

Sirion slowly walked across the room towards the bed. He'd treated Adrianna so coldly, and remorse spiked through him. *It's not her fault that I was forced to fight Sydonnia– not her fault that Joselyn had died with him. I hate myself for bickering with her and keeping her away from her companionship with Dinim. I just can't help thinking he will find what I have so foolishly lost...*

His voice came hoarsely out of a dry throat even though he'd been drinking all night. "Adrianna? Adrianna, I'm sorry." He fell to his knees beside the blanketed hump, placing a hand where he imagined a shoulder might be. He slowly turned her towards him, brushing wisps of pale hair from her face. She resisted, and when he felt wetness on his fingertips, his chest constricted.

"*Shendori*," he whispered. Without another thought he pulled her towards him. Tucking her head beneath his chin, Sirion held her tight. Her body trembled within his embrace, and he rocked back and forth. He stroked her hair as he murmured into her ear. "I'm so sorry. It was wrong of me to shut you out, but I just hurt so much..."

Adrianna found herself in Sirion's arms, her head resting on his leathered chest. He whispered to her in Hinterlic, his voice tight with suppressed emotion. She allowed herself to be rocked within his embrace, but said nothing, not knowing what to say, or if she really wanted to say anything at all. And then he was stroking her hair, caressing her back and sides. Her tears stopped and she began to relax despite not knowing what to think, not knowing whether she should allow herself the luxury of his touch.

Adrianna closed her eyes. She could hear each breath he took and felt each beat of his heart where her hand rested at the open vee of his leather. Warm tears escaped her lids and ran down her cheeks, her chest aching every moment she spent in his arms. *Dear gods, thank you for giving his friendship back to me! Thank you, thank you! I've missed him so much!*

She couldn't deny it. Despite her resolve to forget what they had shared together that night in the Sherkari Fortress, the memories were always there. She didn't know what Sirion had been thinking, but it didn't really matter. He was much older than her by many years, and he came from an entirely different culture. They had very little in common, especially regarding their professions. She was alright with that, as long as they were friends.

Adrianna knew she should pull away and stop her insanity, protect herself from the heartache she knew lay just around the bend. Just as she was about to do just that, Sirion tightened his grip around her waist and put his face in her hair near the curve of her neck. She felt the raw emotion, sensed it eddy gently around them, the stirrings of passion within an answer to what she felt from the man holding her so tightly against him. Her breath caught in her throat. *Oh gods, what is he doing? This isn't what was supposed to happen!* She struggled within herself, and just as she felt that she might win her battle with desire, Sirion pushed the hair away from her neck and kissed the sensitive skin.

Her belly constricted into knots and she suppressed a moan of dismay. She ran her hands over his chest, over the stiffness of the studded leather vest he wore. He hadn't bothered to remove it after he and the Wildrunners went back to the Snorting Gorgon to help clean up their mess and to pay for the extensive damages they had wrought. The vest was the maximum amount of protection he was willing to use. He'd once told her that anything heavier impeded his ability to be an effective ranger. She moved her hands up to his shoulders, over the ornate clasps that bound his cloak, and then tentatively ran her fingers through the thick hair that rested against his neck. Adrianna felt the warmth of his breath as Sirion's lips moved from her neck to her jaw. Her heart fluttered in her chest and she moved her face just enough that her lips brushed his...

Sirion took her face in his hands and lay down beside her on the bed. His kiss was deep and passionate, and she tightened her fingers in his hair. This reaction seemed to fuel him further, and he ran his hands over her back and hips, seeking to bring her closer. The tears continued to flow, unchecked, down her temples. *What am I doing? Why am I doing this?*

Sirion gently rolled Adrianna onto her back. She kept her eyes closed, not wanting to see, just to feel the sensations washing over her with every touch. He pulled his lips away from hers and softly kissed each of her eyelids. She momentarily felt his hesitation and anxiety swept over her for a moment. His voice was a whisper that she didn't expect to hear, "Shendori, please forgive me. I was a fool. Please believe me when I say I would give my life for you."

Adrianna opened her eyes and regarded him without filter, without barrier, brimming with emotion. "Why are you doing this to me?"

Sirion became still and just stared into her eyes. She needed affirmation, couldn't stand to feel him touching her this way without knowing what his intentions were. She couldn't handle a repeat of their tryst in the fortress, no matter how nice it had been.

He replied with confidence she didn't expect to hear, in a low, husky tone. "I love you, Adrianna. You have always been the only one for me."

Adrianna searched his face, not believing what she'd just heard him say. His expression remained solemn as he regarded her through pools of molten amber and she found the sincerity she was looking for. Tentatively, she reached out and placed a hand on Sirion's face, tracing the contour of his jaw with her fingertips. When she approached his lips, he turned towards her fingers and kissed them, his eyes never leaving hers.

She took the initiative and pulled him towards her. Her kiss was hesitant, and he responded by deepening it, his tongue darting between her parted lips. With each passing breath their passion grew. She felt his hands at her waist, her hips, and then her backside. She pressed closer to him and he groaned in her ear. He imprisoned her with his hands, pressing her into his hardening groin. A tingle of fear passed through her, but it was gone almost as swiftly as it had come. Despite the events that had recently taken place, she knew Sirion would never hurt her.

Despite what had happened to her in the past, she felt safe. She *trusted* him.

Once again Adrianna brought her hands to Sirion's chest, wishing the leather was gone. She wanted, *needed,* to feel the warmth of him. As though he read her mind, Sirion tore himself away from her just long enough to unbuckle the vest and slip it over his head. He tossed the leather aside and then brought himself back to her, finally giving her the opportunity to revel in the warmth of his body pressed so close. He moved his lips from her mouth to her throat, and when she rolled her head back, he continued down to the hollow of her neck.

Holding her with one hand at the small of her back, Sirion slowed his movements, bringing his other hand to the laces of her tunic and loosening them. He slowly and deliberately pulled the garment down over her shoulders, his amber gaze smoldering with desire. His hands brushed gently down her arms as he continued pulling down the tunic, his eyes searching hers for any hint of uncertainty or fear.

In spite of the rapid beating of her heart, a calm came over her. Sirion had somehow become more than the hardened warrior. He was the hesitant, tender lover. As he hovered above her, he brought his hand over to hers where it lay on the blanket. He then brought his lips down to meet hers once more.

His kiss was intense, unlike any they had shared before. Adrianna closed her eyes as he threaded his fingers through hers. The sensation was overwhelming, but she didn't miss the feather-light touch of Destiny telling her this was meant to be.

THE RING

The group traveled northeast across the plains south of the Sheldomar Forest. Spirits were high as they rode, for their number had grown since leaving Entsy. After serious deliberation, Triath, Anya, Sorn, and Naemmious had decided to join their ranks. After hearing the account of their trials, the remaining Wildrunners felt it to be the appropriate thing to do. Not only did they want to stand by their old friends, Sirion and Dinim, but Thane was a threat to many. His defeat would save the lives of countless innocents. At first Dartanyen was reticent to accept their aid, for he hated to involve any more people for whom Thane would develop a death wish if they failed. But when Triath kindly and firmly explained that they weren't asking permission to join the cause, Dartanyen heartily took Triath's arm in the gesture of comradeship.

Between themselves and the Wildrunners, the group had enough silver and gold to purchase several larian and a couple of lloryk. With most of the remainder, they bought supplies and weather-appropriate clothing and bedding. With the approach of cold weather, they also invested in a tent. Along with the one Naemmious carried, it would offer just enough room for everyone should the need arise.

As the group moved towards Driscol, they developed a pattern for travel. They rode hard much of the day, letting the larian rest once at midmorning and again for a late midday meal. After that, they allowed the animals to pace themselves before stopping in the early evening. They had deliberately chosen animals that were hardy and able to endure long distances at a rapid pace. They had also chosen animals that would be able to tolerate the company of a corubis. Although Dramati was often scouting ahead with Sirion, the animals still had to deal with the presence of a predator in their midst.

Late afternoon saw Sirion and Anya looking for a suitable campsite. Meanwhile, Dartanyen and Sheridana hunted for rock fowl and ptarmigan that made their homes in the low-lying scrub. By the time the sun was beginning to set, a good site had been located. While Adrianna and Amethyst saw to the lloryk and larian, Tianna and Triath were busy building the fires and preparing for the evening meal. Zorg, Armond, Dinim, Sabian and Sorn would set camp and Naemmious would often busy himself by drawing out the arenas for the evening weapons practice.

Since their first evening of travel, Sirion had resumed Adrianna's sparring sessions. By the time she was finished with the animals, Sirion had the opportunity to rest after scouting all day. Some nights, many of the others would participate as well. Sheridana, Armond, and Zorg were the ones who would practice most often, usually with their swords, but sometimes Dinim and Triath would join in. Sometimes Tianna, Sorn, Amethyst, Sabian, and Naemmious would spar with other weapons such as the dagger, scimitar, or axe. It was a good time, and it increased group cohesion and companionship.

As the evenings passed, Sheridana and Dartanyen discussed the weapons practices during their turn at the watch. Both were pleased to realize they agreed on many aspects of the way battles should be fought and the methods they could use to pull the group together. They developed a plan they could utilize in battle, one that would maximize everyone's skills. It wasn't long before they brought it before the rest of the group. Everyone recognized the logic in Dartanyen and Sheridana's plan, and within a few nights, everyone was adjusting well to the strategy sessions.

It took the group almost a fortnight to reach the lands surrounding Driscol. Along the way, they passed through several towns and villages. All of the residents whispered of an undead monster that rode a black steed made of smoke and ash. He led a party of men who laid waste to every place he encountered as he swept through Monaf. By the time the group reached the outskirts, they had learned that Thane was near the city of Celuna. It was readily apparent they had been traveling towards one another, like an unseen power had determined that they should meet sooner rather than later.

The group set camp inside a cave situated within a small wooded area. As the nights grew chillier they took the extra measures to find a campsite that had some barrier to the winds. They had the tents, but it was so much easier to find something they wouldn't have to work to erect. Tianna walked among the trees, foraging about in the vegetation. She hoped to find some wild onions that would go well in the stewpot this evening and she might as well restock her clover supply. By midday on the morrow they would be walking the streets of Driscol and have the opportunity to replenish much of their stores. Yet, she didn't mind hunting for many of the herbs herself. Besides, it gave her a chance to be away from the rest of the group for a little while.

Since leaving Entsy, Tianna fought an internal struggle. She had put both Sirion and herself in an awkward situation with her untoward actions toward him the night of Adrianna's abduction. He'd come to apologize to her since then, and she had done the same. She could tell he felt remorse for what he had done, but Tianna underplayed her emotions. "You know how I am, given to flights of fancy at slightest whim. My father can vouch for that." Sirion's expression was skeptical, but he'd accepted her words. Adrianna had also approached her. Tianna tried to explain what had happened, but Adrianna didn't really understand any of it. In the end, all that mattered was that her friend lay in the embrace of the one man Tianna had ever truly loved. She didn't hate Adrianna for it, but she didn't like her for it either. It was simply an aspect of the struggle she endured daily as she traveled with the group. To make it worse, she suffered the glances from everyone else, including the Wildrunners.

It only served to increase her frustration.

Tianna knelt to pull back a xinthafroz bush and murmured with delight. Beneath the leaves of the large shrub, she had found the vine of a hybanthis flower. She carefully picked up the vine, following it with her eyes until they beheld one of the tiny flowers. The bloom was gorgeous, emerging only at the end of summer. This vine was carrying its last blooms of the year, and soon they would be falling to the ground. Tianna plucked the beautiful pink flower, and placed it into her pouch. This plant had special properties, ones that were not entirely understood. However, the flowers were needed for a drink she knew how to prepare, one that could be blessed by the goddess to help the person who drank it the ability to see into one's inner being, to realize one's true feelings. However, if the drink was made too strong, the person would suffer a distorted perception of their feelings and become ill.

As Tianna continued to pick the flowers, she was sure not to touch the blue thorns adorning the vine. They were known to produce the same effects as a hybanthis drink, and could make one terribly sick. It would take days for the poison to leave a person's body, and during that time they would have a high fever. They would feel their emotions surge at any excuse, and may even lose control completely. Everyone was different, so one could never tell how they would react until they had been poisoned. However, Tianna wasn't about to find that out for herself. As soon as she acquired enough flowers, she left the area and returned to the rest of the group.

Tianna walked into the small cave and sat in front of the stewpot, suddenly remembering why she had gone foraging in the first place. She sighed heavily and then shrugged. The stew would have to go without this evening. She stirred the contents of the large pot, then removed a ladle-full and sampled it. She nodded to herself. It was good, but definitely could have used the wild onion.

Suddenly hearing a shout, Tianna glanced up from the stew and looked in the direction of the ongoing spar. Sirion had disarmed Adrianna, and had grabbed her from behind. He picked her up and she shouted again, kicking her legs. "Put me down, Sirion! Put me down!" Smiling, he acquiesced, and then spun her around to face him. For a moment, he just stared at her, then he placed his face alongside hers as though he whispered something into her ear.

Tianna tore her gaze away from them, returning her attention to the stewpot. In all of the years she'd known him, she'd never seen Sirion so happy. Everyone was getting a chance to see a side of him no one knew existed. Adrianna had brought that side of him into being. Tianna was happy for

Sirion, but wished it had been she who had been able to make him complete.

As the sun set on the horizon, the group prepared their bedrolls for the night. Triath and Amethyst situated themselves near the cave mouth for their watch. Adrianna was glad Sirion had found it, for it was rare they got the chance to rest unhindered by the elements. Lying on her bedroll beside him, they were the farthest back into the interior. She was about to drift off to sleep when she heard a noise. It was a dry, raspy sound that emerged from deep within the cave behind her. For a few moments it stopped and she began to think it was nothing, but then she heard it again, accompanied by a long, deep hiss.

Adrianna put her hand on Sirion's chest. "I think I hear something."

Suddenly she felt his arms wrap around her and they were rolling towards the cave entrance. Sirion stopped once they hit one of their companions, and he quickly got to his feet. Stalker in hand, he faced the dark cave interior. Adrianna and a disturbed Dartanyen stood up and looked in the same direction. The thing emerging from the darkness was frightening to behold. It was long and reptilian, colored a reddish brown. Its head was a hideous cross between a lizard and a raptor, and two thick black horns sprouted from brow ridges overtop yellow eyes. The jaws were huge, sporting several long sharp teeth.

Sirion slowly began to back away from the creature, Adrianna and Dartanyen following suit. Glancing back, she noticed that most everyone else was trying to make it to the front of the cave. The wyvern hissed again and raised its head, narrowing its yellow eyes. The full length of its body had become visible. It had four legs, much too small to be of much use, which was why it used its belly upon which to slither like a snake. Its leathery wings were folded along its back. More than half of the creature was made up of its tail, which Adrianna noticed had a thick knot at the tip. From it protruded a sharp stinger.

"Adrianna," Sirion whispered, "get behind me–"

The wyvern attacked. Sirion separated Stalker into two blades, and the ring of steel echoed throughout the cave as Sheridana, Zorg, and Armond drew their swords. Adrianna saw one arrow, and then two, as Anya and Dartanyen fired with their bows. She barely managed to move out of the way of the charging wyvern, narrowly missing its sharply clawed feet as it lurched past.

From within the depths of his concentration, Dinim saw Adrianna just narrowly miss being crushed. He was afraid for her, yet continued weaving the magic of his spell. He was about to cast it when something strong struck him across his upper legs. He flew backward and landed on the ground just outside the cave. He lay there for a moment, slightly dazed, and then felt the pain in his legs. He levered himself up to reach down and feel if they were both still in one piece. It was then he noticed another pain. He lifted his other hand off of the ground to find a thorny vine lying beneath it. With an eloquent curse, he uprooted the plant and threw it away from him. He then clutched at the bloody hand, the blue thorns having cut deep into the palm.

Dinim felt a slight sense of vertigo, but slowly stood up and turned back towards the battle. From his position just outside of the cave, he saw the wyvern lash its tail at Zorg, the big warrior jumping over the barbed tip, and bringing his sword down onto the thick flesh just above it. The creature gave an agonized shriek, taking its attention away from a cornered Sheridana. Armond hit the beast with his glowing blades, visible shocks of electricity coursing through its long body. Already weakened by the missile spell that Adrianna had cast, the deep wounds caused by Naemmious's wicked flail, and Sirion's attacks, the wyvern expired quickly. Holding himself up against the cave wall, Dinim watched as the creature slumped over onto its side and took its last breath.

For several moments there was silence as everyone looking at the downed wyvern. Then Anya looked up at Sirion, a deep frown on her face. "I thought you told us this cave was safe."

Sirion's expression became one of chagrin and he shook his head. "I'm sorry. I scouted the place out before I brought you here, but I obviously missed something."

"Yeah, a really big something," she groused.

"I know. I'm sorry."

"Hey, everyone makes mistakes," said Dartanyen. "Let's just clean up this mess."

Naemmious, Zorg, Armond, Dartanyen, and Sorn set to work moving the large carcass out of the cave. Tianna busied herself with treating everyone's injuries, Sabian and Dinim needing the most help. Adrianna and Sheridana tended to the lloryk and larian while Sirion and Anya went back into the depths of the cave, just to be sure nothing remained. Once satisfied the place was clear, they returned to the camp.

Eventually, everyone settled down for sleep again. Sorn and Naemmious sat down for their watch, taking the last hour of Triath and Amethyst's shift. Through narrowed eyes, Dinim watched as Adrianna lay down beside Sirion. His bound hand throbbed despite the soothing cream and clean wrapping Tianna had applied to it. He'd been curt towards her and gave clipped answers to her inquiries about the wound. He wasn't usually so irritable, but maybe he was just overly tired and needed to get some rest.

Dinim lay on his bedroll and just stared into the darkness.

7 Thaliren CY593

The group traveled northeast through the foothills after leaving Driscol. They stayed there only one day and night, not wasting any time to gather the necessary equipment and supplies for their journey through the Ratik Pass. The library was meticulously searched for any information, but when nothing was found, Dinim looked for someone who could tell him the whereabouts of the man he knew who might be able to help them– an old mage by the name of Paxil. The information wasn't difficult to obtain; all he had to do was find a shop dealing in the magical arts. It was harder to find the shop than it was to learn where the mage resided.

Dinim and Adrianna rode towards their destination via the precise directions given to Dinim by the shop owner. They had left the rest of the group behind over a half an hour ago, not wanting to bring everyone should their numbers make the old man nervous. It was rumored that Paxil possessed the ability to know things without seeing or hearing about them. It was like a foresight, but not, simply a *knowing*, and through the decades he'd been sought by many. No one knew how old he was, for he seemed to have always been around.

He was also known to be more than a bit insane.

Dinim glanced back at Adrianna for a moment before turning back to the path. He didn't want her company– would much rather have been alone, but Dartanyen had insisted he take someone along with him. Adrianna had immediately offered and he'd inwardly cringed. He wasn't in any mood to deal with the emotions he felt whenever she was near, not to mention, he'd been dealing with a vague malaise since the skirmish with the wyvern. The only upside to the situation was the expression on Sirion's face when it was agreed she would accompany him.

Dinim held up a hand for her to stop when he saw it. The house was old and dilapidated, hardly a fit structure in which to take up residence. He sensed the power surrounding the place, and he knew that magic was keeping the small cabin from falling to the ground. Dinim and Adrianna dismounted and bound their larian to the healthiest looking scrawny tree. Slowly they approached the cabin, and when they reached the door, Dinim put out a hand and rapped on it.

Adrianna glanced around as they stood there, straining to hear any sounds from within the cabin. If the windows hadn't been clouded with decades' worth of dirt and grime, she might have tried peeking inside. Hearing nothing, Dinim knocked again. Nothing. He pressed his lips into a thin line. "Damn, he must have known we were coming and–"

"I sure did know that you was comin' to pay me a visit."

Adrianna had to put her hand over her mouth to keep from crying out as she turned to face the white-haired, squinty old man standing behind her. She couldn't believe she hadn't heard him approaching. Beside her, Dinim wore an expression of consternation and relief. "Are you Master Paxil?" he asked.

"In the flesh," replied the old man, regarding them critically from his good eye. "Please, come inside– and don't worry, the place won't fall down on you." Paxil cackled and clapped his hands together, stepping between them to open the door.

Stepping through, Adrianna had to give her eyes a moment to adjust to the lack of light. Paxil lit a candle and set it atop one of several cluttered tables. There were shelves along the walls, ones that were just as disorganized and littered as the tables. As she walked further into the room, she tripped over something. She looked down to realize there was precious little walking space, the floors having books, parchments, and various baubles lying everywhere.

"I know why you have come here."

Adrianna began to frown. She'd heard words similar to those before, spoken by one Ami Rayhana. She didn't like their portent, nor the fact that others seemed to know more about her than she knew herself. However, she held her tongue.

"Indeed. We have a powerful enemy, one we wish to know more about," replied Dinim.

"Lord Thane is the least of your problems," Paxil hissed, narrowing his eyes. "He is merely a pawn, one created by a power far greater than the world has experienced before. Aasarak has the Box of Death, and has used it."

Adrianna felt a chill crawl up her spine. She glanced at Dinim to find that his expression had turned stony. The mage came closer, squinting and scrutinizing them with his rheumy eye. He examined Dinim only cursorily, but stopped in front of Adrianna. He opened his good eye wide, and the effect of one eye clear and the other clouded by cataract was eerie.

"Ahhhh," the old man exclaimed. "I know you. How did you come to be so far from home, my dear? I am sure your mother misses you."

Adrianna stiffened. *The rumors are right; this man is indeed crazy. How could he possibly know me? I've never met him before. And he obviously doesn't know my mother, otherwise he would know she's dead. For a man who knows everything he seems not to know much at all.*

"My mother is dead, Master."

"Ah yes, such a shame it was. So much potential wasted."

Adrianna suppressed a sigh. They had only been there a few minutes, but already she was ready to leave. There was nothing this man could tell them.

"Please, Master. Have you any information that can help us against our enemy? Even now he hunts us, and he is close," said Dinim.

"I know how close he is!" snarled Paxil. But then in a calmer voice, "And

177

yes, I suppose I can help you." Paxil turned away from Adrianna, making his way over to one of the messy shelves. He shuffled some things around a bit. "While the master has been busy, the creation has been in pursuit of a personal vendetta. Such is the way of Azmathous. Revenge is their priority. Aasarak should have known that, the fool." Paxil withdrew a small box from the clutter. He then walked over to Dinim and handed it to him.

Dinim slowly opened the box. Inside, nestled upon a bed of dark velvet, was a bronzed ring engraved with silvery whorls. Dinim picked it up and examined it closely. Then his eyes widened in wonderment. "Is this what I think it is?"

Paxil smiled. "Probably. But I am not a mind reader, you know." The old man chortled for a moment, and then continued. "What do you think it is?"

"This is the Ring of Aboleth."

Paxil cackled again. "Right you are. You are a smart one, well read."

Dinim frowned. "Are you sure you want to give this up?"

Paxil shrugged his skinny shoulders. "It is for a good cause, eh?"

All Dinim could do was nod. Adrianna remained silent. *What is so great about this ring? And why does Dinim seem so hesitant? If the ring can help us, he should take it.*

"But Master, it is the only one in existence. How did you come by it?"

Once more the old man shrugged. "I don't even remember anymore. I have so many things, and so many tales to go with them, they all seem to mesh together now. You know, old age and all."

Dinim nodded. "Thank you. This... this is a great gift. You must think us trustworthy."

"We all must put our faith in something. I am old. I don't have much of a future. But countless others *do* have one. You and your comrades have the power to bring about a new era. That, my friend, is worth fighting for, worth believing in, worth trusting someone to make the right decisions."

"But what if we aren't strong enough?"

Paxil's expression saddened. "Then the world as we hope it to be will never exist. Strength comes not only from the body or from the mind, but from the heart."

Adrianna stared at the old man. Suddenly he didn't seem so crazy anymore. He spoke with a wisdom he'd learned through the ages. *Who knows how long this man has lived? And he is so old, it's difficult to even tell his race. Is he faelin, human, or something in between?*

"How do we fight someone who is already dead?" she asked. "We know he has unfathomable strength, the ability to instill mindless fear, and exaggerated attributes he possessed as a mortal man."

Paxil turned to her. "Just because he is dead doesn't mean he can't be killed again. Thane is not a god. He is a construct, one created by an even greater evil. As a creature of darkness, he will gather most of his strength and powers during the night. However, even then he can be destroyed."

Adrianna nodded, hoping for more. She was disappointed when the old man clapped his hands together.

"Come, your companions await you. I have helped you all I can." Paxil walked towards the door and Dinim and Adrianna followed. When he opened it, the light from outside almost blinded them for a moment. Dinim turned. "Thank you, Master. I hope that we will be able to meet your expectations."

"I have no doubt," replied the old man, glancing at Adrianna. Then he was waving them away. "Come again sometime when you don't need me to give you anything. I like companionship every now and again, you know."

Adrianna and Dinim waved back to the man, then walked towards their larian. They untied the beasts and began to lead them away. They turned back to the cabin to have one last look, but the house was gone, as though it had never been there.

The two made their way back to the group. They walked side-by-side, their larian trailing behind. Dinim was silent and she felt the tension radiating off him. A distance had suddenly grown between them and she missed their easy-natured camaraderie. Even now he seemed un-approachable, but she spoke anyway, hoping to bridge the gap.

"What a strange old man. Now I know why he lives so far removed from the rest of civilization."

"Yes," Dinim agreed. "Not to mention that he probably doesn't want to be robbed. Did you see all of those books? They were probably originals! And all of those artifacts– who knows what he had hidden in there." Dinim stroked his chin thoughtfully. "Well, on second thought, Paxil probably isn't concerned with being robbed. It would be effortless for him to keep others out, especially with that *Cloaking* spell he has on the house."

"He said he was expecting us. So he blocked the spell for a while so we could find the place?"

Dinim nodded. "Most likely."

For a few moments they walked in silence, then she remembered the ring. "Dinim, tell me about the ring Paxil gave us. Do you really think it can help against Thane?"

Dinim frowned and turned to her. "We aren't going to use that ring."

Adrianna frowned in return. "Why not? Paxil seemed to think it could be of use to us."

Dinim sighed heavily. "Paxil is old and crazy. He doesn't realize that none of us is strong enough to wield the ring."

"Tell me, Dinim. What does the ring do? How do you know so much about it?"

He looked away and stared ahead at the path. "It's called the Ring of

Aboleth. I learned about it several years ago while I was studying under Master Tallachienan. It is an object of great power, and no one seems to know exactly where it comes from or how it was created. I think that Tallachienan has some ideas, but he would never share them with me."

"But what does it do?"

Dinim turned to look at her again. "They say the ring has been infused with the power of life itself."

Adrianna raised an eyebrow. "The ring is alive?"

"No, but it has the power to bring life forth."

"You say that as though it is a bad thing."

"Well, it can be. As mortals, it should not be up to us to decide upon the emergence of life."

Adrianna smirked. "But Dinim, we do that every day. We have killed men, caused the life to leave their bodies. And every day, somewhere there is a woman giving birth, bringing new life into the world."

Dinim frowned again and stopped walking. "No, this is different."

Adrianna stopped as well and turned towards him. "Well explain it to me, then."

"Just imagine if a bad man had this ring in his possession. What might he do with it? He could perhaps use it to bring back the lives of his companions lost in battle, or perhaps countless others and make himself an army of warriors who are beholden to him. Perhaps he would bring to life things that were never meant to have it, such as a sword or a cloak.

"The point is, the ring can be used to do great evil, and even one with the best intentions can do wrong. Great power like that can be enticing, and can make one thirst for more. Once started, one may never be able to stop, the temptation too difficult to ignore."

Adrianna shook her head. "But the ring can do great good as well, Dinim. Our mission isn't just about us. It's about all the people Thane won't hesitate to kill if we don't destroy him. If the ring can help us do that, then isn't it worth the risk?"

He pursed his lips. "No."

Her tone was exasperated. "Why not?"

"Because the temptation may take us over the edge. We would then be a liability. We could put countless others in danger, and then what purpose would the ring have served? None. We would be right back where we started."

Adrianna crossed her arms over her chest and stuck out her lower lip. "I don't share your opinion."

Vexed, Dinim gave an explosive sigh and threw his hands in the air. "So what? What do you know anyway? You are but a girl, thinking that everything is black and white, like words in ink on a page. Well Adrianna, let me break it to you. The world is in color! This is not a child's game. The ring is dangerous, and not intended for ones like us."

"Why did you take it from Paxil then?" Adrianna spat. "You think you are so high and mighty, that when you use it yourself one day, you won't succumb to the same temptation as others?"

"No," Dinim shouted in return. "I took it because it was a gift. When next I see Master Tallachienan, I will give the ring to him."

Adrianna stepped closer to him. "And in the meantime, you are going to allow us to risk our lives? You know what we're up against. So does Paxil, and that is why he entrusted the ring to us. How many of us will die in this fight?"

He stepped back. "Shut your face. You have no idea what could happen. Whoever wields the ring– they could become like another Aasarak, making the decision of who lives and who dies. That kind of power could turn a good person into one who does only evil things."

"You are being a fool, Dinim," she said, stepping close to him again. "If you never take a chance in life, how do you ever expect to win? The ring is not inherently evil, only it's possible for a person to do evil things with it." Adrianna's tone became more emphatic. "We could anchor the wielder, give him the support that he needs to return to us."

Dinim shook his head. "No, I will not allow it. I understand your argument, but it just isn't worth it. We will fight Thane as though we knew nothing about the ring."

"I am not asking your permission, Dinim. This is my mission and I say we use it."

Dinim smirked malevolently. "This isn't your mission anymore, Adrianna. It has become everyone's mission. And *I* say we will never use this ring."

Adrianna seethed. She couldn't believe Dinim refused to see beyond his faulty reasoning. "Damn, you are a coward. I should have seen it from the start. I can't believe–"

Dinim snorted. "*I'm* a coward? What a joke. *You* are the weak link, Adrianna. You are a little girl playing in an adult's world. You are always afraid, hoping that the rest of the group will step up for you. I have yet to see you really make your own decisions. You have no confidence, and even the rest of the group has wondered if you are up for a fight."

Adrianna took in the scathing words. She stepped back, the rictus of rage that took over his features making her nervous. Her anger was still there, but it was tempered by the little ring of truth she heard in his words.

"You are a little idiot, Adrianna. You have no idea of the gamble you would be taking to use that ring. But do you care? No. You can barely see past your own selfish desires. You would take one threat and exchange it for another, possibly more malignant one, just so you can be finished with your responsibility. Well, this is what I think about you and your dung-eaten

181

mission!"

Adrianna heard the murmuring of a spell being cast. She felt the shift in the air around her, the answer of magic to one who could summon it. She stared at Dinim. His hands made symbols in the space before him and he reached into his pouch of spell components. *What is he doing?* Adrianna looked around, trying to figure out why he would cast a spell. She saw nothing out of the ordinary, but then began to get a feeling of imminent danger.

Adrianna looked back at Dinim. The expression on his face was terrible, all semblance of reason gone. He looked like a crazy man. Suddenly she felt a burning sensation on her upper arm. She slapped her hand over it, feeling the shape of the golden serpent beneath the fabric of her blouse.

Then the spell was cast.

Adrianna watched the energy as it raced towards her, and she recoiled in shock. Suddenly all she could see was a rainbow of vibrant color. The spell struck her and she was thrown back, back, back... An impact thrust the air from her chest and darkness reigned.

She was dead, and it was her friend who had killed her.

"Adria! Adrianna!" The shout came from behind her. She stirred and felt the grass beneath her fingertips. That was strange. If she was dead, why would she be lying on the ground? "Adrianna?" The voice was louder now, more insistent. She opened her eyes and her vision swam, the sky above her swirling about crazily. Then the face of Anya was there too, tilting this way and that. "Adrianna, are you all right?"

"I... I think so," she replied, sitting upright.

"I saw the eruption. What the Hells was it?"

Adrianna's eyes widened and she pushed Anya to the side, searching desperately. Dinim was standing where she remembered seeing him last. He was staring at his hands, an expression of bewilderment on his face. Anya turned to look where Adrianna was staring. "Is he all right? What happened here?"

Adrianna quickly stood up and gestured to Anya. "Come on, we have to get back to the others."

Frowning, Anya contemplated her solemnly. "Where are your larian? You left with two of them this morning."

"They must have been frightened away by the spell." Adrianna turned and began to walk.

"The spell? Adrianna, what's going on here?"

Anya grabbed her arm but Adrianna tore herself out of the other woman's grasp and regarded her intently. "I don't want to take the time to explain this to you right now. Let's just get back to the group."

Anya held up her hands. "All right, fine. But what about Dinim?"

Adrianna cast Anya an intense glance, one that brooked no argument.

"Leave him."

Anya stared at her for a moment and then began to walk. "The group is this way."

Adrianna fell in behind Sirion's sister, her mind in a state of confusion and turmoil. He had meant to kill her. Dinim hadn't just cast a light spell to merely frighten her. He had smitten her with a high level incantation. Adrianna rubbed at her upper arm, the pain still there. The serpent rested right over the sore spot. She still couldn't believe what had happened. Maybe it wasn't Dinim back there. Maybe it was another doppelganger and the real Dinim was trapped somewhere, needing their help.

After a short while of walking, Anya and Adrianna reached the group. The larian were loaded and ready for travel. Dartanyen stood up and approached them when they strode into camp. "So, did you find out anything useful?" He looked beyond her and Anya. "Where is Dinim?"

"He's still back there," Adrianna said in a low voice.

Dartanyen looked back to her and frowned. "Back where?"

Adrianna gestured behind her. Anya put her hands on her hips and stared at her with an expression of agitation. Dartanyen glanced from one woman to the next. "What in the Nine Hells is going on?"

"That's what I want to know," said Anya.

"What's up? Did we find out anything that can help us?" asked Sirion as he walked up to them.

"I saw an eruption of... of some kind of energy," said Anya. "I ran towards it, afraid that perhaps someone was in trouble. I saw Adrianna lying on the ground. I thought she was hurt."

Dartanyen turned back to Adrianna. "Did something happen?"

Adrianna nodded and swallowed heavily. "Dinim attacked me. He cast a spell. I don't know why I'm still alive. We left Dinim back there, where it happened."

Dartanyen and Sirion looked at one another and then began to head in the direction Adrianna indicated. "Armond and Zorg, grab your weapons! We have trouble," shouted Dartanyen.

The two men jumped up with their weapons in hand, running to catch up with Dartanyen and Sirion. Adrianna turned to Anya. "I'm sorry. I just wanted to get as far away from him as soon as I could."

Anya patted her on the shoulder. "It's all right. I would have felt the same way."

Tianna watched the men jog into the trees. She just shook her head and continued perusal of her herb pouches, continuing her inventory. Moments later, a commotion started coming from the direction the men had taken. She heard a few shouts and then, "No, don't touch me! I'm fine!" Dinim stumbled into the camp, his hands in the air before him. Beside him were Sirion and Dartanyen, followed by Armond and Zorg.

Sirion glanced quickly about until his eyes alighted on Tianna. "I think he might be sick."

Tianna frowned and approached.

"I tell you, I'm fine," he argued.

She put a hand on Dinim's brow, and her frown deepened. "Sirion, you're right. His skin is damp and he has a fever."

"Bring him over here," said Sorn, lying out his bedroll.

Tianna nodded, and once Sirion had him situated there, she went to her larian to get her medicine bag and water pouch. She poured some water into a cup, and then sprinkled some greenish powder into it. She swirled it about until the contents were mixed, and then handed it to Dinim.

He took the cup and drank as though he hadn't had water for days, not even bothering to ask what she'd put in it. When he was finished, Tianna set the cup aside and took his injured hand in hers. Dinim jerked the hand back. "I'm fine, Tianna. Let's just go. We have a lot of ground to cover today."

"Dinim, I need to see your hand. It might be infected. That could be the cause of your fever."

Dinim rolled his eyes and slowly held out the hand. Tianna slowly removed the bandages, and then inspected the wounds. The deep lacerations were red, but not infected. She looked closer at the wounds, seeing exactly how deep they went. The muscle had been deeply penetrated, almost as though he'd fallen on something very sharp. "Dinim, tell me again how you got these cuts."

"I got hit by the wyvern, and I fell. You should know that."

"But what did you fall on?"

"Some type of wretched bush." Dinim frowned. "Or maybe it was a vine. I don't remember."

She became still and regarded him intently. "Did the vine have thorns?"

Dinim was thoughtful. "Yes, as a matter of fact, I think it did. I could swear they were blue, but I know that can't be right. I've never heard of a plant with blue thorns." He chuckled mirthlessly.

Tianna took a deep breath. "Dinim, I think you've been poisoned."

"What?"

"The hybanthis vine makes toxic secretions. When the thorns penetrate the skin, the poison enters the open wounds. The effects are varied, but usually cause a general feeling of illness and a fever. Some people even have a heightened sense of emotion."

"I suppose I haven't really been feeling very well. I've been having a lot of strange dreams, and my thoughts..."

Tianna nodded. "Yes. That night after the skirmish I noticed you were a bit testy. I attributed it to the fact that you were probably in some amount of pain. I had no idea that you had been poisoned."

Dinim frowned and looked at the ground for a moment. "Could this be why I cast the spell at Adrianna today?"

"What?" Tianna looked at him in shock.

He looked into her eyes. "I cast a spell. I didn't mean to. Well, actually I did, but it was almost like I couldn't control myself..."

"Dinim, what kind of spell was it?" she interrupted. "It was just a minor one, right?" Tianna looked at him, her eyes pleading with him to tell her that it was a lesser incantation.

"No. It was one of the most powerful spells I know."

Tianna put a hand over her mouth. "Oh gods."

With eyes full of devastation, Dinim took her other hand. "Tianna, you've got to help me. Please cure me of this."

"The toxin can take several days to leave the body."

"I implore you, tell me it was only because of the poison that I attacked my friend."

Tianna shook her head. "I can't. The effects of the poison only act upon what is already there. Whatever you were feeling towards Adrianna was of your conception. The anger that was there was purely yours. The poison only magnified this emotion, making it so that you were unable to deal with the intensity of it." Tianna swallowed heavily. "Then you reacted in the best way you knew how."

Dinim stared off into the space before him, his eyes wide with the horror of what he had done. "I can't believe she is still alive. All I remember is, for that one moment, I wanted to kill her..."

From his seat on her larian, Sirion turned around to look at her, his lips curving into a smile before turning back to the path before him. A flutter swept through her for a moment and she dug her fingers into the thick fur around Dramati's neck. Sirion had insisted she ride him, for the corubis would protect her with his life if need be. Sirion didn't trust Dinim in their midst, not while the poison coursed through his veins. Until it was proven otherwise, he wanted Adrianna as far from him as possible.

It wasn't long before the group was stopping for the night. Adrianna helped Amethyst as best she could with the animals. The girl had learned fast and needed very little guidance now. It was a good thing because there were more lloryk and larian to tend since the Wildrunners joined them. When they were finished, Adrianna went to sit on her bedroll. Despite the cold, she stripped off her blouse and tunic to look at the golden serpent circling her arm. Red skin peeked from around the ornament surrounding it, and she raised a brow. *So, that's reason it's been hurting so much today.*

Adrianna bit her lip as she tried moving the serpent. Much to her surprise, the metal easily gave. The thing slithered to a new location higher up on her arm and, once settled in its new location, regarded her from sparkling ruby eyes. Adrianna stroked the smooth scales before focusing on the burn. It was an angry red, and the skin was peeling away from it. She touched it gingerly with her forefinger and cringed.

"Adria, what are you doing? Its freezing out here!" Sheridana walked over and crouched beside her. "Ouch! What happened?"

She gestured to the serpent. "When I was struck by Dinim's spell, my arm burned. I think the serpent caused it."

Sheridana nodded. "I agree. I believe it's what saved your life."

Adrianna gave a brief nod.

"Well, it looks like it might get infected. I'm getting Tianna."

"No, I'll be fine. I don't want to bother her."

"You can't be serious! You still won't talk to her?"

Adrianna threw up her hands. "She won't talk to me either!"

"Well, that's ending now, because I'm going to get her."

Adrianna cursed beneath her breath and watched her infuriating sister get the healer. Tianna picked up her medicine bag and came over right away. Her expression shifted to hurt when she saw her arm.

"Why didn't you tell me sooner?" asked Tianna.

"I didn't know it was like this until just a few moments ago."

Tianna nodded and sat down beside her. She dug around inside the bag until she found the jar she was looking for. She opened it and smeared some of the contents onto her fingers. "This will hurt as I apply it."

Adrianna crinkled her nose. "It stinks."

Tianna's eyes sparkled. "It's supposed to."

She smiled and rolled her eyes, looking away as Tianna rubbed the salve onto the burn. She saw Sirion staring from the other side of the encampment and when he saw that she'd noticed, he gave her an approving nod.

When Tianna was finished, Adrianna lay back on the bedroll. Her thoughts shifted to Dinim and her eyes sought him out. He sat on his own bedroll, his shoulders slumped and his eyes downcast. His words continued to echo through her mind and she dwelled on the way her comrades perceived her. *Did he say those things just to hurt me, or are they true? I know they like me, but that isn't what worries me. I want them to see me as an equal in battle, and I just don't know if they do.*

Early the next morning as the group prepared to travel, Tianna approached Adrianna with the stinky salve. "I know it smells bad, but it will heal the burn in next to no time." She frowned. "Did this object give you the burn?" she asked, pointing to the serpent.

Adrianna nodded. "When Dinim began to cast his spell, I felt a burning sensation on my arm. Thinking back on it, I've come to realize it must have protected me from the spell because I became surrounded by a protective shell." Then she frowned. "But I really don't understand it. I've been hit with other spells before, and the serpent didn't react to those at all."

"Perhaps it's simply the particular spell that Dinim cast. Maybe it protects the wearer from spells of a certain type or caliber."

"Yes, perhaps," Adrianna conceded softly.

Tianna watched her intently for a moment. "You know he was poisoned."

Adrianna nodded. "I know."

"He's not entirely to blame. The effects of the hybanthis often make one feel overwhelmed."

Adrianna gave a sigh. "I know. I heard your explanation." She shook her head. "But I can't entirely absolve him of his transgression. He cast a lethal spell, Tianna. Without this talisman, I would have died. Despite the poison, there was a part of Dinim that was still there, a reasoning part of him. Yet, he cast the spell anyway. I can't just forget that."

Tianna nodded. "You're right. In your position I would probably feel the same, but I know Dinim deeply regrets what he did."

Feeling the tears beginning to build, Adrianna shook her head and lowered her eyes to the ground. "It's just not enough."

Tianna only patted her shoulder, and walked away.

The group traveled another day and camped at the entrance into the Ratik Pass. The cold was made worse by the winds that swept through the cleft in the mountains, chilling them in their thickest cloaks. Everyone huddled near each other and the fires for warmth. The pervading attitude was solemn, many of them remembering the last time they'd been there. They had barely escaped alive the first time, and now here they were, about to plod through it once more.

Making a concerted effort, Adrianna stopped scratching at the peeling flesh on her arm. A volume rested on her lap, one she'd borrowed from Dinim before he'd almost killed her. She tried to focus to the page open before her, tried to read the words. But her preoccupied mind understood nothing of what they said. At first, no one knew about the Ring of Aboleth, save for herself and Dinim. When asked questions about their meeting with Paxil, its existence was never mentioned. Neither she nor Dinim spoke about the ring, and it continued to lie, waiting, somewhere within Dinim's leather belt-pouch.

Until tonight.

The evening meal was eaten and everyone began to settle down for the night. Sirion continued to sit at the fire with Dramati, talking to Sorn and

Triath. Amethyst and Triath were usually the first to take watch, so it wasn't unusual to see her still awake and walking about camp. No one seemed to pay the girl any heed when she seated herself beside Adrianna on the bedroll.

For a few moments there was silence. Adrianna felt her chest tighten with the enormity of what she was about to do. She spoke in a low voice. "Amethyst, there is something I am hoping you can do for me. It's something I would never ask you to do unless I felt it to be of utmost importance."

The girl leaned forward slightly. "What is it?"

"The morning Dinim and I went to see Paxil, the old man gave us something. It's a ring, a magical ring. It has a power that we may be able to help us against Thane."

Amethyst frowned. "Why didn't you tell us about this before?"

Adrianna lowered her voice even more. "Because the ring is the reason why Dinim and I started to argue. He feels the ring is too powerful to use, and that it may cause more harm than good. However, I feel it is worth the risk if it will save the lives of people in this group."

"He has the ring, doesn't he?"

Adrianna gave a silent nod.

Amethyst's voice was solemn, "You want me to get the ring from him."

"Yes. Dinim is not willing to use the ring. He didn't even tell Dartanyen or Triath about it. I'm afraid that if we don't at least try, and people die in the battle against Thane, I will never be able to forgive myself."

Amethyst nodded again. "I will get the ring for you, Adria."

"Are you certain? You feel the same way that I do, then?"

"I trust you, Adrianna. I know that you would never do something to bring harm to us. I believe you will make the right decision."

She stared at Amethyst, a lump beginning to form in her throat. "Thank you. That means a lot to me."

The girl grinned. "Give me a couple of days and I will have the ring for you."

"All right. Let me tell you where I think it might be..."

My Immortal

T raversing the pass was onerous, and travel patterns changed with the shift in environment. Riding astride quickly became a thing of the past as the animals began to have trouble maintaining their footing on the rocky path. Instead, the beasts were loaded with the much lighter burden of travel packs and other equipment. Sirion and Anya didn't scout ahead as much, and stayed with the rest of the group off and on throughout the day. The nightly watch was split into four sessions instead of three to accommodate everyone's heightened fatigue.

Dawn had barely lit the sky when everyone was packing their bedrolls for another day of travel. The chilly air permeated Adrianna's clothes and she tucked her winter cloak more snugly around her. She turned when she heard someone getting everyone's attention. It was Dinim.

"I just wanted everyone to know I've been studying a spell that can enable me to enchant weaponry. It will help us against the Azmathous."

Dartanyen's eyes were bright with enthusiasm. "I noticed you've been reading a lot. This is great!"

"Maybe you can try out your spell on Zorg's sword!" suggested Armond.

Dinim nodded. "Everyone will need at least one magic-infused weapon to use against the Azmathous. Normal weaponry will hardly touch them."

"You needn't worry about mine," said Sheridana, holding up her blades. "Destroyer is set and ready to go."

Armond hesitated, sending Sheridana an inexplicable glance before indicating his own blades. "I'm good too."

"Amethyst could probably use something on her daggers," said Dartanyen. "And I could use something on my new arrows."

Before long the group was moving through the pass. They stopped at midday to rest and eat a small meal before continuing on. For the first time since their argument, Dinim approached Adrianna. He sat beside her on the ground, and when she couldn't ignore him any longer, she turned to him. He stared at her out of troubled eyes. Dark smudges characterized the flesh beneath his eyelids and the lines of his face were deeper than she remembered. Her breath caught in her throat and she swiftly stood.

Dinim followed. "Adrianna, wait. I won't ask you to forget what I've done, but please consider–"

She held up a hand and he stopped. Her voice was quiet. "Please don't do this. Just... just stay away from me." She turned and walked away from him. Dinim didn't pursue her, and she was glad of it. His nearness made her stomach turn, the hurt of what he'd done still too strong for her to accept.

That evening the group set camp early. Zorg handed his blade over to Dinim, who then began to work on the enchantment. Adrianna regarded him for a moment as she sat on her bedroll removed from the rest of the group. She had her spellbook open and in her lap, pretending to read what was written there. But this time, she didn't even attempt to look at the words, instead focusing on something else. Within the crook of the binding rested the golden Ring of Aboleth.

Adrianna touched the glittering artifact with the tip of her forefinger. It had a rare beauty, the three interconnected shards of onyx surrounded by at least a dozen diamonds. Even with that slight caress she could feel the power nestled deep within. *Dinim is right to be wary of it. Even me, with my relatively narrow scope, can sense that I can be sucked away by the power of this ring and never return. Dear gods, I'm afraid, but I have so little choice. Thane's power is great, and I... we... need something to counteract it.*

Adrianna looked up from the ring and caught Amethyst's gaze as the girl regarded her from across the encampment. Barely an hour ago, Amethyst had solemnly presented her with the ring. It was only then Adrianna glimpsed how much it had taken for her to steal the ring from Dinim. Both knew it was wrong to use one's skills against a member of one's company, yet they had done it anyway. Amethyst was feeling the weight of her transgression, and Adrianna felt guilty for placing her in that position. However, Adrianna couldn't accept full blame. Of her own free will, Amethyst had chosen to steal the ring and bequeath it to her.

With a slight nod Adrianna sought to dissipate Amethyst's disquiet. She then took in the rest of the group: Sabian studying his books, Tianna concocting another strange potion for them to drink, Anya and Dartanyen plucking the feathers of the meal they had procured, and Sorn and Triath erecting one of their tents for the night. Adrianna took the ring in hand. Now that it was in her possession, she needed to tell the rest of the group about it. They deserved to know, and they needed to have a say in the decision to use it against Thane. She feared their reaction towards the fact that she and Dinim had kept the existence of the ring a secret, and dissension over whether or not to use the ring would possibly cause a rift in their ranks. Dinim had shared some very good points with her during their argument, and she could see others sharing his views. This bothered her, for the group could ill afford to be divided now. They were close to their confrontation with Thane, and the rift could cause the group to lose cohesion in battle. *Maybe I should make the decision by myself. I don't like the idea, but is there really another way? Besides, wasn't it Dinim who said I need to step forward and make my own decisions?* Adrianna frowned. *Am I letting my anger with him cloud my reason? I can't allow myself to do that because I'll be doing myself and my comrades the greatest of disservices.*

"Adrianna, are you all right?"

She closed her hand over the ring as Sirion seated himself beside her. She glanced up at him, noting the expression of concern on his face. Adrianna nodded and looked back down at her book. "Yes, I'm fine," she lied.

Sirion's frown deepened. "You don't look fine."

"I think I'm just tired."

Sirion nodded and enveloped her hand in his. For the briefest of moments a thought went through her mind. *We are holding the ring together. What if the wielder has an anchor, one keep her separate from the sheer magnitude of the power of the ring? It was one of my arguments to Dinim. He seemed to think it was a dumb idea.*

"You know I'm here for you." He gently brushed her face with his fingertips.

She felt a tingle race through her body, an answer to his caress. She smiled and put her head on his shoulder. "I know."

Sirion put an arm around her and held her close against him. His embrace slowly began to settle the turmoil in her mind. She had a difficult decision to make, but it didn't have to be at this very moment. Sirion was a strong and solid warmth against her, and she felt safe. With her other hand she threaded her fingers through his, and he gave a little squeeze. Her thoughts leaped forward to the nighttime when they would share some privacy under the cover of darkness. She imagined the fiery passion of Sirion's kisses and her body tingled again. She shoved aside ruminations of the ring.

She would think about it tomorrow.

Adrianna wrapped the winter cloak more tightly about herself. It was getting colder each day they spent in the pass. Not only were they going higher, but they were getting closer to the cold season. Soon they would encounter cold rains, and possibly even snow as they continued upward. Adrianna pressed herself closer to Sheridana's side, seeking the warmth of another warm body. Her sister passed her a pair of gloves and Adrianna took them gratefully as she pulled up the fur-lined hood of the cloak.

Once waking that morning, the burden of the decision she needed to make descended. For most of the day it weighed on her mind, but she kept returning to the same series of thoughts. She needed to tell the group about the ring, and she needed to do it soon. However, she would insist upon its use. Dinim would repudiate her, but she would consider her next course of action when she had an idea about how the rest of the group felt about it. If everyone was entirely against it, she most definitely wouldn't use it. But if there was a split...well, she would have another decision to make.

Late afternoon shifted into early evening. A suitable site was found and the group stopped to prepare camp. Having decided to enchant some of Dartanyen's arrows, Dinim settled down to study his books. His work with Zorg's blade had taken most of the previous night, but with the break of dawn, it was complete. He only got a couple of hours' sleep before the group started to move for the day. Now he seemed utterly drained. The energy it had taken for him to harness the magic to enchant the weapon had taken everything out of him, not to mention the lack of sleep. However, Zorg had been greatly pleased with his blade, and Sabian had congratulated him on a job well done. Dartanyen and Triath agreed, clapping him heartily on the back. Dinim smiled and took it all in good stride, pleased by his accomplishment. Once, she may have been happy for him. Now she didn't care.

Once again, Adrianna sat on her bedroll, removed from the group. Everyone had eaten their evening meal and they rested around the fire. Adrianna held the Ring of Aboleth in her hand, the chain from which she had suspended it twined between her fingers. Now was the time.

Adrianna stood up, and Amethyst's gaze swung to meet hers. The girl squared her shoulders for the events about to unfurl and gave a nod indicating her support. Adrianna steeled herself for the possible battle, and subsequent decision she would have to make. She approached the circle of her comrades seated about the fire. There was a space made for her, but she ignored it, continuing to stand. People started looking up at her, and after a few more moments she had everyone's attention, her expression telling them she had something to say.

"I have a confession to make." Adrianna paused and everyone continued to watch her. She noticed puzzled expressions on a couple of faces, but she continued. "There was something that Dinim and I didn't tell you about our visit with Master Paxil."

Adrianna saw Dinim's expression turn into a bewildered frown. She noticed his body tense, as well as those of some of the other men. "Master Paxil gave us something, an object that can possibly help in our fight against Thane."

"Why didn't you tell us about this before?" Dartanyen's question echoed that of Amethyst just a couple of nights ago.

Adrianna looked from Dartanyen, to Dinim, and then back to Dartanyen. "Because it is the reason why Dinim and I argued after our visit with Paxil. It's the reason why he cast that spell."

For a moment there was silence. Zorg glanced around before speaking. "'Tis alright. You're tellin' us now. What is it?"

Once again Adrianna glanced at Dinim, saw him digging around inside his leather pouch. She opened her hand to reveal the ring lying in her palm. "It's the Ring of Aboleth."

Dinim pulled the small box out of his pouch. His gaze was icy as he realized the ring wasn't inside, and he stood from his place. "Adrianna, I can't believe you have done this. I can't believe you stole the ring from me."

Dartanyen also stood, his frown deepening. "Adrianna, you actually *stole* this ring from Dinim?"

"No, *I* stole it," said Amethyst, also rising.

Dartanyen glanced from Dinim, to Amethyst, and then to Adrianna.

Adrianna felt the tension rise, but she couldn't stop now. "I asked her to steal it for me. Master Paxil gave us the ring so we could win our fight against Thane. Dinim feels we should not use it, the power being far too great for any of us to wield safely. However, I have a differing opinion."

"Adrianna, you don't know what you're doing. Give the ring back to me," said Dinim holding out his hand.

Adrianna shook her head. "No Dinim. No matter what the risk, I believe we should use the ring. It's not a decision for you to make alone."

"Well it's not a decision for you to make either," interjected Sabian.

Adrianna nodded. "I know."

"Then why did you have it stolen?" asked Armond.

"Because I was afraid that, upon asking, Dinim still would not relinquish it."

"All right," said Dartanyen. "Let's get down to the point. What does the ring do?"

Dinim's voice was rough. "It infuses the wielder with the ability to bring forth life. I know that it sounds like a good thing, but it's not necessarily that. The power is addictive and can take away the wielder's ability to reason properly. The person could go mad, using the ring to perform acts that seem right in his twisted mind, but are actually of the greatest evil." Dinim turned back to Adrianna, his voice desperate. "Please, give me the ring. It isn't worth it."

Adrianna stepped back from the circle. "It *is* worth it, Dinim," she said, her voice rising in pitch. "This ring could save lives... all of our lives. Doesn't that mean anything to you?"

His voice also rose. "Of course it does, but that may not be all that happens."

Sirion finally rose from the fire. "Adrianna... Dinim, let's talk about this."

"No!" spat Dinim. "You don't understand. The wielder could become lost in the power of the ring. There may be no turning back–"

"But what if you're wrong?" Tears began to fall down Adrianna's face. "What if there *is* a way to come back? What if–"

"Just give me the damned ring!" Dinim lunged towards Adrianna, only to be caught by Armond. Frantically, she scrambled out of reach. Her ankle twisted, and with a cry she fell. Very slowly, Triath began to make towards her, his hands outstretched. "It's all right. We will talk about this. Why don't you let me have the ring..."

Adrianna shook her head and scooted further away. *Triath will take the ring and there will be nothing left, nothing that can save us from the doom awaiting us. We have such a small chance against my father. I don't know how much more the ring has to offer, but it has to be better than nothing.*

Adrianna unfurled the fist clenched around the ring. She stared at it for a moment, and then back up at Triath. Behind him, she saw everyone was up in arms, upset about what had just been revealed. She could hear none of what was being said despite the volume of the voices. Adrianna took the golden artifact between her thumb and forefinger, gazed at it with all the faith she had within her. "Adrianna, no..."

She heard Triath call out as she slipped the Ring of Aboleth over her finger.

Then she heard no sound at all.

The rush was all-encompassing, sweeping through her veins and touching every part of her in a single burst of fire. She felt energized like never before, felt the magic all around her, migrating to her without the barest hint of beckoning.

Then she began to hear again, to see, and to touch. She felt the ground beneath her, saw her comrades where they stood, staring, less than a farlo away.

"Oh gods, what have you done?"

Adrianna heard Dinim's voice and turned towards it. The expression on his face was one of fear and disbelief. She picked herself up from the ground, dusting off her cloak and trousers. She felt her heart pounding in her chest, the accelerated rate of her breaths. "I feel so... so strange." She looked down at her hands, saw the ring circling her middle finger.

"Adria, are you all right?"

She turned to Sirion. His brow was creased with worry. She nodded. "Yes, I think so."

He put his arms around her and she leaned into him. It was done. She wielded the Ring of Aboleth. She might have made a grave mistake, but she hoped she hadn't. Their future rested on it.

The group traveled silently through the next day, everyone keeping to their own thoughts. The events of the previous evening weighed on everyone's minds, in particular, the sacrifice that had been made. Dartanyen was worried about Adrianna, and what exactly she had done when she put that ring on her finger. They had entered a smooth portion of the pass, and they were able to ride astride. He allowed himself to fall back until finally he was riding beside Dinim and Tianna. Both turned as he sidled in between them.

Dartanyen finally spoke. "What's going to happen?"

Dinim shook his head. "I honestly don't know."

"All right. What *could* happen?"

"Adrianna has placed herself at great risk, and possibly the rest of us too. She may not be strong enough to withstand the power of the ring, and we will have a situation on our hands when the battle with Thane is through."

"Situation. What type of situation?" Dartanyen growled in frustration. "Speak plainly with me, Dinim."

"Adrianna may become so wrapped up in the power she discovers in the ring, she may be unable to return from it. She could begin to make her own decisions of life and death, and ultimately become an even greater threat than Thane."

"How do we stop that from happening?"

Dinim frowned. "We can't."

Dartanyen regarded Dinim intensely. "There must be a way."

"If there is one, I don't know what it is."

"Damnation!"

"I'm sorry. I wish there was something–"

Dartanyen shook his head angrily. "If you are going to feel sorry for someone, feel sorry for Adrianna! If this 'situation' comes about, we might very well be seeing her last days." He kicked his larian and galloped back to the front of the group. He saw Sirion approaching to give them the word on where they would camp for the night, and rode to meet him. They traveled for another three quarters of an hour before they came to a place where the pass began to widen. Then they reached a small glade. The place was not as rocky as most of the rest of the pass, and several trees had managed to take root and grow.

Adrianna followed suit as everyone dismounted and prepared to make camp. The winds had increased, and the narrowed space offered by the pass increased their strength. From where she stood near Sheridana, Adrianna looked over at Sirion across the clearing. The winds whipped the hair about her face, and she pulled it aside to see him staring at her. His expression was solemn with an undertone of fear. She knew it was because of the ring. She caught his gaze and instantly saw the love reflected there, tempered by sadness. She was about to go to him when she was nudged in the ribs. Adrianna turned to her sister.

"Give us help with this fire?"

Adrianna nodded, and with one last glance at Sirion she knelt beside

Tianna on the other side of Sheridana, trying to offer a block from the wind. The air didn't smell like rain, but dark clouds were fast approaching and it was getting colder. Dartanyen, Triath, Armond, and Sorn were attempting to pitch the two tents that they had purchased before leaving Driscol. Beyond them, Zorg and Naemmious were holding the ropes of the lloryk and larian while Amethyst was looking through the bags for the picks needed to remove the rocks from their feet. Nearby, Dinim and Sabian tried their luck with a second fire. Surely, between the two groups, at least one of them would succeed.

The winds began to blow even harder, hitting them with a chilly blast. Adrianna looked into the direction from which it was coming. The air had a strange feeling about it, one she couldn't quite describe. It was then she heard it, a keening wail. A brief moment later, the others heard it as well, and all began to look in the same direction. The sound became louder, chilling them to the bone, suffusing them with an unnatural fear. Adrianna knew what it was without ever hearing it before.

It was Thane telling her he knew she was there and that he was coming.

Sheridana looked up and the two women regarded one another through wide eyes. Adrianna reached out and took her sister's hand. Tears slipped down Sheridana's face and Adrianna could feel the same on hers. Hearing a shout, they stood and turned towards the center of the clearing where everyone was gathering. Once all were there, Dinim spoke over the noise of the winds. "The Azmathous are in the pass!"

"How much time do we have?" asked Armond.

Dinim shook his head. "It's hard to say. I don't know how far he is. It could be as soon as a couple of hours from now, or maybe even sometime tomorrow. But this much is certain: Thane will not attack us during the day because his power is greatest at night. If we get through tonight without encountering him, then we will be safe until tomorrow night."

Sirion moved to put an arm around Adrianna's waist. "If we make it through the night, then I think we should stay here. It is a good location, and it would be best if we made Thane come to us instead of meeting him in another, possibly less advantageous, location."

Dinim nodded in agreement. "Yes, that would definitely be best. I will be able to finish the enchantments on Dartanyen's and Anya's arrows tonight, but then I will need to rest tomorrow. I will need all the sleep I can get before the encounter."

Dartanyen put a hand on Dinim's shoulder. "Will do, Dinim. We will stay here. It should give us a chance to prepare ourselves both mentally and physically." Then he shrugged. "All we can do is wait."

"Yes, wait and pray," said Triath.

Miraculously, the night passed and then the following day. The only person to really get any rest was Dinim, so drained he had no choice but to sleep.

Everyone knew he would be weakened before their battle. The energy it had taken for him to cast the enchantments couldn't possibly be replenished with just a single day of rest.

The winds continued, albeit not as forcefully as the night before. Regardless, it was almost impossible to keep the fire going. Everyone ate from the rations in their packs and sat around to conserve their strength for the upcoming fight. Weapons were sharpened and polished around episodes of talk that focused on previous exploits, prowess in battle, and good friends. It was a time for camaraderie, for reminiscing, and for humility. Adrianna spent most of the day with her back resting against Sirion's, her fingers threaded through his. Both of them watched the others, their banter lighthearted in spite of the surrounding tension. She was happy to see the bonds that had been forged among them, strong bonds that could last a lifetime if they lived that long.

All the while, the group felt the approach of Thane and his undead minions.

When the afternoon began to shift into early evening, they cleared the area. Travel packs, bedrolls, and other pieces of equipment were put aside. The lloryk and larian were tightly tethered a distance behind them down the pass. Sirion bade Dramati to stay with them, commanding the corubis that he was not to enter the fray, no matter what. Armor was strapped into place, and weapons sheathed along hips and thighs, across backs, and within boots.

Then they waited some more.

With the lowering of the sun, the cold winds once again swept through the small clearing. No one made a sound. Darkness slowly descended, and with it came the Azmathous. They sat upon steeds made from darkness found only in the deepest of shadows. Mist swirled from their nostrils and from beneath their cloven feet. Over the winds, the phantom jingling of bit and rein could be perceived. Steadfast, the group held their ground.

The enemy had them surrounded within the blink of an eye. There were seven of them, including Thane. Most were warriors, indicative by their attire. Armor, helms and gauntlets were all black. Two of them were different, however, wearing black robes and cloaks. They could only be the mage and the rogue. Thane rode forward, removing his horned helm. Adrianna could only imagine what Sheridana was thinking at that moment, beholding the face of their father in all of its glorious hideousness.

"At last we meet again," said Thane, his voice redolent of the wail they had heard the night before. He looked from one daughter to the next and grinned widely. "The two of you have found one another. How lovely. You have cost me a lot of time, Adrianna. But perhaps it will be worth it now that I don't need to track down your sister. You did all the work for me."

Adrianna stiffened defensively despite knowing he sought only to goad her, to make her lose her concentration. She began the incantation to her protective spell, knowing that Dinim and Sabian were doing the same. Thane narrowed his eyes and raised his hand. Dartanyen and Anya took the cue and readied their bows. "Fine, no more talk. I will crush you as I had intended when last we met. This time there will be no leniency."

The shadow lloryk charged. Dartanyen and Anya fired their first round of arrows. As the missiles raced through the air, they multiplied into four times the original number. First one, and then another of the death warriors was struck by the magical arrows. Many of them bounced off the black armor, but a few penetrated between the plates. Two of the warriors fell backward off their mounts, clutching at the shafts. The steeds galloped away from their fallen riders, but the knights were fast to rise, pulling the arrows free of their undead flesh.

By then the two unhindered warriors were upon them and the battle was officially engaged.

Zorg leaped into action, swinging his mighty broadsword at the legs of an approaching shadow lloryk. The dark steed screamed and faltered, the knight upon its back thrusting himself away from the falling beast. Zorg took the advantage, springing towards his enemy, slashing at the warrior. However, the other was quick, blocking Zorg's attack with his shield, and then following with a massive swing of his mace.

Sheridana made her way to Zorg just after the mace knocked him to the ground. She had just enough time to place herself in front of her companion as the knight struck again. She blocked his mace with Destroyer and kicked out with a well-aimed foot. The enemy stumbled back, but after swiftly righting himself, the knight swung his mace again. Sheridana managed to dance past and swung her blade in a curved arc.

The death-knight howled as she cut into him, the sound sending a trill of fear coursing through her. She felt the effect of the death wail tapping at her mind, seeking to paralyze her. She refused to let it in, but overcoming the power of the wail was the least of her problems. The enemy was much too fast. Spinning back around to face her, the knight struck her in the ribs with his mace. Sheridana cried out as she fell, only vaguely recognizing that Zorg had somehow risen, and that he was standing over her broadsword raised in defense.

From behind the protective circle of her warrior companions, Adrianna finished her second incantation. It was a simple missile spell, but she had become stronger over the moon cycles of studying and practicing her craft. The magic sprang from her fingertips and five glowing projectiles arced towards the only knight who had not lost his mount. To her discouragement, the missiles fell away before striking, demonstrating an unexpected immunity.

Adrianna found her attention abruptly drawn to Dinim when a sphere of fire rolled away from him towards the two death-knights who had been the first to lose their mounts. The flame encompassed the dark warriors, and Adrianna waited to see if it would have an effect on them, hoping to cast her own *Flamesphere* spell if it did.

Then, walking just outside the effect of the spell, she saw Thane.

She felt a creepy cold sensation move up her spine. *He is coming to kill me, just as he promised.* The flames of Dinim's spell dissipated, revealing the two knights who had been caught within the conflagration. Their armor was scorched, tendrils of smoke escaping from between the plates, but they were still hale enough to fight.. Thane continued towards her, and Adrianna began the incantation to her own *Flamesphere* spell. Behind Thane, she noticed the dark-robed figure of the death-mage. Even from this distance she could feel the Talent he possessed, a master of necromancy in his death, just as the knights were warrior masters in their deaths.

Dartanyen and Anya shot another volley of arrows just as she cast her spell. The fire swathed Thane and the death-mage, but before it could burn to its full intensity, she saw the energy gravitate to the mage, swirling into him. Taking the magic of the spell into himself, the mage spoke only a single word as he then cast the *Flamesphere* back at her.

Adrianna's eyes widened, and she heard the shouted exclamations of her companions. She felt a familiar burning sensation on her upper arm as the flames enveloped her and anyone who happened to be near. Just like before, a prismatic shell surrounded her. The fire burned around her, yet she didn't feel the heat. Then the flames were gone. Before her, Dinim and Dartanyen lay huddled on the ground, scorched from the fire.

Oh gods...

Adrianna looked away, back up to where she remembered seeing her father last. Her heart lurched in her chest and she quickly stepped back. Thane was swiftly advancing towards her, malicious excitement reflecting in his blue eyes. His sword was drawn, the weapon like none she had ever seen before. It wasn't a smooth blade, but instead had a serrated edge that would shred a man on its way in.

All of a sudden, Sirion was there. He positioned himself in front of her and gripped his quarterstaff at its center, both hands touching. Barely a moment later he held two blades, one in each hand. Sirion crossed the swords before his chest and stood there, battle ready.

Thane chuckled as he stopped in front of them. "A champion; how sweet. You think you can protect my daughter from me? I shall enjoy killing you almost as much as I will her."

Sirion said nothing, continuing to hold his stance. Adrianna shook her head, the words refusing to come forth. *No, Sirion...*

Armond advanced towards the death-mage. The dark sorcerer was largely immune to their weapons, despite the enchantments. He also had the ability to take the energy of the spells cast against him and throw it back. *But maybe, just maybe, I still have a chance. My Talent enables me to harness magical energy into the structure of my weapons, different than the way a typical spellcaster affects the energy of the world around us to create something new. Perhaps I can strike the creature when nothing else can.*

In the nearby distance, Armond saw the mage take notice of him. Narrowing his eyes, the dark sorcerer began to chant the words to a spell. Armond faltered. *This being can crush me with hardly any effort.* His focus became entirely broken when someone rushed to his side.

Sabian thrust something towards his mouth, speaking loud enough to be heard over the sounds of the battle. "Armond, eat this!"

He turned his face away, yet continued to watch the death-mage from the corner of his eye. "What the Hells is it?"

"Just do it!"

Armond opened his mouth and Sabian thrust the substance inside. Armond almost gagged and his eyes watered. Just then, the dark mage cast his spell. Beside him, he felt Sabian tense, and Armond instinctively did the same. The spell slammed into them, and the force of it nearly sent him to the ground. However, nothing else happened to him. After recovering from the initial shock, Armond looked around. Sabian lay unmoving on the ground at his feet, blood seeping from the corner of his mouth.

Sabian cast a protection spell on me, but left himself vulnerable?

Armond had no more time to think about his comrade as the death-mage swept upon him.

Amethyst threw the dagger at the dark warrior wielding the battle-axe, the one fighting Naemmious. It was one Sorn had given her, one infused with Dinim's magic. The dagger struck true, piercing the warrior's throat. The knight staggered back, and Naemmious saw his chance. He struck the knight with his flail, splitting the skull. As he fell, the knight disintegrated into dust, leaving behind only the black armor he was wearing. The battle axe fell to the ground beside it.

Amethyst grinned, pleased with how little effort that had been. Maybe these guys weren't so powerful after all.

Suddenly she felt something wrap around her throat, felt it tighten into a stranglehold. She was jerked back, and she fell to the ground on her back. She clutched at the thing around her neck, a smooth, pulsing, fleshy thing that continued to be held by the dark-robed death-rogue standing over her. She staring into the hood, and seeing the visage there, tried to scramble away. The vein-like whip constricted. She wanted to scream, but no sound could come out. Amethyst rose to her knees, clawing at the garrote as it continued to cut more deeply into her neck. Her vision dimmed and her head swam. She felt her life seeping away...

All of a sudden it loosened. Amethyst pitched forward and her face planted into the rocky ground. She saw Sorn standing over her attacker. Behind him stood the man with the black eyepatch, his one eye staring intently at the death-rogue.

Without warning, the enemy flew through the air, finally hitting a large boulder about a farlo away Sorn rushed after, and before the enemy could even begin to stir, he was standing over the rogue. Gripping his shortsword with both hands, Sorn sheathed the weapon into the dark-robed chest. Writhing, the creature let loose a hideous wail, and Sorn stepped back, his hands clutched over his ears.

Amethyst shook with uncontrollable fear, and where he knelt beside her, Triath did the same thing. He had unwrapped the whip from about her neck, grimacing with the strangeness of it. It had a rubbery consistency, and was colored deep red with shocks of purple. It seemed to have a life of its own as it slipped through his hands and writhed over the ground. Just as suddenly as the wail began, it stopped. Triath regained control and looked over to where Sorn stood. The man was looking down at the black hooded cloak that had once been worn by the rogue.

It hurt to breathe. Sheridana struggled to get herself moving as the knight lunged for Zorg again. He barely had a chance to recover from the previous blow before another was inflicted. The death warrior was much too powerful, and much too fast, for a single mortal man. *Oh gods, where is Ian now when I need him the most? The true bearer of Destroyer? My mate and the father of my child?* She recognized the armored figure, now knew with absolute certainty it was Thane who had murdered his own brother. Adrianna had told her in Krathil-lon, but now it was so much more real.

Oh gods... why did Thane commit such a heinous act against his own brother? And now he wanted to kill his daughters too...

Hatred swelled through Sheridana as she lifted herself slowly from the ground, the pain in her side excruciating. She made it up just in time to see Zorg get hit with the mace once more, the wicked weapon finally putting him down. Destroyer in hand, Sheridana wavered where she stood, willing herself forward. It was then she saw the other knight, one wielding a longsword. He came to stand over the prone form of Zorg for a moment before plunging his blade downwards.

"Nooooo!"

Disregarding the pain, Sheridana swung with all her might. The head rolled off the shoulders of the knight with the mace, his body collapsing beside Zorg. She moved just in time to avoid being hit by the sword wielder, and just as she was about to collapse, the half-oroc, Naemmious, was there to take her place.

Sheridana fell back to the ground, clutching her side. She watched Tianna rush over to the fallen form of Zorg. The healers movements over him at first were quick, almost frenzied. But then slowed to a stop.

Something was terribly wrong.

Thane lunged at Sirion, swinging his wickedly serrated blade. The ranger parried the attack, following up with a thrust of his own. Thane blocked, and then pushed forward, forcefully sending Sirion flying back to land over a farlo away. Almost instantly Thane's gaze sought Adrianna out, and he advanced towards her once more. Sirion scrambled up from the ground and flung himself towards Thane. Again the attack was blocked, and Sirion was thrown back. Adrianna had the powerful urge to flee, but knew it would do her no good. Thane would find her, and then he would kill her.

Adrianna watched Sirion get thrown to the ground for the third time. He'd been injured before coming to stand with her against Thane and a circle of deep red stained his studded leather along the side. This time he didn't rise, and fresh blood welled from his temple. Warm tears spilled down her cheeks, turning icy as they traveled to her neck. Thane held her in his sights and came towards her in long strides

Adrianna glanced down at her hand. *I know nothing about this ring, save that it gives the wielder the ability to give life. What could it do against someone who not only was dead, but had used the vilest of means to make himself one of the undead?*

Suddenly Thane was looming over her. He sheathed his blade before grabbing her by the fabric of the cloak gathered around her neck and lifting her up. She grasped at the gauntleted hand, the spikes at the knuckles biting into the soft flesh of her throat. High enough that she could see over his shoulder, Adrianna saw Sirion struggling to rise again. She was shaken like a rag doll, and she refocused on the hideous face of her father. "I will break you with my bare hands," he rumbled. "You are so small and so weak, just like a newborn babe. It seems like forever I have hated you. Just as I contributed to your beginning, I will now be your ending."

Adrianna struggled to breathe, her heart hammering against her ribs. She turned her face away from her father, unable to stand the reek of him. Her chest burned with the power of her emotion; she could scarcely believe what her life had come to, and how it would now end. She saw the stark contrast of her pale hand clutching Thane's black gauntleted one, saw the golden ring around her finger. Adrianna closed her eyes, focusing on the Ring of Aboleth. *Gods, I have no idea how to tap the power of the ring, or how to—*

But then it was there, as though it had merely been awaiting the weight of her thoughts.

Like a mighty river, the power flowed through her. She felt strangely charged, just like she had the evening she placed it on her finger for the first time. She opened her eyes and turned back to her father. He was speaking, but she couldn't hear his voice, couldn't hear *anything* over the deafening surge coursing through her. Still dangling from his grip, Adrianna took her hand from Thane's and slowly reached out to him. In that moment she heard only the beat of her heart and the breaths she took. She felt the pain of the burn around her upper arm, the prick of Thane's gauntlet beneath her chin, and the strange feeling of lightning flooding her veins.

Adrianna reached out to Thane, and for the first time in her life, she touched his face. Once, it could have been a loving gesture, one that a daughter would bestow upon her father. But now it was only instinct that told her to touch him there, one of the few places not covered by metal. Thane's eyes widened with shock, and his mouth stopped moving. Adrianna began to feel another sensation, minimal at first, but quickly becoming something monstrously terrible.

Thane and Adrianna became frozen in place, the Ring of Aboleth circling them in its power. The unnatural life force began to leave Thane's body, a pale ghostly light that seeped from his face and into the hand that touched it. When Thane was finally able to let her go, Adrianna dropped to the ground. But as she crouched there with her hand outstretched to Thane, the blue glow continued to flow into her. The sensation was horrific, and the pain intense, sweeping through her like a storm. And when she could no longer withstand the torment, she cried out in agony.

Then it was over. The blue glow dissipated, and Adrianna slumped to the ground. Thane stood over her, his arms held out to his sides. His expression was one of incredulous anger. "What have you done?" he roared.

Weakly, Adrianna lifted her head from the rocky ground. Her vision swam, and it was difficult to focus. She could barely move, her body heavy as though a pile of rocks weighed it down. As though in slow motion, Adrianna watched as Thane unsheathed his sword. Face contorted with rage, he swung the blade over his head in an arc.

Suddenly his expression changed. His eyes widened in shock, and his body shuddered. It was then Adrianna saw the tip of a sword poking through the break in the black armor between his chest and abdomen. It was bathed in blood. *Thane had become mortal again.*

Adrianna just managed to roll out of the way as his body fell. She looked up to find her sister standing where Thane had just been, holding her bloody blade in her grip. Adrianna moved his arm off her as she shakily rose to her feet. Dropping her blade, Sheri stumbled over to her and the women embraced, each one leaning upon the other.

By the gods, it was finally over.

When they finally parted, Adrianna took in the scene surrounding her: Tianna tending to the fallen, Naemmious supporting Anya as they made their way over to Sorn, and Triath carrying Amethyst over to the place where Sabian lay. Adrianna still felt energized, and despite the suffering she'd endured when she used the ring against Thane, she felt somehow larger than life. Her pains had melted away, and she felt a sense of invulnerability that invigorated her to a height she had never experienced before.

Adrianna walked among her comrades, saw the burns on Dinim and Dartanyen, the jagged laceration around Amethyst's throat, the series of cuts that marred the flesh of Naemmious' arms and chest, and the deep wound in Sheridana's side. She felt pity for them all, wishing they had come through the fight as unscathed as she. Obviously they were weak, pathetically frail in comparison to the fortress she had become.

Adrianna heard her friends speaking to her, calling out. But she merely passed them by, somehow drawn to a place removed from them. And then she saw him lying there, alone on the cold rocky ground. Adrianna walked over to Zorg and then crouched over his lifeless body. His face was ashen, and his pupils fixed and dilated. When she put her hand on him, she felt the warmth had already begun to leave him. But she also felt something else– the rush of power flooding her mind, telling her that it need not be this way, that she could bring her companion back into the world of the living.

Adrianna placed her palms atop Zorg's chest. His heart was no longer beating, and his air-sacs no longer filled with the breath of life, but she could change that, make it so that death had never come. Behind her, Adrianna heard the voices of her other companions, but for some reason, they seemed as though they came from a great distance and she couldn't understand the words they spoke. Adrianna shook her head, dissipating all of the voices save for one. It was the one she had heard before in an argument, a terrible argument. Ah yes, it was the man Dinim.

"No... please... don't know... wrong..."

She could hear only snatches of what he tried to say, his voice filled with a pleading quality. She struggled to understand what he was saying, but then his words from their argument came flooding back: *"The ring can be used to do great evil, and even one with the best intentions can do wrong. Great power like that can be enticing, and can make one thirst for more. Once started, one may never be able to stop, the temptation too difficult to ignore."*

Suddenly, Adrianna found her mind clearing, as though it had been covered by a thin veil. She found herself with her hands resting on Zorg, her desire to bring him back to life manifest in her mind. Adrianna shook her head, and then took her hands away from Zorg's body. No, she would not bring him back. His time had come, and he had died for their cause. She didn't want his efforts to be in vain, and she didn't want to do him a disservice by bringing him life when he had died so valiantly for the lives of others. Sadly, Adrianna rose from Zorg's side. The others would see to his funeral pyre. She would not bring back Zorg, but there were other places to go, places that needed her power, places that needed the life that the Ring of Aboleth could bring. And she had become the master of that power, above the puny efforts of other mortals. Adrianna felt the power, allowed it to suffuse her. She reveled in the sensations, the intoxicating vibrations it brought.

Sirion stood by as the glow encompassed Adrianna. He was afraid, and when he glanced around at the others, he found that they were as well. Adrianna had left Zorg, somehow overcoming the temptation to use the power of the ring to bring him back to life. But she had decided on another course of action.

"I will go... leave this place and find another."

Sirion stepped towards Adrianna. He could feel the raw power encompassing her, the unharnessed magic. He was afraid, but he couldn't simply stand by and watch her leave. He wouldn't lose her, not this way. He had faith that she would be able to break away from the temptation of the ring. If she could master the power of the artifact to decide not to bring life back to Zorg, her good friend, then she could do it again and resist the temptation to leave.

She just needed someone to help her realize that.

"Adrianna... Adria please listen to me. I need you to stay with me. These other places, they don't need you the way I do." The tone of his voice was almost desperate as he spoke in an effort to reach out to her. "I have come to love you so much, love you in a way that this power never will, despite the emotions it imparts. You have opened up a part of me I never knew existed, and without you I will never feel this complete ever again. I can't let you leave this way, because I'm unable to live without you." Sirion stepped closer, disregarding the heat surrounding her. "Adrianna, you have to fight this, be stronger than you have ever been before. I will be here by your side, just as you have been by mine. I will never let you go."

Sirion took a deep breath, and then launched himself into the glow enveloping Adrianna. It was hot... so hot, but he took her in his arms. He put his face beside hers so that his mouth was by her ear. "I know there is a part of you that hears me, Adrianna. I need you, want you, and love you with every breath I take."

Sirion clutched Adrianna close, embracing her within the sweltering inferno. He brought his mouth to hers, kissing her with a passion he demonstrated only when they were alone, in the deepest part of the night...

Adrianna felt the ferocity of Sirion's kiss despite the intensity of the waves surging through her. She matched it with blazing passion that set all her nerves tingling all the way to the tips of her fingers and toes. The arcane waves began to cool, the magic tempering enough to allow her thoughts to break through the shroud covering her mind. Her vision cleared, she could hear again, and she felt the sensation of Sirion's studded leather beneath her palms.

Suddenly feeling weak, her knees buckled. Sirion caught her in his arms and rested her gently in his lap. Adrianna found herself staring into his amber eyes and saw the love reflected there. Her voice was a whisper, "You came for me. I hoped you would."

He kissed her gently. "You questioned that?"

She reached up and caressed his face with her fingertips. "I'll try not to question you again."

Sirion curved his lips into a grin before wrapping his arms tightly around her, as though he never wanted to let her go.

The cavern reeked of death. He liked it that way; the stench of rot and decay filling his nostrils day in and day out invigorating him. The cesspool before him burbled from deep within, a rank bubble of globular material popping sickeningly on the greenish surface. Reaching out a hand, he pointed a long knobby finger towards the pool. The appendage lengthened upon demand, and once the tip of his jagged fingernail reached the surface of the murky liquid, he began to swirl it around in a circle. The corners of his mouth turned upwards in the parody of a grin, knowing he would be pleased by what he saw within the pool.

As the image came into view, his smile widened with pleasure. Before him was his army, the greatest one he had ever created. Deep within the catacombs below, his legions waited. When the winds swept through the caverns just right, he could hear their eerie moans and smell the nearly overpowering stench of their decaying flesh. With the awesome power he harnessed with the Azmathion, he had bade them rise from deep within the ground, dead, but now undead. At his disposal, he had human, faelin, halfen and oroc warriors from past battles, knights who had fought for their kingdoms, and common men who had fought for their friends and their families. Not least among the horde, there were heroes who had once fought for all that was good. Now they all would fight for the Deathmaster, he who had brought them back from death to have some semblance of life once again.

Lord Aasarak turned away from the pool, and he slowly made his way to the upper tier of the cavern. It was there he had brought into undead life his most magnificent creation– Thane Darnesse. That man's intense anger and hate had made him ripe for the picking and Aasarak couldn't help himself from taking the opportunity to barter for Thane's soul as he lay dying in the forest all those moon cycles ago.

As Thane sold his soul, Aasarak had become his new Master. Mere days after Thane's rebirth, Aasarak began to realize the strength his new creation possessed. Thane quickly became his right hand, a force with which to be reckoned. Under Aasarak's guidance, Thane brought organization to the undead he had raised. He had also brought into service the clans of oorgs that surrounded the immense caverns in which Aasarak had made his lair. With his fear aura alone, he had managed to make them work to clear the catacombs within which his armies now resided. Thane was placed in command of the other Azmathous Aasarak created, and many a time he set them loose to wreak destruction wherever they chose.

Much to Aasarak's dismay, all of that was short-lived. As time passed, Thane seemed to have only one thing on his mind. Vengeance. Aasarak saw that Thane's desire for revenge was too often at odds with the commands he gave. But Thane was smart, and for a while, he had found ways to combine his two priorities: his allegiance to Aasarak and his personal vendetta.

Aasarak growled deep within his throat. He hated that he'd been unable to control Thane despite the depth of his power. As Thane got closer to his target of revenge, he had become ever more detached from his Master. In the end, there was no chain strong enough to bind him, and so Aasarak let him go. It was intriguing that Thane's target had managed to be the one to end his existence, and even more, that it happened to be Thane's own daughter.

Even someone as twisted and evil as Aasarak had a difficult time believing a man could hate his own offspring so much.

Lady Adrianna Darnesse.

Yes, he was quite familiar with her. Even more intriguing was that she was the one who played such a pivotal part in the renewal of each Cycle of Odion's Curse. For four Cycles encompassing over half a millennium each, he had fought against her and the group of rag-tag companions with whom she allied herself. He had defeated her every time. As each Cycle passed, Aasarak had grown in strength and power. The next Cycle, he would better know how to harness Thane more effectively and put the warrior's strength to much better use. Hells, the only reason Adrianna had been able to defeat her father was because of the Ring of Aboleth.

Damn that artifact! Aasarak had thought the ring to be gone long ago. And somehow the young sorceress had found it and managed escaping the temptation to succumb to its addictive power. It seemed that this Cycle she was stronger than she had been in the previous ones. A little over two decades ago he had briefly considered saving himself some hassle and having her hunted down and killed during her infancy. However, he had summarily dismissed the idea as being more effort than it was probably worth. Rash actions often had unforeseen consequences during each Cycle. Removing this one person he could defeat may have brought forth a champion he could *not*. Better to wait and defeat her at the preordained time, as he always did.

It wasn't until more recently he recalled the prophecies of Johanan Chardelis. He suspected the rantings and ravings of that idiot were about the girl, but he didn't bother to consider hunting her down, thinking surely she would be in the possession of the sorcerer Tallachienan Chroalthone. It wasn't until Aasarak realized she was the focus of Thane's hate that he knew otherwise. He could only speculate why the young god had chosen against taking her under his aegis for a third time.

Oh well, it was of no consequence. He would defeat Adrianna and her comrades yet again. The addition of the Wildrunners to the group was a new development to occur just this Cycle. It made him wonder what little pebble had been tossed into the water to create such a large diversion from what had always transpired before. There were always pebbles, little differences from one Cycle to the next. It was the same people, living and dying, living and dying. No one was immune except the gods...

Aasarak narrowed his eyes. He might find the Wildrunners more formidable, but with his own increased power and his army larger than ever before, he would crush any possible opposition. The puny machinations of Tallachienan and his dragon friend, Trebexal Phesakmet, meant little to him, and they would fail just as they had in previous Cycles.

Aasarak reached the uppermost tier of the cavern and approached the Azmathous warrior waiting there. The death knight was tall, with tangled ropes of long brown hair escaping his helm. Hodorin was not as powerful as Thane, but Aasarak hoped that, with time, he could get close. He made a brief gesture and Hodorin nodded in affirmation to the command, turned on his heel, and left to gather the other Azmathous.

Aasarak felt the corners of his mouth turn up into another smile, imagining the destruction soon to take place. It was good... very good.

PART TWO

PROLOGUE

Tallachienan sat at his desk, poring over the message Dinim had left in his notebook. He sensed there were some things Dinim left unsaid that didn't include the particulars of Lord Thane's defeat, things that were lost in translation when one communicated with written words alone. However, in spite of this drawbacks, the device had turned out to be ingenious, and the best thing he'd invented to use in order to communicate with his journeymen after they left the citadel for other pursuits. They all carried notebooks similar to the one that sat before him, and when they wrote a message on the pages, he could see the same words written on the pages in his own tablet. He would then be able to write a message in reply and an open line of communication established.

Several moon cycles ago, when Dinim had been imprisoned by Aasarak, Tallachienan was quite put-out. Not only was Dinim unable to communicate via the notebook, but whatever magic had been used to incarcerate the young mage also kept Tallachienan from seeing him in his Vision Orb. Tallachienan knew something foul had happened to his journeyman. Certainly, he could have gone looking, and would have if more time had passed, but he'd hoped Dinim's training would ultimately free him. Tallachienan was pleased to know that his training was precisely what saved Dinim from Aasarak's priests and enabled him to defeat his jailor.

Tallachienan tapped his fingers on the desk. Similar training was what he was supposed to be focusing on now, in particular, Adrianna's training. It was nearly time to bring her to the citadel, and final preparations needed to be made. He'd waited too long already.

Tallachienan had finally completed his mission to bring the other three students he'd been tracking into the citadel. For the first time in the history of his program, other than Adrianna, two of them were women. The other was a man. Historically, his students were all of Cimmerean descent, but out of these three, the man and one of the women were not. It would take some time for his older students to adjust to the change, but he had faith they would all learn to accept one another.

And then there was Adrianna. She would be like a star that had fallen into the citadel, lighting up the darkness like a beacon in the deepest part of the night. In past Cycles she had outranked everyone with her Talent, and he couldn't help but assume it would be the same this time.

Tallachienan closed the notebook just as the door to his chamber opened. In strode Pylar. In every way, the man was his right hand, and without him the place would probably fall apart. Pylar kept order in a place which would otherwise thrive upon chaos, and the students found him a comforting presence that kept many of their fears at bay. "Master Tallachienan, you called for me?"

He nodded. "Yes. Adrianna and her companions have completed their mission, and returned home victorious. It is time for us to make the final preparations for her arrival."

Pylar nodded in return, a lock of thick red hair falling across his face to hide his left eye. Tallachienan thought he saw something lurking there, an expression he couldn't quite make out. But then Pylar was speaking again, and he let it go. "Of course. Most of the preparations have been made. Only the final stages of the move have not yet been implemented. When we make the Time shift, some of the students may have the power to perceive it, so I think we should cast them to *Sleep* before we begin."

Tallachienan nodded. "Very well. In this capacity you know the students better than I do. We will plan for the move a fortnight from now; that will give us plenty of time to be sure that nothing goes wrong. Once the move is complete, we will need to be careful that we don't enter the places we spoke about. Do you remember?"

Pylar nodded. "I have told Coaxtl as well. The citadel is vast. It shouldn't be a problem."

"Good. In only a few more weeks, Adrianna will come, and her training will begin anew. This time I will see to it she succeeds." Tallachienan rose from the desk, placing the notebook dedicated to Dinim back in its spot on the shelf with the others. His gaze drifted to another notebook, an old one removed from the others. He hadn't the heart to take it away, and so it had remained there throughout the centuries. He stopped to caress the binding thoughtfully before turning away and walking through the door leading out onto the balcony.

Tallachienan looked out over the stark landscape surrounding the citadel. It suited him, this desolate place. Some called it called it the Land of Black Ice, a place to which few would go, much less live. But here he was, making it his home, and none contested him for it. The cold stone bit into his palms as he leaned into the winds, his cloak billowing behind. Beyond him was the rest of his fortress, that place to which he soon would be unable to go.

Soon, with the help of his good friend, Charlemagne, he would manipulate Time– go back into the past to train his students. As a result, he would be forced to stay out of a large portion of the citadel. It was within those walls that his past self resided. That man was unaware of the decision he would make in years to come, that he would stall in his decision to take Adrianna as his apprentice– forced to train her in the past so that she would be ready to combat the evil that resided in her future.

Strangely enough, the citadel itself seemed to know what Tallachienan was doing. It was odd, he knew, but he had lived there long enough to realize a few things about the place. There was something about the citadel, a *knowingness* that he could only interpret as consciousness. He was aware of how the walls seemed to shift at times, how there were sometimes unexplained bursts of energy, lost objects suddenly found, and other strange phenomena. For most of his adult years, Tallachienan had lived there. The citadel had come to know him, and he felt comfortable behind the stone walls. He knew the place, knew it almost as intimately as the back of his hand. So the last Cycle, when Adrianna came, he noticed a change in the aura of the fortress. For some reason it reacted to her presence. Tallachienan was pleased. It was almost like the citadel recognized her as its Mistress, just as it knew him to be its Master.

Yet, he knew better than to believe he held any authority over the place. The citadel had a mind of its own.

Regardless of the past, Tallachienan was pleased that he would be the one to mold Adrianna once more. With her innate Talent, and the skill that he would bequeath to her, she and her allies would finally break the curse that had shadowed the world for almost as long as he could remember. It was so much more than just her survival at stake. With her victory over Aasarak, a new age could begin. Tallachienan couldn't help but believe that, this time, Adrianna and her companions would save Shandahar from centuries of incarceration and give life to an untold future.

In short, the world could cease to repeat itself for a sixth time. But at what cost would the victory be won?

HIDDEN ENEMY

8 CHANTEREN CY593

*T*he wind whispered softly through the silver trees. A hush had fallen, and all that could be heard was the rustle of her white ceremonial cloak as it moved over the leaf-littered ground. She looked down at the winter ivy clutched in her gloved hands, the dark green leaves a stark contrast against white satin. She couldn't bring herself to lift her eyes, for she knew his gaze would be waiting Once meeting, the depths of his eyes would suck her within and she would become lost... lost within a pool of amber. The pool was warm, and the love she found there complete. Yet, Adrianna wanted all of her wits about her for one of the most important ceremonies of her life.

Finally, she stopped. The pair of fur-lined suede boots that entered her line of vision told her that she now stood before Sirion. It was easy to obtain some idea of what he was thinking, for she had finally come to realize that a whisper of the connection she once shared with the beast Cortath had remained when Sirion was transformed back into a man. He urged her to look up at him, wanting to see her face, to look into her eyes. Then his thoughts were running with him– the touch of her lips on his, the feel of her hair through his fingers...

Adrianna slammed her barriers up as the heat rose to her face. Damn Sirion! Will he always have this power over me? *His passion was all-encompassing, and in the deep of the night, that was fine. But even during the daylight hours she would find herself thinking of him, and their nights of passion would come creeping up on her. Most of the time, she could chuckle it away, but sometimes it was a burden. Sirion often took pleasure in seeing her so discomfited.*

Adrianna kept her head lowered, and as Sirion took her ivy-laced hands in his, the shaman began to speak. He spoke in Hinterlic, the melodic nuances of the language flowing from his lips like a lazy mountain stream. Most of the Wildrunners wouldn't understand what was being spoken, but she hoped the finer nuances and tones would somehow get through to them. It was a passage that spoke of love, trust, and the deepest of commitments. It was a passage reserved only for a time such as this one, when a man loved a woman and wished to speak a promise. As Sirion held her hands in his, Adrianna felt the power of the shaman's words sweep through her. The winds stirred in the treetops and the soft, auburn fur lining the hood of her cloak caressed her face. The sounds the winds made became musical in quality and Adrianna felt Sirion's thumbs stroking the tops of her gloved hands. She sensed the magic of this place, the grove where all of the Promising Ceremonies took place.

The shaman finished speaking. Once again, there was a hushed quality in the air, tinged with a hint of expectancy. Putting a hand at her waist, Sirion pulled her towards him. In a moment of surprise, Adrianna looked up into his handsome face. His eyes captured hers and his lips curved up into a smile of triumph. He lowered the hood of her cloak. Just as she knew she would, she melted towards him, already becoming lost within the depths of his gaze. Sirion wrapped his arms around her, steadying her as she leaned into him. Adrianna breathed deeply, inhaling his familiar, spicy musk. Then she felt the pressure of his mouth on hers, his lips entreating her to let him in. She responded and felt herself being swept away in the moment, the first moment they would share in an entire lifetime of moments together.

Adrianna stood on the balcony of the alcove she inhabited within the Sherkari Fortress, smiling at the memory. A gentle wind swept through, moving the treetops overhead. The silver leaves rustled and danced, and she watched as several of them drifted into view, falling to the ground far below. Her eyes were captured by her hand resting on the balustrade. Around her middle finger was the beautiful ring Sirion gave her just yesterday at the Promising Ceremony. The silver-wrought leaves were perfect in every detail, each one intricately interwoven with the next. It was a symbol of his love and his devotion. It was his promise that she would one day be his wife.

Adrianna leaned over the balcony, looking around out at her surroundings. Above, beneath, and alongside her, Adrianna saw balconies that belonged to other alcoves. Interconnecting bridges spanned from one giant tree to the next, affording people the ability to travel freely throughout the fortress. This was indeed a wondrous place, for it contained sights one would never see anywhere else upon Shandahar. To her, the magic surrounding the fortress was palpable, and most likely helped to regulate the climate within the boundaries. However, it was still very apparent winter was quickly approaching. The climate control only protected the inhabitants from the coldest of winter winds and the strongest of rainy gales. Blankets and furs were piled high on the beds, glow-spheres had been removed from summer storage, and the warmth-giving ales and brews taken from their places on the shelves.

Adrianna snuggled deep within Sirion's oversized cloak. It was hard to believe her life had come to this. Sirion was more than she could ever have hoped for. There were so many things that could have kept them apart, yet here they were, making plans for a future together. It seemed like many moon cycles had passed since she and her companions defeated Lord Thane. However, only a mere two fortnights had gone by. In truth, it was difficult to believe they had survived the encounter, and even more that she had been so pivotal in his demise. The Ring of Aboleth currently rested inside the magically locked box inside the cabinet by the bed. Sirion had been the one to remove it from her finger after bringing her back from the brink of arcane insanity.

The first days after Thane's defeat were spent in recuperation. Dartanyen, Dinim, and Sabian had been dealt the most damage and Tianna spent most of her energy on them before falling into exhausted sleep. The most able bodied went in search of materials, and a platform was slowly built from the scant resources found in the rocky pass. By the second night, everyone was recovered enough to gather around it. After holding a brief ceremony, Zorg's funeral pyre was lit. It took most of the night to burn. In the end, all that lay on the blackened heap was his enchanted broadsword.

When everyone was fit enough to travel, it took the group several days to reach the city of Sangrilak. Upon arrival, they found themselves in the midst of celebration. The news of Thane's defeat had traveled faster than they ever could have imagined. The city-folk had gathered at the Inn of the Hapless Cenloryan, the favored inn of the Wildrunners, and everyone applauded their victory. People from Elvandahar were also there, including Carli and Fitanni. Over the course of the following days, other people had come, people representing several of the provinces within the realm of Monaf. The Wildrunners were given gold and other tokens of goodwill from the people Thane had devastated.

And that is what they had become... the Wildrunners.

Despite their initial protestations, the people continued to call them by that name. After a few days it didn't really seem to matter anymore. By the time their stay in Sangrilak was done, the group had even begun to call themselves by the legendary name. If it was so important to people that the Wildrunners still be in existence, who were they to deny them that?

After five days' sojourn in Sangrilak, Sirion decided it was time to return home to Elvandahar. He had responsibilities he needed to handle upon his return, not to mention, monitoring any progress made against remaining lycan in the area after Sydonnia's death. The rest of the Wildrunners agreed to return with him, feeling it was the perfect place for a sojourn before deciding where they wanted to go next.

Adrianna smiled to herself. Home. Yes, she could very easily consider Elvandahar the place she would think about whenever she heard that word. Already she preferred the forest trees to city streets. She enjoyed living in a place with very few walls, where she could look up into the sky on a clear night. She loved the rustling of the leaves in the breeze, and the creaking of thick branches when the winds were strong. She loved the scent of the lichens that grew on the trunks of the oldest trees, and the sight of shimmering silver leaves made more iridescent by early morning dew.

Sirion beside her made it complete.

Dinim stared at the open tome Sabian and Armond placed before him. He sighed and rubbed his eyes wearily. Truth be told, he had been too long at this task and desperately needed a break. But he had given himself no such respite. He knew he was close– their literature search had taken them so far. And now, here lay the culmination of all of their efforts: the Rod of Atlenbos.

Early on they had stumbled onto a reference of the rod, and upon further study, Dinim realized it might be something worth researching further. Now, looking at the descriptions on the pages before him, he realized all of their work was finally coming to fruition. Many of the books had vaguely alluded to the artifact, but with several days' worth of perseverance, they had finally found clues that led them to this one. And here it was, a full description of the artifact, including a crude representation on the leading page.

Dinim skimmed over the text while Sabian and Armond looked on. Only Dinim had the ability to read the ancient script written on the pages– having received training in the ancient languages from Master Tallachienan when he was an apprentice. It was written in an early form of Denedrian, not too different from what the language was today. However, in order to decipher the details of the notes, one had to know how to translate the different meanings of some of the words. Depending on the context, one word could have two entirely different meanings, or two very different words could have the same meaning. It was all sometimes very difficult to translate, especially when it came to some of the earlier prophecies; but Dinim somehow always figured it out.

Finally Dinim looked up from the pages. "This is it!"

Sabian and Armond looked at one another and grinned widely. All of them had put in long hours of hard work, dedicating themselves to a task Dinim said was worthy. This rod could be the defining factor in their fight against Aasarak. Now all they had to do was procure it, and then learn how to use it.

First arriving to Elvandahar, Dinim had received a nocturnal visit from his mentor. Usually Master Tallachienan communicated to him via the notebook, but in some rare instances he would make a physical appearance. Tallachienan had warned him about Aasarak, that the dark sorcerer's grasp of the Azmathion had grown significantly and that his necromantic activity was causing trouble in the northern realm of Tusbir. The warning had spurred Dinim into action; knowing he was in the best place in all the faelin realms to conduct arcane research, he plunged himself into the task of finding something that might help them in their endeavors against Aasarak.

The Master had also told Dinim that his preparations for Adrianna were almost complete, and that he would soon be coming for her.

Dinim closed the book and then sat back in his chair. "Let me look over this tonight. The text should give me an idea of where we should start looking for the rod. Once we know where we'll be going, we can tell the others what we know and begin to make preparations."

Armond and Sabian both nodded and began stacking the multitude of books, loose parchments, and scrolls they had looked through into piles on the tables. Then they left the library to seek the sanctuary of their alcoves. Not much later, book in hand, Dinim also left. He walked through the corridor, thinking about how he was going to tell Adrianna about Master Tallachienan's plan for her. She would balk at the concept of leaving the group, especially when they had the threat of Aasarak looming over them. But that wasn't all. She was Sirion's betrothed now. She would be loath to leave his side in spite of the benefits she would reap by studying under a man as powerful as Tallachienan Chroalthone.

Dinim sighed as he turned a corner and entered his alcove. Adrianna wasn't the easiest person for him to talk with these days. Ever since their argument about the Ring of Aboleth, she had been distant and withdrawn. He didn't really blame her. He would have killed her had she not been wearing the serpent talisman. Whatever that thing was, it had also protected her from the spell thrown back at them by the Deathmage in their battle against the Azmathous. Strangely, there were spells that it didn't protect her against, and Dinim was left wondering about the true nature of the talisman. Where did it come from? What was its primary purpose? And why did it pick and choose when to offer its protective powers?

Dinim set the book onto the nearest table. In spite of some rather skeptical prior assessments of her, he had to admit Adrianna had handled herself well in her fight against Thane. She had persevered against a man who had murdered countless others, not to mention he was her father. Against his wishes, she had taken the ring and used it to her advantage in a battle that could have cost the lives of more than just one group member. Because she had taken the risk, only Zorg's life had been forfeit. Dinim still felt the risk of using the ring wasn't worth the potential consequences, but he wouldn't change the outcome of that fight for anything. During their initial argument about the ring, Adrianna had suggested an anchor for the ring wielder, someone who could help that person resist the temptation the ring offered. He had ignored her, thinking her a silly girl with very little experience. Ultimately that very strategy had held true and Sirion had brought Adrianna back from the brink of insanity, the love they shared conquering the pull of the ring.

Now, as Dinim sat back and reflected on it all, he had nothing but respect for Adrianna. She had stepped forward and taken the role of a leader at a time when it was most needed. He regretted his cruel words during their argument, as well as his unfriendly thoughts and subsequent action that would have killed anyone else. He respected her as a person and as a magic user. He respected the relationship she shared with Sirion, knowing it was the only thing that could have possibly saved her from the ring.

But in the end, Dinim still wished it had been him.

11 CHANTEREN CY593

He stood alone amongst the trees. From out of his Daemundai talisman, he took the tiny communion orb, held it aloft, and began the words to his spell. He carved the runes in the cold air before him, his warmer breath forming a surrounding mist. Under different circumstances he would have carried the staff used by mages who served the Daemundai. The communion orb would have been set within a four-pronged claw at the top, enlarging upon contact with the staff. The runes wouldn't have been needed, and the incantation wouldn't have been as difficult. But here he was without his staff, fearful the rest of the group would recognize it for what it really was, especially Dinim. But he gladly went without, for he had successfully infiltrated the group, and subsequently made his discovery about the man they called Triath.

Sabian completed the words to his spell, and the runes circled the floating communion orb. The sphere began to glow red and the runes dissipated. As the orb began to enlarge, the glow became brighter. Then the voice of the leader of the Daemundai emanated from it.

"What newsss have you for me, ssservant?" The priest's voice was roughly sibilant, almost reptilian in nature.

"None yet, sire. The group still rests in Elvandahar. I have yet to receive sufficient opportunity to influence Triath."

Sabian heard a hiss and then the mehta snarled, "What in the Hellsss iss taking them ssso long?"

Without thinking, Sabian replied in a soothing voice, hoping to calm the priest who had taken the place of Gaknar after his unfortunate demise against the Wildrunners. "Their battle with Lord Thane was brutal, sire. Wounds need time to heal. The sorcerer Dinim Coabra is conducting a search for an artifact that may help them in their fight against Aasarak."

The mehta would not be mollified. "I exsspect the daemon-walker to be under your influensss within a fortnight! He will be a valuable asssset to the fold and it isss a shame the other one wasss ssslain. Don't let the sssame fate take thisss one, or you will sssuffer a sssimilar one."

Sabian inhaled sharply, knowing the threat was not an idle one. "I will endeavor to do as you command, sire." With that he ended the transmission, snatching the communion orb from out of the air in front of him. The orb immediately shrank in size, and when Sabian placed it back into the talisman, the red glow had begun to recede. He then put the talisman in his pack near the bottom, not wanting to take the chance that anyone in the group would see it.

Sabian made his way back to the fortress, thinking about when he had first made his discovery about Triath. It was when they were in the city of Entsy after Sirion's battle with Sydonnia. There was a scene that had taken place at the inn, one that was later described to him by Dinim...

Alone in the room he had to himself, Sabian caught bits and pieces of a commotion, and after a few moments, decided to see what was happening. He rose from the bed and looked out the window to see Sirion rushing down the street. He then caught a glimpse of deep purple. The girl, Amethyst, hung from the upper trellis of the inn. He watched her drop, crouching when her feet touched the ground. Then she sprinted down the road after Sirion.

Having nothing better to do, and his interest substantially piqued, Sabian went in pursuit. Using a Transformation *spell, he took the form of a blood raven and flew into the cool evening air. It wasn't long before he caught up to the others. He was surprised to ultimately find Sirion in the company of a small group of individuals that he quickly realized were what remained of the Wildrunners.*

Sabian landed on a nearby awning. From the hasty conversation he surmised there was another group in town as well. The Wildrunners referred to this group as their "doubles", and after only a few moments more of deliberation, they went in pursuit of them, having ample reason to believe Adrianna might, somehow, be in their clutches. All the while, Amethyst had remained hidden and followed them not far behind. Sabian was careful not to be detected by the young rogue, and continued to follow as well.

It wasn't long before they reached the Snorting Gorgon Inn. Luckily it was a small establishment and had only a single level. Sirion, Triath, Naemmious, and Sorn separated and circled the building. Using the trellis, Anya swung up onto the roof. From his lofty position, Sabian watched as she moved slowly across the expanse. Suddenly noticing the presence of another, Sabian instinctively called out a warning to Anya, but all that emerged was a raucous squawk. It was too late when Anya discovered she wasn't alone on the rooftop. Anti-Sorn tackled her, and they both fell, alerting the others inside the establishment.

Even from his height, Sabian heard Sirion curse eloquently in Hinterlic. Naemmious barreled through the front door, followed by Sorn, Sirion and Triath. Sabian alighted onto the balcony of a nearby building, transforming back into his natural self so as to save his strength should he need to make a fast retreat. He saw Amethyst pressed against the wall of the same building, waiting to find the best time to enter the Snorting Gorgon. As the Wildrunners infiltrated the establishment, mayhem ensued. Shouts and curses accompanied the patrons as they poured out the front door, most of them of the unsavory variety. It wasn't but a moment longer before Amethyst was running across the street and entering the inn. Sabian leaped off the balcony and followed her inside.

For a moment he stood unobtrusively in the entry. Amethyst slowly circumvented the melee, pressing up against the walls and hiding behind tables as she made her way to the hallway from which anti-Sirion had emerged. Meanwhile, Sorn engaged anti-Anya, and Naemmious fought with anti-Arn. Both Sirions strained at one another, their struggle so intense it was felt in the air surrounding them. Out of the corner of his eye, Sabian saw Triath use the rear door of the common room, the one that led back into the kitchens. Sabian considered going around the fight and following him, but thought better of it when Naemmious threw anti-Arn against the adjacent wall. Sabian felt the impact, and he wasn't even touching the offended wall. He made the decision to go outside and walk around to the rear of the building to enter the kitchens that way. His curiosity demanded that he catch at least a glimpse of the fight that would take place, knowing that Triath's double must be there somewhere in order for him to leave the rest of his comrades so easily.

Sabian exited the establishment, and under the cover of the darkness, he made his way to the rear of the building. Once there he stopped, the scene that met his eyes one he would never forget. Bathed in torchlight, Triath and anti-Triath stood half a farlo apart from one another. There were few differences between the two men. One man had been derived from the other, and in that respect, the two should have been identical. But where Triath's character was most of what was benevolent and moral, the persona present in his double was equally as evil and destructive.

Right away, Sabian noticed that the patch Triath wore over his eye was absent in that of his double. He assumed that it was because Triath had sustained the injury after his double had been created. He watched as the two men sized one another up, slowly beginning to circle one another. He saw the features of anti-Triath's face harden into that of someone in deep concentration. Sabian then felt a sudden clap of energy reverberate through the air, and Triath went flying into the stone wall of the inn.

Anti-Triath leisurely strolled over to where Triath lay against the side of the building, and when he was close enough, pushed the toe of his boot into Triath's side. "Do you honestly think you are powerful enough to defeat me?" Anti-Triath began to chuckle, but the laughter was short-lived when Triath grabbed the other man's leg and pulled him off his feet. Anti-Triath thudded to the ground and a moment later Triath was on top of him, slamming his fist into anti-Triath's face.

With only the light of the torches to see, Sabian strained to get a closer look at anti-Triath. There was something strange about one of his eyes. Sabian got his chance when he felt another clap of energy and Triath was, once more, sailing through the air, his body slamming into the wall of the building. Anti-Triath rose from the ground, and when the man looked into the light just right, Sabian could see what was so strange. One of his eyes was completely black. Viewing it even from a distance, he could sense the soullessness about it, feel the evil emanating from it. And from somewhere in the gut of his being, he knew a daemon lived inside this man, or at least the essence of one.

"You stupid fool! You have no chance against me. I have harnessed the power of the creature who attacked us, and it is I who will be the victor this night!"

Triath screamed and put his hands on the sides of his head. Sabian felt the energy compressing towards Triath and marveled at the power anti-Triath possessed. This man had psionic ability, the power to manipulate the energy of the world without the use of magic. Anti-Triath appeared to be using a Mindblast, creating a cone of energy directed at Triath's mind with the hope of incapacitating him. But it seemed Triath had some power of his own. After only a few moments longer of holding his head, he lowered his hands and looked up at his adversary. Sabian felt some of the energies gravitate towards Triath and surround him. He figured it was some kind of Psionic Shell, a basic skill psionicists used to protect themselves from the power of others. It seemed Triath was exceptionally skilled with this particular ability, for the look of concentration on anti-Triath's face was acute as he used all his power to try and breach Triath's defenses.

Sabian felt giddy with the discovery he'd made. The only creature he knew that had psionic ability was a merzillith, an intermediate daemon from one of the Nine Hells. Not only was the daemonic essence present within the "evil" Triath, it existed within the "good" Triath as well. Triath must have encountered a merzillith prior to the creation of his double, and when the "evil" Triath emerged, he must have felt the power within, just waiting to be unleashed. Somehow, "good" Triath had managed to keep the daemon at bay, but not entirely. Triath still had some of the daemon's abilities, just not to the extent of his double.

Anti-Triath grinned malevolently. "So, it seems you have some power after all. Well, you won't be able to keep it up for long. I can feel your concentration waning, even now."

Sabian glanced at Triath and saw how anti-Triath had made his deduction. Triath was obviously in some amount of pain, and the gash in his head from his meeting with the wall of the inn surely didn't help any. Blood from the wound ran thick and dark down the side of his face, and he would need to see Tianna as soon as he made it back to the Golden Griffon.

Just as Triath's shell began to fail, anti-Triath leaped to take advantage. With the power of his mind he created a whip and cracked the invisible weapon against his opponent. Triath flinched from the blow, and any clothing in the way parted with the impact. As Triath fought the realization of what was happening, anti-Triath cracked his whip again, laughing insanely with the pleasure it *provided.*

Again and again anti-Triath beat his opponent with the Psionic Whip. *Triath's shirt hung in pieces from his body, and thin lines of blood marred the flesh of his chest and arms. Sabian continued to watch the interplay, almost forgetting about the battle going on inside the inn, focusing entirely on the combat before him. He saw Triath's confusion pass into anger, felt a shift in energy, and then the slight compression of the air that heralded a Psionic Force. But this time, instead of seeing Triath being knocked off his feet, Sabian saw anti-Triath being hurled through the air. The other man slammed into some barrels arranged against the wall of the inn.*

Triath wasted no time as he rushed his opponent. Drawing his dagger, he tackled his double as he struggled to rise. He straddled anti-Triath's back, pushing his face into the dirt. As the other man attempted to reach behind and grab at him, Triath took the offending hand, slammed it down on the ground beside him, and embedded the dagger into the palm. Anti-Triath gave a blood-curdling shriek and began to struggle ferociously. Noticing some cloth sacks lying next to him, Triath picked one up and shoved it over anti-Triath's head, drawing the ends of the sack around his neck. The other man struggled even more, his body writhing and bucking in a mad attempt to dislodge Triath.

After a while, the struggling finally receded. Breathing heavily, Triath grabbed the cloth around anti-Triath's neck, forcing his opponent's shoulders and chest up off the ground. "So where is your magnificent power now?" he hissed. "Not used to being human now, are you? Damned daemon inside can't see out with this sack over your head."

Suddenly Triath went still, and for a moment his eyes were blank. Sabian wondered what was happening. Despite his weakening state, anti-Triath was probably attempting another psionic attack. But then Triath was in motion once more. He slammed the enemy's head onto the ground and cursed, spittle flying from his mouth. "Effin umberhulk dung! You can't paralyze me now!"

He withdrew his dagger from anti-Triath's hand and roughly rolled the other man over and repositioned himself on top. In vain, anti-Triath attempted to grab him while he used his empty hand to grope at the sack. Once Triath had found what he was looking for, he raised his dagger over anti-Triath's face, and with a downward plunge, sank the dagger deep.

Once again, anti-Triath emitted a terrible shriek. This time it seemed almost inhuman. With the last vestiges of his waning strength, anti-Triath succeeded in bucking Triath off. He stood up and clawed at the cloth sack over his head. The dagger held it firmly in place, and Sabian could see that the weapon was embedded in one of the eyes... the evil eye. Blood soaked the side of the sack, and it was quickly spreading downward.

Anti-Triath stumbled in the direction of the inn, which Sabian finally noticed had caught fire. He had ignored the signs of the fire before, disregarding the odor of something burning during the battle he had just witnessed. Triath finally rose and watched as his double stumbled to the inn and found his way through the open door. Sabian could see that the fire had already reached the kitchen, and as anti-Triath made his way through, the combustibles within exploded.

Triath recoiled, drawing his arms up in front of his face. Not wanting to be caught there, Sabian darted back around towards the front of the inn, knowing that Triath was soon to follow. As he ran, he cast his Transformation *spell, again morphing himself into the form of the blood raven. He flew back to the Golden Griffon Inn and awaited everyone's return.*

Now, as Sabian made his way back to the Sherkari Fortress, he felt a measure of dismay at the loss of the evil Triath. He would have been quite a commodity, a great tool the Daemundai could have had at their disposal. That is, if Sabian had found some way of swaying the man to his cause. However, even if he'd explained himself fully to anti-Triath, describing his association with the Daemundai, Sabian would most likely have been killed anyway, just for the simple pleasure it would have given the other man. That was the nature of a Merzillith, and Sabian knew it was something he would have to control with Triath when the time came.

Dinim walked through the quiet library, glad that there was no one else about. It would be difficult to speak with Adrianna, but he couldn't procrastinate any longer. Any time now, the Master would come for her, and she needed to know what to expect. She would undoubtedly be surprised, for she'd had no contact with Master Tallachienan before. She would wonder how the sorcerer had learned about her and why he had chosen her out of so many others across Ansalar.

Dinim paused when he finally saw her and took a deep inward breath. Adrianna had made it abundantly clear she wanted nothing to do with him, and he had subsequently kept away. He'd briefly entertained thoughts of leaving the group, but then thought better of it, knowing they would need him in the battle ahead. Setting aside his emotions, he had stayed for the greater good of the cause. If not for that, he would have been gone weeks ago.

Hesitantly, Dinim approached. Adrianna looked up from the book she was perusing, her expression neutral. He glanced at it and saw the depiction of a silver dragon adorning the cover. He then looked back up to her face, noting her shielded demeanor. Dinim smiled pleasantly despite knowing it wouldn't quite reach his eyes. "I've been searching for you. You can be rather difficult to track down, you know."

Adrianna closed the book and tucked it beneath her arm. She regarded him intently for a moment before she began walking towards the library entrance. "Why are we meeting here Dinim? What is so important, or not, that requires my amateur attention?"

He winced. "Actually, it is rather important."

Adrianna continued walking for a moment longer before stopping and turning to face him. She regarded him expectantly, patiently waiting for him to tell her what was on his mind.

"You may be more than a little surprised when I tell you this. It came as a surprise to me, and I know Master Tallachienan rather well..." He cringed again at the memory of how he had treated her and simply trailed off.

Adrianna's brows furrowed. "What is it?"

Dinim nodded an apology, but some part of him was proud that she stood up to him rather than dismissing him. "Over the past several moon cycles I've been keeping Master Tallachienan apprised of our activities. On several occasions I spoke to him about the people with whom I've been keeping myself, including you. It seems he has garnered quite an opinion of you and wants you to join him at his citadel as his apprentice."

Dinim watched her intently as he said the last. A series of expressions passed over Adrianna's face before she finally settled upon a single emotion. She shook her head as she made her reply, her eyes continuing to mirror her incredulity. "Dinim, you know I can't leave. Our mission against Aasarak is my primary concern right now. How can I–"

Dinim held up his hands, forestalling any additional comments. "Adrianna, I understand how you feel about leaving the group, but let me tell you how important this decision is. An apprenticeship with the Master isn't one to be dismissed lightly. Very few people are asked to study with him, and many would give an arm or a leg to do so. You will gain knowledge and skill you've only dreamed about, and with that type of power you will have the capacity to aid the group in so many more ways. Ultimately the decision is up to you, but in my opinion, you would be a fool not to accept."

Adrianna frowned and narrowed her eyes. "As I recall, you seem to think I'm a fool already."

The words slammed into Dinim like an umberhulk wagon. He wasn't prepared for the pain he heard in her voice, or the bitterness. It was suddenly difficult for him to breathe, and he had to clear his throat before he could speak once more. "Adrianna, please let's–"

She shook her head. "You're right. Let's not go there." She sighed heavily and took a moment to refocus. "My answer remains the same. The Wildrunners need me now, and I won't desert the group so that I can cater to my own desires and garner some bit of personal satisfaction. Don't get me wrong, under any other circumstances I would leap at this opportunity, but not right now. There is too much at stake."

"But that's just it! The group doesn't need you right now. I've discovered the location of the rod I told Sirion about, and we can take the journey to obtain it without you. We can spare you for a few moon cycles while you study, and by the time you return to us, we will be ready to fight Aasarak. You will have some heavier arcane weaponry under your sash, and you might be able to turn the tide of the battle in our favor."

Adrianna pondered his words for a few moments and finally nodded. "I will speak to Sirion about it. Once I have his opinion, I will let you know what I've decided. Are you sure you won't need me for the journey?"

Dinim nodded. "Have some faith in the rest of us. We can get the job done. Then we will figure out how to use the rod. When the time comes, we will move against Aasarak. When Master Tallachienan has deemed your studies complete, he will return you to us wherever we may be."

"But are you sure he wants me? I've already been apprenticed under another master."

Dinim shook his head. "Yes, but your time was cut short. You never completed your final test in the Sorcerer's Tower. Master Tallachienan will show you another level of spell-casting, one that is known by few others. You will undergo your tests with him, and once they are complete, you will leave his side to make your mark in the world as a journeyman."

Adrianna nodded. "All right. I will let you know."

Dinim nodded in return. She turned and began to walk away. "Adrianna..."

She stopped and looked back over her shoulder. Dinim swallowed heavily before continuing. "I am sorry for everything that has happened between us, and I wish that you could find it in your heart to forgive me."

Adrianna was silent for a moment before she replied. "I *have* forgiven you, Dinim. But it's not so easy to forget."

Dinim silently watched as she walked out of the library. His heart ached at the sadness he saw in her eyes when she responded to his plea, and it cut him to the core of his being. He hoped one day he could make everything up to her, and perhaps, just perhaps, she would finally allow herself to forget.

On the Road Again

Sirion was silent as he walked beside Adrianna. The day was cool and brisk, typical for this time of year. Soon the snows would come, and most people would remain in their homes for the duration of the winter season. However, now that the general location of the Rod of Atlenbos had been discovered, the Wildrunners would be leaving Elvandahar within the week and the warmth of a well-kept fire would be a thing of the past.

Sirion mulled over the things Adrianna had just shared with him. An apprenticeship with Master Tallachienan Chroalthone was nothing to take lightly. Sirion had heard of the man many times during his four and a half decades, and some people even believed him to be more than a mere mortal. He was one of the most powerful sorcerers to walk Shandahar, and if Adrianna were to accept his tutelage...

As the moments passed silently by, he knew he was taking longer than he should to reply, but he honestly didn't know what to say. A part of him wanted her to take the apprenticeship, to learn all she could from this man and become as successful in her profession as Sirion was in his. He wanted her to be all she could be, and if that meant leaving his side for a time, then so be it. She was young, and this was the time in her life when she should endeavor to make herself into the sorceress she wanted to become, the one she was *destined* to become.

Yet, there was another part of Sirion that didn't want her to go. The situation was reminiscent of one he'd encountered many years ago with the young druidess, Joselyn. At that time in his life, he was still busy making a place for himself in the world. It had been his decision, as well as Joselyn's, to focus on their professions instead of their personal relationship. It was a decision he'd never truly regretted.

But Joselyn *had* regretted it, and that regret ultimately ended her life.

Adrianna wrapped the fur-lined cloak more tightly around her and cast a sidelong glance at her companion. *What is he thinking? I mean, I know he doesn't mind my Talent, and I believe he even respects me for it. But will he let me go? I don't know how he feels about me furthering my education, especially now that the group has decided to find Aasarak and put an end to the treachery he concocted with constructs such as Thane.*

For a moment she thought she saw an expression of strain pass over Sirion's features, but dismissed it when it disappeared more quickly than it had come. She began to doubt herself. *Maybe I'm being selfish for mentioning this. Maybe I need to stop entertaining silly thoughts of apprenticing under Master Tallachienan, no matter what Dinim said.* Unfortunately, that was easier said than done. Tallachienan Chroalthone was more than just a well-known figure in arcane history. He was a paragon in his field of expertise, and very few people even knew or understood what that field was. She had read about him in one of the texts she was asked to study whilst an apprentice under Master Tallek. All throughout the book there were references made to the man, including his outstanding merits as a spellcaster and his subsequent rise to power. It wasn't until later she learned he was a god...

Adrianna was about to tell Sirion she wouldn't be taking the apprenticeship, when he spoke. "When will you be going?"

The pair stopped to face one another along the forested path. Adrianna closed her mouth and shook her head. "I don't know. Dinim and I didn't speak of the details."

Sirion nodded thoughtfully. "Let me know when you find out." Adrianna nodded in reply. "Sirion, are you sure–"

"Shhh." Sirion stepped forward and placed two fingers over her lips. "Yes, I'm sure. You need to do this. It isn't just coincidence that one of the most powerful wizards to influence the world has asked you to be his apprentice. It's your destiny."

She shook her head. "My destiny is with you, Sirion."

He let his fingers caress her lips before letting his hand return to his side. "I hope so. One day we can be together, but not yet." Sirion took her hand within his. "For many years I have pursued my dreams and made my mark in the world. But you have yet to do that. I won't be the one to hold you back. Now your time has come. It is your turn to chase your dreams, and when you return to me, we will have all of the days remaining in our lives to be together."

With her heart in her throat, Adrianna stepped close to Sirion and put her arms around him. Sirion returned the embrace and they stood there for a few moments, each absorbing the warmth given by the other. Adrianna smiled as they parted, and Sirion returned the gesture. Yet, his demeanor was quick to shift into one of solemnity.

His tone was almost hesitant. "Adrianna, I've been thinking about what we should do with the Ring of Aboleth."

"Adrianna frowned. "What do you mean?"

"It is an artifact of awesome power. I am sure that the temptation to use its power is still there, lurking inside your mind."

A mixture of hurt and anger coursed through her. "Sirion, are you trying to say you don't trust me?"

"No, it has nothing to do with me trusting you. It's the ring I don't trust."

Sirion watched Adrianna take a step back, releasing her cloak to place her hands on her hips. The cloak flowed around her in a crimson wave, and her eyes flashed with indignation. He suddenly remembered just how beautiful she was when she was angry.

"Sirion, one does not place trust or distrust in inanimate objects. The truth is that you don't trust me with the ring and that you want me to get rid of it."

Sirion sighed. "Adria, those who have learned it still exists will come in search of it and will try to wrest it from you. It is dangerous to keep it in your possession for this reason alone. Those with whom you keep company will also be at risk as long as you have it. Yes, I think you should rid yourself of the ring."

Sirion said the last with his hands resting at his own hips. His voice had risen as he made his argument, and he could see the effect it was having on Adrianna. She pondered over his words, and within moments he saw she understood the reasoning behind them. However, she wasn't happy about the decision she was being forced to make. It was obvious she wanted to keep the ring with her, perhaps thinking it was safe from the machinations of others as long as it remained within her benign possession.

For several moments silence reigned. Sirion thought about her predicament. *She is probably wondering how she can rid herself of it, yet continue to keep it safe from others at the same time. Who can she entrust with it, or where can she take it where she can be certain it won't be disturbed?*

Sirion then had an idea. "Adrianna, why don't we take the ring to Andahye? Perhaps there we can find a place where it can be locked away. There must certainly be a place; it *is* the seat of arcane power this side of Ansalar."

Adrianna looked up at him with a thoughtful expression, tinged with an air of irritability. "I would rather not go there. Perhaps we can take the ring back to where Dinim and I first acquired it. Master Paxil kept it safe for so long, maybe he won't mind taking it back into his possession."

"Perhaps, but now the existence of the ring has been made known once again, as well as the location. You need to accept the possibility that Master Paxil won't want the ring with him, especially now. It will be easy to trace it back to him, and those who would hunt you down will also hunt for him."

Adrianna sighed heavily. After a few moments her shoulders slumped as though the weight of the world suddenly rested on them. "You're right. Paxil probably won't want it back, and it would be wrong for me to expect him to take it." Adrianna paused before continuing. "Damnation! I so much dislike the prospect of returning to Andahye!"

Now it was Sirion's turn to frown. "Why? Was it so bad for you there?" He reached out and placed a consoling hand on her arm.

Adrianna turned away and began to walk along the path once again. Sirion fell into place beside her. Adrianna recaptured her cloak and brought it around herself. "No, it really wasn't so bad. But the only person who made that place worthwhile for me is dead and gone. I had very few friends while I was there, and many of those have probably gone by now. I left rather precipitously, and I have much to answer for. I suppose I have to face up to my mistakes sooner or later."

Sirion's grip on her arm tightened. "You don't have to face them alone. I will be there with you."

Adrianna glanced at Sirion for a moment before nodding and casting her eyes back to the ground. "I know."

It was then he realized her trepidation not only lay with Andahye, but the path they would use to make it there. In spite of her initial resistance, Sirion pulled her close to his side as they walked. She rested her head on his shoulder and slowed her pace. The words Adrianna spoke next were a whisper of sound that seemed as though it came from the winds that swept along the leaf-strewn path.

"I love you, Sirion."

Triath solemnly regarded himself in the looking glass. He took in his appearance: the snug dark blue trousers, crisp white shirt, and matching light blue vest with darker stitching. His body was in excellent shape; his legs lean and muscular, his belly flat, and his chest finely sculpted. His light brown hair just touched the tops of his shoulders, and he sported a finely chiseled jaw line. He had the nose of a nobleman, and his eyebrows arched gracefully over cerulean blue eyes. No, eye.

He had only one eye.

As Triath frowned, he became disgusted with the image in the glass. Once upon a time he had been a vision of perfection: every lock of hair in place, his brows arched just so, his eyes mesmerizing in their intensity. And when he smiled, the world smiled with him. But no more.

The daemon had taken so much more when he took Triath's eye.

Triath stepped closer to the looking glass, studying every line of his face. His gaze was inadvertently drawn to the scar on his cheekbone that disappeared beneath the black patch that covered his eye socket. Triath touched the scar with his forefinger, tracing it to the patch. When he lifted the patch from its place, he swallowed convulsively.

Once again Triath regarded himself. One eye was blue, the other black as pitch. He hated that lifeless orb resting nonchalantly in his face like it belonged there. Something had happened during his ill-fated battle with the merzillith daemon, something he couldn't entirely remember. He knew only that it was magic.

After the battle, Triath had been forced to bed-rest for several days. Laura took care of him, cleansing the wounds that the daemon had inflicted upon his chest, arms, and face. Not to mention the empty socket where his eye had once been, having been torn out by the daemon before it died a hideous death. After a while, Triath was able to tend to the socket himself. Laura showed him how to apply the salve so as to keep it moist until it healed and how to change the bandage when it became soiled. It was at that time Triath began to notice something strange happening to that eye socket, and within several more days, a new eye had filled the void.

It took Triath a few days longer to tell the rest of the group about the emergence of the new eye. He didn't know why he waited– perhaps he was afraid it would cause them to react in the same way he had. And when he finally showed them what had occurred, he saw his fear was well-founded. The shock and dismay expressed on his friends' faces was enough to send him into moody contemplation, and he seriously considered cutting the new eye out of his socket. It didn't belong there, but in the face of an evil daemon, one that lay dead several days in the swamps south of Tambour.

But Triath didn't remove the eye. Mayhap he was too afraid of the pain he would endure only to have it grow back again. He continued to wear the patch, and after a while, began to realize that when he removed the barrier, the eye didn't see the world the way his 'normal' eye did. The view was different, so alien it was difficult to describe. Instead of seeing the dimensions of things, in all their many colors, he saw things in within a single plane consisting of shades of blue, brown, and grey. Oftentimes his vision was hazy, but he could distinguish the thermal properties of a given object. And then, if he left the patch off for long enough, he began to see weird things– things floating around at the periphery of his vision, things that were drawn to him, touching him with feather-light familiarity. Their caress was one he never wished to experience again, yet he had also realized his powers became magnified with the removal of the patch.

Yes, powers. Not only had he gained the eye of the daemon, but many of the abilities of the creature as well. The daemonic powers that had nearly defeated Triath during the fight had begun to manifest within *him*. The powers were varied, and he knew that the secret to learning them all meant he needed to remove the patch entirely. However, he found himself unwilling to do so. He wasn't certain he was prepared to suffer the consequences of that action.

Triath continued to stare at his reflection. The man in the glass looked strange, no longer quite human. Within the very fiber of his being, Triath knew he was no longer the man he was before that battle. Something had come and taken up residence within him, something so fearful he didn't dare think overly long about it. But think about it he did, knowing that it was there lurking deep inside him like a coiled serpent. It waited for the opportunity to spring from its hollow, to wreak whatever havoc it could on its surroundings.

Triath reminisced about another time and another place... his fight with his double in the city of Entsy. His double had removed his eyepatch, allowed the creature within free reign. And Triath had experienced firsthand the things that he would be able to accomplish if he were to do the same. That man had wielded such power, had mastered so many of the creature's abilities in so short a time. Yet, it was the daemon that lived inside anti-Triath that had ultimately been his undoing. Anti-Triath had lost touch with his human self, and when Triath put that sack over his head, the man hadn't known what to do. Triath had reached out with his mind, felt the disorientation that his enemy was feeling, the inability to suddenly start using his human senses to take back control of the situation. And so, despite anti-Triath's power, Triath had won the fight and lived to see another day.

Triath gazed into the black eye, so much wanting to discover its secrets, yet afraid to do so. It was so deep despite the absence of soul. All of a sudden, something within him began to rise and started to reflect within the depths of the daemon eye. Triath kept himself in check, refusing to acknowledge the abrupt desire to flee, to place the patch back over the eye. It rose higher, and Triath recognized it as the serpent having found its opportunity. Triath trembled, feeling himself become suffused with strange sensations he had only felt flutters of heretofore. From out of the black eye he began to see a darkness about himself reflecting within the looking glass, something that would be imperceptible to a mere human eye. The room began to look hazy, and he felt a wrenching in his mind.

Triath clutched his skull, closing his eyes with the pain. The thing within him continued to rise, seeking to overcome him. He felt power and began to get an inkling of what lay within, waiting to be tapped. Triath opened his eyes and once again saw himself in the glass. He saw his hands clutching his head-saw his normal human eye, and then his daemon black one. He became angry, hating the emotions coursing through him, fear and denial paramount. In the glass, Triath noticed a vase on the table next to his bed. Despite the pain and the rising darkness, Triath reached his mind towards the object...

The vase flew off of the table. Triath moved his head just in time before the thing hit the looking glass. Shards flew in every direction and Triath fell to the floor. Scratching at his face, Triath maneuvered the patch back over his eye, hiding it from the world once more. The thing within him began to recede, as did the pain in his skull. Several moments later, Triath finally stood. Pieces of the looking glass crunched beneath his boots as he walked across the floor to the bed. He slumped down onto the furs and breathed deeply. *What the Hells is going to happen to me?*

16 Chanteren CY593

The Wildrunners traveled south towards the Denegal River. Once crossing it, they would journey towards the Bryton Hills. Travel there would be more difficult and slow paced. Dartanyen projected it would take them approximately three weeks to make it to the northern border of the hills. They would then search for the ancient temple to which Dinim's references referred. There were some crude references made to the terrain surrounding the temple, but for all they knew, the decades had changed the landscape and the clues no longer existed.

Early that morning the group had left the city of Alcrostat. Many farewells to family and friends had already been made, but the parting was difficult nonetheless. For a while they rode together as a whole, but by midday, the time for them to separate had come. It had been decided that, while the larger part of the group went in search of the rod, a smaller contingent would accompany Adrianna to Andahye, where she would place the Ring of Aboleth in the protective custody of the Varanghelie Vaults.

Sheridana had been instantly wary of the idea. She simply wasn't prepared to part with her sister again, especially so soon after being reunited. "Are you sure this is a good idea? Maybe we should all go."

Sirion had shaken his head. "We will be fine, Sheridana. Besides, it would be a waste of time and resources if we all went. Sorn, Amethyst, and I will be ample protection for Adrianna on her journey to Andahye. The rest of you should focus on obtaining the rod. Once our two groups have each completed their mission, we will meet back in Elvandahar unless we agree otherwise."

Sheridana had continued to frown. "Perhaps I should go in place of Amethyst or Sorn–"

"No, Amethyst is still in training. It's important she learn all she can from Sorn before we meet with Aasarak. Besides, your skills are best suited for the mission involving the rod. The group will need your strength and skill with Destroyer."

Sheridana had pursed her lips with perplexity. She was certain Sirion was just saying that so she would stop making such a fuss. He wouldn't step down from his position as Adrianna's chief protector, no matter what argument was put forth. Besides, the rest of the group seemed content with the division, so she didn't have much clout.

Sirion had then placed a hand on her shoulder, his gaze intent. "Adrianna will be safe with us, I promise you that."

Sheridana remembered those words as she watched her sister ride away. Adrianna took one last look behind her as she, Sirion, Sorn, and Amethyst disappeared among the trees. In spite of Sirion's reassurances, Sheridana had the sinking feeling that it would be quite a while before they were together again.

For much of the day they rode in silence, the weight of recent farewells weighing on everyone's mind. It was soon apparent to Sheridana that she wasn't the only one who disliked parting company with Adrianna. After a while she moved her larian to walk alongside Dinim's. He must have been able to tell what she was thinking because he started speaking without her having to say anything. "It's dangerous for her to go on a journey like that without me," he said with a shake of his head. "She's at risk while she carries that damned ring, and gods only know who or what they might encounter on their journey. I know Sirion thinks he is her best defense, but..." His voice trailed off.

"But what?" she asked. "Isn't it best she take it to the safest place possible? You said yourself it is unknown for anyone to have the ability to break into one of the Varanghelie Vaults."

Dinim nodded solemnly. "Yes, they are protected by the strongest of magicks, and only those with power and wealth are able to keep things there. It was good of King Thalios to provide the gold necessary to store the ring."

Sheridana shrugged. "So what is the problem, then?"

"It isn't the destination that bothers me. It is the journey itself. I'm sorry, but I don't trust anyone other than myself with her safety."

The last he said rather obstinately with a stubborn set to his jaw. Sheridana just stared at him for a moment, an eyebrow raised. Not more than a few weeks ago, he had tried to kill Adrianna with one of his most powerful spells, Yet, she understood. She had suspected once before, but never really knew for certain– Dinim was in love with her sister. It was no small wonder why he was so disturbed by the parting. Sheri simply patted his shoulder and moved off after a while when it looked like they might try to find a place to rest the animals.

For several more days the group journeyed through southern Elvandahar. Despite the deepening cold, the traveling was easy, the larian keeping a good pace. Naemmious' lloryk was one of the largest Sheridana had ever encountered, but he was a gentle beast and carried the massive form of his rider without slowing them down. The half-oroc had proven to be a good ally and companion. In spite of Naemmious' often menacing countenance, he was gentle at heart and Sheridana felt drawn to him. He responded to her in kind, and a strong friendship had sprung between them on their journey to Elvandahar after the battle with Thane. The same had happened with many other members of the merged groups. Over the weeks since their fight, Amethyst had become somewhat of an apprentice to Sorn, and Anya and Dartanyen had begun to share a camaraderie. Sheridana was glad to see it, for she had heard the story of the friendship he'd shared with a fallen comrade they called Bussimot. Sheridana couldn't help but remember Zorg's company, and she knew Armond felt his loss more than any other.

As they traveled, Sheridana focused upon the environment through which they passed. Elvandahar was a beautiful place, full of intriguing plants and animals. In the deeper parts of the forest, leshera were most prolific. They were slender beasts, with short brown hair, delicate heads, thin legs, and large dark eyes. However, the graceful creatures were often elusive, so a person tended to catch only a glimpse of one before it was gone, bounding off into the trees. A couple of times the group heard the snorting and shuffling of a bruin. They were careful to keep their distance from the large animal, skirting the area respectfully as they passed. Bruin were often difficult to deal with in an encounter, and no one wanted an altercation that could ultimately cause its death.

As the group began to approach the borderlands, that place that marked the end of the forest and the beginning of the steppes, the environment began to change. The trees got smaller, and the grasses thicker. The diversity there was greater, the plants and animals of the plains coexisting in this place with those of the forest. Here one could find a greater abundance of shaggy grey wemic, for resources there were bountiful. The nights were never silent, the packs calling to one another in the twilight hours and well into the darkness. In this area one could find wild boar as well. Sheridana was immediately repelled by the animals. They were a strong reminder of their larger cousins, the alothere, and with those she had endured bad experiences in the past. The wild boar were aggressive, and ugly. She would just as soon hunt one for her dinner than bother evading them.

In all, it took the group approximately eight days to finally reach the timberline and the border of Elvandahar. Another half-day would get them to the Denegal River. They would camp there until the next morning, and then take a ferry across. Once on the other side they would be in the kingdom of Karlisle. Sheridana had never been there before, and it would be a new experience. Rumor in Elvandahar had it that relations between them and the humans that ruled Karlisle were tenuous. Many believed that their king, Geronfrey of Mondemer, was going insane. That was just hearsay, but nevertheless, they would be careful whilst in Karlisle– keep out of trouble, and not make any noise.

The small group of travelers journeyed north from the Terrestra River. The first snows began to fall, and the temperatures dipped and continued to slowly plummet through the day and into the night. Without the protection of the trees, the cold winds were swift, seeking access to the warm bodies beneath their thick winter cloaks. Only eyes could be seen beneath the furred hoods, scarves covering the rest of their faces from the cold. The larian were covered with thick blankets beneath their riding pads, which extended all the way down to their knees. Amethyst hoped the snows wouldn't last long, for if it got deep enough, the blankets would need to be rolled up. The poor animals would be even colder than they were already.

The group stopped by a small copse of trees and began to set up camp for the night. First they worked to pitch the tent Sirion had brought with him from Elvandahar. It was just big enough for the four of them, with little space left over. It might have proved stifling in the summer, but when it was this cold, the warmth of other bodies close by was appreciated.

Once the tent was under control, Amethyst went to the larian and saw to their comfort. The animals stood close together for warmth. She removed the travel packs and riding pads from each one, rubbed each back briskly with the palms of her hands and a curry brush, and then gave everyone a couple handfuls of grain. She then removed a large blanket from one of the packs and draped it over the three animals. Wanting to make sure everyone was well, she patted each nose and looked into each mouth before heading back to the tent.

Amethyst stepped inside and was relieved to be out of the cold. Adrianna had brought in the travel packs and laid out everyone's bedrolls. Outside, on the leeward side of the tent, Sirion and Sorn had built a fire and were preparing a warm brew. It was several more moments before the men came in with a pot of steaming tea. Adrianna retrieved their flask of mead and poured some of the pale brown liquid into the pot. Sorn swirled the contents around as he seated himself on his own bedroll, on the far side of Amethyst's. Sirion also sat down and Adrianna opened the food pouches. Sorn filled four mugs and passed them to everyone.

Adrianna took her mug. The brew was warm and bubbly as it went down her throat. Within moments, her body began to feel the effects of the invigorating drink, and the cold began to recede. They passed around the bread, cheese, roasted nuts, and dried berries. They had restocked their supplies at a large village near the Terrestra River, and even spent the night in the barn of a friendly livestock keeper. The smell of the animals hadn't bothered them as they received a good night's sleep. The next morning they had given the man a gift of silver for his generosity, thanked his family for the loaf of fresh-baked bread, and then boarded the ferry to cross the river.

The next village was located just outside of the Sheldomar Forest, a day's ride from their present location. If they made haste in the morning, and rode quickly throughout the day, they would reach it by nightfall. They would then be able to purchase a few more supplies before entering the forest.

Adrianna didn't look forward to traveling through Sheldomar. Memories of that place had haunted her for longer than she cared to realize, and entering the forest again was not something she cherished. She knew the fear was unrealistic, but it was a primal fear, one over which she had very little rational control. She kept reminding herself that, this time, Sirion was with her, as well as Amethyst and the new friendship she had found in Sorn. They all would stand by her should the need arise.

When the meal was finished, they packed away the remaining food. Sorn and Amethyst began talking about an aspect of her training and soon were deep in conversation. Adrianna settled down with a book and Sirion set about examining his weapons and equipment. It was at these times, usually before their meal had been taken, that they would have a practice session with their staves. She had learned much from Sirion since the first afternoon he'd invited her to spar with him, and she was glad they had continued the instruction while in Elvandahar. Tonight, however, with the snow coming down, it would be difficult to practice. Adrianna hated to think that their sessions would be coming to an end, but accepted the possibility.

The cold temperature and the rigors of the day wore on them more heavily than usual, and it wasn't long before they were preparing for sleep. The temperature within the small tent had risen, and the walls of the structure kept the winds away. Once ready, they blew out the lanterns and settled themselves beneath their furs. Adrianna pressed her body close to Sirion, and he wrapped his arms tightly around her. In the darkness he found her lips and kissed her tenderly. She responded to him in kind, a warmth settling within the pit of her belly that had nothing to do with the drink she had imbibed earlier. She reveled in the feel of his embrace, and she never wanted to imagine a time when he wouldn't be by her side.

Four days later found them riding through the Sheldomar forest. Despite her dislike for the place, it was easier to travel there than in the borderlands. The small road was relatively clear and the trees afforded them some respite from the weather, blocking some of the wind despite the absence of leaves. The snows had lasted only a couple of days and then subsided, the temperatures climbing slightly upward again after the storm passed. Sirion resumed her training with the staff, warning her that the next time the snows came, he wouldn't put a stop to the sparring. He told her that it would be good for her to learn how to cope with inclement situations, that it would make her body stronger and her mind more alert to her surroundings during a match.

Adrianna was glad that Sirion was so interested in teaching her all he knew about the staff. More than once she wished she had her own weapon, in particular the staff Master Tallek had given her while she was his apprentice. She had left that weapon in her room at Volstagg's inn when she had first returned to Sangrilak after her arcane training in Andahye. It had been overlooked during the drama unfolding with Thane, and then forgotten when they returned there for a brief stay after his defeat. The staff had been constructed just for her, and it would have been nice to use in her lessons with Sirion. Adrianna knew she was getting closer to mastery of the weapon; at the end of each spar Sirion was slightly more winded than he was the last. This fact gratified her, and she sensed that Sirion was happy too, pleased she cared so much to learn what he had to show her.

Adrianna looked forward to the end of every day when she could practice with Sirion, yet she became more wary the deeper they rode into the Sheldomar Forest. The slender road twisted and curved ahead of them, and she couldn't help remembering the last time she'd traveled this path, a journey that had ended in great loss. Her first mentor had died in the ambush that succeeded in taking her hostage. Nahum had given his life to protect her, but it wasn't the only thing she had lost...

For most of the day the group rode in silence. Adrianna sat on the back of her larian, her gaze flicking here and there, alert to any change in the environment around them. Amethyst rode beside her while Sorn took the rear. In the distance ahead of them were Sirion and Dramati, checking the road to be certain it was clear for their passage. Adrianna trusted them, but still couldn't keep from examining every shrub, tree, or rock they passed. That night, they set up camp a bit later than usual. The weather had been friendlier than in previous days, and they had decided to cover more ground. It meant weapons practice would be left out that evening, but it wasn't often they made the decision to keep moving, and more than once they had even set their camp early. So, the evening meal was quickly prepared in the semi-darkness and promptly eaten. Soon after, the group settled down for the night. With the milder temperatures, they chose not to pitch the tent, leaving the sky open and the stars winking at them from above.

Adrianna lay there for quite some time, staring into the sky. She knew they were close to the place that had dominated her worst nightmares for so many years. There was a negative feel about this place. The tragedy of that night, and the days that followed it, had been burned into her memory. She wanted to shuck the cloak of pain, but somehow it remained despite her attempts to be rid of it. Adrianna turned on her side, away from Sirion toward Amethyst's back. She watched as the blankets over the girl rose and fell with her rhythmic breaths, telling Adrianna that she had already fallen into sleep. Behind her she could hear Sirion's breaths also beginning to even out. He shifted closer to her back, finding a comfortable position for rest. Beneath the furs she felt his warm hand slide around her waist to rest at her belly. Adrianna closed her eyes, also feeling the effects of fatigue. Yet her fears kept sleep away, and she stayed awake for some time after the others were deep into their slumber.

How long she lay there she couldn't say. She only knew that time passed because one moment it would be light, the scattered rays of the sun touching her naked flesh, and the next it was dark, the pale light of the moons only vaguely reaching her beyond the leafy canopy above. When she was able, she painstakingly removed the remains of her tunic and stuffed it between her legs, blood from the wounds she'd sustained deep inside continuing to trickle forth. At first the pain was more acute and she gave all her attention to breathing. After a while it became just a terrible ache. She wondered why the wild animals hadn't smelled the blood and come for her. Even they would have been preferable to the agony of lying there on the ground, dying a slow death.

Perhaps two days passed, maybe three. It was then she knew it was only a matter of time. She was chilled where she lay, but she didn't have the energy left to even try to move. The insects had come, and she felt the pain as they ate at the raw rope burns on her wrists, the cuts on her face, and the deep lacerations on her chest and belly. Somewhere in the depths of her mind she knew only something magical could save her from death.

Then it came. Fever ran rampant through her battered body and old blood soaked the cloth between her thighs. Black and blue bruises covered the fair skin of her neck, chest, and ribs. The lacerations were surrounded by hot, dark red flesh. Like a creature from a wondrous dream, the unicorn came to her. The beautiful animal stood over her, looking down at her broken body. Then he lowered his head- brought it closer, closer, closer. His soft muzzle touched her swollen face, gently breathing over her eyes, nose, and mouth. And then it was lowering even more, stopping only when the tip of his long, spiraled horn touched the oozing wound on her belly.

Adrianna lay, unmoving before the unicorn. She was dead, and the mystical creature had come to bear her away into the Netherworld. She felt comforted by this, knowing unicorns were heavenly beasts and only came to those who were good of heart and pure of soul. It was her mind's way of telling her that everything would finally be all right, and that she would find peace at last.

But then, all of a sudden, Adrianna began to feel a sensation of warmth suffusing her abdomen. The feeling intensified, accompanied by excruciating pain. She tried to cry out, but all that emerged was a croak, her throat so parched from lack of water that nothing else would come. Then, just as suddenly, the pain was gone, and the area of warmth began to encompass her ribs, pelvis, chest, and thighs. Her entire body became bathed in the warmth afforded by the magic of the unicorn.

For a long time Adrianna lay there, luxuriating in the sensations surging through her. The agony had subsided, and when she moved, there was significantly less pain. Finally more alert, she opened her eyes more widely and saw the horn of the unicorn glowed a soft yellow. A realization began to dawn on her, and her mind began to whirl. Perhaps she wasn't dead after all, and this unicorn was real.

Finally the sensations ceased. The glow receded from the horn, and after a few moments longer, stopped entirely. The unicorn hung his head, his muzzle once more caressing Adrianna's cheek. She could sense the fatigue surrounding the beast, and knew it had given all of its strength so she could live. She slowly lifted her hand and gently touched the beautiful white face. The beast closed his eyes and sank onto the ground beside her. Adrianna continued to stroke the soft fur of the wonderful creature for a few moments, but then her own tiredness took over. The darkness of a healing sleep swept over her and she was free of pain for the first time in what seemed like forever.

For three more days they had traveled through the Sheldomar Forest. Adrianna's memories continued to play over and over again in her mind but she ceased to fight them. The events that had unfolded after that terrible night following the ambush were agonizing, but that time was passed. The unicorn had seen her suffering and chose to aid her, a mystical creature who was her savior. For that she would always be profoundly grateful, for the beast had given her a part of himself that day– the will to endure despite the deep sorrows that drowned her heart and the shadows that enveloped her soul.

For two days the unicorn carried her through the forest. In the middle of the first day, they reached a freshwater stream. They drank thirstily before Adrianna cleansed herself in it. It felt good to wash away the dirt, blood, and remnants of rape. She still felt the pain of that night, for the unicorn hadn't been able to heal her entirely. She could feel a sickness within her, lying deep inside, waiting to spring forth. However, the unicorn had saved her life at great cost to himself, and he slept nearby while she bathed. He was tired, profoundly so, yet he carried her weary body through the forest in the direction of Andahye. Somehow he knew the magical city was her destination.

After the second day, Adrianna began to feel the fever come upon her once again. With what energy he could muster, the unicorn set his horn to her once again, healing her so that she would be able to survive and walk upright for the remainder of the distance to Andahye. The next day she did just that, feeling better than she had since before the ambush. Despite the continued bleeding from the place between her thighs, she was strong.

For almost three more days, Adrianna and the unicorn walked slowly towards Andahye. The unicorn didn't leave her side until they came to the forest outskirts. Once out in the open, the beast could travel with her no longer, but only one more day of walking remained between them and the city. Adrianna bade the unicorn farewell, wrapping her arms around his neck and sobbing into his silky fur. She sensed the sadness emanating from him and knew he would miss her as well. She knew she would never see him again, for unicorns were rare. It was unheard for a person to see a unicorn more than once in his or her lifetime, and most people didn't get to see one at all.

After that, Adrianna journeyed alone. She deviated from the main path, just as Nahum had told her, and remained ever watchful for any signs of danger. By the time she finally reached the rock-strewn area in which the city could be found, she was feeling the effects of fever again. She remembered the specifications Nahum had taught her– the precise location of the entry into the city, as well as the words she needed to speak in order to gain access.

In her fevered state, it took her another half day to find the two large boulders with the image of a trio of stars inscribed into each one. Adrianna struggled to speak the words that would open the gates into a city she had never seen. She breathed a sigh of relief when the area before her was suddenly the path into the main thoroughfare of Andahye. As she stumbled onto the street she took one last look behind her, taking in the late afternoon position of the sun, the rocky field that she had recently searched...

And it was then she caught a glimpse of silvery white behind a boulder in the near distance, testimony that the magnificent unicorn had never truly left her side.

4 Saliren CY593

Sheridana focused her thoughts upon any and everything but her far away friend and daughter. Thinking upon Carli and Fitanni, safe but without her, lead her down melancholy avenues she could not afford. Instead, she stayed intent upon on the here and now of her life.

For over two days the Wildrunners had traveled through the Bryton Hills. The journey there was a relatively easy one; the weather had stayed fairly neutral, and they had encountered no trouble. The caravans they had passed while they traversed the plains on their way to the hills paid them virtually no heed, the merchants and other travelers intent on their own business as they made their way towards the port city of Tambour. That area between the Denegal River and the Bryton Hills sported a wide road, easily accommodating the heavy traffic passing from the cities of Velmist and Cartagena to the port. Nervously, they had waited for someone to panic at the presence of a half-oroc amongst them, but no one seemed to take notice. Perhaps it was the time of year to which they owed thanks. As a result of the colder temperatures, most people were hidden from the prying eyes of others within their winter cloaks. The only thing that would really draw anyone's attention was Naemmious' height. As it turned out, it never became an issue.

Once into the hills, travel had become slightly more difficult. The lloryk and larian bore most of the burden, slowing their pace as they were forced to walk the uneven terrain. The weather thus far had been mild, but they were barely into the winter months. Sheridana knew that when the snows came, it would be even more difficult. However, she hoped they would fare better than Sirion, Adrianna, Sorn, and Amethyst. Their friends traveled further north and had probably encountered their first snowfall already.

Sheridana sat on her bedroll, silently watching the activities of her comrades. Over the last three weeks she had noticed a group dynamic beginning to take shape. Triath was the one that usually prepared the evening fire, and Tianna the one who prepared the meals. An easy friendship had begun to develop between the two, and their laughter was pleasant to hear after a long day of silent riding. Many evenings, Anya and Dartanyen went in search of fresh meat while Armond saw to the animals. Most of the time Sheridana would join him. She found Armond to be a somber individual, not appearing to be interested in any type of conversation with her despite her initial efforts to be friendly. After a few evenings of initiating conversation and not receiving much response, she stopped speaking to him, getting the distinct feeling that he didn't like her, although she knew not why.

During the day, the dynamic was slightly different. Sheridana rode at the front of the group with Dartanyen. Together they usually decided the route they would take, often dictated by the landscape. Sometimes they would notice tracks or other spoor that would be an influence, most often the result of their desire to avoid the thing that produced it. The rest of the group followed behind, usually in pairs. Customarily Dinim and Sabian rode next, followed by Triath and Armond, and then Tianna and Anya. Bringing up the rear would be Naemmious. Sheridana and Dartanyen were often the ones who chose a suitable encampment site. However, sometimes Anya would suggest one if she happened to see something as they passed by. The others simply followed suit, usually uncaring as to the location of camp, as long as they remained out of the wind.

Sheridana shifted on her bedroll, more tired today than she had been of late. Perhaps she would ask Tianna to take her place with Dartanyen at the watch this night. Her eyes sought out the other woman and found her at the other side of the camp, speaking with Triath. Tianna was an easygoing person, and got along with everyone. She was the group's caretaker; when anyone felt ill, it was to her they went in search of herbal remedies. When anyone was injured, it was to her they went to seek healing salves and ointments. And when anyone just needed someone to listen, it was to her that they went in search of an ear.

However, Sheridana had noticed there was really no one in whom Tianna could confide, no one to listen to her woes, and no one to offer a lending hand. There was a melancholy about Tianna, and she often wished she could help. However, nothing she could say or do would help the other woman, for only time could heal a broken heart. Despite the love Tianna felt for Sirion, he couldn't return that emotion, for he had found something greater in the heart of her sister. Adrianna and Sirion were magnificent together, and Sheridana couldn't have asked for anything better for Adrianna.

She let her gaze shift to the man with whom Tianna was making conversation. Triath was an interesting character, one she had yet to figure out. He was an extremely handsome man in spite of the black patch he was forced to wear over one eye. He had only once alluded to the daemon that had removed the eye and a deep scar visibly extended below the confines of the patch-testimony of a brutal battle. She had glimpsed what resided beneath the patch, and the image of that sight had burned itself into her mind. The socket was not empty, like she had thought it would be. Instead an eye rested there, entirely black. The eye bored into her, making the blood run cold in her veins. A chill raced up her spine, and she felt there was something not quite right. But then Triath had readjusted the patch, covering the eerie eye. He'd caught her staring at him, but said nothing as he went about his business. She wondered about it afterward, but as yet, she hadn't mentioned her misgivings to anyone else. Triath had already proven his loyalty to the group when he fought by their side in the battle against Thane. She didn't want to make him feel that she didn't trust him, even though she hadn't been able to do so since the day she saw the eye.

Sheridana sighed and then found her focus coming to rest upon Dinim. His dark brows pulled together into a frown as he deliberated over his scroll. He'd unfurled it, and was turning it this way and that, apparently trying to decipher something about the image, which looked like it might be a map. She watched his frown deepen as he intently pored over it. He was so different from the man she had met only a few moon cycles ago. He had been much more social then, talkative and humorous. But now he was withdrawn, hardly ever spoke to anyone, and rarely smiled. His once quirky nature and light-hearted attitude were things of the past. The consequences of his actions against Adrianna weighed heavily, and her heart went out to him since realizing he cared so deeply for her sister. Even up to their departure, Adrianna could hardly bring herself to speak with him, the pain of his attack still too much for her to endure. Dinim had made his mistakes, and now he paid for them. She only hoped he wouldn't have to do so forever.

Sheridana refocused her gaze when Sabian sat down next to Dinim. The other man took the scroll and began to study it as well. Her eyes narrowed slightly. Sabian was a quiet man and usually kept to himself. There was very little that anyone really knew about him, and she thought that a trifle odd. He'd been with the group longer than she; yet, anyone didn't even know where he was from. He was a magic user and had known Dinim in his early days when he was an apprentice. However, as of yet, no one had seen but a fraction of his skill. Sheridana felt that he was probably more powerful than anyone knew.

Coupled with his secretive nature, this could prove to be deadly. For all she knew, they had a weapon they didn't know how to use. She would have to talk to Dartanyen about it, ask him what he thought of the situation. They had already begun thinking about an endeavor to bring this group together into a more cohesive unit. As it was now, they would be nothing against the power of Aasarak. They would need to know the strengths and weaknesses of every member of the group in order to succeed.

And that would be only half of the battle.

THROUGH THE PORTAL

The Master sat within his massive oak chair, memories of the fourth Cycle running through his mind. He'd been happier than he was since his beloved sister, Briyana, was alive, and he'd finally allowed himself to live in the present. Adrianna was his apprentice, but she'd come to him, her white nightgown falling over the curves of her small body as she settled onto his lap. He remembered the feel of her skin beneath the gown, remembered her response to his caress. He remembered her words, spoken so long ago, yet remaining fresh in his mind.

"I do swear, that I'll always be there. To give you anything, and everything, and I will always care. Through weakness and strength, happiness and sorrow. Through all space and all time, I will love you with every beat of my heart."

She had cupped his face in her hands and kissed him. He remembered the passion they'd shared that night, the fire that burned between them. The love they shared was so strong, nothing could have parted them.

Then she'd gone into battle and died.

The fourth Cycle came to its bloody end and the fifth one began. Tallachienan lived his life as a rebel, breaking many friendships and making even more enemies. He was a rogue spellcaster, perfecting Dimensionalism into the school that it was today. But he could never forget that he'd let the woman he loved fall at the hands of a sordid necromancer, a daemon hybrid sorcerer who lived and breathed the dark arts.

Tallachienan was aware the day Adrianna was born. He could feel it deep within the depths of his mind, her essence calling out to him before she'd even emerged from her mother's body. In his pain he discarded her, determined not to let her back into his heart. He feared he would lose her, yet again, at the end of the Cycle.

Adrianna passed through childhood and then into adolescence. The time that he should have gone to pursue her for training came and went. Talent generally made itself known at the onset of awakening, the time when every faelin child began the physical and mental developments he or she would endure as they shifted into adulthood. He could have taken her any time after that, as he had in the third and fourth Cycles. But not this time. This time he did not come, hoping to wait as long as possible before he had to take her. He'd thought that, if he waited until she was a bit older, he might not find it in his heart to care for her again. However, as the time passed, he began to realize he was making a mistake. By giving in to his selfishness, he was taking away the precious time he would need to train her, and to give her the best chance possible in her fight against Aasarak.

Now the time had come. Tallachienan could wait no longer. He had to begin her training, and he had to take extraordinary measures in order to ensure that she had the best and most complete training possible. This Cycle he had taken Dinim early, and because he had chosen to take Adrianna late, the two had not apprenticed together. This Cycle would provide a different dynamic. Because Tallachienan had waited so long to take her, Adrianna had sought out alternative arcane training. She would have to unlearn much of what she had been taught by her previous Master, and this could prove to be difficult. Nevertheless, he had no one to blame but himself, and the only reason he knew that much was because Dinim had relayed the information to him via his Travel notebook. Dinim had been excited to tell Tallachienan about the extraordinary woman he'd met, a woman with so much untrained Talent that he could hardly stand it.

Tallachienan shook his head. Just by reading Dinim's words written in the notebook, he could sense that his apprentice already had feelings for the girl. It had been that way in the third Cycle, and they'd been lovers for a time until she left the citadel to meet her destiny. In the fourth Cycle, Tallachienan had claimed her for himself, and any relationship that could have formed between them was terminated. This Cycle Tallachienan thought that, with the proximity in which that had found themselves, Dinim and Adrianna naturally would have formed a relationship just as they had in the third. However, Tallachienan had the impression that they had not. He could only speculate as to what kept them apart.

Tallachienan stood from his chair. Preparations needed to be made. He had put them off for far too long. He'd placed Adrianna's life in danger when he waited so long to begin her training, and the measures that he would now have to take in order to train her were extreme to say the least. Even though he would like to do so, Tallachienan couldn't turn back Time. He would just have to manipulate it slightly, with the help of a friend of course. Perhaps then he could tip the scales to their side for once, giving him the chance to train Adrianna the way he should have in the previous two Cycles. He would have to be harsh, but the price was well worth it.

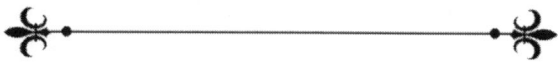

Adrianna read the message on the small scroll, the script inked in very precise handwriting. She would recognize it anywhere, for it was that of Master Garsheim, the Headmaster at the Vanderlinde Academy. Sirion moved to stand behind her and put his hands on her shoulders. "The Masters will meet us at the vaults at midday," she said.

Sorn rose from his seat at the table, laying his napkin beside the remnants of his breakfast. "Amethyst and I will have a look around the city while the two of you are busy with that."

Sirion gave him a warning look. "I'd be careful if I were you. This isn't any ordinary city."

"I don't need any trouble. I have enough of it as it is already," said Adrianna.

Sorn held up his hands in a gesture of acquiescence. "Trust me, we won't be looking for trouble. We will keep our hands to ourselves."

"Please Adrianna? I promise we will be good." Amethyst's expression was one of hopefulness.

Adrianna sighed. "Fine, but meet us back here for the evening meal."

Amethyst smiled gleefully and Sorn gave a slow grin followed by a small bow. "Of course, mi'lady."

Adrianna chuckled. "I'm going to get ready. I'm sure the masters want to meet with me about more than just the Ring of Aboleth. I left the city quite precipitously after Master Tallek died."

Sorn just nodded as she walked out of the small dining room and into the foyer of the keep Master Tallek had left her upon his passing. In spite of the memories of loss it evoked, she was glad she had it. She and her comrades could rest there as long as they chose, in the comfort of a home instead of an inn. Sirion followed her to the suite Tallek always used. It had been cleaned periodically during her absence by the skeleton crew she had paid in advance of her departure all those moon cycles ago, but none of his belongings had been removed. The only disturbance the books, scrolls, and clothing had suffered was to be placed in their rightful spots.

Not for the first time, Adrianna just stood there and looked around the chamber. There were so many memories, and her beloved master was no longer there to share them with her. His favorite cloak still hung on the hooks by the door, a pair of boots lay beside the bed, and the books he'd used during her training sat on the wizened oak desk. Sirion moved up behind her and put his arms around her shoulders. "Are you all right?"

She nodded and swallowed past the lump in her throat. "I think I will be."

He turned her around to face him and pulled her close. She lay her head on his chest and just luxuriated in his embrace– reveled in the warmth of his arms, the scent of his hair, and the thump of his heart. "I *know* you will be. You haven't allowed yourself the chance to grieve for him. Take some time after your meeting today to do that."

She nodded. He held her for a few moments longer before he pulled away. "I'm going to get some water for your bath."

She shook her head. "You don't have to do that."

"I know, but I want to."

247

She looked up into his eyes and saw the sincerity there. "All right. Thank you."

He smiled. "It's not a problem. I'll be back in a bit."

Adrianna sat down by the window and let her thoughts take her away. It didn't feel like any time at all passed before Sirion was back with large buckets of warm water that he poured into the tub on the other side of the room. She undressed and stepped into the bath. With the soaps she brought with her from the Sherkari Fortress, she washed her hair and body. When she was finished, she beckoned for Sirion to share the bath with her, unwilling to let the water go without him getting in.

Finally they were ready to go. Adrianna and Sirion walked through the city streets. It was just as she remembered it, with sprawling academies, soaring towers, wide streets paved with unfamiliar substances, interesting shops, and eccentric shopkeepers. The Varangheli Vaults were located in the center of Andahye, and before they were remotely close, Adrianna could feel the magic protecting the place. Upon arrival, guards wearing Savanlean plate opened the doors for them, and once inside, Adrianna couldn't help looking back at Sirion.

His expression was much as she thought it might be.

Fluted columns stood at the sides of a large chamber, supporting a vaulted ceiling carved in bas relief. The golden stone was so smooth it felt like marble, and it was polished to a high sheen. The floor was pale, almost white, zigzagged with metallic gold veins, and at each corner of the room stood a statue depicting the twin gods of wealth and fortune.

A faelin man wearing a golden robe approached. "How may I help you, mi'lady?"

"I'm here to meet the headmaster of the Vanderlinde Academy."

"Of course, mi'lady. Right this way." The man offered a small bow and led the way across the chamber and up a flight of stairs to the second floor. He took them to a small room where ranking masters of the academy awaited her.

Master Garsheim was the first to speak. He inclined his head and gave a smile that never reached his pale eyes. "Lady Adrianna, I am glad to see you well, especially in light of what you have recently been through."

She regarded him solemnly, easily seeing past the pretense. She never knew why he didn't like her, and now it simply didn't matter anymore. She had come for a specific purpose, and before long, she would be gone again, his academy free of whatever stench she brought in her wake. She returned the gesture of greeting. "Thank you, Master. I appreciate the sentiment. You and your council were the first persons I thought of when my betrothed mentioned he wanted to find a resting place for the Ring of Aboleth."

Garsheim's eyes flicked to Sirion, who stood apart in the corner of the room nearest the door. "Your betrothed is a wise man."

Adrianna remained silent.

He continued. "The Ring of Aboleth is a dangerous artifact."

Her tone was tight. "I am very aware of the dangers of the ring."

Garsheim nodded. "Yes, I suppose you do. Where did you get it?"

"It was given to me by a man called Paxil."

Garsheim tried to hide the frown that took over his face. "That's a name I haven't heard in many years. Where did you find him?"

She deliberately avoided the question. "I believe it was more that he *allowed* us to find him."

"I see. And he just simply gave you the ring?"

Adrianna hesitated. She wasn't willing to share her history with Dinim with a bunch of people she didn't care much about. "Yes."

Garsheim noticed her hesitation, but was perceptive enough not to pursue it. "And where is the ring now?"

She turned to Sirion. He stepped forward and placed a nondescript brown pouch in her hands. She opened it and dropped the ring into her palm. The engraved silver whorls glinted in the light cast by the lanterns and floor braziers.

Garsheim stepped towards her and hesitantly took the ring from her open hand. He raised it to the light and the other masters came closer to inspect it with him. "It certainly is the Ring of Aboleth."

Adrianna frowned. "You doubted?"

"You wouldn't believe how many amateurs come to me saying they have an artifact, when in actuality, it is nothing."

Adrianna had a sharp retort but bit her tongue.

"You made the right choice to bring it to us. Andahye is the best place for arcane objects of such significant power."

"I certainly hope so Master Garsheim."

He raised a steel grey brow. "You doubt?"

This time she couldn't stop the words from tumbling from between her lips. "I doubt every man with power such as yours, power that can change the lives of others so easily."

His blue eyes fixed onto hers, and she remained still and unwavering. The other masters looked back and forth, their discomfort shown only by the almost imperceptible stepping from foot to foot. Garsheim knew exactly whose life she referred to, even if the others did not. Finally he gave a nod. "Wise you are, to be so hesitant. Enemies among us masquerade as allies all the time. You are right to question me, for you don't really know me. However, your Master did. Tallek may not have always agreed with me, but he trusted me."

She remained impassive. "That is the only reason I stand here before you today."

Garsheim nodded. "We shall place the ring here, within one of the most highly fortified vaults. It is costly–"

"The Realm of Elvandahar is willing to help. I have the gold to pay for several moon cycles."

Garsheim nodded. "I have much respect for this act of generosity. It is good of King Thalios to help. Come, let us place the ring in safety and move on to other matters."

An account was made and a small vault chosen. Adrianna and Master Garsheim watched as the ring was placed safely within and locked. A key was provided and given into the safekeeping of Garsheim with the understanding that he needed the permission of Adrianna and fifty percent of the council to use it. Everyone returned to the Vanderlinde Academy and Adrianna was questioned about her precipitous departure and subsequent absence from the city after Tallek's death.

"There was nothing keeping me in the city. I had family I hadn't seen in many years back in Sangrilak."

Garsheim's tone was solemn. "But did you ever finish your Final Tests?"

Adrianna was contrite. "No, I did not."

Silence reigned for a moment. "I thought as much. However, the other masters and I have heard the trials you have been through and have decided to exempt you from the formalized tests. We are pleased to present you with the badge of Journeyman, and your name shall be written in the annals of the Vanderlinde Academy and rendered undisputable."

One of the other masters stepped forward and presented her with the badge. In silence she accepted it. Finally she gained the voice to speak. "Thank you. I never expected such an action on my behalf. Master Tallek would be pleased."

"Indeed, it is the least we can do to honor him and the apprentice he chose to succeed him."

Adrianna frowned. "What do you mean, 'succeed him?'"

Garsheim frowned. "He didn't tell you? Tallek was taking only one last apprentice before his retirement. It is understood that a wizard's final apprentice is the one who will be left to succeed him, the one whom he believes will be all he can teach them, and more. That apprentice is the culmination of all of the master's work over his lifetime, and will one day take his place at the Academy."

Shock swept over her and made her voice small as she replied, "No, he didn't tell me." Everything suddenly slipped into place: Journeyman Tannin's hatred of her, Tallek leaving the Keep in her possession, his hesitation to take her as his apprentice all those years ago when she stood before the Vanderlinde Council with the hope she would be selected as an apprentice. Even though she had passed their tests, she was very untried, and a potential loose cannon. He had placed so much faith in her, more than she ever realized.

She felt a gentle hand on her shoulder and looked up into the eyes of

Master Garsheim. It was the first time he'd ever looked upon her with any sympathy or care. "He didn't have the time to tell you. His time was cut short. But I want you to know, you are deserving of his teaching. Very deserving. He would be proud of you."

A painful lump formed in the back of her throat and she fought back tears. "Thank you."

10 Saliren CY593

The Wildrunners made slow progress through the hills, but their quest for the rod had begun in earnest. Beside Triath, Armond rode in silence, knowing they would be stopping soon to set up the evening encampment. The sun would soon begin its descent, and there would be only so much daylight left to prepare a fire, cook a meal, and tend to the animals. Within moments, Dartanyen was calling a halt; Anya had found a suitable campsite. Armond dismounted from his larian and led the beast a suitable distance away from the site. After a few moments, everyone else brought their own lloryk and larian to the spot Armond had chosen, and then left the animals to be tended while they went about their own duties.

As was her custom, Sheridana came to join him in his endeavor to tend the beasts. Armond glanced at her as she approached, then turned back to his business. At the beginning of their journey, she had made polite conversation, most likely in attempt to get to know him better. His responses had been rather short and clipped. After several evenings of being rebuffed, she stopped trying to make conversation with him at all, focusing instead upon the animals they tended. Armond was fully aware of what he had done, and he even felt some remorse. He wasn't a very talkative person and generally kept to himself, but he'd been unfriendly towards Sheridana, and he didn't really know why.

From beneath lowered eyelids, Armond contemplated the woman working beside him. It would have been very easy for her to choose to go hunting with Anya and Dartanyen, for Armond had seen her proficiency with the bow. Instead, she chose to help him with the animals. Each beast needed to be looked over for signs of stress, rubbed down after a long day's work, watered, and then fed. It was very apparent she didn't enjoy this task. She very rarely spoke to the animals, and patted each one only after she had completed her duty to that individual. It was much different for Armond, who somewhat enjoyed the job he had chosen, and spoke to each of his animals as he examined, rubbed, and fed them. It seemed he had an affinity for the beasts that made the work so much easier. Armond watched as Sheridana picked up each of the feet of the larian she rode, inspecting them for injury. He had to concede she cared about the beasts, for she was thorough in her work, making sure each animal was hale and healthy. She just simply didn't enjoy tending them at the end of every day, and simple conversation with him would have made her work at least somewhat endurable.

But Armond had shot her down right from the start. Now he didn't quite know how to rectify what he'd done.

After examining the larian's feet, Sheridana moved to the belly, feeling it for signs of distension, and then to the mouth, looking inside for any sores. Armond patted his larian and whispered to the animal while feeding him from his hand. He then sprinkled the rest of the grain onto the ground in front of the beast and moved on to the next one, the lloryk ridden by Triath. Once again he glanced at Sheridana and noticed she still wore her breast plate, having chosen to see to the animals before tending to her own needs. Armond forced himself to look inward, to really think about it and find out why he distanced himself from her, and why he refused to give her even a fraction of his time.

He'd been rather surprised to discover Adrianna had a sister like Sheridana. The two women were as different as night and day in appear-ance as well as personality. Where Adrianna was rather peaceful and reserved in her demeanor, Sheridana was often stubborn and forthright. Adrianna was always willing to listen to what others had to say, often took the advice given by her peers, and was generally easy to talk with. Sheridana was the opposite. She was boisterous, hardly ever took anyone's advice, and not always easy to approach. Adrianna was soft- spoken, and adamant only about things that were of great concern to her. Sheridana was often loud and outspoken about almost everything.

In consideration of the differences between the two women, it was not difficult for Armond to realize that Sheridana possessed all the qualities about a woman he disliked. He preferred his women calm and collected, cool and serene. He liked them tender, caring, and companionable. Adrianna had all of those qualities while Sheridana had none. However, working here beside her, Armond couldn't help but feel some degree of attraction.

Sheridana was a beautiful woman, quite distinct from her sister. Where Adrianna had hair as pale as Steralion, and eyes a deep brown, Sheridana's hair was so dark it was almost black, and eyes a cerulean blue. Adrianna was soft and rounded in all the right places. Sheridana was firm and muscular, built like the warrior she was. Armond wasn't drawn to her the way he was to Adrianna, but there was something about her that intrigued him nonetheless.

Armond recoiled with this revelation, almost wishing he hadn't been moved to think so deeply about her. Yet, he'd felt guilty about his treatment of her, and wanted to know why he had responded so coldly towards her. Now that he'd figured that out, as well as some other things, he felt irate. *How can I be attracted to someone who is all I never wanted? She is certainly pretty, but her personality leaves much to be desired. Or does it? Damnation!*

Once more he glanced at Sheridana. She wiped the back of her hand across her forehead, and when it came away with sweat, she thought to wipe it on her tunic. When she found that she still wore her breastplate, she stared at the offending hand in mild disgust. Armond couldn't keep the smile from tugging at the corners of his mouth, and when she realized he was watching, her gaze swung to him. Quickly he turned away, not wanting to give away the fact he'd been gawking.

Armond quickly and efficiently completed his tasks, seeing to his animals and then tending to his own needs. Tianna was preparing the evening meal and Anya and Dartanyen were engaged in a friendly spar. Armond watched them for a moment, seeing that both were proficient with the sword, but neither of them really good at it. Armond knew he could best either one of them in only a matter of moments. He knew that Sheridana could best them as well, probably with one arm behind her back. It was then he realized how interesting it would be if they were to ever decide to spar against one another. The idea intrigued him, but he dispelled it quickly enough. Yes, she would be a worthy opponent, but it would be a bad idea for them to be pitted against one another. It could create tension if one of them was found to be better than the other, especially since both of them were so competitive and had advanced proficiency.

Armond made his way over to the fire and accepted the bowl of stew Tianna handed to him. He thanked her and then sat down to eat. His thoughts kept returning to Sheridana, and he decided he would just continue to keep her at a distance. He didn't need this type of complexity in his life right now, especially in light of what the group faced in the near future. Besides, just because he was physically attracted to the woman didn't mean that he actually *liked* her. Of course he didn't like her.

In spite of the cold and possibility of foul weather, the small group only stayed in Andahye another couple days before heading back towards Elvandahar. Once out of the city they moved through the Sheldomar Forest, the trees protecting them from some of the chilly winds sweeping down from out of the north. The second night found them setting camp early so that Sirion and Dramati could have the time to find something for the stewpot before it became too dark to hunt. In companionable silence the others prepared for the night. Amethyst tended to the larian and Adrianna poured some water from her flask into the cooking pot. She watched as Sorn made the fire and then set the pot over the newborn flames.

She tiredly sat back on her heels and waited for the water to boil, sifting through her pouches of herbs to find the ones she would use to prepare the tea

Tianna had taught her how to make. She carefully measured everything out, and had just finished her preparations when the water was ready. She put everything into the pot and watched the steam rise. It had been a long day, and she was so, so tired...

At the periphery of the camp, a large burst of light suddenly flared. Startled, Adrianna stood from her place beside the fire. Before knowing what it was, she began to incant the words to a protection spell. Within moments the light was dimming, but she continued, faltering only when she saw a man standing in front of an oval of subdued light. He wore black tunic and trousers covered by a maroon robe that was tied about his waist with a navy sash. Shoulder-length black hair was tied back from a handsome face, and he regarded her intently from deep lavender eyes. When the man spoke, she found her gaze drawn to his sculpted lips.

"I am Master Tallachienan Chroalthone and I'm here to begin your training. Are you ready?"

Adrianna blinked, startled. *My training?* A part of her had forgotten he was coming, and perhaps she'd been a bit afraid he would decide not to take her as his apprentice after all. As a result, she'd kept thoughts of the training out of her mind. In truth she'd never expected him to come to her this way, at a time when she wasn't even in the comfort of her home, but out in the middle of the wilderness...

The man waited. She knew he expected a reply. He continued to regard her, his gaze unwavering. She glanced over at Amethyst, whose mouth was hanging open in awe, and then at Sorn, whose eyes were almost popping out of his face. "I... what about my comrades? They..."

Tallachienan interrupted her. "I will return you to them when your training is complete. They will just have to finish their journey without you." He paused a moment before continuing. "Nevertheless, if you don't wish to accompany me, I will leave you here with your companions."

Adrianna watched him as he spoke, the unsaid words dangling between them. If she were to pass up this chance, he would not return again. She could see he wished to leave right away, and that it was an effort to maintain the portal shimmering behind him. Aggrieved, Adrianna considered her situation; Sirion had not yet returned to the camp, and she wanted so much to say goodbye.

"Go ahead, Adria. We will tell Sirion when he gets back."

She looked over at Sorn and noticed he'd had recovered from his stupefaction. He gestured her towards Master Tallachienan and the waiting portal. She rushed over to her belongings and slung her pack over her shoulder. Then, for a moment she stood there, uncertainty rooting her to the spot. *Sirion. I so much want to see him before I leave...*

"Lady Adrianna, we must make haste. The portal is closing."

She turned back to see that, indeed, he spoke the truth. The portal was becoming smaller, and had begun to lose some of its light. Quickly she made her decision.

She walked closer and stopped when she stood in front of Tallachienan. She inhaled deeply before speaking. "I am ready, Master."

He held out his hand to her, palm up. She hesitated momentarily before taking it. His long fingers curved around her hand and Adrianna felt a curious tingle race up her spine. Together they turned and walked into the portal. Once more she felt a twinge of uncertainty. She had no idea what she was walking into, and this time her companions would not be standing behind her.

The walk through this portal was vaguely similar to the one she experienced from Krathil-lon. The wrenching sensation was much heightened, and the moments that passed seemed so much longer. The bright whorls of color were almost blinding and she had to close her eyes against them. She stumbled when they finally emerged from the portal and a steadying hand was there at her elbow. She remembered Sirion being the one to catch her the last time, and her heart instantly ached for him.

Collecting herself, Adrianna looked up at the imposing mountain range surrounding her and then at the dark fortress nestled among the rocky cliffs. A cold wind blew, and her hair whipped about her face. The towers and spires soared high into the sky, and some of them even seemed to touch the clouds. It was huge, and she surmised that it could possibly be the size of a small city. Adrianna felt a chill of apprehension sweep through her. When she turned to glance at Master Tallachienan, she saw that his face was expressionless. She could sense a disquiet about him, as though he was about to do something troubling.

Adrianna turned away to focus once more upon the vast citadel. This place would be her residence for the next several weeks. She felt a hand on her shoulder, and then the Master was turning her around. The landscape shifted, and she was suddenly standing within a courtyard. Given the new perspective, Adrianna felt dwarfed by the magnificent structure and looked up at it with awe.

"This is my home. I hope you will enjoy your stay here." Adrianna lowered her gaze only when Tallachienan took her elbow once more and led her through the courtyard. As they approached, the front doors of the castle opened, and out stepped a man.

"It is good to see you home again, Master." The man bowed as he spoke.

Tallachienan nodded in return. "It is good to see you as well, Pylar."

The man turned towards Adrianna. She inhaled swiftly once seeing his eyes, colored a golden yellow. She had never seen eyes quite like them before. His skin tone was a deep bronze, and his hair the color of flame. He stood more than a foot-length taller than she, slim, but well-muscled and built for power.

"Adrianna, meet Pylar. He is one of the citadel guards. He also aids the apprentices when it is necessary for their instruction." Momentarily, Adrianna saw something flicker within the depths of Pylar's eyes as he bowed before her.

"Welcome, my lady. I hope that I may help to make your stay here a more pleasant one." Adrianna smiled and nodded. She then returned her gaze to the Master. Somewhat imposingly he stood by, silently watching her, almost as though searching for something. Then, with a flourish, he extended an arm towards the opening of his home, encouraging her to precede him into the castle.

As Adrianna stepped inside, the strange feeling that she'd been there before overcame her. She frowned, shaking herself free of the sensation. That was impossible; she'd have known if she'd ever stepped into a place such as this. Hanging on the walls were magnificent tapestries. They depicted all manner of things, from beautiful landscapes to great battles. Each appeared to be made of the finest materials, with gold trim at the edges. The floors were covered by splendid, richly woven rugs with varying hues of orange, crimson, purple, and maroon. Massive chandeliers hung from vaulted ceilings and curved staircases led to the next storey.

Adrianna slowly followed Master Tallachienan out of the lobby, through a side corridor, and into the largest room she had even seen. She could have fit the entirety of her old home in Sangrilak inside it. She stopped and found herself rotating in place, taking in the magnificence. There was but one thing that was dissatisfying about the place: it was so *dark*. Torches cradled within ornate sconces hung on the walls. All of them were lit, but darkness continued to shroud the place within its blanket. Involuntarily, her body shivered slightly.

"Are you ready for your first day of training?"

Adrianna returned her gaze to Tallachienan and she saw his eyes flash. It was a challenge. Was she up for it? She had traveled through the Sheldomar Forest all day and she'd only just arrived at the fortress. She hadn't the time to bathe, rest, or even eat a meal.

"But Master Tallachienan, she–" Pylar began to object.

The tone of Tallachienan's voice was a warning. "Pylar..."

"I am ready whenever you are, Master," she replied.

For a moment, she thought she saw a smile tugging at the corners of his mouth, but then it was gone as swiftly as it had appeared. Was it her imagination? As he held her gaze, Tallachienan held out his hand. She hesitated only a moment before she took it. Once again she felt a zing sweep through her, the same tingle she'd experienced when first taking his hand to walk into the portal. Her heartbeat accelerated, and her body trembled. She frowned as she contemplated this unexpected reaction. Somehow she would have to learn to control it. She didn't want to have to deal with this every time he touched her.

Adrianna heard the incantation to a spell and was suddenly standing beside him in the center of a large, dimly lit room. A strangely patterned, circular rug filled more than half of the floor space, and the walls were paneled with polished red wood. The room was empty with the exception of a few braziers against the walls. Tallachienan led her to the center of the rug. Adrianna then watched as the man closed his eyes and began to speak. His voice was deep and rich, filling the room as he chanted another spell. The breath of magic began to eddy about, and the flames in the braziers flickered. She felt the power move about them as he continued. The eddies became a breeze, and Adrianna felt errant strands of her hair moving against her cheek. In awe she turned in place, reveling in the power Tallachienan called, having never felt the likes of it before. He reached into a crimson pouch at his side and pulled out a fistful of– something. He flung the contents of his hand into the winds he created. The space before them was suddenly littered with what looked like millions of tiny stars. Tallachienan then stretched out his arms in front of him, his palms faced outward. Slowly he began to draw them apart. About half a farlo away appeared a long, silver, vertical thread. As the space between Tallachienan's hands increased, so did the width of the thread. The thread became a slit, and the slit became an oval that rippled in the air. Meanwhile, the breeze had become a whirlwind. Adrianna's cloak whipped about and the fires in the braziers were extinguished. Before them stood a shimmering silver portal. The space around it was charged, and the winds swirled madly around it.

Tallachienan dropped his arms to his sides. He spoke loudly to her over the sound of the winds rushing about the room. "This is what you will strive to accomplish as a student under my tutelage. This portal leads to a place unlike any you have ever seen, or could even imagine. Some would call it a "dimension", but it is so much more than that." He paused, seeming to contemplate what he would tell her next. His eyes fastened onto hers and he regarded her intensely. Then he continued, "There are several such places, each wonderful and horrible in their own way. In some of them, time passes very slowly, while in others it goes by quickly. Each place has its own denizens, some neutral, some chaotic in nature. I will take you to a few of these places to give you a taste of what it means to choose the path of a Dimensionalist.

"All that you learn from me will be a means to this end. When you leave me to begin to journey on your own, you will only have an inkling of the power it will take to open one of these portals. Even more power will be needed to actually step through. Only several years of study and accomplishment will grant you that." Tallachienan paused. "Are you sure you wish to continue? It will take much hard work and dedication in order to succeed as a Dimensionalist. I can return you to your companions if you so desire."

Adrianna regarded him intently. *Hells, I've already told him I am ready. Does he wish for me to reply in the negative? Does he mayhap think me unworthy? Why would he bring me all the way here, just to turn around and return me home again?* She raised an eyebrow, her voice firm. "Master, I am ready to continue."

For a moment he looked into her eyes. Then, once again, he held out his hand. Adrianna took it without hesitation. "The first day of your training begins here," he said as they stepped through the portal.

It took a moment, but Adrianna realized that she stood in the room from which they had started. She swiftly turned around, but the portal was gone as though it had never been there. She turned to the man standing beside her and found him watching her. Tallachienan had shown her six of the twenty-eight known "dimensions", only a glimpse of the complex universe in which they lived. As they passed from one place to the next, she hadn't really realized the passage of time. Pass it did, however, but exactly how much was uncertain.

He saw the question in her eyes and answered it before she had a chance to say it aloud. "Eight days have passed in this world while we Traveled."

Adrianna frowned. *How can that be? I would have known if so much time had gone by. Or would I?* She remembered the incident in Gaknar's temple, back when she'd first met Dartanyen, Zorg, Bussimot, and Armond. Together they had come so close to death's door and slept the healing sleep of magic for several days before finally awakening.

"Come, I will escort you to your chamber," said Tallachienan. "You will now tire very quickly, for your body has begun to realize the trick we played." In a rapidly growing haze of fatigue, Adrianna nodded.

Placing his hand at her waist, the Master helped her onto a floating disc that somehow materialized before them. It carried them down several corridors, each one blurring before her eyes as they passed. It seemed only a few moments went by and they were stepping off the disc to stand before a large door.

"Thank you for the journey, Master Tallachienan. It was amazing, and much like you said it would be. I'm not sure I've ever learned so much in such a short span of time before. I look forward to the next one" Adrianna smiled, turned to look at him, and suddenly began to fall.

Tallachienan quickly took her around the waist and supported her against his side as he knocked on the door. Seemingly of its own volition, it swung open, the hinges protesting softly. "It was my pleasure." Fatigue weighed her down like a thick, wet, winter cloak. He helped her over to the bed, guiding her as she tumbled onto the satiny softness. His voice was like a whisper when he spoke again. "Sleep well, Adrianna."

Tallachienan stood over her for several moments. *By all that's in me, she is just as beautiful as I remember.* With the utmost of care, he straightened her on the bed, removed her boots, and pulled the blanket up to her chin before leaving her quarters. Pylar was already aware of their return and he would be responsible for Adrianna's care until she awakened from her Travel-induced sleep. But that wasn't to say he might check up on her himself a time or two...

Tallachienan rode a disc to his chamber. He poured himself a glass of wine and slouched down into his favorite chair, stretching his legs before him. It had been a long time since he'd experienced true fatigue. He'd left mortality behind long ago, if even he'd ever had it, and with it went the encumbrances that accompanied that state of being. However, he knew he should still sleep. He'd found over the decades that, if he chose not to rest, he was unable to cast the same caliber of spells with the same ease and fluidity that he could when he was well rested.

However, he didn't wish to sleep, and instead chose to ponder the young woman with whom he had just taken on her first Traveling excursion. Just as she had been in the third and fourth Cycles, Adrianna was intelligent and quick to understand the principles he placed before her. She keenly remembered the things he taught and applied that knowledge from one world to the next. Moreover, she was resourceful, industrious, and more than happy to learn all he had to teach her. She was like a sponge, sucking up every morsel of information he shared. Tallachienan grinned as he envisioned her beautiful face lit up with a passion that he hadn't seen since he trained Dinim.

Ah yes, Dinim. Tallachienan frowned. He'd been unable to establish communication with his most gifted student. It had something to do with the fact that he now resided within the past. He had taken his students back in time in order to have ample opportunity to train them, especially Adrianna, before events in the future took unalterable turns that not even the most gifted of individuals could rectify. The apprentices didn't know it as of yet, for he hadn't seen the point in alarming anyone. He might decide not to tell them at all, for if he were to do so, he might have to explain the state of the world in their own time. He didn't have the heart to tell them it would soon be gone. The world as they knew it irrevocably altered to fit the desires of the wicked, and evil would reign unchecked across the lands.

There was only one hope for the world, and it lay in the indistinct ramblings of prophecy.

Tallachienan knew that the group who now called themselves the

Wildrunners would fail without Adrianna. He also knew they would possibly fail *with* her as they had in the other Cycles preceding this one. However, he hoped this time would be different. He'd wished the same thing the last Cycle, but when the same failure was still met, Adrianna's death cut him to the core of his being.

Tallachienan gave a heavy sigh and took a swallow of wine. The weight of the world rested heavily on his shoulders. So much depended on him, that he train Adrianna well and impart to her everything he knew. It was going to be more difficult this time, for he'd noted a lack of self-confidence that he didn't recall her having in the previous two Cycles. He drummed his fingertips on the arms of his chair. He wondered what had caused that and cursed himself for not monitoring her activities in the past. He dared not do it now; time travel made him vulnerable to his enemies, and of these he had many.

Tallachienan sighed again, his mind shifting to other concerns, particularly his Echelon One students. Ryaltar had been the first from his newest group of apprentices to come to the citadel. Tallachienan had found him within the bowels of the world, severely beaten down and abused. His was a situation very similar to Dinim's, except that Dinim had dealt with his liberation differently. Unlike Ryaltar, Dinim had chosen not to take up the yoke of bitterness, his desire to excel encompassing his personal universe. Tallachienan hadn't bothered to think that not everyone would be like Dinim, and he'd begun to find this type of negativity common among his male Cimmerean students.

Ryaltar seemed to be the worst so far.

Next had come Sobrar. His situation hadn't been as tenuous as Ryaltar's, but questionable nevertheless. The mental abuse he'd suffered from the faelin who raised him had affected his self-esteem and confidence. Tallachienan took both young men on their first Travel almost three moon cycles ago. Before that, they had been with him for almost two years. Since they'd received no prior magical training, he'd had to start at the beginning with the basics.

Eighteen months after bringing Ryaltar and Sobrar, Tallachienan went to collect Tridium. She was Cimmerean, but she was also the first woman he'd chosen for instruction. He hadn't noticed her for her quickness of mind, although she had that as well, but for her unusual compassion, uncommon among Cimmerean females. Ultimately, he respected her most for her strength of character. Despite what went on around her, she didn't accept such iniquitous ethics for herself. After bringing her to the citadel, however, Tallachienan found he'd created a problem. The Cimmerean men within residence resented her being there. They felt she had invaded their safe haven, not realizing it was a place of safety for her too. Despite this dilemma, he had left soon after to collect Yasmin, the first non-Cimmerean to enter his program. He felt no reason why he should limit the knowledge to the

Cimmerean race, feeling that if he did so, that Dimensionalism as an entirety would suffer. He was relieved to discover that nothing untoward had happened during his absence, but dismayed that Yasmin's appearance added fuel to the fire. Not only was she a woman, but a woman of another race.

Once seeing the two women settled, Tallachienan brought Myan to the citadel. He, also, was of another race, but that didn't seem to affect the young Cimmereans as much as the fact that women resided among them. They accepted Myan within their ranks, but continued to exclude the two women, especially Tridium. Somehow, they finally learned to accept Yasmin, perhaps because of her race; but Tridium was simply a constant reminder of what they had suffered in the Underdark. This did not include Sobrar, for he hadn't been raised within Cimmerean society. Unfortunately, much to Tallachienan's consternation, he just fell into following the leader.

Tallachienan swirled the contents of his glass before taking a long swallow. Not only had he to deal with Ryaltar, Sobrar, and three new students, but he also had four Echelon Two apprentices. He would often find Mosodj, Dlamini, Yazton, and Mebrak with Ryaltar and Sobrar. They seemed to have many of the same prejudices against Tridium, although not quite as intensely. The six young men had begun to spend much of their time together while he took Myan, Yasmin, and Tridium on their first Travel. When they returned ten days later, he found that the group had become rather close-knit. Tallachienan was glad they had found companionship, but concerned that Ryaltar might cause trouble within the larger group in which he now found himself.

It was two moon cycles later that he decided the time had come to get Adrianna. The moment was right; she was ready for instruction and her companions wouldn't need her for their excursion to obtain the Rod of Atlenbos. Once she was finally here with him at the citadel, he'd impulsively decided to take her on her first Travel right away. He half expected her to decline, for she'd neither seen her quarters, broken her fast, nor rested. But when she accepted his challenge, he'd found himself strangely pleased. He wished to test her, to take her to the brink of her limitations. He wanted to make her the best, better than she had been in the fourth Cycle.

Tallachienan clenched his fists on the armrests of his chair. This time, he wanted her to live.

IMPOSSIBLE ASSIGNMENT

Adrianna slowly awoke in an unfamiliar place. Hanging above her there was a filmy beige canopy, the fabric draping downward to encompass the bed on both sides. She moved the fabric aside with a heavy hand and allowed her eyes to peruse the room. It was big, much larger than any she had ever been given for her own use before. At one wall there was a cloak rack, a large cabinet, and the entry door. The adjacent wall sported a large window. Next to it was a sturdy oak desk with a bowl of fruit sitting on it. She looked to the wall opposite the bed and saw three more doorways.

She sat upright in the bed, scrunching up her face and groaning to herself as she moved. *Damnation, how long have I laid here?* Much to her fascination, the bed moved with her as she shifted, the surface rippling beneath her. It was a strange sensation, one that made her feel as though she floated on a sturdy surface of water.

Finally managing to stand, Adrianna felt a plush rug beneath her naked feet. It felt good between her toes, the thick, soft fibers sticking up between each one. It ended as she wobbled over to the door nearest the desk. The stone floor was cold, but it was the chill in the air that made her realize she was naked but for her smallclothes. Adrianna opened one of the doors to discover that the room behind it was bare except for some torch brackets along the walls. She closed the door and moved towards the next. It was a closet. The area became illuminated somehow when she stepped inside. There were pants, blouses, dresses, tunics, robes, cloaks, and various other garments of all colors and styles, neatly organized on the shelves. She followed as the closet curved to the right, the shelves now holding all sorts of footwear. There were also many shelves of accessories, such as cinch-belts, sashes, and cloak fasteners. At the end of the closet she came to a door. Opening it, she saw that it led into a room with a large pool at its center. Against the wall closest to her was a vanity table. Set atop it were various combs, brushes, hairpieces, and face paints. Inside the drawer there were all types of soaps and creams. She walked around the pool she assumed was a bath. Several people could easily sit within at the same time. Through the door at the other side of the room, she found herself once more in the bedchamber.

Considering, Adrianna turned back and regarded the pool. It would do her good to bathe. She shucked her smallclothes as she walked back into the bath chamber. Placing them on the floor beside the steps, she descended into the warm waters. She felt her muscles relax as soon as the waters swirled gently around her ankles, thighs, and finally her back and shoulders. She allowed herself to luxuriate, taking a sweet-smelling soap found at the pool's edge to her hair and body. After scrubbing herself clean, she floated in the water for a short while longer.

Suddenly, from the corner of her eye, she saw movement coming from the bedchamber. She became still for a moment but then remembered where she was. It was probably someone who had just come to check on her. Relaxing again, she called out. "Hello? Who's there?"

From the other room she heard an answering voice. "It is only I, Pylar. It's good to see you up and about. The Master was beginning to concern himself over you. I will leave you to your privacy. However, if you wish it, I will bring something to eat."

"I will be done in just a few more moments, and yes, a meal would be very much appreciated."

She heard the man leave her quarters, closing the door behind him. She sighed and allowed herself the luxury of floating just a short while longer before getting out of the pool and drying herself. She then made her way to the closet, wondering about her own clothes. Where were they? Not that she would have worn them; they had eons worth of dirt embedded in the fabric. Adrianna stood there for quite some time, debating what to wear, especially since she had so many options from which to choose The towel drooped to her waist as she rifled through the clothes with the other hand. A few moments later, she heard Pylar enter. "Lady Adrianna, I hope you don't mind that I took the liberty of choosing your dishes. I know what you have been through, and what your body needs to recuperate. I also brought you some tea. It is quite good actually..." Pylar's voice became louder and Adrianna belatedly realized he was approaching the open closet. Before she could cover herself, he had entered.

Adrianna fumbled with the towel, covering her modesty and the scar on her chest. She watched as his face turned from its natural bronze tone to a deep, rich red. He quickly averted his eyes. "My lady, I apologize. I didn't realize... didn't think..." Pylar quickly took himself from the closet.

She gripped the towel closely about herself, suddenly feeling self-conscious. However, she also felt sorry for poor Pylar, who now stood, mumbling, outside the closet.

"...I'll just go now." Pylar's low voice had moved closer towards the door.

"No, wait a moment!" Adrianna quickly pulled a pale yellow tunic from one of the hangers, followed by a matching pair of trousers. "I don't know where I'm supposed to go, or when I am supposed to do whatever it is that I am supposed to do!" Adrianna stepped from the closet, pulling the tunic over down over torso. She regarded the flushed countenance of Pylar. "I don't even know what time it is. I feel as though I've been asleep for a week!" She grinned and then pushed her legs into the light-weight trousers.

Pylar cleared his throat softly. "Well, not quite a week. Only about three days."

Adrianna stared at him. "Three days? I've been asleep for three days?"

Seeing the look of alarm on her face, Pylar was quick to reassure her. "Maybe not quite three days. Perhaps more like two and a half. Or maybe three days, but just two nights." Pylar paused, realizing he wasn't helping. "The Master was beginning to fret a little, but he feels better now, knowing you have awakened. Most people sleep about two days, but you must have been tired before you took your trip." Pylar paused again. "You have nothing to worry about. You will be well by the end of the week."

Adrianna turned back to the closet, her mind in a daze. No wonder she'd had so much trouble climbing out of bed. She had been sleeping for over sixty hours. She shook her head as she grabbed a green sash from a hook and a pair of brown soft leather boots from the rack, before returning to Pylar, who waited patiently. She found him standing beside her desk. Resting on it was the tray of food he had brought, as well as two large books. Suddenly feeling very hungry, she hastened to the desk. The tray was covered with a variety of meats, breads, cheeses, vegetables, and fruits. She picked up a chunk of bread and began to eat, not caring how good it tasted, just so long as it was edible.

"What are these books?" She picked one up. The cover bore no title, but when she looked on the inside, in bold type, it read, ASTRALON. She quickly surmised what the other volume was about– Cansandia, the other world to which the Master had taken her.

"Master Tallachienan bade me bring these to you. He suggested you begin reading them right away, for you are to be tested on the material contained within them before you begin your Formulations and Mathematics classes."

She raised an eyebrow. "When will that be?"

Pylar lowered his eyes for a moment, before responding. "Approx-imately eight weeks from now."

Adrianna made no reply. He returned his gaze to her, watching her riffle through the pages of the book. He forbore telling her that the rest of the Echelon One class had almost completed them since they had arrived many weeks ago. He felt sorry for her, knowing that the Master was going to push her to get her to catch up with everyone else. Pylar was sure that Tallachienan felt that her previous training and experience would aid her, but Pylar knew better. Her previous training wouldn't help her much here, and in many ways would probably prove to be a hindrance.

Adrianna closed the book. "So, where am I supposed to go? What am I supposed to do, and at what time am I to do it?"

"The Master told me to just bring you to him when you were ready. Finish eating and we will go."

She grabbed a piece of cheese and stuffed it into her mouth. She'd found she wasn't able to eat much, her stomach feeling full after only bread and a few tubers. Pylar eyed her critically. "It's typical for people to be hungry, but unable to eat much after Travel." He then shook his head. "But, my dear, you must eat more than this. You will surely wither away upon such skimpy sustenance."

Adrianna grimaced. Her stomach felt so distended that she felt slightly ill. Pylar picked up a papas fruit from the tray. "At least take this with you. Before you know it, you will be hungry again." He held out the pink orb. Hesitantly, Adrianna placed it within her pack, along with her spellbook, stylus, ink, and parchment. She then followed Pylar out of her chambers.

Once in the hallway, a floating disk appeared. She vaguely recalled riding one with Master Tallachienan upon her return. Pylar stepped up onto it, gesturing her to follow. As it began to move, Adrianna grabbed his arm. He turned and smiled. "The disks just take a bit of getting used to. You're going to love having them because the citadel is so large."

The disk accelerated slowly until reaching a steady speed. After several moments it finally stopped at a set of double doors. Pylar jumped down. "Here we are." Adrianna followed suit, and once standing beside him, Pylar pushed open the door. She saw the Master seated at a desk at the front of a small lecture hall. Several other persons were seated haphazardly among the dozens of available chairs, and they looked towards them as she and Pylar entered.

Tallachienan inclined his head. "Good day. You rested well, I hope?"

"Yes, I'm well. Thank you," she said as she regarded her peers. Three of the five students were Cimmerean, two men and a woman. The two Cimmerean men sat in a group with a young man that appeared to be of Savanlean descent. The Cimmerean woman sat next to another woman, this one appearing to be Terralean in origin. It seemed that the students had divided themselves this way purposefully. Nearer the back of the room, she saw two more Cimmerean men that were obviously older than the rest.

Adrianna returned her attention to Tallachienan. Seated beside him was another man. He had a pale golden complexion, with hair a dark shade of brown. His eyes were stunning, colored a pale silvery-gray. He regarded her intensely for a moment before returning to his book.

Tallachienan gestured towards the chairs. "Have a seat, Adrianna." He pointed to the rear of the room. "The two men in the back are Masters Tambrith and Brenner. They will be your Sage Knowledge instructors." The two Cimmereans nodded solemnly as she glanced in their direction on her way to an empty seat.

Tallachienan began to pace at the front of the room, his hands behind his back. "For some of you, I know I should have had this discussion earlier. However, I was awaiting the day when you would all finally be here together before me. You will discover, if you haven't already, that I don't like to repeat myself. I find it exceedingly tedious, and I'm sure I speak correctly when I say you probably do as well.

"Some time ago, I founded a school of magic. I never coined a term for it, but others began to call it Dimensionalism. It's not an entirely accurate term, but it stuck, and even I use it. In more recent years, I have begun to teach other people what I've learned. It's been a new experience for me; however, I find it important that others know about the true nature of the universe around us.

"As you all now know, the universe contains other worlds other than the one upon which we live. Others call these worlds 'dimensions', but actually this is not the case. These worlds exist in the same fashion as does our own. I now know of almost thirty such worlds. When I first began to realize their presence, I made it my life's work to research them, and once I did so, realized they were places from which I could procure power.

"There are three systems of which I have knowledge. Our own system is called Tharmagellan's Gate, and the two neighboring systems are known as the Seven Heavens, and the Nine Hells. Our system has four primary planets: Shandahar, Cansandia, Astralon, and Mistygia. Each of these has its own moons, and in all make up twelve 'worlds'. In the Heavens there are also four primary planets, each with its own moons, totaling seven worlds in that system. The Hells have five planets and four moons, totaling nine worlds. Everyone has already embarked upon their first Travel to Astralon and her two moons. We have also seen Cansandia and the two moons belonging to that planet. We will visit Mistygia and her moon sometime in the future, and at that time we will also visit the three moons of Shandahar. For the most part, moons tend to be devoid of life, but many of them contain elements that aren't found upon any of the primary planets.

"As a Dimensionalist mage, I obtain my power not only from our world, but from the other worlds as well. This accumulation of power from more than a single source makes my spells more potent. Other wizards have become jealous of the power available to those who apprentice with me. Over the years they have become vengeful and often violent. This is why it is important for us to always work together and learn to trust one another. When the time comes, we may need to fight. Unfortunately, this is the way of a Dimensionalist. It is a harsh world outside these walls, and we need to know we can rely on each other."

Tallachienan paused to look around the room before continuing. "Since everyone has completed the first phase of other-worldly Travel, the six of you will be divided into two groups. It is within these groups that everyone will learn the meaning of teamwork. Everyone will get to know their team members well: their skills, special abilities, strengths, and weaknesses. At the end of your training here, not only will you have an individual test, but a group test as well." The Master pointed to the wall at the rear of the chamber.

"In the back of the room there are two carts. Each one has three sets of the Sage Knowledge series of text. There are four volumes within each set. The assignment is for each of you to read the set and write a synopsis of each chapter in each volume." Tallachienan held up a thick stack of parchments held together by clips. "This is the protocol by which you are required to write your synopses."

Tallachienan walked among them, handing each student a clipped portion of the stack. "Your assignment is due at the end of next week." He paused once again, his gaze settling on Adrianna. "You are dismissed to begin your assignments."

While everyone looked through the parchments, Tallachienan stopped beside her. "Adrianna, you will need to catch up on your mathematics and physics. You should report to Masters Merlow and Kramer starting next week. There are separate texts you will receive from them. You will also get individual instruction from me every five days, beginning tomorrow. I will see you one hour after daybreak." He then turned and walked back to his desk, picked up what he'd been reading before Adrianna entered the room, and left.

Adrianna chanced a look around. None of the students had moved from their seats. By the expressions on their faces, they all appeared to be just as disgruntled as she was about their assignment. She glanced back at the carts loaded with books and shook her head. It wasn't feasible. There was no way anyone could read that amount of material within the small time allotted.

Adrianna turned back to see the two other women approaching. They sat down in chairs near hers. "You were late," said the Terralean. "The Master was beginning to get restless behind his big desk." She grinned wryly and glanced pointedly at the desk at the front of the room. Her pretty face was round, framed by short, dark brown hair. Her eyes were also brown, with lashes so long they touched her cheeks when she closed them. She wore a blue robe that was open at the front to reveal a short, sleeveless pale purple tunic.

"Perhaps even slightly agitated," continued the Cimmerean with a raised eyebrow. "I saw him frown a time or two." She also wore a blue robe. It was embroidered with gold thread and a yellow sash wrapped it about her middle. Beneath it she wore a beige blouse and matching trousers. Her beautiful black hair lay in silken waves over her shoulders and down her back. With lavender eyes a similar shade as Dinim's, she regarded Adrianna and extended her hand. "I'm Tridium."

Adrianna took the proffered hand. "I am Adrianna. And I assure you, my tardiness was unintentional."

The Terralean woman smiled. "I'm Yasmin. So what was the cause?"

Adrianna grinned in return, suddenly deciding to be feisty. "I was lazy and decided to sleep in. Besides, it gave me the perfect opportunity to make a grand entrance, did it not?"

"Well, it definitely caught *their* attention," said Yasmin, looking toward the three young men. Adrianna and Tridium followed suit. The two Cimmerean men just glanced in their direction before returning to their discussion, expressions of disdain etched on their faces. The Savanlean just regarded them in a neutral fashion for a moment before returning to his protocol.

Adrianna cringed inwardly. "Is it always like this?"

"For the most part, yes," replied Yasmin.

"Well, it's because of me," stated Tridium.

Adrianna raised an eyebrow. "Whatever for?"

Tridium regarded her speculatively. "It is because of the way Cimmerean society works. They can't understand it can be different between men and women when the chance is given." Tridium looked down her lap and then continued. "In the Underdark, women rule in a matriarchal society. Men aren't treated very well, and they oftentimes suffer greatly for no reason."

Adrianna was familiar with the conditions of which Tridium spoke. She remembered Dinim telling her about the abuse he'd sustained from his mother and subsequent betrayal by his brother. Adrianna nodded. "I have a friend. He told me about his life before he was trained as a sorcerer."

Tridium returned her gaze to Adrianna. "You have a Cimmerean friend? From home?"

Adrianna smiled wryly upon thinking of Dinim. For the purposes of this conversation, she would call him her friend, even if it was far from the truth. "Yes. He was the one who told me about Dimensionalism and that Master Tallachienan would possibly take me as his apprentice."

"Is he handsome?" asked Yasmin.

Adrianna grinned and nodded, knowing how her admission would be taken by the women.

Yasmin's blue eyes sparkled. "Hmph. Seems to me he could be more than just a friend."

Adrianna flushed. "Well, not him..." She let her voice trail off.

"Oh. So it is someone else, eh." Yasmin began to smile widely.

"What's his name? What does he look like?" asked Tridium, leaning forward.

Adrianna couldn't help but return the smile. "His name is Sirion. He is a Hinterlean ranger hailing from the realm of Elvandahar."

Yasmin regarded her with wide eyes. "So, you have a relationship with this man?"

Adrianna nodded. "Besides my sister, he is the best friend I've ever had." She heard the wistfulness in her tone and a twinge of loneliness arched through her. "We have been Promised." She extended her hand. "He even gave me his signet ring."

Tridium took her hand to look at the ring. "I've heard what they say about the Hinterlean rangers. They supposedly can't be tamed."

Adrianna nodded. "Yes, I know. Many have told me that nothing is more important to a ranger than his freedom. But Sirion... he is different."

"Or maybe," said Tridium, "it is *you* who is different."

Adrianna's brows furrowed with thoughtfulness. "Perhaps." Looking up, she saw the men getting up to make their way to the back of the room. The three women rose from their own seats and followed suit. Once reaching the carts, Adrianna heard Tridium give a heavy sigh. Again, she thought of the impossibility of the assignment. Speaking quietly to herself Adrianna complained, "How in the Hells are we going to accomplish this? It's insanity to think–"

"It *does* seem to be a rather daunting task, does it not?"

Adrianna turned to find the Savanlean man standing behind her. He was handsome, with slightly canted cerulean blue eyes and silvery-white hair. He wore a pale blue woolen tunic and trousers, overlain by a dark blue cloak.

"Indeed," she replied pensively, her hand at her chin.

"This is impossible," exclaimed Tridium. "How are we going to finish this assignment within just two weeks?"

"You definitely won't if you just stand there and yammer about it," said the taller of the two Cimmerean men as they moved away with one of the carts. His hair was short and had been combed into spikes. The other Cimmerean man chuckled behind his fist at his companion's words. His hair was cropped so short that he didn't need to comb it at all.

Adrianna just stared after them a moment as they made their way out of the room. "Effin calotebas dung," she spat beneath her breath.

The Savanlean chuckled and shook his head. "My name is Myan."

Adrianna turned back and grinned in response. "I am Adrianna."

"We're in the same group," he said.

Adrianna glanced at the two Cimmerean men and saw Yasmin rushing to catch up with them as they left the lecture hall. She surmised that the groups had been determined during the days she'd been asleep. Adrianna walked out of the lecture hall, she and Tridium analyzing the volumes of books on the cart while Myan pushed it.

Adrianna looked down the corridor. "Won't it be a long walk to our chambers?"

Myan shrugged. "I don't mind the walk. It's a pleasant change from the floating disks."

Adrianna nodded and continued alongside the cart. A couple times Myan examining a small book from inside his small shoulder pack, but she was too tired to ask about it. She'd just slept for three days and didn't understand why she was tired already. In spite of the conversation, she began to drift after a while. She didn't know how long passed before Myan's raised voice brought her back to attention.

"Adrianna?"

She looked up and found his hand circling her upper arm, his face close to hers with an expression reading mild concern. They had stopped in the middle of the hallway. She shook her head and yawned. "I'm sorry. It's just that I'm so tired. What did you say?"

His brows creased. "I've asked you three times now. Where are your quarters located?"

"I... I'm not sure."

Seeing the worried look on her face, he patted her arm. "Don't worry about it. I'll look it up." Myan pulled out the small book once more, saying her name in an undertone. He pointed down the hall. "It's this way, not very far from ours."

"That's good. It will be easier for us to study together." said Tridium. "So, the burning question is, how are we going to accomplish this?"

Adrianna tried pulling herself up from the dregs of fatigue. She looked from one companion to the other– both were rather disturbed about the assignment. However, much to her chagrin, she found that she hadn't the strength to care. "Gods, I'm so tired!" she exclaimed.

"Well, it's no wonder," said Myan. "You just got back from your trip. Everyone is tired after Travel."

"But I slept for three days!" she objected. "One would think that I would be well rested!"

Myan and Tridium frowned. "So, you were telling the truth when you told Yasmin and me why you were late," she said.

Adrianna nodded.

"That's quite a long time to sleep," said Myan. "We only rested for a couple of days, but maybe you were just tired before you went."

Adrianna thought back. She had been traveling in the middle of winter, just back from her ordeal in Andahye, when Master Tallachienan came to take her to the citadel. The memory made her ache for Sirion, and that she'd been unable to tell him goodbye before she left.

"Yes," she said disconsolately. "I was terribly tired from a long day of walking in the cold. I didn't get a chance to rest."

Myan frowned. "Why not? You must have known it would be hard on you if you didn't."

"I didn't get the chance to think about it. Right when I got here, the Master requested that I accompany him. I didn't receive the opportunity to rest."

"I got the chance to settle in for a few days before the Master took Yasmin, Myan, and I on our Travel," said Tridium.

"Yes, I remember," Myan replied in a low tone.

Adrianna had a surge of petulance. "Well, you were lucky." Then, feeling badly about her irritability, she said, "I'm just going to rest for a little while, and then I will think about our problem. I can't function in this condition."

Tridium regarded her solemnly with an expression of concern. The same was reflected in Myan's cerulean eyes. Once more they stopped walking. Adrianna turned to find they stood in front of the door to her chambers. "Our rooms are just a little ways down this hall," said Myan with a brief gesture. "When you awaken, just come to my room. You should have a book like the one I use somewhere on your desk." He paused. "Sleep well."

"Thank you," she replied, opening the door. Tridium waved as the two of them moved down the hall. Adrianna immediately went to the bed and fell onto it. Before the rippling motions had a chance to cease she was asleep.

Adrianna awoke with a crick in her neck. She rubbed the sore spot and tiredly rolled out of bed, stumbling when the blanket caught around her ankle. Wearily, she made her way into the bathing room and washed her face with a cloth and warm water. After a few moments she returned to the bedchamber. She walked over to the window and leaned on the casement as she took in the view. Early morning shadows played among the lonely hills, and the high mountains rose, dark and imposing, beyond. The skies were empty, save for some storm clouds and the occasional hawk drifting along on the air currents. She looked down, away from the skies, the mountains, and the hills– closer to the citadel. There was the courtyard, the one she'd entered through with the Master, but then she saw another, one much larger, with what appeared to be a garden. *Maybe I can go there sometime...*

After a while she left the window and seated herself in the chair in front of the desk. She picked a rumo from the bowl of fruit sitting there and bit into it. She spit out the bumpy, purple skin, but the inside was wonderfully sweet. In no time it was gone. She noticed a lonely book resting on one of the shelves. Taking it in hand, she opened it to the middle. There, revealed on the pages, was a two-dimensional image of what appeared to be a segment of Tallachienan's massive citadel. As she looked closely at the picture, it began to change. A three-dimensional image finally appeared, containing a blinking red dot in the nearest tower. Her eyes widened with delight. She flipped to the front of the book and saw there was a page with instructions on how to use it. Without reading it, she flipped back toward the map. She smiled to herself, vaguely remembering what Myan had said about it.

Then, all of a sudden, she remembered something else. *Oh gods, I'm supposed to meet Master Tallachienan for my first session of individual instruction!* She jumped up and rushed to the closet. As she searched for suitable attire, Adrianna shucked the yellow tunic she'd slept in. She hurriedly took the first things to come to hand, pulling a red tunic from its hook and wrapping a yellow sash about her waist. She slipped some sandals on her feet and then began to tame her unruly hair. In the middle of plaiting it, there was a knock on the door.

She quickly composed herself before speaking. "Enter."

Pylar strode in and gave her a smile. "I know you are unfamiliar with the citadel, so I have come to escort you to the Master for your first session of individual instruction. He bids that you bring your spellbook." Adrianna nodded as she hurriedly completed braiding her hair. She then grabbed her cloak and her journal, following Pylar out the door. They stepped onto the disk awaiting them outside her room, and within several minutes they stood at the doorway to a spacious, carpeted hall. It was a plain room, containing only a couple of cushioned benches and a table at one end. On the table rested a tray with some cups and a pitcher. There were two other doors in the room, each one at opposite ends. The doors were closed.

"Good day, Adrianna. I hope you slept well." Startled, Adrianna turned around to see Tallachienan walking through the door from which they had just entered.

"Yes, thank you." Adrianna watched Pylar as he left her side and quit the room, closing the door softly behind him. Almost immediately, she began to feel uneasy without someone else in the room with herself and the Master. She didn't really know why, for she'd been alone with the man before during her first Travel. She glanced back to find him watching her intently. He was unmoving, his hands behind his back. He was handsome... very much so. She couldn't help but be enchanted despite feeling that such a response was misplaced. Her heartbeat involuntarily increased in his presence, especially when he looked at her as he did now, his lavender eyes studying her pensively. She wondered what exactly it was about him that caused her to react this way, radiating such a powerful aura that he intimidated her.

Then she remembered. The man was a god. Of course he would intimidate her.

"You brought your spellbook as I requested?"

Adrianna handed him the journal and stood by, uncertainly looking about the room as he thumbed through it. He asked her about a few of the spells, the frequency of her usage and the components she used during casting. He then returned the journal and pointed to her upper arm. "I sense you have an item of arcane significance. Could you please show it to me?"

Adrianna nodded and pulled up the sleeve of the blouse she wore beneath her tunic. She felt the warm metal of the serpentine artifact beneath her fingertips as she revealed it to the Master.

Tallachienan looked from her face to the serpent, and then back to her face again. His expression was impassive. "I will need to suppress its power while you are here. When you leave, I will remove the *Suppression* spell."

Grudgingly, Adrianna nodded. It had saved her life on at least two occasions and she was loath to part with its magic. Tallachienan took her arm with one hand. The other hovered over the golden serpent coiled around her arm. It stared balefully at her from ruby eyes, and Adrianna felt a twinge of unease. The object was meant to protect her, and here she was, giving permission to remove that protection. Realistically she knew that the serpent couldn't feel emotion; it wasn't even alive. But she couldn't help but think that it felt betrayed.

Somehow sensing her unease, Tallachienan offered an explanation. "I don't want any of my apprentices using items of arcane value. They may interfere with your training, or may cause harm that I may be unable to foresee. I have installed other *Suppressors* in and around the citadel to prohibit my apprentices from using certain spells. It is all arranged for your safety, and to maximize your learning capabilities."

Adrianna said nothing. The area beneath his cupped palm over the serpent glowed briefly. When he was finished, he stepped away and once more placed his hands behind his back. He then began to pace in front of her. Adrianna had the distinct feeling that he was about to lecture to her.

"Dimensionalism is a very different type of school from the ones about which you are accustomed to hearing. When a Talented individual decides to become a specialist, he chooses a school from which to study his magic. Although every sorcerer has the power to cast any spell within his level of experience, it is intensely difficult for a specialist to cast a spell opposite to his school. Do you know why this is so?" Tallachienan stopped in front of her.

Adrianna shook her head. "No, Master."

Tallachienan continued pacing again. "Every master has his own individual style of spellcasting, passing it down to all of the apprentices he takes. It is the same with schools of magic. Each school teaches their students methods that facilitate the casting of certain types of spells. Naturally, because the methods are so specialized, they will exclude some spell types.

"Mages don't have this problem. A mage can cast any spell. However, because he does not specialize in any single spell type, a mage is neither the best diviner, nor the best illusionist. He is just someone who knows how to do almost everything, but is not *exceptional* at any of those things. Mages aren't taught short cuts, or any other specialized method of casting spells. Nonetheless, they are still taught by someone. That someone has his own way of casting spells, a certain way of thinking about the way a spell should be cast. A master passes this on to his students. Master Tallek passed his individual signature down to you. But now you will learn *my* signature. I will teach you a unique way of spellcasting."

Tallachienan stopped in front of her once more. "As you well know, the world around us is suffused with energy. This energy can be tapped and harnessed, but only by those with an inborn ability we call Talent. There are varying degrees. Yours is very strong, or you would not be here today. Only those of the highest caliber can even dream of achieving what you will one day."

Adrianna stared in surprise. She'd never considered herself as a particularly strong Talent despite Nahum's insistence. Yet, who would know better than a god?

"The way a Dimensionalist casts his spells is different from any other magic user. He doesn't specialize in one of the traditional eight different schools of magic. Not only does this make him different, but the source from which he obtains some of his magic also makes him unique. Unlike every other wizard or mage, a Dimensionalist doesn't just take the energy around him and shape it to his will. Instead, he uses the energy to create a doorway. This doorway enables him to reach within and take what he desires, be it fire, water, or sand. If the element of his desire exists upon this world, he can take it from where it exists and bring it to himself to use as he wills.

"When you cast a spell, you shape the magical energy of the world into what you desire. You use words, body movements, and spell components, such as a feather or a shard of crystal. The energy forms itself into what you command. It replicates fire: the appearance of fire, the smell of fire, the heat of fire. It envelops you, and makes you invisible to other creatures. It forms a missile, an orb of light, or a ray that causes weakness in your enemies. The way you cast many of these spells will not change. The art that I will teach you encompasses only some spells. However, it will open another world to you. When you learn to cast your primary spells in the fashion of a Dimensionalist, you open for yourself the means to which you will learn how to Travel to different places, places apart from the world upon which you live. I have already taken you to six such places. This makes the Dimensionalist a master of worldly travel, an individual who knows not just *one* aspect of the universe in which we live, but *many* of them."

Tallachienan stepped away from Adrianna. He softly spoke the words of a spell and held out his hand. Within a few moments, he held a small orb of flame in his palm. "This flame is one that a mage would cast." He then stepped away from the fiery orb. Beside it, he held out his hand again, speaking the words of another spell. The air around his body glowed momentarily, and before she knew it, the Master held another flaming orb within his palm. It appeared more quickly than the first orb, and seemed to be fuller and brighter. "This is a flame that a Dimensionalist would cast."

With a sweep of his hand, the orbs were gone. Tallachienan continued, "A Dimensionalist actually takes the material he wants from the place in which it exists. The mage simply bids the energy make a replica. With years of skill, it takes less time for the Dimensionalist to open his doorway and extract his fire. Not only that, but the fire is real, not something shaped on command. The fire of the Dimensionalist is brighter and hotter.

"When a Dimensionalist casts his spell, it has two parts. The first is the opening of the doorway and extraction of the desired material. The second is the channeling of the material into the desired form. A Dimensionalist will extract his fire and bring it unto himself. He will then shape the fire into the form that he wishes it to be.

"I am going to teach you the way a Dimensionalist casts his spells. You must unlearn what you have learned in order to succeed. We will begin with the basics– the opening of the doorway, or portal, and the extraction of the material. We will learn how to channel and form that material later."

Tallachienan turned to look at her. "Watch me."

Adrianna studied his body movements and listened to the words he spoke. The Master was graceful as he moved, and his voice was a rich bass. She felt the energy in the room, the raw power that Tallachienan evoked. The air beside him began to ripple, similar to a pond's surface when a small stone is thrown. Beyond the ripples, she vaguely saw the image of a flame. The flame leaped to the portal and peeked through before the opening was suddenly gone.

He turned back to her. "Now, visualize where you wish to obtain your flame. It can be from any source you know. For example, that fire over there." Tallachienan pointed to one of the large sconces on the wall opposite them. "Repeat the incantation after me."

Adrianna replicated his movements and stored the words he spoke into memory. At his command, she did it again, this time speaking the words for herself. It took her a couple of tries to control her movements and to remember the words he taught her. Finally, she felt the stirrings of energy, but nothing more.

"Try it again."

Adrianna repeated what she had been shown, and once more, the energy failed to rally.

"The incantation you speak will open the doorway to that place from which you wish to gather your flame. You then must use the energy to beckon your flame to come to you. You must visualize it in your mind, down to the smallest detail." He nodded for her to continue.

Once again, Adrianna spoke the incantation, and this time accomplished the creation of a small ripple in the air. The energy had stirred a little bit stronger, but nothing more happened.

"Try again," said Tallachienan. "You can do it. All you have to do is concentrate."

Adrianna paused. She closed her eyes, beginning to feel her weariness, but willing the magic to respond. Her body was still, her hands at her sides, her breathing shallow. She then took a deep breath and began the sequence once more. She knew the meaning behind all of the movements, as well as the incantation. The incantation was simply a request. The movements of her body and the power of her mind urged the magical energy to come to her. Nevertheless, it refused to move.

"Reach out to the energy with your mind. Seduce it to you and weave it into your spell."

Adrianna shucked her cloak and loosened the laces of her blouse. Wiping the sweat from her brow, she tried again. Several times more she unsuccessfully attempted to cast the spell. With each consecutive failure, the Master became more impatient while she became ever more frustrated.

Tallachienan's voice finally rang throughout the room. "Stop. That is enough."

Adrianna stopped and turned. She felt the tension surrounding him, the pent up power. For a moment she was afraid of him, not for the harm that he could do to her body, but her mind. Yet, she was attracted to him anyway, regardless of his anger and frustration towards her. She squared her jaw. She hated that.

Tallachienan sighed heavily and shook his head, his jaw tightening. His voice was a low growl. "Be sure to work on this. You are dismissed."

Adrianna was silent as she extricated her cloak from the Master's on the floor. She patted her face and neck with it as she walked out of the room without saying anything to Tallachienan. On the other side of the door she met Pylar. In silence he escorted her to her chamber suite. Ordinarily she would have spoken, but not after what she'd just been through.

Once reaching her chambers she stepped off the disk and looked up at him. Her tone was solemn. "Thank you." Pylar simply gave a slight bow. He looked like he might say something, but she didn't give him much of a chance, entering her room and closing the door behind her without a backward glance.

Adrianna grumbled through her tears as she threw the cloak onto the bed. *What is wrong with me? Really, this can't be so difficult. At least the Master doesn't seem to think so. And he was so terribly harsh. He encourages me to succeed, but offers no words of kindness. He simply told me all the things I was doing wrong, not bothering to mention anything I may have been doing right.*

Adrianna removed the sweat-dampened blouse, tunic, and trousers as she moved into the adjoining room. Moments later she was stepping into the thermal pool. The warm waters were relaxing her muscles, and she had to keep herself from succumbing to the temptation to close her eyes and simply float. When she finally stepped out of the pool, she donned a robe and sat on the edge of the bed. She combed her hair and plaited it. She then picked up the first volume of her assignment and settled down to read.

After only a few moments Adrianna yawned and rubbed her eyes. How she could possibly be so tired, she couldn't entirely fathom. Sure, the Master had worn her out with spell-casting exercises, but she'd slept half of the day yesterday and all of the night. She sat up in the bed, placing a pillow behind her back, and began to read anew. Again, she yawned.

With an irritated sigh, Adrianna left the bed. She sat at the desk and opened the book once again. She read a few paragraphs before her mind wandered. *How are the Wildrunners doing? It has to be terribly cold by now, and maybe snowing. Have they gotten close to the rod? And Sirion, does he miss me?*

Adrianna looked at the signet ring that circled her middle finger and then tightly closed her eyes. He was truly her other half, possessing some of the traits she lacked most. He had strength of character and was a good advisor and leader. He knew how to get what he wanted without letting anyone else stand in his way. He was also a good friend.

Adrianna wiped the tears from her cheeks. She was silly, sitting here and thinking such things, making her life in this place more difficult to bear than it already was. It was then she realized she didn't really wish to be here, living behind these cold stone walls. The citadel was so dark, gloomy, and foreboding. It shrouded her with a veil of melancholy. She was certain the absence of her comrades didn't help. *It might be better if the place had some color to it, some light, something...*

Adrianna found herself returning to the bed, book in tow. Once more, she settled down on the covers and opened it to the appropriate page. Her eyelids became heavy and, within moments, she'd inadvertently fallen asleep.

She walked. The halls were dark and cold, as though the light and warmth had been sucked out of them. The citadel was vast, much more so than she'd ever imagined, and full of voices just out of the range of her exceptional faelin hearing. She stopped, straining to hear. The words flowed into one another to make it sound like soft mumbling. She closed her eyes and focused. Then she heard it.

"Adriaaannnaaaaa..."

She jerked awake and blinked her eyes free of sleep. Her heart thundered against her ribs and her breathing was fast. Shaking her head free of the dream, she looked at the light streaming in through the window and quickly rose. She went to the closet and chose an ensemble consisting of a light brown, ankle length skirt with a white blouse and red cinch-belt. She slipped a pair of brown sandals on her feet and then went over to the fruit bowl. She thought about what she had to do that day, and grimaced. She would love the opportunity to get to know the citadel a little better. However, the decision wasn't really hers to make, for she had but only one *real* choice. She had to study. There were so many books to read in so little time.

Adrianna licked the juices from the fruit off of her fingers and once again picked up the first book of the four-volume series she had to read within the next twelve days. She didn't even want to think about the texts on Astralon and Cansandia that she needed to read for the test coming up in eight weeks. It was virtually impossible. How in the Hells she was going to read all of these books inside of twelve days was beyond her. It usually took her at least eight days to read a book this size, and that was without interruptions. Thus, it would take her at least thirty-two days to read the series. That wasn't including the synopses she needed to write!

She rolled her eyes and began to read. Two pages later found her slamming the volume shut and putting it down on the desk. *For the life of me, I just can't concentrate! I can't remember a single thing I just read.* Restlessly, she drummed her fingertips on the desk. *What the Hells am I going to do?*

A knock on the door saved her from further ruminations. She got up and opened it to find Myan and Tridium in the hallway. The young man didn't wait for an invitation before crowding past her into the room. It was obvious he was agitated as he immediately began to pace the floor. More sedately, Tridium followed. Adrianna cast her a questioning glance as she closed the door. Tridium just shook her head and crossed her arms at her chest.

Myan dramatically lamented, turning towards the two women. "That man has placed a scourge upon us all!"

Adrianna frowned. "What in Shandahar are you ranting about?"

"The spells! I can't cast my spells! This is quite a conundrum!" Myan didn't wait for a reply before he began pacing the floors again.

Adrianna turned to Tridium. "We figured we would try to use magic to buy ourselves some time– you know, cast some *Quicken* spells," she said. "When Myan cast the spell, nothing happened. I mean, we could feel the energy there, but when the incantation was completed, the energy was gone. It had somehow dispersed."

Adrianna frowned. "Most likely it is because of the *Suppression* spells Master Tallachienan cast, or mayhap he has written a *Spell Block*."

Tridium regarded her questioningly and Myan stopped his pacing to listen as well. "What do you mean?" she asked.

"Master Tallachienan probably has a *Spell Block* on this place. It's a security measure. Not just anyone can come behind these walls and cast spells. I'm sure he has many enemies in high places."

Enlightened, Tridium nodded. However, Myan continued to be agitated. "Damn! How can we work in a place that is so limited? That spell is the only thing I can think of that will allow us to complete the Master's wretched assignment."

Tridium closed her eyes and sighed heavily. "If only we could steal time."

"Yes, well, we can't," spat Myan venomously. He put his hands to his face, rubbed his eyes, and swept his fingers through his already tousled hair. It was then Adrianna realized how tired he was. She saw the dark circles beneath his eyes, and the paleness of his already pale complexion. It was obvious he'd been awake all night.

Adrianna felt a little bit guilty, for she'd hardly begun to study the texts at all. She held up her hands, hoping to forestall a potential argument. "Listen, I understand you're upset, but I haven't quite had a chance to assess the situation yet. Besides, I have to study." She gestured toward her pile. Tridium nodded and headed for the door, Myan hesitantly following. "I'll come by your room a bit later."

Myan nodded as Tridium opened the door. They stepped out and Adrianna closed it behind them. Then, just as Myan had done, she swept her hands through her hair. She stifled a yawn. She couldn't possibly be tired again already! She sat down on the floor beside the books. She opened the first volume once more, fingering through the pages. There was a thought that she couldn't get out of her mind, something Tridium had said.

"If only we could steal time." Adrianna said the words aloud, toying with the notion. *What if we don't need a spell? What if we can steal time without the use of magic at all?* Adrianna folded her knees to her chest, resting her chin on them. She inhaled slowly. *If only we could steal time.* Her mind jumped to her Travel with Tallachienan. She recalled the knowledge she'd learned– vast stores of knowledge she had yet to find the time to catalog in her mind.

"Time," Tallachienan had said, *"is purely relative. One finds that it differs from one place to the next, that it moves at different rates at different climes. Time on Shandahar is much the same as it is on Cansandia, but on other worlds, very different. For example, on Shandahar, time seems to go by more slowly than it does in any of the Heavens, but in relation to the Hells it is just the opposite, going by at a much faster rate than in any of those."*

A brilliant flash swept through her mind and she smiled. Excitedly she rose, and on her way to grabbing a light cloak from her closet, she heard another knock at the door. She answered it to find Pylar standing there. She stepped outside into the hall with him, and seeing the questioning look in his eyes she said, "Let's go to Myan's chambers. I think I've figured out how to finish our assignment!" She smiled conspiratorially, and with a grin he preceded her to her destination, knowing she probably didn't yet know where it was.

Adrianna knocked on Myan's door once, and after a moment of waiting, knocked again. Myan finally answered: clothes rumpled, pale hair mussed, eyelids drooping. She smiled up at him, placing her hand gently on his chest as she walked past him into the room. She saw Tridium sitting at Myan's desk, poring over a volume. She walked over and closed the book. The other woman scowled as she looked up at her. Adrianna just continued to smile. "I've figured out a way to solve our problem."

Tridium glared while Myan continued to stand at the door, rubbing his face with his hands. Pylar had entered and stood at the center of the room, watching and listening. Adrianna waited for her revelation to sink in, allowing her comrades to wake up from study-induced coma. After a moment, Myan abruptly took his hands from his face. "What? You have the answer?"

Adrianna just nodded. Myan paused before shutting the door, glancing into the hallway as though he heard something out there. Then his face broke into a smile, and he rushed over to her. He took her shoulders in his hands. "How? How did you do it?"

"It just came to me. Remember when Tridium said that she wished we could steal time? Well, I continued along that vein, remembering what the Master had taught me while we were Traveling. I then put two and two together, realizing that it is to another world which we need to go in order to solve our dilemma. We will take the time we need by residing in another world, a place in which time moves more quickly. By the time we reach our deadline while in that other place, we will have stolen at least twice the amount of time that we would have spent had we stayed here. At that point, we will return to this place, our assignment completed."

"Adrianna, this is excellent!" exclaimed Tridium.

"It is very dangerous in other worlds," stated Myan. "I assume we plan on going to one of the Heavens?"

Adrianna nodded and Pylar cleared his throat. The three looked towards him, almost having forgotten he was in the room. "That is where I come in. I will guide and protect you during your stay within the world you choose."

The students smiled and patted one another on the shoulder, Myan and Tridium congratulating Adrianna on a job well done. Adrianna reached out to Pylar, placing her hand on his arm and drawing him in. His eyes brightened when they included him in their circle of comradeship. He turned and his gaze locked onto hers. They regarded one another, and for just one moment, Adrianna felt the feather-soft touch of familiarity sweep over her. Then it was gone. Pylar gave her a small smile, one that held a twinge of sadness.

Before she could say something, Tridium was patting her shoulder. "We need to decide which of the Heavens we wish to visit. It was your idea, so you choose!"

"You will most certainly want to choose from the ones that will give you the best opportunity to study, as well as having the least amount of dangers," said Pylar.

They all looked to her, and Adrianna suddenly felt self-conscious. Unlike these people, she knew nothing about the worlds of which they spoke; she hadn't had the time to even find out the names of the worlds comprising the Seven Heavens. "I..."

Seeing her discomfiture, Pylar spoke on her behalf. "Well, we must remember that Adrianna has been here only a short while. She may not know about the Heavens quite the way you do."

"Yes, Tridium, why don't you choose?" said Adrianna.

Tridium beamed with pleasure.

"Mayhap I could work out the mathematics," quipped Myan. "We need to make sure we don't overspend our time there. We don't want to overshoot our deadline!"

"Well, I shall leave that up to you then," said Adrianna. "In the meantime I think I will go and collect some of the supplies we will need for our trip. I figure that we can leave as early as tomorrow morning."

"Yes," agreed Tridium with a sparkle in her eyes. "I think I will retire from my books for the remainder of the day. It has been much too long."

"Then we will meet here at sunrise tomorrow morning," said Pylar.

Everyone nodded in agreement. Tridium picked up her books and followed Adrianna out of Myan's chamber. The two women waved as they parted ways, walking in opposite directions down the corridor. Adrianna thought about Pylar as she made her way back to her quarters. She wondered why he'd seemed happy one moment, and so sad the next. Sometimes when he looked at her, he had an aura of such melancholy, it was as though he'd lost someone dear to him.

Once in her suite, Adrianna went over to the window and looked out across the landscape. She still had yet to see the sunshine. Although it was light outside, it was a muted, shadowed light. Once more, she wondered what made this place so dark, even to the occlusion of the sun. But she wouldn't be concerned about it for now. She looked forward to leaving the next day, and was excited about the prospect of visiting yet another new world.

Just as planned, they met at daybreak in Myan's quarters. Everyone carried his or her own packs. Even Pylar carried a pack, as well as a spear that was almost as long as he stood tall. They ventured to the kitchens, where they took much of what they would need to sustain themselves while they were away. Several days' worth of food found its way into their packs, and by the time it was all stored away, the group sported at least four packs each.

Feeling like overly laden umberhulks, the threesome followed Pylar, each on his or her own disk. After a few moments longer, they approached a set of doors. Everyone stepped down and when Pylar opened them, they walked into a massive chamber. It was soon apparent that the room was part of a laboratory. The shelves contained large tomes, strange apparatus, and arcane devices of several types. The tables contained much of the same, as well as varying shapes and sizes of flasks, vials, jars, and bottles, all of which contained some strange thing or another. To the left, the students saw other rooms adjoined to this central one. On the right there were several bookshelves and the doorway to another small room. It was there that Pylar led them.

Adrianna, Myan, and Tridium found themselves approaching a large well built of stone. Around it, reaching almost to the lip of the well, was a circular ceramic dais engraved with elaborate runes. "This will take us to any world we wish to go, without having to worry about the complex casting of spells," said Pylar. "It is one of the greatest things the Master has ever created. Merely concentrate upon your destination, and it will take you there."

Adrianna paused before the well and then seated herself on the ledge. It was made of some type of gray rock with streaks of silver. Dangling her feet into the hole, she looked down and saw she was unable to see the bottom. She looked back up at Pylar only to find him sitting quietly beside her, a protector even at that moment. She smiled wanly at Myan and Tridium sitting on the other side, who looked back with the same expression of nervousness she felt.

"So I'm to go first?" Without waiting for a response, she gripped her packs securely, concentrated on her destination, and thrust herself from the ledge.

For a moment, Adrianna had the sensation of falling, and then there was only darkness.

EPILOGUE

With a sense of trepidation Tallachienan placed his hands on the Vision Orb. For a brief moment he contemplated not watching, but then swiftly discarded that notion. There was no way he *couldn't* watch. He was too emotionally invested now, his love for Adrianna so strong he couldn't bear not to know exactly what was happening to her. The greenish colored mists within began to eddy about, and after a few moments they parted to reveal an entrance set into a rocky cliff face. The image took him through a long passageway that finally led into a massive cavern. It was lit by torches set in large metal sconces hammered into the stone walls. Within the cavern's center was a still pool, and all around stalactites and stalagmites cast eerie shadows that shifted and wavered against the walls.

The image slowly moved into the cavern and a group of people came into view. Tallachienan knew all their names, for Adrianna had talked about her friends in her communications with him via her Travel notebook. He watched as the group warily shifted themselves into formation: Adrianna, Dinim, and Tianna made up the middle, Sheridana, Zorgandar, and Bussi took up the front line, and Armond, Amethyst, and Dartanyen covered the rear. With barely a whisper of sound, dread priests and necromancers that had aided Aasarak in the creation of his army oozed from out of the shadows. The two forces regarded one another for the barest moment, and then the battle began.

Adrianna and Dinim cast their first spells, a distraction to give the fighters an advantage. The halfen, Bussimot, held his battle-axe at the ready, while Sheridana, Zorg, and Armond did the same with their swords. The *Flamespheres* leaped from their hands, arcing over the group to strike the oncoming enemy. Tallachienan imagined the screams of the priests that were burned by the twin infernos. The moment the flames subsided, Adria and Dinim were intoning their next spells while Dartanyen and Amethyst shot volleys of arrows at the unwitting enemy. Two or three of the dark robed priests and sorcerers fell and then the fighters rushed forward.

Right from the start it seemed to be a losing fight. Despite her location in the center of the group's protective circle, the young cleric Tianna was the first to go down. It was obvious she was the target of the enemy's initial attack when first one lance of dark energy struck the woman, followed swiftly by another. Tianna fell to the floor, her rich chestnut hair framing a face beautiful even in death. The priests that killed her also died a quick death, Zorg and Armond making fast work of them. Those priests knowingly forfeited their lives so the group would be greatly weakened. Indeed, without Tianna there to call upon her goddess, no one could be healed.

Her concentration broken, Adrianna cried out as her companion fell. With a sinking heart, Tallachienan watched her turn in place to see the remaining destruction materialize. Since no sounds could be transmitted to him from the orb, he could only imagine the shouting of the other fighters, the clash of metal, and the wails of the injured and dying. Zorg was the next to surrender his valiant life to the cause. The big man staggered and fell, clutching his chest as Aasarak emerged from the darkness before him. The Deathmaster had his hand outstretched, having touched the warrior with only a single finger...

Tallachienan saw the fear washing over Adrianna's face, the minute trembling of her body as she watched Bussi fall next, his battle-axe nothing against the massive scythe wielded by a gruesome Azmathous warrior. He watched her attempt to concentrate on another of a long line of spells she had already cast, her brow furrowing with the effort. However, the noises of the surrounding battle seemed to muddle her mind, and after another moment she quickly glanced about to get her bearings. When Adrianna turned back again to focus, Aasarak was suddenly gone. Even Tallachienan hadn't seen the sorcerer leave the battleground. He noticed a gleaming arrow arc through the air where the wizard had stood, but it continued its flight, unhindered until it finally hit a stalagmite rising from the cavern floor.

Adrianna glanced around the cavern, desperately trying to find Aasarak. She visibly flinched when she saw Amethyst lying not far away, a pool of bright red blood surrounding her. Once more Dinim cast another spell, the vibration of it causing two stalactites to come loose from the ceiling and come crashing to the floor. When the Deathmaster used the opportunity to re-emerge from the shadows, Adrianna rent the air with her magic. The sizzling bolts left her fingertips only to be deflected. Aasarak laughed at her puny efforts as the last of his nefarious priests fought what remained of the group. It was then Sheridana suddenly swept at him, seemingly from out of nowhere. She struck out at him with her longsword, only to find the blade stayed by his hand. Aasarak struck back at the young warrior, and Sheri flew back with the force of his blow, hitting the ground about a farlo away.

With a sense of desolation beginning to creep over him, Talla-chienan continued to watch the battle. The terrible carnage lay all around, dark robed priests and sorcerers littering the blood slicked ground. Sheridana tried to rise after Aasarak threw her back, but the master sorcerer wasted her with nothing but a gesture of his hand. The broken bodies of Dartanyen and Dinim lay another farlo away. Ultimately they had both died of multiple stab wounds to the chest and back, but seeping abscesses and blisters covered their skin, courtesy of the dark arts. Tallachienan felt Dinim's loss acutely, for the young Cimmerean man had been one the best apprentices to walk the hallowed halls of his citadel... the male counterpart to Adrianna.

Terror consumed him as Tallachienan watched Adrianna hit Aasarak with everything she knew. Nothing seemed to faze the despicable sorcerer. He could see the desperation cross her blood-smeared features, and he shook with what was about to unfold. Adrianna was suddenly engulfed in smoke. She choked on the thick vapors and soon started to suffocate. Weakened, she stumbled forward, seemingly towards a voice Tallachienan couldn't hear. Just as it seemed she would pass out, the thick cloud began to recede. Armond's tall figure strode towards Adrianna and she ran to his side. He put his arms around her, but a moment later she was pulling away and looking at a deep wound in his side. The black tendrils of his hair shrouded the man's face, but Tallachienan was able to make out the pain and fatigue reflected in Armond's green eyes.

The smoke rolled away, and in its place came Aasarak. The sorcerer's black hooded cloak whipped about as chaotic air currents swept by in response to the flow of magical energies. Armond placed his shining blades between them and the approaching menace. As Aasarak stepped towards them, Armond backed away, Adrianna pressed in close behind. Tallachienan saw the trembling in the man's body, as well as each labored breath he took. This was the end. Every last one of their companions lay dead on the ground. Adrianna placed her hand on Armond's arm, a gesture of reassurance that she was still there and that it wouldn't be his fault when he failed in what would come next.

With his heart trapped in his throat, Tallachienan watched as Adrianna sank to one knee and cast her last spell. The magical energy flew from her fingertips. It struck Aasarak and he screamed into the *Void*. Any mortal man would have been sucked within, but the Deathmaster resisted. When the vacuum finally receded, Tallachienan saw that her magic had finally caused harm to Aasarak. Finally the sorcerer had become weakened enough to feel it.

But it didn't matter. Time was on Aasarak's side. The energy around the comrades stirred as it moved towards the dark sorcerer. Armond dropped one of his blades and crouched low, falling to one knee and reaching out for Adrianna. Weakly she clutched at her comrade, burying her face in the side of his tunic beneath the protection of his arm. The energy arced through the air and raced towards them. Armond balanced his sword to meet the oncoming threat. Tallachienan caught the last expression on Adrianna's face, one of desolation and intense sorrow. He wished he could have known her thoughts the moment she took her last breath.

Tallachienan closed his eyes and screamed in agony, the sound of it sweeping through the corridors of the citadel. The very foundation of the place shook with the power of his emotion. It reverberated throughout the mountains, across the seas, and over the plains. It echoed throughout all space and all Time, never to reach the one for whom it was meant.

GLOSSARY OF TERMS

Aertna (airt-na) – that place faelin-kind believe to exist within every man somewhere between his mind and his soul

Alcrostat (al-kro-stat) – the largest city within the realm of Elvandahar - residence of the Sherkari Fortress, home to the King

Alothere (al-o-thayr) – large porcines that are cousins to the wild boar – they live in the forests and steppes of the temperate regions of Shandahar

Andahye (an-duh-high) – mystical city located at the northern edge of the Sheldomar Forest – it is the place where many mages receive their arcane training

Ansalar (an-sal-ar) – one of the three continents of Shandahar – it is the most inhabited

Azmatharcana (az-math-ar-kana) – a mystical tome that delivers many necromantic secrets, including those contained within the Azmathion

Azmathion (az-math-ee-on) – the arcane artifact that gives Aasarak much of his power – it is a geometrical work of art, and one must work the puzzles contained within it in order to divine its secrets

Azmathous (az-math-us) – the most powerful of Aasarak's undead creations – with the power of the Azmathion, they are reborn and are able to retain the skills and abilities they possessed in life

Behiraz (be-heer-az) – a worm of gargantuan proportions, it lives beneath the ground finding it's prey by the vibrations they make upon the surface – swift and deadly, very few survive an encounter

Buffelshmut (buffel-shmut) – a slang term for buttocks

Burbana (bur-ban-uh) – a small ermine-like animal with exquisitely soft fur

Calotebas (kal-o-tee-bas) – a large foul-tempered herbivore that lives near swamps – the taste of their flesh is equally as repugnant as their personality

Cenloryan (sen-lor-yan) – a creature made of the twisted magic of the Kronshue, it has the lower body of a lloryk and the upper torso, arms, and head of a human

Chag (chag) – a drink made from the large seeds of the chagatha plant, which grows in the more southern regions of Ansalar

Chamdaroc (sham-dar-ok) – a shrub that grows within Elvandahar and other forested regions of northwestern Ansalar – it has small white flowers that are said to have intoxicating qualities

Cimmerean (sim-ur-ee-an) – one of the faelin sub-races – also known as 'dark' faelin, they live in vast labyrinths below the surface of the world

Common (com-mun) – the universal language across most of the main continent of Ansalar

Cortubro (cor-too-bro) – a realm situated north of Elvandahar

Corubis (kor-oo-bis) – large canines that have tawny fur with dark dappling – they live in packs headed by an alpha male, but many of them find companionship with faelin, especially hinterlean rangers

Croxis (krok-sis) – a plant that has hallucinogenic properties, often making the person feel a false sense of well-being – the extract is called croxian

Daemundai (day-mun-die) – an organization of those who strive to give daemon-kind influence and power in Shandahar

Daladin (dal-a-din) – a Hinterlean house in the trees

Denedrian (den-ed-ree-an) – one of the human sub-races – they are largely nomadic, originating from the western plains and deserts

Dimensionalist (dim-en-shen-al-ist) – a sorcerer who specializes in otherworldly knowledge and travel

Doppleganger (dop-pel-gang-er) – a bipedal being once thought to be made of magic, it is a daemon that has the ability to shift its shape into any humanoid between four and eight feet tall – it is a master of trickery and disguise that works for the most powerful of sorcerers

Elvandahar (el-van-da-har) – large forested region in the vee of the Terrestra and Denegal Rivers – it is ruled by hinterlean faelin, and bears the largest population of these people

Esfexanar (es-fex-an-ar) – a deadly poison often used to subdue someone – it causes the person to fall unconscious and to have after-effects such as slurred speech and tiredness

Eukana (yoo-kana) – a mixture of assorted nuts and dried berries that Hinterlean rangers carry on long trips

Farlo (far-low) – the equivalent of several feet

Filopar (fil-o-par) – one of the five domains of Elvandahar

Fistantillus bush (fist-an-til-lus) – a plant bearing poisonous thorns that can make a person violently ill for several days

Grang (grang) – slightly shorter than halfen, these small, bony humanoids live primarily on the steppes - they are primitive and voracious, but not very smart, their greed often getting in the way of thieving strategies

Griffon (grif-fon) – large animals that have both feline and avian features – they are friendly and intelligent, and can often be found in the company of druids

Hamzin/Hamza (ham-zin/ham-zah) – the title given by the King to the one who rules within one of the five domains in Elvandahar

Helzethryn (hel-zeth-rin) – one of the dragon sub-races – at maturity their color ranges from pale gold, to deep bronze, to fiery red – they have the highest propensity towards *bonding* with other species

Hestim (hes-tim) – one of the three moons of Shandahar

Himrony (him-ron-ee) – a type of grass that grows abundantly throughout the central Ansalar – the preferred vegetation of larian

Hinterlean (hin-ter-lee-an) – one of the faelin subraces – they live in treetop villages within temperate forests

Hralen (her-ay-len) – the name used for the household staff within the Sherkari Fortress

Humanoid (hue-man-oyd) – any creature that walks upright on two legs (bipedal)

Hybanthis (hie-ban-this) – a vine that has poisonous blue thorns – poison has brain-based affects that heighten a person's emotional state, making emotions difficult to handle

Isterian (iz-ter-ee-un) – the name used for the guards that keep patrol throughout the Sherkari Fortress

Karlisle (kar-lyle) – the human realm neighboring Elvandahar on the other side of the Denegal River

Kleyshes (klie-shays) – one of the five domains of Elvandahar

Krathil-lon (kruh-thil-lon) – a forested glen located within the southern reaches of the Sartingel Mountains

Kronshue, Brotherhood of the (kron-shoo) – a 'technological' society that dominates eastern Ansalar

Kyrrean (kie-reen) – large blond felines with dark brown dappling and oversized paws – they make their existence on the warm temperate plains and borderlands

Larian (layr-ee-an) – with only minor differences, these are smaller cousins to the lloryk – they are able to carry faelin and most humans

Leschera (le-sher-uh) – very gentle, larian-sized, deer-like creatures that grace the temperate woodlands

Lloryk (loor-ik) – large muscular equine-like creatures that are able to carry humans and small orocs – they are omnivorous and beneath the top coat of silky fur, have modified hair shafts that appear similar to scales one would see on a reptile

Lycanthrope (lie-kan-throap) – one afflicted with the disease of lycanthropy – they are humans, faelin, or hafen that can transform into animals (beginning with prefix *shir* - wemic, althothere, or kyrrean) – the disease is spread through the bite

Lytham powder (lye-tham) – a component used in a spell that creates a noxious vapor

Mehta (may-tuh) – the title given to the leader of the daemundai

Meriliam (mer-il-lee-am) – one of the three moons of Shandahar

Merzillith (mir-zil-lith) – otherwise known as a mind flayer, this intermediate daemon is from one of the Nine Hells – it has psionic power, the ability to use the energy of the world in a way that is different from the Talent possessed by mages

Mirpur (mir-poor) – one of the five domains of Elvandahar

Monaf (mon-af) – the human realm neighboring Torimir on the other side of the Ratik Mountains

Morden (mor-den) – one of the halfen sub-races – they live in deep caverns within the mountains

Murg (murg) – an alcoholic beverage distilled from fermented cane sugar

Necromancer (nek-ro-man-ser) – a sorcerer who focuses on the darker aspects of spellcasting

Nefreyo/Neiya (nef-ray-oh/nay-yah) – the familiar terms used for nephew and niece

Oorg (oorg) – one of the humanoid races of Shandahar, they are even larger than orocs and are often called giants – they often fight with brute strength alone, but aren't good with any type of real strategy

Oroc (or-ok) – one of the native races of Shandahar – they are muscular and broad, standing at least six to seven feet tall – faelin are their greatest enemies, and the two races find any excuse to maim and kill one another

Pact of Bakharas (bak-hair-us) – an agreement between daemon and dragon kind that does not allow one or the other too much influence over Shandahar

Papas fruit (pay-pas) – a small pink orb about the size of a nectarine – it grows on the papas tree, which is prevalent throughout the temperate borderlands of Ansalar

Ptarmigan (tar-mig-an) – a squat, grouse-like bird that is often hunted for its flavorful meat

Rathis (rath-is) – the leaves of this plant are known for their pain-relieving capabilities

Recondian (re-con-dee-an) – one of the human sub-races – they mostly live in the central regions of Ansalar

Reshik-na (resh-ik-na) – an order of druids that lives within the Elvandaharian domain of Filopar

Rezwithrys (rez-with-ris) – the largest of the dragon sub-races – at maturity their color ranges from silver to steel blue to metallic violet – they have a propensity for magic

Samshin/Samshae (sam-shin/sam-shay) – the son/daughter of the hamzin or hamza

Sangrilak (sang-ri-lak) – a very diverse city located in the northwestern quadrant of the realm of Torimir

Savanlean (sav-an-lee-an) – one of the faelin sub-races – they live in majestic cities built into mountainsides located in the more northern regions of the Ansalar

Shagendra (shuh-gen-dra) – the root from this plant can be used to make a person's mind vulnerable to suggestions – also causes general lethargy, dulls the senses, and slows reflexes

Shockwave (shok-wave) – a game that is popular throughout the continent – involves cards, bones, and no small amount of strategy and luck

Steralion (stir-a-lee-an) – one of the three moons of Shandahar

Tabanakh drink (ta-ban-ak) – a drink prepared by the druid elders as a right of initiation for their tyros – it has properties that exaggerate the visions of those who are so gifted

Talent (tal-ent) – (adj)the ability that some people possess to harness the energy of the world and use it – (n)someone who uses magic

Talsam (tal-sam) – the root from this plant is ground into a powder from which a pain-relieving tea is made

Tankard (tank-erd) – a vessel for holding liquid – it is the equivalent of approximately two mugs and is usually used in taverns

Terralean (ter-a-lee-an) – one of the faelin sub-races – they inhabit many of the borderlands between the forests and steppes and are the most widespread

Thalden (thal-den) – one of the halfen sub-races – they live within the temperate hills

Thritean (thry-teen) – very large silver felines with black striping and six legs – they live in cold northern forests

Tobey (tow-bee) – a small, goat-like creature – many nomadic peoples breed them for the creamy textured milk they produce

Torimir (tor-eh-meer) – the realm neighboring Elvandahar on the other side of the Terrestra River

Tremidian (tre-mid-ee-an) – one of the human sub-races – they live on the eastern side of the continent

Trolag (trol-ag) – one of the humanoid races of Shandahar, they are tall and stooped, their long, gangly bodies covered with dark brown wiry hair – they have the ability to heal quickly

Umberhulk (um-ber-hulk) – large, stout burden beasts with thick umber colored skin virtually devoid of hair – used to pull carts in cities, towns, and many times even in caravan trains

Varanghelie Vault (vair-an-gay-lee) – a highly protected storage facility located within Andahye – it is where many people keep their most valuable possessions

Wemic (wee-mik) – in some places better known as wolves, these animals appear to be distant cousins to the corubis – they run in temperate to sub-arctic forests and have never been tamed

Wraith (rayth) – a corpse that has been re-animated – they are mindless, following the commands of their necromantic masters – their bodies are ravaged by the effects of decay and they wield only the simplest of weapons

Wyvern (why-vern) – a large snake-like creature with four stubby legs and a poisonous barbed tip on its long sinuous tail – it lives in shallow caverns in temperate climes

Zacrol (zak-rol) – the equivalent of about a mile

About The Authors

Tracy R. Chowdhury (aka Ross) was born in the small town of Tunkhannock Pennsylvania in 1975 and moved to Cincinnati Ohio when she was twelve years old. Growing up, she was an avid reader, especially of fantasy and science fiction, and she loved to write. She attended college at Miami University in Oxford, Ohio and studied her other passion, Biology. She graduated in 2002 and worked in cancer research for several years. During that time she picked up her love for writing again, and in 2005, her first book, *Shadow Over Shandahar- Child of Prophecy*, was put into print. With the help of her co-author, Ted Crim, the sequel was published two years later.

Tracy currently lives in Montgomery, Ohio. She is married with eight children, a big dog, and four cats. She does home renovation work, and in her 'spare' time she continues to write and promote her books. In 2011 the novels were picked up by a small press, and her original duology was remastered and separated into smaller volumes to make a series. More books have followed, as well as several short stories. And now, she and her husband own their own publication company! More information about the books can be found on her website at www.worldofshandahar.com, and she can be found on Facebook and Twitter.

Ted M. Crim was born and raised in Cincinnati Ohio. He spent most of his early youth in Over-the-Rhine, but moved to upper Price Hill when he was about eight years old. He was always interested in fantasy role-play, and enjoyed playing Dungeons & Dragons with his friends. When he was a junior in high school he went into a vocational program called Animal Conservation and Care located at the Cincinnati Zoo & Botanical Garden. He received his certificate in 1989 and worked in animal care for several years.

It was during that time Ted met his good friend, Tracy, and they shared an interest in Dungeons & Dragons. She was a writer, and it was upon the first campaign they played together that her first book, *Shadow Over Shandahar-Child of Prophecy*, was based. Together, they brought the world and the characters to life into a novelized format. He attends many of the conventions and festivals at which the books are sold, and goes by the moniker, Pirate Ted!

Ted is currently working on his new fantasy series and gaming system. More information about the books can be found on his website at www.worldofshandahar.com, and he can also be found on Facebook.

OTHER BOOKS TO ENJOY:

Imagine living over one hundred years without a home, without a family, without responsibility. Imagine being alone in the wilderness with nothing but memories of the long ago past. Imagine dreaming of the day you might find something worth living for... worth dying for.

Elvish Jewel.

Found within these pages is a wonderful assortment of tales and adventures from some of the most memorable people in the world of Shandahar! Come and meet Sirion as a young lycan hunter, Thane before he became corrupted by the greatest of evils, Sorn as a young rogue tempted by love, and Dartanyen before he meets up with the Wildrunners! You will meet some new people too, and experience the depth and richness Shandahar truly has to offer!

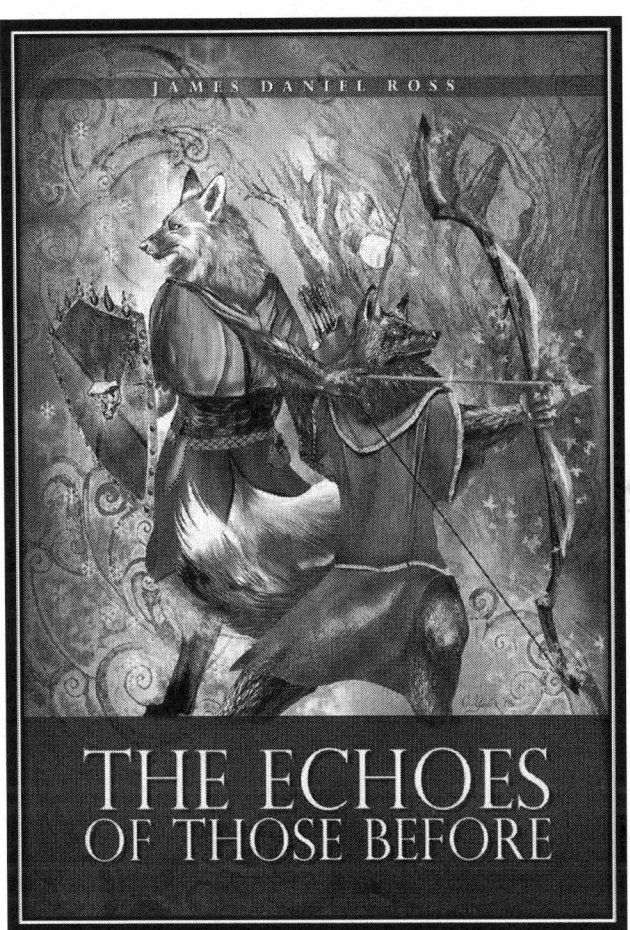

THE ECHOES
OF THOSE BEFORE

Hungry. Feral. Remorseless.

Demonic creatures have crawled from their hives for the first time in thousands of years. They seek their prey relentlessly, seemingly invincible, swarming across the world to blot out whole nations.

Two young men, an orphan and a maverick, will pick up one of the most powerful weapons ever forged by Those Before and stand against the rising tide of darkness.

Follow this pair as they venture from the safety of the Fox Vale, into the cold embrace of the big wide world.

Nine year old Sam is having terrible dreams every night. The house cats, Freya and Odin, find out that goblins are stealing away all his good dreams and leaving the bad ones behind. There is darkness and danger around every turn. How can the cats stop the goblins and win peaceful nights of sleep for their human friend?

This a story about one cat's courage to defy the evil lurking in the shadows, her indomitable will to see it defeated, and most all, her love for the boy that she calls her own. This a true tale of friendship in its purest form, one that audiences of all ages can enjoy.

Ages 8-12

SONG OF CHAMPIONS

JAMES DANIEL ROSS

In a world beset by nightmares, another is coming. Two of the mightiest nations in the world are clashing in a war that will shake the Great Veddan River Valley to its core. The fae elves and the bronze dwarves look upon one another as foreign and alien, their conflict fueled by dark powers and bigotry. Pride and misunderstandings foil peace at every turn, and two star-crossed lovers shall suffer as their people descend into bloodshed.

AND FORTHCOMING:

Seth and Kaila: writing partners, friends, lovers. Their relationship is a rocky one, and an arguement sends Kai out into the night in tears.

A terrible accident leaves Seth suddenly facing the worst days of his life. Deep within the embrace of a coma, Kai struggles for her life, her mind trapped within the world she and Seth have created. And as the days pass, she continues to weaken.

The only thing keeping Seth from insanity is their book manuscript, and as the love of his life slips closer to death, he is desperate to finish what they started together. As their darkest hour approaches, Seth finally realizes what might save Kaila's life, and it is a race against the clock before she is lost forever.

VISIT THE WEBSITE AT
WWW⬚WINTERWOLFPUBLICATIONS⬚COM
FOR

BREAKING NEWS
FORTHCOMING RELEASES
LINKS TO AUTHOR SITES
WINTERWOLF EVENTS

Made in the USA
Columbia, SC
03 July 2022

62707333R00183